THE FATAL GIFT

ALEC WAUGH
has written more than forty books. They include:

NOVELS

The Loom of Youth (1917)
Kept (1925)
So Lovers Dream (1931)
The Balliols (1934)
Jill Somerset (1936)
No Truce with Time (1941)
Unclouded Summer (1948)
Guy Renton (1953)
Island in the Sun (1956)
Fuel for the Flame (1960)
The Mule on the Minaret (1965)
A Spy in the Family (1970)

SHORT STORIES

My Place in the Bazaar (1961)

TRAVEL

Hot Countries (1930)
The Sugar Islands (1958)

AUTOBIOGRAPHIES

The Early Years of Alec Waugh (1962)
My Brother Evelyn and Other Portraits (1967)

MISCELLANEOUS

In Praise of Wine (1959)
A Family of Islands (1964)
Wines and Spirits (1968)
Bangkok: The Story of a City (1970)

THE FATAL GIFT

A Novel
by
ALEC WAUGH

'The fatal Gift of beauty . . .'
BYRON

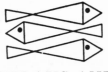

FARRAR, STRAUS AND GIROUX
NEW YORK

Copyright © Alec Waugh, 1973
Manufactured in the United States of America
Library of Congress Catolog Card Number: 72–97081

ISBN 0–374–15380–9

First American publication 1973

FOREWORD

This is a work of fiction, the life-story of the second son of an obscure but affluent English peer, who was born in 1903. It is told in the first person and the narrator, the 'I', is myself. No actual events have been dramatised, with one exception. My brother Evelyn did in 1924 bring a girl to Oxford and take her, dressed up as a man, to an undergraduate 'binge' which was raided by the proctor and his bulldogs. The subsequent story of that lady—a fortunate and happy one—was entirely different from that of Judy.

I have introduced one or two real people by their actual names. My hero going up to Oxford in October, 1922, would certainly have met Evelyn and Brian Howard, in New York in 1930–31 he would have been seeing Claud Cockburn, and as a staff officer in Cairo in 1942 he would probably have met Robin Maugham. I could see no point in finding pseudonyms for them.

Nor did I see any point in finding a pseudonym for Dominica. The island is unique and this particular story could only have happened there. In Dominica my hero would have met Elma Napier, John Archbold and Stephen Haweis, so I have written about them as I would have done, and indeed have done, in a travelogue. I think this is legitimate in a novel, and I hope the reader will not be confused.

It is, I repeat, a work of fiction.

ALEC WAUGH

1

It was raining, as I had guessed it would be. Though the month was April, Dominica is the wettest island in the Caribbean. Its mountains attract the rain. It has over three hundred rivers. I opened my umbrella as I came down the gangplank. I hurried across the tarmac. A hand, waved from the verandah, reassured me; though it was six years since we had met, I had never ceased to regard Raymond Peronne as one of my closest friends, and I had expected that my air letter announcing that a professional need for copy was to bring me once again to Dominica, would be answered by such a cable as the one I got, 'Thrilled your visit come as soon as you like stay as long as you like.' But I had not known whether he would be fit enough to undertake the two hours drive over the mountains. That was why the waved hand reassured me. He was in good health.

He was awaiting me beyond the customs shed beside a low red Alfa-Romeo two-seater; a car admirably suited to the island's steep, sharp curves; a car, too, that striking a note of unostentatious affluence, was typical of its owner. Tall, upright, elegant, Raymond Peronne was as handsome now in his seventieth year as he had been when I met him first as an undergraduate at Oxford.

His clothes were as appropriate as his car: dark green slacks, a white linen jacket, patterned in green by broad, thin-lined squares; a white silk shirt with, at his throat, a dark green polka-dot cravat. His panama hat was bound by a bright madras. As he crossed from the parking lot, his face was lit by the smile that was peculiarly his own, a welcoming smile that both accepted and dismissed the manifold chances and changes of the world. In essentials he had not altered in half a century, and his welcome was typically casual.

'You've come at the right time for the mangos. I expect you remembered that,' he said.

Mangos are wonderful in Dominica; so are most fruits for

I

that matter, grapefruit in particular. Rose's Lime Juice started there.

'I'm in time for the Cassia too,' I said.

Its brilliant yellow stabbed the dark green of the country-side. Till I had visited Dominica I had not realised how many shades of green there are. The mountains that surrounded us as we drove, looked like a single solid background with one shade of green mingling with another, as on a painter's palette. But I knew through many trips on foot how that seemingly solid background was split by valleys, so that a house that seemed only a mile away was separated from you by a succession of deep gorges.

The sun broke through the clouds and a rainbow curved above the mountain road.

I looked about me with fond recollective eyes.

'I hadn't forgotten how beautiful it is,' I said.

He smiled.

'All the same, I'm surprised at your coming here for copy. I should have thought that you'd have found more in St Lucia and Grenada, with all those new hotels.'

'But that's precisely why I'm here. I wanted to see the one island that has missed the tourist boom.'

Dominica had missed it because, although one of the larger islands, it has no beaches on the leeward coast and bathing on the windward side is dangerous. It holds no attractions for the package tourist.

'That's so,' he said. He seemed satisfied with my explanation, and there was no reason why he should not be. The writer's quest for copy is an unassailable alibi. Why should he suspect that my presence here was due, not to an editor's whim, but to a son's curiosity. 'I've got to find out what's biting the old boy,' his son, who is also my godson, had insisted. 'Why won't he come back to England? Has he got some ghastly illness and is ashamed to see us? Is he mad with me about my marriage, though he pretended not to be? Is he tied up with some fearful floosie? Has he gone broke? I've got to know. You're the one person who can go there without making him feel suspicious. The estate will foot your bill. We've got to know.'

Already I had found the answer to one of my godson's questions. Clearly Raymond had not contracted some disfiguring tropical complaint.

I acted in terms of my rôle of a professional writer in search of copy.

'I've given myself two weeks here,' I said. 'I want to see all I can.'

Twenty-five years back, in a piece called 'Typical Dominica', I had tried to explain the particular magic that this island has held for so many and such diverse eccentrics. I wrote of three friends in particular, Elma Napier, Stephen Haweis and John Archbold. Elma Napier was the daughter of the Sir William Gordon-Cumming who had been involved in the Tranby Croft baccarat scandal. She had settled on the north-east corner of the island. She had become involved in local politics and had been elected to the Legislative Council. She had written several books. Stephen Haweis was a scholar and a painter who had lived the life of a recluse after losing most of his money in the 1929 Wall Street Crash. John Archbold was a youngish, rich American, who had come to the island on a cruise shortly before the war. He had meant to leave that night, but a sudden unaccountable impulse had moved him to stay on and purchase an estate. A typical Somerset Maugham situation, but Archbold was not a beachcomber. He had developed his estate as a sound business proposition. His presence on the island contributed substantially to its congeniality and prosperity.

I asked about them. 'I can't expect to find Stephen here,' I said. He had been very frail on my last visit.

Raymond shook his head. 'He checked out three years ago, but Elma's fine. She celebrated her eightieth birthday the other day. She finds it difficult to get about, but those blue eyes haven't lost their sparkle. We're going out to lunch next week; Daphne's fine too.' Daphne was Elma's daughter and a fond friend of mine. 'She runs a bar restaurant in town. One great piece of luck. John Archbold's here, in cracking form. We're dining there tomorrow. Maybe you won't find things so very different,' he concluded.

Certainly his own home was not. Six miles north-east of

Roseau, Overdale stood back from the Imperial Road, a two-storeyed wooden villa that had been built on the foundations of an old plantation house. The ruined tower of a sugar mill stood behind it. In front was the stonework of a low garden wall, with large curved flower pots at its corners. Between it and a curved 'welcoming arms' entrance a ragged lawn was shaded by a widespread mango tree. A verandah ran round the house. Bougainvillea, purple and rust red, trailed over it and between the upper windows. The house stood above a valley. The jungle between the house and the stream was a tangle of trees and plants, bananas and bamboos, from which four coconut palms towered. There was no formal garden. The short drive from the road was lined with crotons. The west wall of the house sheltered and protected a miniature orchid house. 'I've got some rather remarkable flowers,' Raymond said, 'but they're hidden away in corners. They are for the house. One doesn't sit about in gardens here.'

It was nearly forty years since I had come here first. It had altered as little in that time as had Charminster, his home in England. In neither case had there been any necessity to improve or add.

From my window I could see across the waters the majestic outline of Martinique, where a hundred and ninety years ago Rodney, in a one-day battle, had saved the British Empire. It was the same room that I had had on my last visit, a bare room with practical wooden furniture, its white walls decorated by the work of local painters—a flower design in oils by Daphne's husband, Percy Agar, and a water-colour landscape by Stephen Haweis—I have its twin sister in my flat in Tangier.

As I came downstairs I looked round the hall for signs of a woman's presence—a floppy hat, a shopping basket. I did not see any. It looked as though I had found the answer to the second item in his son's questionnaire.

My punch was awaiting me. I had drunk passion fruit occasionally, but simply, as I have drunk orange juice at breakfast. I had never taken it in as a punch. It was rich and sweet. Nutmeg scattered on the surface enriched the flavour

4

of the rum. It tasted like a dessert, but I could feel its strength.

After a single sip I raised my glass to Raymond.

'In not so long now we shall have known each other for half a century.'

He had come to Oxford in the October of 1922. My brother Evelyn, as he has told in his autobiography, had come up a term late for his year, in the preceding January. In November, he arranged for me a small party of his special friends— Harold Acton, Peter Quennell, John Sutro, Robert Byron, Christopher Hollis, Hugh Molson, Anthony Bushell, Claud Cockburn, Terence Greenidge, Richard Pares. About a dozen, and every one of them is well known today. I found them all likable and lively. But the one who struck me most was Raymond, not only for his good looks, though they were remarkable: he was tall, long-legged, broad-shouldered, with reddish hair, grey eyes, a long straight nose, rather a wide mouth, very white teeth which you only noticed when he smiled, a clear complexion, indicative of health. Yes, he was strikingly good looking, with two particularly striking traits: one, a characteristic that was to stay with him all his life—an air of effortless composure in which was implicit the assumption that living was on the whole an agreeable business. At ease with himself, he put others at their ease. Enjoying life, he liked everyone who contributed to the sum of it. That was his first distinctive characteristic. The second, which also stayed with him all his life, was his air of masculine maturity. This was not so noticeable later because he shared it with many others; but in Oxford, in that set, it was practically non-existent.

As many autobiographies have witnessed since, there was in that set a strong homosexual undertone. Most of them had led at school celibate monastic lives. Any deviation had been punished by expulsion. A conspiracy of silence had been maintained. Then suddenly the Public School sixth-former became an undergraduate to whom everything was permitted. Most of them passed through a homosexual phase which in the majority of cases was completely shed when

5

they entered adult life. In that respect Raymond was markedly different from his contemporaries. He never passed through that phase.

This difference was of considerable irritation to several of them, particularly to Brian Howard. In recent years Brian has appeared in a number of memoirs and a large biography of him has been issued, *Portrait of a Failure*. Before he died by his own hand, when he was close on sixty, he had exhausted the patience of nearly all his friends. Many people considered him the original of Ambrose Silk in *Put out More Flags* and Anthony Blanche in *Brideshead Revisited*. In part he was. In *A Little Learning* Evelyn described him as having, at the age of nineteen, 'dash and insolence ... a kind of ferocity of elegance that belonged to a romantic era of a century before his own.'

He was petulantly irritated by Raymond's absorption in the other sex. 'It's maddening,' he said. 'I could have been crazy about him, oh, but my dear how crazy. But what do you think happened: at the age of fourteen, fourteen I ask you, he was seduced, and by his aunt; by his aunt. I ask you. He hasn't looked back. What chance for little me?'

I cannot remember what we talked about, Raymond Peronne and I, at that first meeting, but I do remember having in his company a curious sense of being where I belonged. I have since learned that he gave that same sensation to many others.

Afterwards I asked Evelyn who he was. 'A younger son,' he told me. 'His father's a Baron, Peronne of Charminster; the brother was killed in the war, but that brother had a son, which rules Raymond out.'

'I've never heard the name.'

'Nobody has. It's a Huguenot family: took refuge in the Netherlands, came over with William of Orange: that's how it got ennobled: rested on its laurels ever since. His father's as obscure as any eighth peer could be. But he's rich, all right, which is as well for Raymond.'

'Isn't Raymond very bright?'

'He's bright enough.'

'Then why should it be so lucky for him to be rich?'

'Because he doesn't have to force himself into a career that may prove uncongenial. There are so many openings for a young man with ability, with connections and with money.'

'Such as?'

'You know—so many things.'

I did not, but I let it pass.

'Raymond can afford to wait,' Evelyn went on. 'He doesn't have to accept the first good offer that comes his way.'

'I hope I'll be seeing more of him.'

'You will. He'll be around.'

Evelyn was right. He was. I myself went up to Oxford every term, and Evelyn's friends were constant visitors at Underhill, my father's house in Hampstead. Raymond was one of the most regular. I saw as much of him as I did of anyone during 1923. But we did not become more than close acquaintances until the hilarious occasion in the following January when Evelyn brought down a female to an Oxford 'blind'.

Her name was Judy Maine. She was then in her early twenties, prettyish, little, with brown, bobbed hair. In retrospect I see her as typical of all those young girls who invaded London after the war: eager, idealistic, resolved to put the world to rights. She might have been a character out of an early Aldous Huxley novel, *Crome Yellow* or *Antic Hay*. She had read Marx and Freud. Dostoievsky was her bible. She had taken a degree in history in a provincial university, Reading or Bristol, I cannot remember which. She supplemented a parental allowance with a succession of odd jobs for idealistic projects which tended to fold or reduce their staff within a few weeks of her joining them. She was a member of the 1917 club, of which Ramsay Macdonald was the first President, and she despised everything that the Victorian age stood for, the age whose 'selfishness and short-sightedness were responsible for the war': she had come up to London resolved to rid herself of the inhibitions that had frustrated her maiden aunts. That project at least she had achieved.

She had a minute flat at the top of a converted house in Bloomsbury. Its divan was piled high with cushions, its walls were lined with sagging bookshelves; it had orange curtains.

I had met her at the Caves of Harmony, a club in Charlotte Street run by Elsa Lanchester and Harold Scott that figures in *Antic Hay*, and that once a week gave dances which were enlivened by a cabaret: Morris dancing, character songs and one-act plays.

At the end of the Christmas Vac. I had taken Evelyn there, asking Judy to join us. They made friends quickly. In those days I played Rugby football every Saturday. 'In two weeks' time,' I said, 'we're playing Reading University. Why don't I come on and stay the night at Oxford.'

'I'll give a party for you. It'll be a good way of getting the new term started.'

'What wouldn't I give,' she said, 'to have Gyges' ring and go to an Oxford blind.'

'There's no need for Gyges' ring. You can come on your own.'

'A girl isn't allowed in College after dark.'

'You could dress up as a man.'

It was a typical Evelyn fantasy and we devoted quite a while to the discussion of how she should be dressed. She was slim, but she was not unrounded. It was finally decided that plus fours, being voluminous, would provide the best disguise.

I was not of those who had profited from the release of Judy's Victorian inhibitions. We met irregularly, but most weeks we had a telephone conversation. Towards the end of the week she was to ask, 'Do you think that Evelyn's serious about my going up to Oxford?'

'I shouldn't have thought so, why?'

'I heard from him today. He wanted to know what train I'd catch.'

'Evelyn's one for carrying a joke through.'

'Would he be surprised if I turned up?'

'I think so, yes.'

'What would he do?'

'He'd pretend that he knew all the time you'd come.'

'Would he be annoyed?'

'He'd respect you for taking up his dare.'

'I've a very good mind to go.'

'You do just that.'

But I did not believe for a moment that she would. I could not have been more surprised at being met at Oxford by Evelyn, Raymond and an object that it took me several seconds to identify as Judy. She was appalling. She looked barely human. The plus fours hung below her calves, barely an inch above her ankles. The coat, of a different material, could have gone round her twice. Instead of a collar and tie she wore one of the high-necked pullovers that were just coming into fashion; it hung in thick folds over her bosom; her hair was contained within a cycling cap. An untidy, improbable composition, but what made it grotesque was the unhealthiness of a face washed clean of make-up. I have heard people described as 'the kind of thing you find under a stone'. That is exactly how she looked. She filled me with nausea. I could barely look at her. But to my astonishment she was having an entirely different effect on Raymond.

We dined at the George. Raymond was the host. He was in the highest spirits. He was responsible for her make-up and was delighted with his achievement. 'Doesn't she look wonderful? I thought her something of a dream when she got off the train this morning, but now there's all the difference in the world: I don't know how she'll ever have the heart to be a girl again.'

In the restaurant she had had of course to take off her cap. Her hair was plastered down with brilliantine. Caked on the back of her neck, it increased her air of unhealthiness. I could not think why the management did not turn her out.

All this happened in 1924, but I have never seen in a whole half century since anything that looked so degenerate. Nothing, however, could diminish Raymond's delight in her appearance. I had never seen him so ecstatic. He plied us with wine. The party became very gay, so gay that by the time that we had reached our port, I had begun to see Judy through Raymond's eyes. 'There's no one like her, is there,

9

there couldn't be anyone so special.' Special, well, she certainly was that. There was no one like her. I let my glass be refilled. By the time we left the hotel, I, too, was in an anapaestic mood.

Evelyn's party was being held in a graduate's rooms in King Edward Street. There were about ten guests. Bottles of burgundy stood along the mantelpiece; there was some tawny port, and a bottle of cognac. Everyone had already dined, but there was a cheddar cheese, three loaves of bread, a dish of butter and a fruit cake.

The party soon became extremely noisy. I kept as far away from Judy as I could, but my eyes were on her. Evelyn, too, kept away from her, but he played his part as host, bringing up one guest after another to be introduced. 'It's going all right, isn't it?' he whispered conspiratorially. Judy certainly was having a high time. Her eyes were bright; her laughter constant. Raymond never left her side and presently a puzzled guest came over to me. 'What's the matter with Raymond?' he enquired.

'Nothing as far as I know. Why?'

'He's suddenly gone "pi". I was telling quite a harmless story, spattered, I must admit, with a number of four-letter words, but *au fond* a perfectly harmless story, if you follow me. Suddenly Raymond said, "I must ask you not to use that kind of language." What's biting him?'

I chuckled inwardly. It was precisely to hear that kind of language that Judy had wanted Gyges' ring. She was getting what she had come for. It was ironic that Raymond should be trying to protect her aural innocence. As the evening progressed I found myself able to look at her with less dismay. Her cheeks were flushed now and she looked less unhealthy, but her presence was certainly surprising those of the guests who were not in the secret.

'Who on earth is that extraordinary creature Raymond's sponsoring?' I was asked.

'A jockey,' I said. 'Didn't you know he was a racing man?'

'Ah, that accounts for it.'

A few minutes later I was hoping that this explanation would satisfy a more stringent, more perceptive examination.

Suddenly the noise of the party was interrupted by a banging on the door.

'What is this impertinence?' demanded Evelyn. But it was not an impertinence. It was the proctor with his bulldogs. A voice demanded 'silence'.

'I need your names, please, gentlemen, and the names of your colleges.' The bulldogs came round taking names.

'Alec Waugh,' I said. 'I live in London. I am staying at the George.' They took name after name. Finally they reached Judy. They looked her up and down. Would the bulldogs accept her? She lowered the pitch of her voice. 'Mr Stanley Maine, London, staying at the Randolph.' They took her particulars and then moved on. 'Mr Terence Greenidge, Hertford College.' It was a great relief, yet I felt that it implied some criticism of the contemporary *mores* that so repellent an object could pass as a man.

At last, the last name was taken. The proctor spoke: 'I will ask all members of the University to return immediately to their colleges.' The bulldogs watched the members of the University leave the room; Evelyn as he passed me whispered, 'Breakfast at the Randolph nine o'clock. Tell Mr Maine.'

It was a cheery breakfast, though Judy was concerned about her hosts. 'Is this going to get you into trouble? I'd hate it if that happened.'

Raymond shrugged. 'There isn't much that they can do, provided that you're looking likely to make a reasonable showing in the schools. How do you stand with your college, Evelyn?'

'I have my private war with Cruttwell.'

Cruttwell was the Dean of Hertford. Evelyn was to deal with this private war in *A Little Learning*.

'Crutters will be pleased,' he said. 'It will be extra ammunition for the final showdown.'

That showdown was to come in the following September when Evelyn got a bad third in Mods, had his scholarship taken away, and started the period of his life that he entitled 'in which our hero's fortunes fall very low'. But all that was ten months away. Its shadow did not cloud our morning. We sat over the breakfast table until after ten. Then I suggested that as Raymond had a car, we should lunch at Thame, at the Spread Eagle.

'We'll start at noon,' said Raymond. 'That'll give me ninety minutes to show Judy round such of the sights as she has not seen.' As they walked away together down the Corn, Evelyn and I exchanged a glance. 'That seems to have worked out,' I said.

When they returned, it was very clear that they had thoroughly enjoyed their time together. Judy was bright eyed and rather giggly. Raymond was oratorical, talking at length and for effect on abstruse subjects such as 'the case for Greek in elementary schools' as though he were seconding a motion at the Union.

2

Judy and I caught an afternoon train back to London. It had come from the West, was crowded, and we had difficulty in finding seats. We sat on opposite sides of a compartment, two places away. I had brought the *Observer*. Raymond had given her *The News of the World*. 'It is time that you were acquainted with the facts of life,' he said. I studied my *Observer* dutifully, but she let her lurid sheet fall forward on her lap. Her face wore an abstracted look.

We reached Paddington shortly after six. Even for Londoners, London has never been very lively on a Sunday evening. You have to know the city well to know where you can beat up entertainment. Judy and I looked questioningly at one another. She hesitated. She clearly did not want to go home alone. I had a suspicion that she had something to get off her chest. It was up to me to make some suggestion. Pubs would not be open until seven, and after the lunch at the Spread Eagle I was out of funds.

'The cook in my flat has Sunday off,' I said. 'But I'm sure the housekeeper could scramble a few eggs and I've got some wine.'

'This is exactly what I wanted,' she said later, as she settled herself after supper before the fire, her feet curled under her, her head leant back against a chair. 'Now,' she said, 'you can tell me all about him.'

'I haven't much to tell you. Much that you don't know already. He's a second son.'

'That makes him an honourable?'

'That makes him an honourable.'

'And that's how I address him on an envelope? The Hon. Raymond Peronne.'

'That's how you address him on an envelope.'

'But I introduce him just as Mr.'

'Exactly.'

'That seems a pity. Still . . .' She paused. 'The Hon.

13

Raymond Peronne. It'll be the first time I've addressed an envelope that way.'

'So you think that you'll be writing?'

'I think so, yes, don't you?'

'It looked that way.'

'No danger, is there, of his being one of those?'

'Not the slightest. That's what Brian Howard and the rest complain about.'

'Has he a special girl friend?'

'That's what I wouldn't know.'

'You could find out, couldn't you?'

'I suppose I could.'

'I'd be grateful. I'll find out for myself, of course, quite soon. It's one of the things where if anything's going to happen it'll happen quick.'

'How can you tell?'

'It's the kind of thing you always can. You should know that.'

I did not. Though I was twenty-six. It was the kind of remark she was fond of making. I wondered out of how wide an experience she was speaking, or whether she was repeating a remark made to her by another woman; a remark she had found effective.

'It's fun sometimes when you know from the start that it's all going to take time; a gradual getting to know each other, lunches to start with and then dinners, first parties with other guests, then just the two of you; yes, that *is* fun, wondering at the start how long the working-up will take, sometimes hurrying it, sometimes delaying it, playing it by mood. Oh yes, it is fun, that. But,' she paused, a half smile flickering on her lips, 'this kind of thing is more fun, much more fun. I suppose I ought to clear my decks.'

'Are they very cluttered?'

'No, not especially. Still . . .' Again she paused. She was really talking to herself.

'I've heard it said that one of the pleasantest things about the start of a new affair is the walking out on someone who has begun to bore you, but whom you've kept on with out of laziness, and it *is* fun, yes of course that is, but . . . I don't

14

like hurting people, particularly somebody I've . . . When I'm happy myself, I don't like someone else being wretched, particularly when it's because of me they are wretched.'

She was talking, I was now sure, in large part to impress herself. One day, I thought, I'll make use of this in a story, changing it so she won't recognise herself.

I asked her if she would like a glass of port. She shook her head. 'I like wine when I'm eating, not otherwise. I wish you had some Russian tea, but I know you haven't. I'll have to give you an electric kettle for your birthday.'

'That'll be a long time off. July the eighth.'

'It'll have to be Easter then. I can't wait till July.'

She stretched her arms above her head. She sighed, a sigh that came from a deep well of happiness.

'To think that yesterday morning I'd never even heard of him. There was I, eating my breakfast, wondering whether I'd go down or not. You remember how grey and cold it was. The train journey would cost me—I didn't even know how much the ticket was—and two weeks of the month to run before my allowance comes. If anyone even reasonably reasonable had rung me up, I'd have called it off. What I'd have missed.'

'He's certainly good looking.'

'Oh, but it isn't only that. It isn't even that. There's something about him. I don't know what it is. I seem so at peace with him, so understood by him. I don't have to explain myself, and he doesn't have to explain himself. Can you appreciate what a relief that is to a girl? No, of course you can't. Because you're not a girl. You don't know what men are like when they are with girls, always talking about themselves, trying to impress us. He's not like that, not at all: he doesn't seem interested in himself.'

'Perhaps he isn't.'

'Oh, but that's silly. He must be; of course he is. Everybody is. We are all interested in ourselves. I am. You are. Wondering what we really are. He doesn't seem to be. He accepts himself for what he is. Just as he accepts you for what you are. Oh, I do hope that he's not mixed up with some wretched trollop. You'll find out, won't you, as soon as possible?'

'I'll do my best.'

Next day I wrote to Evelyn: but our letters crossed. On the Tuesday morning I received from him an enquiry as to Judy's position in my life. Was she my mistress? The word mistress was not in inverted commas. It was typical of Evelyn to use such an old-fashioned word. Raymond was anxious to know. Judy had 'intrigued' him. That word was put in inverted commas, so was the assurance that he did not want 'to trespass on my preserves'. I was touched by his concern, but not surprised by it. I have often found Americans surprised by the Englishman's refusal to damage a masculine friendship on a woman's account. I sent Evelyn a note of reassurance and rang up Judy. 'You can get your decks cleared,' I said.

During the winter, when I played football regularly, I kept strict training for the last three days of the week, but on the Saturday night, in the vernacular of the hour I 'beat it up' with four or five members of the side. Our usual haunt was Dehem's Oyster bar off Shaftesbury Avenue. Sometimes when the bar closed, two or three of us would go on to the 43.

The 43 was a club in Gerard Street, run by a lady whose two daughters were later to marry peers. It was half a speakeasy and half a brothel. It was at this time in its early days. It was patronised by the world of fashion. It had elegance. It was real. Gossip columnists found useful copy there. It figured in *A Handful of Dust*.

We arrived there rather early. It was one of the places that one went onto afterwards, but to my surprise Raymond Peronne was already there. A female was at his table: otherwise he was alone. He waved to us to join him. A bottle of club champagne was on the table. 'What a pleasant surprise this is,' he said. 'Mabel, this is Mr Alec Waugh and his two friends . . .' He raised the pitch of his voice interrogatively. I gave their names. 'I hope you'll help me finish off this bottle. It isn't very good. Mabel has already switched to her own special poison.'

She was sipping at a hock glass that was filled with a pinkish liquid. It was priced at seven and six, and presumably contained grenadine and soda. Mabel was blonde and slim and undistinctive. You would be unlikely to recognise her at a second meeting unless she was wearing the same frock. On this occasion it was pale and blue, tight-bodiced, with a panier skirt. It was quite smart. She was not unattractive; it was hard to explain why you knew instantaneously that she was one of the hostesses and not a guest.

'Shall we ask Mabel to bring over one or two of her friends? She has some very nice ones,' Raymond asked.

I looked enquiringly at my two footballers. They shook their heads. It was their first visit here. They had asked me to bring them. They were curious to see what it was like. But one glance was enough to tell them that 'hostesses at the 43' were not in their income bracket. Nor, for that matter, were they in mine. 'Another time,' I said.

'Fine. We'll have better talk without them, if you'll forgive me, Mabel.'

'Granted, I'm sure.'

'Let's have another bottle then, and another of your specials, Mabel.'

Mabel sipped it slowly, with apparent appreciation. 'Could I have something to eat?' she said. A sandwich was produced; a thin sliver of ham divided two thin slices of white bread whose corners were turned up. Mabel devoured it as though she were hungry: perhaps she was.

'Any food for the rest of you?' Raymond asked. We shook our heads. We had had an Irish stew at Dehem's, we told him. 'What about some cheese then?'

We agreed that we would like some cheese. The cheese came in small silver paper-wrapped triangles. 'It's the only thing here that's fresh,' he said. He behaved as a host would. Without actually asking questions, he learned that one of my footballers had been at Tonbridge, the other at Haileybury; that they had been too young for the war, that they decided not to go to a University. 'Very wise,' said Raymond. 'Get started on the battle right away. You'll have a three-year start of the rest of us.' They were now qualifying as chartered accountants. They would be taking their final exams in August. The talk moved easily. Time ticked by. By now most of the tables were filled; on the dance floor couples were swaying but scarcely moving. The noise increased. After an hour my football companions took their leave. 'We must be on our way.'

Raymond seemed genuinely sorry when they left. I rose with them. 'I should be going too,' I said.

He waved me back. 'No, stay on another half hour, please.'

He was not mandatory, not insistent, but it was never easy to refuse him.

'There's still half a bottle of this deplorable liquid left,' he said. Mabel in her turn stood up. 'Back in a jiffy.'

As soon as we were alone, Raymond said, 'I'd rather you didn't mention to Judy that you saw me here. She might not understand.'

Did that mean, I asked myself, that he had seen Judy since the Sunday? If he had, what was he doing here? It was clear that Mabel was expecting him to take her home. Had he quarrelled with Judy? If he was planning to take Mabel home, why was he lingering here? When had he got to be back at Oxford. Had he any right to be here at all in term-time?

Mabel rejoined us. Again he turned his attention to her. He had not neglected her while the others had been at the table. He had included her in the conversation, addressing parts of it to her. She had contributed very little. She answered questions, briefly, that was about all. But she had seemed perfectly happy, sitting there, listening; content, grateful that no demands were being made upon her, yet.

'Let's dance,' he said. It was the first time they had. He held her close; she was a good dancer, smooth and rhythmic; so was he, not indulging in elaborate steps, but following the music's beat. His dancing was a form of courtship. 'And this is where I go,' I thought. As soon as the music stopped and they came back to the table, I would make my excuses. It was after two, I had had a hard game of football and I was tired. Now was the time; the music seemed to be moving to a close. It loudened, tautened, another minute and then ...
But before that minute came, there was a sudden noise outside, the beating of something heavy on a door, a raising of

voices on the stairs, then a loud proclamation: 'Ladies and gentlemen, will you return please to your tables.'

The music ceased on a rising scale. Somebody shouted: 'The police: a raid.' Another voice shouted 'Let's get out of here,' but the doors were picketed. The three uniformed policemen who had forced their way through the door had been joined by three plain-clothes men from the floor, spies, presumably, who had given the police the tip off.

'Now, now, quietly please, quietly, ladies and gentlemen; we won't be here for long. Ten minutes and you'll be back to your fun again. We only want to make sure of what you've got in all these glasses. And to take a name or two. We shan't be long.'

He wasn't. In two minutes he was at Raymond's table. He raised a glass. 'Now what would you have here?'

'I wouldn't know, Constable, it was sold to me and charged to me as champagne. But I suspect that it's aerated hock.'

'It's alcoholic, though.'

'Oh, definitely alcoholic.'

'In that case, sir, I'd like your name.'

He put down the glass and opened the notebook that he held in his other hand. He looked at Raymond closely.

'I don't think I need to ask *you* for your name, sir.'

'Perhaps you don't, Constable.'

'The Hon. Raymond Peronne, if I'm not mistaken.'

'You're not mistaken, Constable.'

There was the flash of an electric bulb across the room. The constable swung round. 'No more of that or there'll be trouble.' He turned back to Raymond with a grin. 'I'm afraid that his Lordship may have a surprise when he opens his *Daily Mail* on Monday morning.'

'He's got a strong constitution; I think he'll weather it.'

Within ten minutes the policemen had done their job. From the doorway the sergeant waved goodbye. 'Back to your fun, now, ladies and gentlemen. Make the most of your good time while you can. It may not be for long.'

His prophecy was not to be fulfilled. It was not the first time that the 43 had been raided. Nor was it to prove the last. Even though the proprietor was to serve a period in gaol, the club was to operate until the second war.

The band struck up. Couples were back upon the floor, waiters hurried between the tables. But Raymond looked pensive. 'Will that photograph in the papers trouble you?' I asked.

'Not at home, my father couldn't care less what I do, but it may at Oxford. I got special weekend leave to see my father. There's no explanation for my being here when I should be there. Two raids within a week. I'll begin to think that you're in league with the police.' He sat silent for a minute, then he shrugged. 'Waiter,' he called. 'My bill.'

He put his wallet on the table, took an envelope from his pocket, moved some notes into it, I could not see how many nor of what denomination, and handed it across to Mabel.

'I'm sorry,' he said. 'Please forgive me, but somehow that raid has upset my mood.' He turned to me. 'I've got my car here. I can drive you back.'

It was a cold but a clear night. There were few clouds in the sky and a waning moon was three quarters full. He sat at the wheel, still pensive. 'Somehow I don't feel like driving back to Oxford right away.'

'I'm not too keen on another nightclub.'

'That isn't what I had in mind. Why don't we look up Judy?'

'At this time of night?'

'She keeps late hours. She's quite likely to be reading or playing the gramophone.'

'Shall we ring her up?'

'No, no, she may be asleep; we don't want to wake her. She'd feel she had to ask us over, though she wouldn't want to. Let's drive round and see if she's a light on.'

Her flat was visible from the road. If he knew that, he must have been round to see her, probably that afternoon. Perhaps they had quarrelled over dinner and he had gone to the 43 in pique.

We drove in silence through the deserted streets. I was surprised at his composure. He was six years younger than I, but he seemed six years older.

20

'Here we are,' he said. 'Yes, there is a light on. You ring the bell. I'll stand in the street and wave.'

As he had foreseen, at the sound of the bell a window sash was raised, a female head looked out. I would have not recognised who it was, but he, on the pavement, was unmistakable, with his height and his short, fur-collared coat. 'Wait there a minute,' she called down.

She reappeared with an envelope in her hand. 'Catch,' she called. She flung it out. Its weight carried it over the narrow garden, into the street: a bunch of keys was in it. 'The yale key for the front door,' she called.

She was wearing a flannel nightgown, a very nursery garment. I could see over her shoulder before the gas fire a couple of cushions, an open copy of the Shakespeare Press, blue paper-covered edition of *Ulysses*. She had been reading it, lying on her stomach. She had no make-up on. Her face glowed with happiness, with relieved happiness. She looked no older than fifteen. 'What can I get you to drink?' she asked.

'Is the kettle still on?'

'It is.'

'Then some of that Russian tea.'

'You, tea?'

'If you'd known where I've been spending the last three hours, you'd know that that was the one beverage we could use.'

'Where have you been spending the last three hours?'

He told her. He made a good story of it. He had asked me not to let her know that he had been at the 43. But that was two hours ago, when he had been planning to spend the night with Mabel, two hours ago when he was in reaction against whatever it was that had gone wrong with his date with Judy. They were together now. There had been no episode with Mabel. He could dismiss the whole excursion as a joke.

'I don't know what I shall be seeing in Monday's papers,' he concluded, 'but I'm feeling very grateful to those policemen. But for them I wouldn't be here now.'

It was clearly time for me to be on my way. I had served

21

my purpose. I left my Russian tea half-finished. 'I've played football this afternoon, remember.' No effort was made to make me stay. If it doesn't come to a head tonight it never will, I thought.

It did.

The Times was laid every morning by my breakfast tray. There was no reference there to a police raid on the 43. But at that time I had a half-time employment in my father's publishing house of Chapman & Hall. Monday was one of my office days, and at Earl's Court Station I bought a copy of the *Daily Mail*. It was there all right. On the second page: 'Peer's son in Soho nightclub raid'. A good photograph too. Raymond unmistakably himself. He was highly photogenic. It was not surprising that the policeman had recognised him. I was in the photo too, but I might have been anybody. Perhaps that was a lucky trait. It is better for a novelist to pass unnoticed.

At half-past ten Judy was on the telephone. 'Have you seen the *Daily Mail*?'

'Yes.'

'Isn't it terrible?'

'It's what he expected.'

'Yes, but we all say things like that before they happen. When they do happen . . .' She was in the mood, clearly, for a long, long talk, but Monday was my busy morning. I interrupted her. 'Are you doing anything tonight?' I asked.

'Nothing that I can't cancel.'

'Why not a quiet dinner, then?'

'That would be wonderful.'

She was round very early; soon after half-past six. She was looking radiant. She had so much to say that she could not get it all in order. She would jump from one aspect of the subject to another. 'He's wonderful,' that was the main rhythm of it all, the thread that held it all together. She had not believed that anyone could be so wonderful. Thank heavens that she knew enough about other men to realise how special he was: and it wasn't as though those others had been shoddy men. No, no, they hadn't. It was simply that he was different. That was the main thread, the theme that she came back to always.

But there were other threads, innumerable other threads—the surprise, the miracle of it all. 'The two of you turning up like that. The last thing I had expected. I was feeling so despondent. His sudden leaving after dinner. Everything had been going so well, at least I thought it had. We'd dined at the Isola Bella, one of my favourite places. I love those pictures on the wall. The old half-drunk man, with the monkey taking away his bottle, and the girl with her head tilted back and the butterfly hovering above her lips, so tantalising. We finished with zabaglioni and that yellow Italian liqueur, strega. It was so warm, so cosy, I was saying to myself, "In an hour from now, we'll be back in my flat." He wouldn't hurry, that I knew. But we would be going back there, I was sure of that; and then, without warning, he signalled to the waiter, he looked at his watch. "It's later than I thought. I've got to be back by midnight." It took my breath away. I couldn't think of anything to say. I was silent the whole way back. He didn't ask if he could come in. He didn't kiss me goodnight. Not even a peck on the cheek. I was sunk, I couldn't have gone to sleep. I sat in my chair, staring at the fire. What had gone wrong? What had I said? What had I done? Had he realised suddenly that I wasn't his kind of person? Had he thought my flat awful, cheap and tatty? Question after question. I can't stand this, I told myself. I gave myself a bath, a steaming hot one; but that only made me more awake. If I had taken a drink I would have gone on drinking; but drink's not my remedy. Drink makes me sullen. Yet I couldn't sleep. I had to sleep. I had to take my mind off this. *Ulysses* was on my writing desk. It'd been there five weeks. I had got stuck quarter through. *Ulysses*, that was my solution. I'd break the back of it. That would need concentration. I put two cushions on the floor. I made myself some tea. "Now I'll fight this," I vowed, and I did fight it. Do you know how many pages I got through? Seventy-seven: and I understood them, too. I not only understood them, I enjoyed them. I was so delighted with myself that Raymond almost went out of my mind. No, I can't say that. But I regained my confidence. I wasn't a trivial nonentity who had been turned down by a second son. I was quite a person. I could not only understand *Ulysses*, I could enjoy it. To hell with Raymond. I was having myself a ball. And then suddenly that bell went; and he was down there on the pavement, and I forgot everything that I had thought about him. It was so wonderful.' She paused. 'It couldn't have been more perfect. Even so,' she paused again, 'I wonder why he did go off.'

Later, quite a lot later, I was to ask him that.

He laughed. 'You may not believe it, but I had a twinge of conscience. No, don't look so astounded, I really did. It was all too easy; so much too easy. It couldn't lead to anything. I might be bad for her. We weren't committed yet. There's a point in a love affair where you can back out. That point once passed, you can't. We hadn't passed it yet. If I didn't get out now, I never would. That's why I went to the 43, to find somebody like Mabel, to work it all out of my system. I looked round the room, Mabel was the most my type, and she would have been amusing; I could tell that from the way she danced. But when she came back to my table, and I remembered Judy sitting opposite me an hour earlier at that other table, I couldn't go through with it; not yet, anyhow. It would need a lot of drink before I was ready for that. Heavens, but I was relieved when you all turned up. It gave me a respite. I put it off, and I put it off. Then those policemen came. What a relief they were. Now I had an excuse for dumping Mabel. I didn't want to hurt her feelings. Those policemen, an intervention of providence, they made my mind up for me.'

'Have you told Judy this?'

'Of course. She roared with laughter. It's become one of those little intimate jokes that you build up with someone. If we're dining out together and we're feeling pretty close, you know the way it is, just waiting to get back to bed, and I'd say "about time we got our bill" she'll say, "Let's hurry, before the policemen come and throw you off your stroke." It's fun how during an affair you build up a code language for yourselves.'

24

'Like Swann's cattleyas.'

But that confidence was several weeks ahead. Now we sat before the fire in my flat, she in her first flush of enchantment. 'It's wonderful to have you here so that I can talk about him. Do you know what's one of the most frustrating things for a woman in a love affair?'

'You tell me.'

'That she can't tell a man how wonderful he is. It's not the thing. She would embarrass him. But he, he can tell her everything about herself. Write sonnets to her eyebrows. Moon over her. But a woman can't moon over a man. She's got to have a confidant. Thank God for you.'

She mooned over him, right enough. But half the time she was worrying about that photograph in the *Daily Mail*. Oxford was bound to see it. Would there be a row? The proctor at that party and now this. She'd hate to have him get into a row on her account. She had, clearly, a strong maternal streak. What would his father say? Was he independent of his father? Would it damage his career? What was he planning to do?

I told her that he was reading history. 'But what's that leading to? He must have something definite in mind.'

The telephone rang. It was Raymond at the other end. 'What luck finding you in. Are you alone?'

'Except for Judy.'

'The very person that I was looking for. Can I come round? Right away? Within ten minutes. Fine.'

'You know who that was,' I said to Judy.

She nodded. 'And he's in London?'

'Must be; within ten minutes.'

He was round in less, bright-eyed, breathing a little quickly, with a high colour to his cheeks.

'A whisky, quick,' he said. 'A strong one, with very little soda.'

He drank it standing up, in a succession of gulps. 'That's better,' he said after the first. 'I didn't dare have one before. If there'd been a smash, "Peer's son drunk in car", no, that would have been too rugged: as it is it's calamitous enough. I've been rusticated until October.' He was obviously

25

excited. He was not in the least depressed. He behaved as though he were a hero, the sole survivor from a wreck. He had scarcely greeted us: Judy had not shifted from the cushions. He had not bent to kiss her, just put his hand upon her neck, running his fingers through her short bobbed hair, then standing with his back against the fire. 'I'm cold, cold, cold,' he said, 'an hour and a half to Charminster, then two hours on from there: only time to grab a sandwich and leave my things.'

'What did your father say?'

'He wasn't there, up here in London, debating in the House. He'll be back tomorrow. Relief, on the whole: not that he'd have minded. As long as I avoid what he calls a scandal, cheating at cards, that kind of thing. Spending a night in London is normal for a young man, he'll say. No, he won't mind.'

I asked him if he wasn't hungry. 'No, no, I'm too excited to be hungry,' but when I produced a cake, he welcomed it. He stood with his back to the fire; he wanted to talk, talk, talk.

I had been struck by, more than anything, his composure. And he was still composed in spite of his excitement. He gave the impression still of knowing exactly what he was about.

'What did the Dean say?' I asked.

'You're a novelist. Imagine what you'd have a Dean say to someone like myself who had behaved as I have.'

'Was he angry?'

'Not particularly. It was a set speech. "You haven't been working properly up here," he said. "Let's see if you'll work better in your father's house. When you come back here in October, I shall expect you to be as thoroughly up in your set subjects as if you'd been here." When you come back in October, indeed. I wonder if I shall.'

'But of course you will,' said Judy.

He shook his head. 'I've been doing a lot of thinking during those two long drives. I've been wondering what a University degree will do for me. I'm not a scholar. I'll be lucky if I get a second. I've taken it for granted from the start that I should go up to Oxford and get as good a degree as possible, because that's the routine that's laid down for every Public School boy. His after-life is determined by what he does at Oxford. He wants to make a mark for himself. And his Oxford career is his jumping-off point. But that isn't my case after all. I've got a basic income. I'd be glad to have more money, who wouldn't? But I don't need it. And as for a position in the world, well, even nowadays having a handle to one's name does count for something. People know who I am.'

'But surely,' Judy expostulated, 'you're going to have a career of some kind? You aren't going to live on the past, you're going to be someone in your own right?'

'Of course, but the question is, what? It sounds ridiculous, but I hadn't begun to think about it till today. It's something that I've got to decide about?'

'Where will you stay until October?' That was my inter-polation.

'I'm not sure yet. Certainly not all the time at Char-minster. And that reminds me, I've got to find somewhere to put up tonight. Can I use your telephone? I'll ring up my sister.'

'Why don't you come back with me?' That was Judy's suggestion, and it seemed to take him off his guard. For all his composure, he was not yet twenty-one. But he knew enough to know that the fact you had spent one night with a girl did not mean that there would be a second. It was not until after the second night that you could be certain how the course would run. 'That's dear of you,' he said. 'I'd love to.'

His manner changed. He became less excited, less in the middle of a drama. He moved away from the fireplace, edged past me to the chair against which she was leaning; he put his glass and cake on a low small table, drew her head back against his knees; with his free hand he stroked her head, drawing his long fingers along her cheek. He lowered the pitch and pace of his voice.

'I'll have to do a good deal of thinking during the next eight months. I've got to make up my mind about what I'm going to do. I've not really given it a thought till now. There was no reason why I should. No one's ever bothered about me. Our family life was built round my brother. He would come into the title, he would inherit the house. Everything was going to be his. Our father lived in him. He had no career of his own; the Peronnes have an inherited reluctance to enter public life: a need for peace after those religious wars; he sat and voted in the House but he hardly ever made a speech. An occasional question, that was all. My brother's place in form, his cricket, his batting average: that's what mattered to him. I believe I became a wet bob simply so as not to be in competition with my brother's memory.

'I liked my brother. He was seven years older; as you know there were two sisters in between. With that disparity of age, we couldn't be very close. But he was generous: he never patronised me. He had a glamour of his own, particularly when the war began. He was in uniform within a month, a Grenadier. He was in France soon after Christmas and before Easter he was back with a purple and white ribbon on his tunic, and military crosses weren't dished out with the rations. Then there was Loos, and he got wounded there. With his arm in a sling, he had an added dash of glamour.

'He got engaged to be married; she was a pretty little thing, only eighteen. But I am sure that at any other time my father would have raised some highly effective opposition. As it was, I suppose it was the subconscious knowledge that the betting was against his son's survival, the need for a grandson . . . It was a very short engagement. Within a few months he was fit again for active service. They were married on his last leave; that was in April, 1916. The last letter he got before he went into the Somme offensive brought the news that she was pregnant. It seems unkind to say it, but I believe that when the news of my brother's death came through, heart-broken though he was, my father's chief anxiety was whether that child would be a boy.'

His voice had taken on a different, a deeper tone. It was the first time that I had heard him talk about himself. I had never seen him serious before. Sitting upright in his chair, with Judy's head against his knees, he could not see her face. But I, sitting opposite, could; and as his voice changed so did her expression. Puzzled at the start, it softened, became tenderer. She, too, was seeing him now in a new light. She had fallen in love with him, almost at first sight. He was someone altogether new to her. With his looks, his name, his prestige, it was natural that he should dazzle her. But he had been outside her experience, he had seemed immune from the problems that harassed the world into which she had been born. He had appeared privileged and unique. Now she recognised that he had his problems too. That made him more personal for her, humanised him, yet at the time they were so exclusively his own, so unlike the problems that other young men confided in her, that he lost nothing of his strangeness for her. On the contrary, they accentuated his uniqueness.

Neither she nor I felt the least wish to interrupt. 'It was a strange time for me. I was then just twelve. In the top form at Summerfields. My headmaster broke the news to me in a formal, stereotyped way. He had had to break that kind of news so often. But one of the masters did appreciate my particular position. "If your brother's child should turn out to be a girl, you'll be a Lord." I nodded. Yes, I had realised that.

'Realised it without taking it in. I had never thought of myself as being my father's heir. I had always thought of myself as a second son. I had been perfectly content with what I was. I was fortunate to be so well placed. I had been born under a lucky star. Yet at the same time it would be exciting to be a peer, to take my seat in the House, to make speeches, to be caricatured in the press, to wear regal robes, to attend the coronation, all that kind of thing. Yes, it would be fun, but I don't think I was in the least disappointed when my brother's child was a boy. I shared in the thanksgiving, my father was so delighted; there were such festivities at Charminster. My father forgot that he was in mourning. He started to rearrange the house in terms of having his favourite son's son as his heir. The succession had not been interrupted.

'My nephew had been born in late November. Christmas was given over to these rearrangements. My sister-in-law—

Margaret—had been staying with her parents. He soon had all that altered. "Of course she has to live here," he said. "This is going to be her son's home. He must get adjusted to its being his home as soon as he's aware of anything." He discussed it with me at length.

' "We'll give her your mother's old room. Then the boy, as soon as he's old enough, can have that little room beside her, the same that Adrian had. We must make it up to him in every way we can. He'll soon know what he's lost through not having a father, but we'll have to diminish it as much as possible. We owe that to Adrian."

'I'm not at all sure that my father wasn't, in his heart, rather relieved that he was a widower, so that he could make the house over to Margaret. He could never have done that when my mother was alive. She wouldn't have stood for that. Nor, I guess, would Margaret. My father had another reason for wanting to make Margaret as comfortable as possible— he didn't want her to re-marry. He didn't want his grandson to be brought up by a step-father. Margaret was under twenty. She was pretty enough. My brother left her quite a little money. If she'd been left alone in London, she'd soon have been snapped up, she'd have wanted to be snapped up. But she'd think twice about leaving a house like Charminster.

'My father's been very tactful with her. He's given her all the freedom that she wants—trips abroad, that kind of thing. If she wants to have an affair, and I presume she does, nothing could be easier. My father always assumes in his conversation that she'll be leaving some day. "Of course I'll be sad when you do have to leave me, and I know you will —this is no life for a young girl like you. I'll be delighted for your sake when you find the man who's right for you, but till that day comes we must see that you have as good a time as possible. You must ask young people down here. It'll stir me up. I need enlivening."

'He never questions her about her friends. I'm sure that several of the men who've come have been her lovers. She's having it, not both ways, but several ways at once. Why should she want to marry, when she's already got all the substantial emoluments of marriage, and why should any man want to marry her when he can get all he wants without the responsibilities of marriage? I'll bet that there's quite a number of men waiting for their turn; and why not, after all, the best of luck to her; but you can see, can't you, why I don't want to spend too much time there.'

'You don't like her very much?' I said.

He shrugged. 'I don't dislike her, but, after all, she's taking my brother's and my mother's place. I can't think of Charminster as my home: any more than my father thinks of it as being mine. I don't belong there.'

He paused, half interrogatively, as though he were expecting one of us to speak. We neither did, at first. But the pause continued.

'Where do you feel you do belong?' I asked.

'That's what I've been asking myself during those two long drives. As I've already said, I've never thought much about myself till now, but now . . . well, I've got to come to some decision now—and there's one way in which you can be a help.'

'I'll be delighted.'

'Wait till you know what I'm asking. You wouldn't believe it, but what do you think I've been doing in my spare time, this last few weeks? Writing a novel.'

I was not surprised. I have met very few people who have not at some point in their lives at least started on a novel. And those who have not, usually have a locked drawer in their desk that contains, not love letters but unpublished and unpublishable sonnets. As always in such a situation, I expressed appropriately surprised enthusiasm.

'Fine, how far has it got?' I asked.

'Quite a long way. I'll show you.' He got out of the chair. Beside the coat which he had flung over a chair was a large buff-coloured envelope. He handed it across to me. It contained over a hundred and fifty pages of typescript, double-spaced. It was a neat job of work, with alterations.

'How much of a novel's there?' he asked.

'About half of a short novel.'

'I expect it'll be a long novel then.'

'Publishers don't mind that; if it's good, they'll want it.'

'Would you be able to tell from that amount whether it's the kind of book they would want?'

'I ought to be.'

'How long would it take you to read it?'

'Half a day.'

'Then would you lunch with me on Wednesday and tell me what you think?'

'Delighted.'

'Simpson's, then. Simpson's in the Strand at one-fifteen.'

I was a minute or two early, but he was waiting in the hall. He had not brought Judy with him, I was relieved to see. He went to the point straight away, the moment after he had ordered a large dry sherry for us both. 'Well, what's the verdict?'

I had thought out carefully what I had to say. I wanted to encourage him, yet I did not want him to feel that he was in any imminent danger of immortality. This was the spring of 1924. In the previous summer Michael Arlen had published *These Charming People*, Aldous Huxley's *Antic Hay* had been the most discussed novel of the autumn, D. H. Lawrence was emerging from the shadow of *The Rainbow*'s prosecution and the obscurity of having to publish *Women in Love* in the USA alone, and in a limited edition. Compton Mackenzie, who in the spring of 1914 had been selected by Henry James in a couple of authoritative articles on the modern novel in *The Times Literary Supplement* as one of the brightest hopes of the rising generation, had in the course of an ecclesiastical trilogy explaining how an Anglican parson became a Roman Catholic, lost his hold on Bloomsbury, but *Sinister Street* was essential reading for every undergraduate.

Raymond's novel *The Ungainly Wise*—a title taken from Rupert Brooke's *Mamua*, was cast in the cradle-to-grave technique, but with colour tones from Huxley, Arlen and Lawrence.

It was autobiographical, but with certain key alterations to throw the reader off the scent. The hero was the son of a general who had been knighted. He had nothing, therefore, to inherit. He was the eldest son, but a second child. His mother's love was concentrated upon her daughter. As an army officer his father had no fixed home. He had, according to the demands and exigencies of the service, taken a succession of furnished houses near the place where his Regiment or the staff to which he was attached was stationed. The hero had never felt that he belonged anywhere. His father had been generous and affectionate, but had been too interested in his own career to take a personal interest in his son, particularly when he had come to realise that his son would not follow in his steps.

His mother, on the other hand, had been absorbed in her elder daughter. She wanted her to lead the life she had not led herself; a West Country girl, daughter of a local squire who had seen nothing of London life, she had fallen in love with the handsome young captain she had met at her first Hunt Ball and had married before she was eighteen because his regiment was sailing right away for the Boer War. Her daughter must have everything that she had missed, a finishing year in Paris, a London season, balls and beaux, and then, when she had had a full look at the world, marriage when she was twenty-three to someone rather grand.

No one had made the hero feel that he was anyone of the least importance. It did not worry him at all. He was not jealous. He did not develop a chip on his shoulder. He would not inherit a title or position, but he would one day have the use of a comfortably dimensioned sum of money. His health was good. He had a sunny nature. He considered himself a fate-favoured mortal.

The hero's situation was the equivalent of his own. The story had carried him to the age of fifteen. His youngest sister, a ten-year-old, had just been accorded an attractive Swedish governess. I suspected that her rôle in the hero's life was to be similar to that of Raymond's aunt in his.

The narrative moved briskly. It was told with humour. The hero was *simpatico*. 'I've handed it to my father,' I said. 'I've recommended that we should make an offer for it.'

He grinned. His face expressed relief. 'That's fine, that's

what I wanted to know. I'm going down to Charminster this afternoon. It'll be a useful card to play when I discuss things. Is your father likely to agree?'

'He usually follows my suggestions on a point like that.'

'In that case there's no more for us to say. Let's talk about something else.' But in point of fact there wasn't anything else to talk about, and there was still a lot more that needed saying. 'The usual terms for a first novel,' I said, 'are ten per cent on the first two thousand copies, twelve and a half on the next three thousand, fifteen up to ten thousand, then twenty per cent; and there's an advance on publication of a hundred pounds.'

'Fine, fine.'

'How long do you think it'll take to finish it?'

'I started this during the long vac., in August. I'll have more leisure now. Not more than six months, I'd say.'

'How long will it be?'

'About as much again.'

'How do you plan to finish it, or rather where do you plan to finish it?'

'At the end of his first year at Oxford.'

The age, in fact, that he had reached himself.

'Will it work to anything, will there be any final scene? Any kind of showdown?'

He shook his head. 'No, no, the novel with a plot's old-fashioned. I'll go on till I reach a suitable point for a mental summing up.'

It would, that is to say, stop, not finish. Well, that was in the mode right then.

I did not want to give him the impression that he was launched on a career of affluence. 'First novels don't often make much money,' I warned him.

'Some do, surely?'

'They have to be rather special.'

'And you don't think this is?'

'I didn't quite mean that. I meant that for a novel to be very successful it has to have a news value. It has to be sensational, or controversial, or scandalous. Something that gets talked about.'

34

'A lot of novels that don't fit that description seem to do very well.'

'But not first novels. It takes quite a while to build up a public. A first book attracts critical attention. "This is a writer to be watched" they say. Then there's a second, and they say, "Mr So-and-so is fulfilling the promise of that excellent first book." And his sales go up. Then there's a third and a fourth. The reviews may not be as good. Arnold Bennett said that it's harder to get good reviews for a fifth novel than a first. But the sales keep mounting. Then, suddenly, and no one can tell why or how it happens, there's a breakthrough and the novelist who has just been doing rather nicely becomes a best-seller overnight.'

'That's what you prophesy for me?'

'That's what I hope for you.'

He shook his head. 'Can you see me settling down industriously, turning out a novel a year?'

I couldn't. But I answered him indirectly.

'I've never thought of you as a novelist.'

'Neither have I. Turning out a novel a year. No, that's not my game. When should I find time to live? And what should I find to write about if I did no living? No, no, that's not my line at all. But to write a novel now and then, write five or six novels altogether, that could be an adjunct to a career. Disraeli wrote novels, after all. They were an adjunct to him.'

'Doesn't it depend on what career you pick?'

'Of course.'

'And what career do you plan to pick?'

'That's what I've got to decide during the next seven months. But I can't imagine any career that won't be helped by my having a novel to my credit. That's what I'll tell my father. I'm going down there this afternoon. I haven't heard from him yet, but I'm not expecting fierce reactions. He takes things calmly, and your verdict about my novel is just what's needed as a softener. When will you know what your father's verdict is?'

'He works fast. He makes up his mind quickly. There's a board meeting on Friday afternoon.'

'Could you telephone me after it: at about five o'clock?'

'Of course.'

'I'm coming up on the Saturday to see Judy. Couldn't we meet over the weekend?'

'What about the two of you lunching with me on the Sunday?'

'A very happy idea. Now I must be off. Pray for me this evening. Zero hour's about six o'clock.'

Before lunching with Raymond, I had handed my father *The Ungainly Wise*.

'This is only the first half,' I said, 'but I think you can get a good idea of it. I think it'll do.'

I was dining at Underhill that evening and we went home together. I had planned to talk to him about Raymond, but to my surprise I found that he had already read the book.

'I've read a great many novels exactly like it,' was his first comment. '*Sinister Street* in modern dress.'

'Don't most young writers start that way, imitating someone they admire?'

'Perhaps they do, but I'd prefer to back someone who has something of his own he wants to say, even if he doesn't quite know what it is, even if he is muddled and confused. This fellow is quite well off, you say?'

'He will be very soon.'

My father shook his head. 'The camel and the eye of a needle. How much do you know about him?'

I told him as much as I knew. By now we were within a few feet of Leicester Square tube station. In those days John Wisden, the cricket outfitters and the publishers of the Almanack, had their shop in the same street as the station. 'Only three months to cricket,' my father said.

It was rush hour on the tube. My father got a seat and I did not. I could not read my *Evening Standard* carrying an umbrella and swinging from a strap. I reviewed the arguments with which I could plead Raymond's case. He was, I would point out, a prominent Oxford personality. His book would attract attention there. It would introduce Chapman & Hall to Oxford as a go-ahead firm, interested in the young idea.

There must be someone up at Oxford now who would develop into a prominent writer; though that one might not be Raymond Peronne himself, by publishing Raymond we might lure that exception to our list. That was a prize worth aiming at.

My father, too, had thought out the matter. As we turned to the left, past the Golders Green Hippodrome, up the North End Road, he said, 'There are two kinds of undergraduate writer. There's the one who wants to write and the one who wants to have written. When we're dealing with someone like your young friend, who already has a position in the world, there's a danger that it's only the idea of being a writer that appeals to him.'

That was a point I was ready to concede. But I brought forward my arguments as persuasively as I could. Then I said, 'It's well enough done, isn't it? It's well written, it would bring credit to our list.'

'It wouldn't discredit it.'

'And even if it doesn't do anything spectacular, we can't lose a lot. Any Chapman & Hall novel subscribes seven hundred to the libraries and bookshops. We shall get publicity for it through his name. It would make a subject for "leaderettes"—"Is this how young Oxford feels?" We'll break even if we sell twelve hundred. And we should do that.'

'I suppose we should.'

My father disliked discussions. To him argument was a synonym for quarrel. When he recognised that I was really resolute upon a project—provided that it was reasonably reasonable, he let me have my way.

I then brought up my final proposition, and this, I knew, was the tricky one. The question of the advance. 'It's very rare for one of our novels not to earn fifty pounds in royalties; if one's worth doing at all it's really worth a hundred, and even if in this case he doesn't earn it, we can write down the over-advance as advertising, as a lure to the young idea at Oxford.'

I paused: this, I was well aware, set a dangerous precedent. It was not an argument I could use very often. The use of it now was a cutting into capital. I could not use it again for at least six months.

It was dark and only when we were actually under a street lamp could I see the expression on his face. It was a steep ten minutes' pull up the hill. My father's pace had slackened. He seemed to be leaning more heavily on his umbrella. He looked very tired. I had a twinge of guilt. I should not harry him in this way. Why couldn't I let him have things the way he wanted? He had run his firm well enough for fifteen years.

'All right,' he said, 'that's settled. I'll bring it up at Friday's board meeting.' He said that at the very moment that we reached Underhill. As he fitted his key in the lock, he left behind him all the problems of Henrietta Street. No manuscript under his arm. No 'shop' to be discussed at dinner. He could enjoy his home. Never again, I vowed, never again. Though even as I vowed it, I knew that sooner or later another similar situation would arise, and a sense of duty would force me to present my point of view as forcefully as I could.

At the same time Raymond, as he was to tell me later, was breaking the news at Charminster. His father was in the library reading a detective story. He looked up with a smile of uncommitted welcome. 'Come in, dear boy, you'll find some sherry over there. On a night like this I'd recommend the dark rather than the pale. But you know which you'd prefer. Now draw up your chair and tell me what it's all about. I gather it's not very serious?'

Raymond explained what had happened. 'I see, I see, nothing serious. A bit of a nuisance now, but in five years' time it'll be as unimportant as an attack of chickenpox. Several men during my time were sent down, quite a lot were rusticated. Didn't make the slightest difference to them afterwards. The only question is how you are going to put in the next few months.'

Raymond told him about his novel. 'Now, that's a surprise. You'll be the first Peronne to write a novel. A novelist in the family; well, well, well.'

At dinner, he had his butler open a bottle of champagne. 'Margaret, we must drink a health to this,' he said. He raised his glass as a sign to his daughter-in-law that it was a jovial occasion. There was no suggestion that Raymond was in disgrace; but later, when he had returned to his library, to his thriller, Margaret treated the matter more seriously. 'I hope that you're not too worried about this,' she said. 'We seem to be taking it for granted, but it must be a blow to you.'

He was touched that she should be concerned on his account. He had been relieved that his father had not regarded his escapade as serious, but he recognised that his father's tranquil acceptance of the situation was due to a basic and deep indifference to his son's concerns. His son could do what he liked as long as he did not disgrace the family. But Margaret was worried on his account. She was about the first person who had been since his mother died.

'We must make the best of a bad job,' she said. 'We must have as much fun as we can. We must have amusing parties. Your father will be very cooperative. He's always telling me to bring my friends. "I like young people round me." He'd rather have parties here than me going up to London, leaving him alone. The trouble is that I don't know enough young people. I never had a chance of meeting them. I never had a London season, because of the war. Adrian was the first man I met. At nineteen, when I should have been at a finishing school in Switzerland or Paris, here I was, a widow and a mother, everything settled and sewn up.'

She did not speak bitterly. She had a sunny nature: she was in a way laughing at herself. 'You must have plenty of amusing friends who'd be glad to come here. I'll try and find some lively girls. Let's enjoy ourselves,' she said.

And they could have had a lively time together, he realised that. For the first time he found himself feeling sorry for her. Her life was not as enviable as he had supposed. Had it been, she would not have welcomed the prospect of his presence so whole-heartedly.

'It's silly of me,' she said, 'but until this happened, I hadn't realised that you had grown up. I'd always thought of you as a child.'

He chuckled to himself. He was tempted to say 'Thank heavens that naughty aunt of mine didn't.' But he refrained. Yes, they could have fun all right, but was it the kind of fun he wanted? He could foresee how it would develop. He would be an alibi for her, and she for him. She would find some girl or girls for him, and he would provide her with a selection of young men from Oxford. A succession of foursomes. It was an obvious routine, but was it what he wanted with his brother's widow, with someone who was living under his father's roof? He liked privacy. He did not want other members of his family to know what he was doing.

Chapman & Hall board meetings took place on a Friday at three o'clock. There were only two other directors who attended regularly, the Chairman, W. L. Courtney, the literary editor of the *Daily Telegraph*, and an Oxford Don. Their meetings were very brief. They were followed by a cup of tea. By half-past four they were usually over. At five o'clock my father rang down to me. This was a little later than usual.

My father looked exhausted.

'Did anything go wrong?' I asked.

'Not really wrong. A little difficulty with our Oxford colleague.'

'Over what?'

'He had heard about young Peronne being rusticated. He did not think that his name would bring much credit to our list.'

'Oh.'

' "If the book is good enough to stand on its own feet," he said, "I'm for it. But if we are publishing it in order to attract young Oxford, I think we should find a different magnet." That put me in a rather difficult position.'

Once again that sense of guilt assailed me. Why should I add to his burdens?

'They asked me,' he went on, 'whether I thought the book was strong enough to stand on its own feet. I said it was, but I'm not sure it is. I do hope the book ends strongly. A lot depends on that. Perhaps he'll discuss it with you. I hope he does. You could be most helpful to him. It might make all the difference.'

I promised that I would try. I looked forward to working on the book with Raymond.

Raymond received my news on the telephone without surprise. He expected to have things go right for him.

'That's fine. We'll talk it over on Sunday. I've a new idea for you.'

I had presumed that his idea would be about the book itself. It wasn't; at least not directly.

'I've realised during this three days that I'll never be able to write that book at Charminster. Too much is going on; too many interruptions. I don't associate Charminster with work. I've got to get away. After all, I always have gone away to work. I've not been a day-boarder who does his prep in the nursery. I read a symposium the other day in which various novelists described how they worked. Some of them took rooms elsewhere and went to them every morning, like a lawyer going to his office. One of them said he went away to a small hotel. That didn't seem a bad idea, for me. There's an inn at Dodsbury seven miles away; I could stay there, food found, for eight shillings a day. With drinks and tips fifteen shillings a day would settle it. The trouble is where to get those fifteen shillings. I don't inherit until October. I ran up debts at Oxford. I could get anything on credit there. I don't like to ask my father for money. He isn't stingy, but he expects me to live within my fixed allowance and that is mortgaged—not only up to the next quarter, but to the one after that. He has been so decent about my rustication that I don't want to fuss him about this, and it would fuss him, I know that. I need fifty pounds for three months in that village inn; in three months I could get that novel finished. Now what I was wondering was this: would Chapman's pay me half the advance of a hundred pounds on the signing of the agreement?'

It sounded a simple enough proposition. But I knew my father. One of his strictest rules was 'No advance without a manuscript.' On this one issue he was adamant. 'Authors are always in debt. They only work when there is a reward waiting for them. At heart they are all Micawbers.'

There were a number of battles that I was prepared to join with my father for my friend's sake, but this I could not. Never take the field unless you have a reasonable chance of winning. I shook my head.

'I'm sorry,' I said. 'That's one of Chapman & Hall's rigid rules. No advance without a manuscript.'

'I see.'

He did not seem too crestfallen. He had supreme self-confidence. 'Then I suppose I had better try and find a publisher who has not got such rigid rules. There must be some who haven't.'

'Is this fifty pounds so important?'

'To me at the moment, yes. In a year's time it will be chickenfeed. But now, if I'm going to get this novel finished within three months, I need to have three months on my own.'

I could see his point. Some aristocrats have a patrician disregard for 'filthy lucre'. They feel that the world owes them sustenance. They borrow shamelessly and leave hotel bills unpaid. Others have a *noblesse oblige* attitude. They borrow from moneylenders, not from friends. Raymond was one of those. I could see his point, too, about needing to get away. I had found it impossible to work under my parents' roof at Underhill. That spring I had taken, as I have told, a flat in Kensington. But I was finding it difficult to work there, seven feet from a telephone. I could appreciate his predicament.

'Can you think of any other publisher who if he liked the beginning would be prepared to offer me that fifty pounds?'

As a matter of fact I could. Gerald Duckworth had taken in as a partner a youngish man, Tom Balston, who was anxious to get in on the ground floor with the younger generation. He had signed up Godfrey Winn and Harold Acton. Later he was to enrol Evelyn and the Sitwells. Anthony Powell was to join the staff as Literary Adviser. Balston was a friend of mine. I thought I could persuade him to take on Raymond. Did I want to, though? Ought I to? I had my duty to Chapman & Hall. I had argued Raymond's case seriously. Should I let him go to a rival without a struggle? Then there was the issue of Raymond's own interests. I believed that I could give him the kind of professional encouragement and advice that he could not get at Duckworth's. I had looked forward to nursing him. Might he not, if he had been already half-paid for the book, lose interest in it, scamp the final draft? So much could depend upon that final draft. I did not flatter myself in believing that my being at his elbow would make the difference between a book that was 'just all right' and one that hit the nail upon the head, but I might help. Surely there must be another way of raising fifty pounds?

I hesitated. I looked at him thoughtfully, trying to make up my mind. What ought I to do? What was best for him? What was best for Chapman & Hall? He was lolling in a deep armchair. Judy was, as usual, on a cushion at his feet. Her head was leant back against his knees. Her face wore an expression of utter peace, of complete fulfilment. She was not in fact more than ordinarily pretty, but this morning, rested and refreshed by love, she was touched by radiance, while he, I had never seen him look more handsome, more elegant, more full of *race*. He had the supreme good looks that spring from intermarriages over two and a half centuries between men and women who are privileged to make their choices among the most polished, the most attractive courtiers of their day— choices that had now and then been renewed and revitalised by a caprice for a lady of the stage or a foreign adventurer. He was unique. What did it matter whether his novel was any real good or not, to him or to Chapman & Hall or to the world in general? The prizes of the world were his without his having to earn them. Men like myself who were born to nothing, stood or fell by the use we made of our special talent. But Raymond was not in that position. He might make a great deal of his life or, in view of his opportunities, make very little. But he was running in a different race. Why not give him what he wanted now?

I told him about Duckworth and Tom Balston. 'I'll

43

probably be seeing him tonight at the Phoenix show. If I do I'll have a word with him.'

The Phoenix was a theatre group that in the early twenties produced Elizabethan and Restoration plays on Sunday nights. As a private society, it was immune, like the Stage Society, from the scrutiny of the official censor. It provided scope for a number of actors and actresses, tired of being type-cast, to show themselves in unaccustomed rôles. Isabel Jeans for instance, who was usually cast as a dark-haired vamp, appeared in *The Country Wife* as a light-haired trollop.

It was sponsored by social and literary Bohemia. As I had expected, Tom Balston was there that night. I told him about Raymond's novel. 'Hard though it is to be believed,' I said, 'he badly needs fifty pounds. You'd give him that, wouldn't you, if you liked the book?'

'While your father wouldn't.'

'He has a fixed rule, no advance without a manuscript.'

'Not a bad rule, either. But it can be broken sometimes.'

'I'll have the manuscript sent round tomorrow.'

Next morning I broke the news to my father. 'I'm afraid that after all we shan't have to outrage our Don. We're not getting that Oxford novel.'

'Why ever not?'

'He's declined our generous offer.'

'But that's ridiculous.'

'I told him so. What do you think he wanted?'

'Not a hundred and fifty, surely?'

'No. Much worse. Fifty right away.'

'But that's impossible.'

'That's what I told him.'

'What's he going to do?'

'Offer it somewhere else.'

'With that same stipulation?'

'Yes.'

'He'll never get it.'

'I'm not so sure. I had a word with Tom Balston. He'll give him fifty if he likes the manuscript. The idea appeals to him.'

A puzzled look on my father's face was followed by a grin. He chuckled. 'Poor Gerald, poor old Gerald.' They were good friends, Gerald Duckworth and himself. They had been contemporaries at Oxford. They were both members of the Savile. Their offices were nine doors apart in Henrietta Street. The chuckle surprised me; I had presumed that my father would be somewhat disconcerted to learn that Duckworth was planning to take over an author for whom he had made an offer. I wondered whether he might not question the wisdom of his own iron rule. I was resolved never myself to bring the matter up again, never to remark 'What a pity it was that we lost Raymond.' But I hoped *The Ungainly Wise* would hit the jackpot. In the meantime I hoped that my father would not brood over the situation. The chuckle took me off my guard. I had not realised then what a malicious pleasure elderly men take in the discomfiture of their contemporaries.

Eight years later my father, in his autobiography, as an illustration of the new post-war atmosphere, was to recount the incident of a young manager returning after the armistice to his place of occupation, in the uniform of an infantry officer. His chief, who was also the proprietor of the business, received him in his private room upstairs with an air of genial welcome. But he was hardly prepared for the response. The young man seated himself on the table, took out a cigarette, tapped and lit it, throwing a glance of indulgent patronage around the room. 'Well,' he said. 'I'm not sorry to be back. Now we've got to buck up, all of us, and put a bit of life into this old bus.' The ex-officer's employment ended that afternoon. The chief was Gerald Duckworth. The ex-officer was Jonathan Cape.

When I told my father a week later that Duckworth had accepted *The Ungainly Wise* he chuckled again. 'Poor old Gerald. He'll soon be wishing that he'd kept on Cape.'

As a footnote may I add that Tom Balston's policy paid off very satisfactorily. A year and a half later he offered Evelyn fifty pounds on an unwritten life of Rosetti. The book was delivered, and he was to receive all Evelyn's travel books. He would have received his novels, too, if in his

45

absence, Gerald Duckworth had not been shocked by *Decline and Fall* and let it slip through his fingers.

During the following summer I was to miss Raymond on the visits I paid to Evelyn on what was to prove his last term at Oxford. But through Judy I was to meet him fairly often. He had decided, he was to tell me, not to go back to Oxford. 'After six months on my own it would be a putting back of the clock. I've embarked on other things.' One of the things on which he had embarked was as a wireless announcer—the BBC had not yet imposed its autocratic dictatorship and was run by a group of semi-amateurs operating from Savoy Hill. It was found that Raymond had just the right pitch of voice for this medium.

'How's the novel going?' I asked.

He shrugged. 'The back of it's broken, but I want to put it away for a little, and then come fresh to it. Don't you think that would be wise?'

'Very wise. Most of us when we read our proofs wish we could have the typescript back.' But can't afford to, I felt like adding.

In October I was to ask him again how it was progressing. Again he shrugged. 'An extra month or two in storage won't do it any harm. Let it rest awhile.'

In January my father was to say, 'I've just seen a copy of Duckworth's spring list. I don't see your friend Peronne's book in it.'

'He's lying fallow for a while,' I said. My father shook his head. 'Poor Gerald,' he said. 'Poor, poor Gerald.'

My news put him in the best of spirits.

In retrospect 1925 has come to appear as the start of a glamorous and carefree period. The Bright Young People were starting to take over. Scott Fitzgerald was in Paris, so was Hemingway, getting his material for *The Sun Also Rises*. A pound bought a lot and quite a number of people had quite a lot of them. I had my share, and most weeks I threw a party of some kind, with Raymond and Judy customary guests. They were an attractive couple. There was a glow about her, the result of happiness. She had also a number of new clothes. Raymond had come of age and into his inheritance shortly before Christmas. He must also have had good credit. Judy profited. They looked so happy together that no one looked ahead. He was after all only just twenty-one; she was three or four years older. They could afford to live in the moment; there was no need to wonder yet 'where will all this lead?' Judy's jobs continued to be shortlived, but she had no difficulty in finding a new one when a firm collapsed. She could always pick up the three pounds a week that settled her basic needs of rent and light and heat, laundry and morning coffee. Nothing could have been more 'set fair'. Then, to her astonishment, a Hollywood scout offered her a secretarial job in his Montreal office at seventy-five dollars a week. 'We want someone with an English accent, to give us class,' he said. He had noticed her when she was employed in the Box Office at the Everyman Theatre. 'I've been waiting till the right opening came,' he told her.

'Are there any strings attached?' I asked.

'There always are, aren't there?'

She had slipped back into her rôle of 'the knowing one'.

'At any rate, it'll get me to Canada,' she said.

We discussed it at length over a Russian tea. 'What does Raymond think about all this?' I asked.

'He doesn't know yet; that's something I'd like to have you do for me.'

'Have me do what?'

'Break the news to him.'

It was then I realised that she really loved him. Had she been irritated, offended by his refusal to talk of marriage, how she would have relished the opportunity of walking out on her own terms. Had she not said on the evening after their first meeting, 'One of the great things about starting a new affair is the walking out on someone who has begun to bore you.' Here was her chance of the most satisfactory of all feminine revenges and she was letting it go by.

'I don't know how he'll take it,' she said. 'I've no idea how much it'll mean to him. He may be relieved at getting rid of

47

me so easily. I may have become a drag. If I have . . . well
I couldn't bear seeing a look of relief on his face. On the
other hand it may be a shock to him, he may have gone on
from day to day, not looking ahead, assuming that I'd always
be around. If that's how it is, if he was suddenly to feel he
needed me . . . I don't mean in terms of marriage—no, I
really don't; I've never thought of him in terms of marriage,
though I do realise, of course, that one of these days I must
get married. I'm twenty-four, after all, but that's not what
I was feeling about Raymond. I'm quite happy to go on as
we are, but this trip to Canada is a chance, I oughtn't to pass
it up. If, on the other hand, he genuinely feels he needs me,
he well might after all . . . It's so hard to tell with him, but if he
did need me, I could hardly leave him. That's why I want you
to tell him. He'll be off his guard with you; you'll be able to
see what his first reaction is, and that's what I need to know,
what I've got to know.'

'Which way do you want it to be?'

She shook her head from side to side. 'I don't know.
Honestly, I don't know.'

'Either way I shan't be bringing you bad news.'

Again she shook her head. 'I'm prepared for either,
prepared to settle for either. The moment I know, one way
or another I can carry on. But you will tell me the truth, won't
you?'

'I'll tell you the truth.'

'The absolute and utter truth?'

'The absolute and utter truth.'

I told him the following evening, when we were changing after
a game of squash, which we played once a week at the RAC,
of which he was a member.

'It's exciting news about Judy, isn't it?' I said.

'What news?'

'The job in Montreal.'

'What job in Montreal?'

'For a film company that wants an English voice to give it
tone.'

'It's the first I've heard of it. When's she leaving?'

48

'As soon as possible. They want her in a hurry.'

'A film company. Well, that *is* fine for her.'

His expression could not have been more unconcerned, more personally unconcerned that is to say.

'When did you learn this?' he asked.

'Yesterday afternoon.'

'I'm surprised she didn't telephone me.'

'She tried to,' I lied. 'She couldn't get you.'

'I was out a good deal yesterday. How is she taking it?'

'She's excited, naturally.'

'Naturally. It's a great chance for her.'

It did not apparently occur to him that she would not accept it.

'But didn't he seem surprised?' she was to ask me afterwards.

'Not more surprised than you would expect anyone to be when a friend has a piece of luck.'

'He didn't seem relieved?'

'Not on his account. He was glad on yours.'

'No look of disappointment, of shock?'

'Not that I could see.'

She shrugged. 'That lets me out then, doesn't it?' She took it in her stride; she was well enough content that it had all turned out the way it had. But I did feel that she was a little aggrieved that he had not been a little bit upset. She had been cheated of a scene.

3

That was in 1925. A few months later I completely altered the general pattern of my life. Now making enough as a writer to rely upon my pen, I became a traveller, on a large scale. I gave up my flat, I gave up my directorship at Chapman & Hall's. I was in England less than five months a year. I made new friends, but saw less of old ones. Raymond was one of those with whom I started to lose touch. Whenever I got back I called his number, but he himself was as often as not away. He kept changing jobs; or rather he kept taking jobs that were on a temporary basis; as often as not he was standing in for someone. He had occasional assignments on the air, but he had no fixed executive post. He was, for a time, a part-time gossip writer for the Sketch. Once he sold cars and once he sold insurance on commission. I asked Tom Balston about his novel. Tom shook his head. 'I doubt if he'll ever finish it. Particularly now that he's paid back that fifty pounds.'

I mentioned this to Raymond next time I saw him. 'I was sorry to hear you'd dropped *The Ungainly Wise*.'

'So was I in a way. I ought to have finished it when the idea was fresh. I re-read what I'd written the other day. Too dated.'

'I was held by it when I read it.'

'That was in 1924. The world's changed since then.' As of course it had. The early twenties had been fretted with anxiety by the fear of revolution; so many dynasties had toppled. But in May 1926 had come the General Strike. So this is it, we thought, and enlisted as special constables or engine-drivers. But the strike collapsed and the country drew a long breath of relief and went on a spree—not unlike, so the prophets of gloom warned us, the carnival on which Russia embarked after the St Petersburg massacre in 1906, the *Sanine* period. There was in England no precise equivalent for the New York fun fair of the later twenties when the stock market was booming; there was never that amount of money around in England, but May 1926 to September 1931 was the *Vile Bodies* period of 'the Bright Young People'. No one was taking the future very seriously.

'Are you planning anything particular?' I once asked Raymond.

He shrugged. 'I'm biding my time,' he said.

'Very sensible of him too,' was Evelyn's comment. 'Sooner or later the right opportunity will come. This honeymoon can't last for ever. Let him enjoy it while he can.'

He certainly seemed to be enjoying it. He was as elegant as ever. He never indulged in such sartorial eccentricities of the period as 'Oxford bags'. He dressed conventionally, but smartly. In London he wore a bowler hat and carried gloves and an umbrella. His shoes shone. His suits looked as though he had had them for eighteen months and worn them rather seldom. He never seemed to wear the same tie twice. When he wore tails, his white waistcoat never showed below his coat. He looked as though he had been smiling a few seconds before and would be smiling again in a few seconds' time. Gossip linked his name with those of a number of attractive females. But there were no rumours of an engagement. He was, after all, still in his middle twenties. He had time in plenty.

Friends said of him, 'He has his serious side, you know.' But it was not apparent what it was.

I met his father once. J. C. Squire ran a cricket side, the Invalids, of which A. G. Macdonnell's chapter in *England, their England* is more a photograph than a caricature. Squire led his side against villages and against country houses. In 1930 Charminster appeared on his fixture list.

'I'll be playing against you in June,' I told Raymond.

'What date?'

'The second Saturday.'

'Too bad, I'll be away.'

It was the first time I had been to Charminster. Though no one had been impressed by it when it was built at the end of the seventeenth century, it had by the end of the nineteenth century become one of the houses that were written about and photographed, simply because it had not been altered. In the course of two centuries no one had added a bow window, an elaborate portico, a gabled wing. In that it was typical of the Peronnes who, after the stress of the religious wars, were content to have things the way they found them. It was solid, red brick, rectangular, three storeyed, with ivy trailing between its windows.

The cricket field was within the Park; a small oval paddock, its pavilion shaded by a copper beech. Lord Peronne had his own chair by the scoring table. In the early sixties, he was tall, moustached, handsome, slightly corpulent, with a high colour; he wore loose-fitting tweeds with an Old Etonian tie. I introduced myself. 'I'm quite a friend of your son Raymond.'

'I'm afraid he's not here today.'

'So he warned me. I was disappointed.'

The old man shrugged. 'Never cared for cricket. Can't think why. We've all been cricketers. His brother ought to have played at Lord's that last summer. Cruel luck, catching measles, two weeks before. Measles, I ask you. I said to Raymond when the war began, "Now it's up to you." But he insisted on being a wet bob. I can't think why. Rowing's bad for the heart; luckily he wasn't any good at it, so he gave it up.'

'What about your grandson?'

'Ah, that's another matter. Chip off the old block. That's him over there.'

He pointed out to me a boy in a grey flannel suit who was stretched out on a rug, propped on his elbows, with a bag of raspberries at his side. He was light-haired, fresh-complexioned. 'He was second in the batting averages last term, holds his catches too; what one wants these days. I've been having him coached at Lord's during the Easter classes. Goes to Eton next half. I'll be surprised if he's not playing at Lord's four years from now.'

His voice dropped a tone when he spoke about his grandson. It deepened, glowed, a smile crossed his face. His eyes were tender. It was touching. 'Here comes his mother. You haven't met her, have you?'

She was small, slim, blonde. She was wearing a floppy

52

hat. So this was Margaret. I rose to greet her. Her handshake was firm and friendly. As our eyes met I had a feeling ... but it is impossible to describe that feeling, that meeting 'of a stranger across a crowded room', that instant recognition of affinity: there is no mistaking it, there is no denying it. As our eyes met, she smiled. She feels it too, I thought.

There was a vacant chair beside me, and she took it. 'I've heard a lot about you from Raymond.' Her voice was frank and firm. 'I've wanted to meet you. I like your books.'

'It's a mistake to meet the authors of the books one likes.'

'That's what I've been told. But a friend of mine who knows you said "When you once know him, reading a book of his is just like hearing him talk." I was inquisitive. I asked Raymond to bring you down here. He promised that he would, but he's bad at promises.'

'He's not here often, is he?'

'Not very often, and now he's going to New York in September.'

'I'm going in November.'

'You'll be meeting, won't you?'

'I'll insist on his bringing me down here in the spring.'

'You do just that.'

She smiled. We each knew what was in the other's mind. Six minutes ago we had not met, and now we were on the brink of a romance. We knew nothing about each other, yet we knew each other. I remembered how Raymond had talked about her that day at lunch all those months ago. Here was the reality that he had hinted at. But it wasn't that way at all.

'I've never seen the house,' I said. 'Could you show me round when the game's over?' It was an unforgettable half-hour, though there was not a great deal for me to see. There were suits of armour and family portraits. Watercolour landscapes by Victorian spinsters. The library was stocked by sets of the Victorian novelists and historians. There was nothing very personal about it. 'Has Raymond a study of his own?'

She shook her head. 'His father wanted to fix up a suite of rooms, but he'd have none of it.' She showed me his

53

bedroom, an impersonal room. No photographs. A compactum wardrobe, a built-in hanging cupboard, a writing desk. The pictures on the walls were not his own. Clearly he had not wanted to identify himself with Charminster, to make a home in a house which would one day cease to be his own.

'Does he have no special feeling about the house?' I asked.

'He doesn't want to have any special feeling.'

That was understandable. When his nephew came into his inheritance, he wanted to be able to pack his few possessions onto a single lorry, like a Bedouin rolling up his tent.

'How do you feel about it yourself?' I asked.

She shrugged. 'As a woman always must feel about a house that will one day be her son's. That's a woman's fate, isn't it? In England, anyhow, with the tradition of the widow's dower house.'

She smiled as she said that, a smile that was almost wistful. Our eyes met and our looks held each other. I have seldom felt so close to anyone in my life.

'Maybe this is what I'm looking for,' I thought. I was free emotionally. I did not want to get married. I wanted to travel, to be out of England for at least half the year. I was the wrong man for the vast majority of the women for whom I might have been suitable in other ways. My need for independence made me impossible for the kind of woman—and that is to say the vast majority of women who need a home and 'a man about the place'. But surely for every man there is a woman for whom, no matter what his peculiarities may be, he can be the right one. Perhaps I was right for Margaret. It was a heady prospect.

'I'm booking to be back in England at the end of March,' I said.

'I'll note that in my diary,' she said.

The winter of 1930–31 is not one that New York remembers gratefully. The depression was mounting to its peak, with no end in sight. Soup queues were stretching in Times Square; apples at 5¢ a piece for the unemployed were on sale along the sidewalks. Each day the stock market slid a little lower.

But there were those who managed to enjoy themselves, and I was one of them. In the spring my travel book *Hot Countries* had been a Literary Guild selection. I was in funds. Colston Leigh had booked me for a lecture tour which gave me a chance of widening my knowledge of the USA. I took a furnished flat on the eighth floor of an apartment building that still stands at the junction of Lexington and 36th. I joined a squash racquet club and kept myself in training. I wrote during the morning; every evening there was a party of some kind. I began to feel myself a part of the New York scene. The friendships that I made then have led to the friendships that were later to enrich my New York life: particularly that with Elinor Sherwin, later to marry Wolcott Gibbs. Through her I met the friends who twenty years later were to sponsor me for the Coffee House. Every day was an adventure.

I led a picnic life, very different from the one that John O'Hara was to describe in *Butterfield 8*—it was during my stay that BUT 7431 became BU-8 7431—I moved in far less affluent circles. But most of my opposite numbers were managing comfortably in spite of the depression. The theatre was doing well—and there were some fine plays showing— there were plenty of magazines to pay $150 for an article to $300 for a short story. As often as not the men and women whom I was meeting had some piece of good news to celebrate.

For the most part I was mixing with Americans, but I had two good English friends there in my cousin Claud Cockburn, then on the London Times, and Raymond, who kept no office hours but was vaguely representing—the adverb is the one he used—a firm of London stockbrokers. His employers had provided him with a dapper duplex apartment on Park and 47th and underwrote a share of his expenses. We had a number of friends in common, at whose houses we kept meeting. We also used to manage to see each other on our own at least once a week. We enjoyed comparing notes, and being able to let our hair down. Each of us loved New York, yet when we were with New Yorkers we had a slight feeling of being on parade. The English had not made themselves popular in the USA during the 1920s. They had been patronising and conceited; they had also shown too marked a readiness to let Americans 'pick up the check'. It was up to us, we felt, to show Americans that all Englishmen were not like that. We cast ourselves in ambassadorial rôles.

It was the first time that I had seen Raymond regularly since Judy had left, while Claud and Raymond had scarcely met since Oxford. There was a good deal of reminiscing. There was also a good deal of political talk between Claud and Raymond. Claud was moving towards the left. Within eighteen months he was to resign from the *Times*, join the Communist Party and start his own 'News behind the news' in his mimeographed six-sheet *The Week*; while Raymond, who had spent several weeks in Chicago, had been startled by the poverty that he had found there. He became acutely conscious of the faulty distribution of the world's resources. What had struck him most—and it was something that struck a number of others during the late twenties—was that while people were starving, in Brazil coffee was being burnt on the wharves and in the North Sea fish were being chucked back into the ocean, because they could not be marketed at a profit. 'The system's wrong,' he said.

'That's what I've been telling you,' said Claud. 'Russia's found the answer.'

That, Raymond was not ready to concede. He thought that Mussolini had found a better answer. They discussed rather than argued the issue, amicably; they never came to a conclusion and as often as not they changed the subject before a conclusion could be reached. They had so much else to chatter over. They were as absorbed as I was by the New York scene.

We were each of us at that time involved with New York ladies; we often went out on foursomes, occasionally on six-somes. Claud was courting Frances Hope Hale, whom he was to marry the following year, and whom I was to see, only a few months ago, now as Mrs Herbert Gorham, at the PEN congress at Dublin. She was so warm and lively and attractive, it was hard to believe that forty years had elapsed since those speak-easy days when Claud lived at the Brevoort. Raymond was involved with a tall, long-legged New Englander who was staying with an aunt in a mid-town apartment while she was reading for a Master's at Columbia. For discretion's sake I will here call her Myra Bedford. She had a flat accent that I was later to associate with seaboard society. Raymond knew very little about her background. 'That's one of the fascinations of life over here,' he said. 'In England we all know each other, or know about each other. You're attracted by someone at a dance, you ask her out to dinner; before you've finished the fish, you've discovered what mutual friends you have and before you know where you are, you're having a cosy family chat about Bill and Gertrude, and that isn't why you asked her out. In America, on the other hand, it's the other way. You meet a girl at a cocktail party, there's a flicker and you make a date. Before you're through your second cocktail, you've finished discussing your host and hostess, as far as you know they are all you have in common, so you can get down to the real reason why you asked her out, and start telling her that she's a highly attractive female, and your campaign is launched. It's not till much later that you find you have quite a number of friends in common. Which is an adventure too.'

'And have you found that you and Myra have a lot of friends in common?'

'As a matter of fact I haven't.'

'Aren't you inquisitive?'

'Not really. After all, why should I be? What does it matter who she is, it's what she is that matters. We have a wonderful time together. She makes everything more fun.'

I was not surprised at him saying that. He was related by vague ties of cousinship with half the debutantes that he had met during the seasons when he had gone to dances. Half his conversation with them was ready-made. It must be a relief to him to be anonymous. And there was no doubt that he and Myra were having a considerable ball together. Half the time they were laughing. And when they were talking seriously, there was an intense, concentrated expression on their faces that proved them to be absorbed by what each was saying. They were a striking couple when they danced together, and when they walked together on a bright brisk February afternoon, on their way to a cinema or theatre. They were living in their moment. But I, a spectator, was curious about her.

At 136 East 36th Street Rollin Kirby's daughter, Janet, had an apartment too. She was then married to Langdon Post, an assemblyman in FDR's New York administration. Elinor Sherwin had introduced me to her, and with Lang often away on duty, we fitted into each other's lives, the borrowing of gin from each other when our bootlegger failed us being one of the many practical links we had. I asked Janet if she knew Myra. 'I've never met her, but most of my friends seem to have. Let's look her up in the bible.'

'The bible' was the New York Social Register, which I have always found a fascinating compilation. 'Dilatory domiciles' for example. How was that definition found for socialites who had moved outside the radius of Manhattan? And again, 'Married Maidens'. I looked up Myra Bedford, but the record did not tell me much beyond the fact that she was the daughter of a second marriage, that her father, who was now in his fourth marriage, was living in New York and that her mother, now in her third marriage, was in Cape Cod. I learnt nothing about her father or either of her stepfathers' careers. 'Is she rich?' I asked.

'I imagine,' said Janet, 'that in October, 1929, they fancied that they were ruined; but that by now they've realised that their losses were mainly paper ones. That type lives on the interest on its interest. Now that the dust has settled, they're much where they were in 1926. They're probably better off, because everything costs less. Even bootleggers have dropped their rates.'

I told Raymond what I had learned from Janet. He did not seem interested. He was satisfied with the situation; my curiosity was still alert, however, and during my last week in New York it was given an unexpected fillip. An Englishman like Raymond relished the anonymity that he can enjoy in New York society. He was able to meet social types that lie outside his range in London; while someone like myself, who was not a socialite, now and again found himself, through the accident of a lucky letter of introduction, moving in a far grander atmosphere than any he would know at home. I, for example, had arrived in New York in the previous summer with a letter to Eleanor Roosevelt. I had been invited for a weekend at Hyde Park. I had felt an immediate sympathy for her mother-in-law, Mrs James. During my winter on 36th Street she often invited me to her lunch parties, some of which were quite grand occasions, and in particular the dinner that she gave for Lord Beauchamp, then on his way back to England for a personal drama of whose nature the world was yet unaware. There were twenty-two guests, one of whom to my considerable surprise was Myra Bedford. 'Yes, I know Mr Waugh already,' she said when we were introduced. 'You needn't look so surprised,' she added when we were alone.

'Frankly, I am. You seem to take my being here for granted.'

'I knew that you knew The Dowager.'

'You've never mentioned her.'

'Why should I?'

There was no answer to that.

We sat at different ends of the table. No wine was served; after dinner the men separated into a small library to smoke cigars. When we returned to the drawing room, Myra caught my eye. I went across to her. It was the first time I had been alone with her. On our foursomes and six-somes we had always been engaged in group conversations across a table.

'It's been strange,' she said, 'going round a city that is one's home with three Englishmen for whom it's a foreign city.'

'In what way?'

'That's what I've been trying to figure out while I've been discussing the Governor's showdown with Tammany. Because in one way Claud knows more about New York than I do.'

'Do we take you to places where your style of American wouldn't go?'

'No, it isn't that. One speakeasy's very like another. It's

a different atmosphere. You're looking at it with different eyes. Things are strange to you that wouldn't be to Americans, and vice versa.'

'Can you give me an example?'

'That's what I've been trying to do all evening, and I can't . . . It's all so different.'

'Do the other two, Claud's and mine, feel it?'

'I haven't asked them.'

'You'd never seen either of them before?'

'And shall probably never see either of them again, once you've gone. That's one of the things that's made it so much fun.'

'It has been fun then?'

'Enormously. It's like being in disguise. No, it's not like that. It's more like being invisible. Leading a New York life about which none of my friends know anything—not having them ring up to ask them how I enjoyed *Tomorrow and Tomorrow*. Being in New York this way is as much an adventure as it is for you. It's made New York a new city for me. You may not believe it, but I've never had any affair in New York before. Doesn't that surprise you?'

'Well, yes.'

'All my affairs, they've been—I talk as though I'd had a hundred, but of course I haven't—it's that I've been on my guard here, with Americans, with men who know all about me—it's different in Europe or meeting them on ships, or resorts like Newport, that's like being on an island, but in New York, marriage always seems to come in somewhere, sooner or later. If it's someone in my own world, I begin to wonder why he doesn't start talking about marriage —does he think I'm not good enough for him, does he rather despise me for being . . .? well, it puts a rein on me, I don't let myself go the way I want to—I don't want to be looked down upon. I may not want to marry him, but I want him to want to marry me. That, of course, is with someone in my own world. It's the same thing the other way round, when it's someone not in one's world, someone who's obviously unmarriageable, and that's something that really gives a kick—an affair with a steward on a boat for instance;

there was a barman on the *Ile de France*, how I let myself go with him—but in New York, very soon that kind of man develops a chip upon his shoulder. "Of course you wouldn't marry somebody like me." If you suggest going to an inexpensive restaurant it's "so that you won't see any of your grand friends," he'll say. He becomes impossible. Row after row, and it's such a business to get rid of him. I had that kind of trouble once in Boston with a crazy Irishman, when I was at Radcliffe . . . Never again, I vowed, never in Boston or New York. You can't guess what a good time I'm having now. I've always thought "New York must be heaven to be in love in", and now at last I am.'

So she was in love with Raymond. I had wondered that; while he with her? It was hard to tell. He had once said 'I'm so much in love with life that I can't tell if I'm in love with anyone.'

I made no comment. I did not try to lead her on, to invoke a confidence. I waited for her to start again.

'But of course this can't go on, I realise that,' she said. 'I've got to marry some time. A woman has no life unless she does. And in my case I suppose it should be pretty soon. I'm twenty three, after all. That's a good age for marriage, with someone experienced, but not too much. I want marriage to be an adventure, even though it's something that one has to work at. Everything that's worth while has to be worked at. Like your books. You get the idea for one in a flash—you explained that in that lecture of yours—it's like meeting someone at a party, love at first sight, even though it may not go very deep, though it may turn out a fiasco; there's the first second of exaltation, then there's the routine of courtship; what was that cliché?—at least you called it a cliché in your lecture—two per cent inspiration, ninety-eight perspiration. Most marriages fail, don't they, because couples forget the ninety-eight per cent part of it. Even so there has to be that flicker first—that's what makes it so difficult for me: I meet all these fine, suitable New Englanders, so straight and stern and handsome, so right for me in every way, we understand each other so well. We can talk in shorthand, but that flicker, that sudden recognition of an affinity that has nothing to do with up-bringing—do you see what I mean?'

'The English,' I said, 'have the same problem; we know each other so well, we're like brothers and sisters to one another and then the stranger comes.

'English women say that English men are cold, and Englishmen say the same about English women, but American women don't find us cold, and foreign diplomats are delighted when they are accredited to the Court of St James. I thought it was different here, with every state a little different; here you can get surely both strangeness and familiarity.'

She shook her head. 'When a Texan's meeting a Chicagoan maybe, but in seaboard society, no.'

This was one of my early visits to the USA. I had not then learned the special ingredients of seaboard society.

'I know what I want,' she said, 'but I don't know where to find it. The trouble is that when one does meet a stranger, one realises after a little while that one doesn't know enough about him. One needs to know his background. They all say, you know, that Englishmen are quite different at home.'

'Isn't that what worried Henry James?'

'I'd give a lot to see Raymond in his own setting.'

'I don't think you'd find him very different. Three quarters of the time he's out of England.'

'I'd like to see that quarter. Is he likely to be in England in October?'

'Most likely. October is one of the best months in England.'

'Maybe I'll come across then. Don't warn him, though. I want to take him off his guard.'

I kept my promise. But I did tell Raymond that I had met Myra at Mrs James'. He did not seem surprised, or for that matter very interested. 'I wonder if she's the English equivalent for Elizabeth Ponsonby,' he said. Elizabeth Ponsonby was partly the model for Agatha Runcible in *Vile Bodies*.

I asked him about his summer plans. 'I expect to be over in early June. I want to go back to Chicago first. There are one or two of the Labour Left that I want to meet.'

'You're not going into politics, are you?'

'I might do worse. Something's going to blow up soon, and someone like myself who's not committed and who's independent might have a part to play.'

'Would you run on the left or on the right?'

'On the left wing of the right.'

Which bore out what he had said about Mussolini.

'The Conservatives at Charminster would welcome you as their candidate.'

'That's what I thought.'

'Would you like me to be one of the speakers on your platform?'

'You'd be highly welcome.'

'Your sister-in-law suggested that I should come down and play cricket for the hall against the village.'

'That should send up your stock there as a canvasser.'

'The match will be at the end of August. Will you be there?'

'I'll make a point of it.'

If I were to help him in his campaign, I should have all the alibis I needed for visits there. Would he come to resent my presence? I remembered how he had refused the idea of providing alibis for Margaret, but this was different, or was it? We always excuse ourselves by pretending that our case is different. Time would show. I did not want to forfeit Raymond's friendship.

I outlined my plans; I wasn't aiming to spend more than a few days in England. 'I've an idea for a novel. I want to go down to Villefranche right away to work on it. It should be a ten-week job.'

'Maybe I'll join you there.'

'Do that.'

I only spent a week in England. I rang up Charminster to give news of Raymond. Margaret answered the telephone. I told her that I was going to Villefranche to write a novel. 'Is there any chance of your coming to the South of France?'

'I'm afraid not.'

'Is there any chance of your being in London during the next six days, so that we could lunch?'

She hesitated. 'Well, let's see.' There was a pause. I could guess what was passing through her mind. It would be possible for her to lunch in London. But she was wondering whether it would be a good idea. There would be an atmosphere of haste. Perhaps an attempt to hurry things that would prove fatal; I was glad she hesitated. I was relieved when she said that no, it wasn't possible. She was feeling, as I was, that it was not worth running the risk of spoiling things. Yet she would be grateful that I had rung up.

'You haven't forgotten that I'm going to play for your side against the village?'

'Indeed I haven't.'

'Will your son be playing?'

'For the first time, yes.'

'Quite an occasion, then.'

'Quite an occasion.'

Was there an undermeaning to that 'quite'. I wished that I could have seen the expression on her face. My heart was beating. It was going to be all right. Some things were much better for not being hurried.

4

Raymond arrived in Villefranche half way through June. The Welcome Hotel, as anyone who has read Francis Steegmuller's book on Cocteau will appreciate, was at that time a kind of Club. My brother Evelyn was there, so were Keith Winter and Patrick Balfour, now Lord Kinross.

Raymond arrived off the night train early in the morning. He had had a bad night, sitting up in the centre of a second-class compartment. 'I never spend money on myself,' he said. 'I take buses and tubes when I'm alone.'

But in spite of the night's discomfort, he looked as spruce and as cleanly shaven as any wagon lit tourist. He was wearing *espadrilles* and one of the blue sleeveless sailor's *maillots* that were then the vogue. He came onto the terrace shortly after nine: I had had my first half-past-six swim on the beach below the railway line, had finished my rolls and coffee and was at work upon my manuscript. Evelyn and Keith Winter, late risers, were finishing their coffee and reading aloud to each other, picked passages from the local *L'éclaireur de Nice*. The world was shut away.

Raymond stretched his arms above his head. 'The peace of this, the peace,' he said.

'That's what we find,' Winter said.

'Peace,' he said, 'How I need it, after New York, after Chicago, then London for three weeks, ten days in Paris, Rome next week. Everything going round in my head. I've got to think things out.'

'What things?' Winter asked.

'The whole situation, the economics of it: that's the axis on which it all revolves.'

Evelyn's eyes widened, in an incredulous stare, as though he were saying 'Can such things be? Can such men exist?' It was a habit of his that many found disconcerting. It was singularly eloquent.

'There'll be a crisis soon, there must be,' Raymond was continuing. 'I've looked at things in Chicago, in New York.

Everywhere the same approach to chaos, and no one any-where doing a thing to stop it.' It was the kind of talk that I had been hearing in New York between him and Claud, but it was new to Winter and to Evelyn. 'Unless something is done soon it'll be too late,' he said. It was the same talk again, but it was said now in a new temper. He was restless, impatient: he was desperate to get something started.

'What are you proposing that we should do?' asked Winter.

'Follow the one man who can lead us.'

'And who may that be?'

'Mosley, of course.'

Evelyn's eyes widened to a point of ultimate incredulity. 'Tom Mosley,' he said, on a note that as far as he was concerned, closed the conversation. He sat silent while Winter cross-examined Raymond. Winter was at that time a very close friend of Peter Howard, the one-time Rugby international, who for a brief while was one of Mosley's lieutenants; later he was to enrol under Moral Rearmament. Winter never had the slightest sympathy with Mosley's party, but he was curious to know what Peter Howard saw in it. Evelyn and I sat in silence while the duologue con-tinued. 'Before the summer is out, Mosley will have left Labour as he left the Conservatives. There's no time for compromise. A clear, straight line of action, that's what the country needs.'

This happened over forty years ago. It is now easy with hindsight to find such talk ridiculous. But Mosley had glamour in his youth: glamour, courage and ability, and very many of his ideas were sound. In that early summer of 1931 he did appear to many as the man of destiny. Ray-mond's eyes shone as he talked about him.

'I need to know how they feel in Rome,' he said. 'I've letters to two of the chief blackshirts. They'll give me the clue as to what's happening. Particularly to what's happen-ing in Berlin.'

He stood up. 'I've got to stretch my legs,' he said. 'I'm still stiff after that night journey.'

But there was no stiffness in the pace with which he strode

towards the narrow path that leads past the fortress, along the rocks towards the harbour. He was the embodiment of youth and hope and vigour. 'I was afraid,' said Evelyn, 'that when Raymond took to something serious, he would take to something foolish.'

'You think he's serious about this?'

'It looks so, doesn't it.' And to prove Evelyn's point, Raymond proceeded for the next two days to exhaust us with his prophecies. Two more days of this, we thought . . . but luckily on the next day Fate intervened.

I was sitting on the terrace with my morning's work completed. It was half past eleven. Time for my second swim; I was folding up my *cahier* when a young woman whom I had not seen before came out from the hotel. She looked at me for a moment, hesitated, then came across.

'You are Alec Waugh?'

'Yes.'

'I thought so. I'd heard you were here. No, don't get up. May I sit down?'

She was pretty in a trim, blonde way, in her early thirties or maybe a little younger. 'I'm Eileen Martin.'

The name meant nothing to me, though she seemed familiar. But she was wearing a wedding ring. I might have known her when she was a deb. 'I'm down here because of Raymond Peronne,' she explained. 'They told me at the desk that he was here.'

'He's in that boat over there, he went over to Passable to bathe.'

'Is he going out or coming back?'

'He's coming back. He should be here in half an hour.'

'Good, not too long . . . that is to say . . .'

'Does he know you're coming? He didn't mention it.'

'I know, he didn't know. I didn't want him to. It had to be a surprise. I was afraid he might have gone.'

'He's leaving for Rome tomorrow.'

'I knew that, at least I knew he was planning to. I was afraid he might have gone already: it's a relief to find him here.'

She talked in quick, chopped-off sentences. She took out

a small platinum cigarette case, tapped a cigarette, lit it with a silver lighter, and began to smoke in short, quick puffs that were in tune with her sentences. 'Half an hour, that's a long time. Nervous to sit here watching. Too early for a drink? No, surely not. Lost sense of time in that long journey. Thought I was in Cannes when it was Marseilles. Must have something, now. You'll join me, won't you? What do you usually take here at this time?'

I told her that I didn't drink myself before my second bathe. 'What can I get you?' We agreed that Dubonnet would be appropriate, in view of the advertisement in high blue lettering on the Reserve hotel, DU, DUBON, DU-BONNET, which at that time faced you from the railway station. 'Here you are,' I said. While I was fetching the glass she had finished her cigarette and lit another. She attacked her Dubonnet as she had her cigarette, with short quick gulps, keeping the glass in her hand all the time. 'That damned boat isn't coming any closer: doesn't seem to have moved an inch. Can't stand this waiting, making conversation, finding mutual friends, talking Lords and Ladies; can't keep it bottled up any more, got to blurt it out . . . my husband, damn him, has found out about me and Raymond. Raised hell, kicked me out of the house, in fact, opened divorce proceedings right away, got all the evidence he wants— letters, photographs, the works, pretends to be furious, but I bet he's not, just what he's been waiting for, that bitch Lily, no alimony to pay me now, a Lord's son as the co-respondent. Can you beat it? Now you know why I'm here: had to tell Raymond myself, had to see his expression when I tell him, then I'll know; you see that, don't you?' She finished her Dubonnet in a double swallow, then held the glass out.

'I could use another.'

I was grateful for the interruption. It gave me time to collect myself and absorb what I had been told. By the time I returned, she was more composed. She had started on another cigarette, but she was spacing her puffs and she put down the glass after her first sip at it.

'How long has this been going on?' I asked.

'Two years or so. He goes away so much.'

'Is it . . .?' I paused. How serious was it, I wondered. Was it the real thing—for her? For Raymond it could scarcely be, in view of Myra's intervention.

'Raymond hasn't mentioned you,' I said.

'Of course he hasn't. He's not that kind of man.'

'If it's lasted two years, it must be serious for him.'

'Not necess . . . You know what Raymond is.'

I didn't, but I let that pass.

'He's away so much. If you travel as much as he does, things aren't broken off.'

'Have you been married long?'

'Five years. But it's my second marriage. I'm a war widow. I married very young. I've got a daughter, born after the armistice.'

That made the daughter twelve years old.

'Did you have any children from your second marriage?'

She shook her head. 'No, I can't think why. That was one of the things that went wrong with that marriage, I believe. He wanted a child, a son particularly. Someone to carry on the name and business, he's a wine merchant. He resented my daughter. He was jealous of my first husband because of her. "You've got to be in love to have a child," he'd say. Silly, wasn't it, but that's the way it was.'

'Were you in love with him?'

'It's hard to say. Five years ago. So much has happened since. I wanted to be married; he happened to be around when I was beginning to feel that it was time I married.'

'What about Raymond, were you in love with him?'

'Again hard to say. It was terribly easy to fall for him. His looks are devastating, aren't they? Even as a man you can see that. And then his graciousness, he makes everything so easy and so pleasant; his voice, there's so much warmth in it. He's irresistible—the moment I realised that he'd taken a fancy to me, I knew . . . no playing hard to get, a dead duck from the start. And it's been worth it.'

'What now?'

'Indeed what now? Exactly what I'm wondering.' She paused. She looked across the water: the row-boat was a bare fifteen minutes away. You could almost recognise the faces.

'It's funny to think of him in that boat,' she said, 'with no idea I'm here, with no idea of the news I'm bringing him: with no idea that the next half hour may be the most dramatic, the most decisive in his life.'

'How do you think he'll take it?'

'No idea. That's where he's so difficult. He's so easy, always thinking of you, not of himself: making no demands; I don't mean, always asking you what you want to do, that's boring. One wants to have one's mind made up for one. But the way he plans things, you can always tell that he was asking himself "What does she want?" At the beginning I'd tell myself, "he really loves me. He always thinks of what I'd like." But later I've come to think, "That's only because he doesn't care". He's so indifferent to how it all turns out that he can save himself trouble by jollying me along. If he really cared, wouldn't he insist on having his own tastes, his own interests catered for, on a fifty per cent basis?'

'Would you like to marry him?'

'Only if he really wanted it. You see . . .' She paused 'I recognise that I'm not a catch for him. I'm three years older. I've got a daughter, a twelve-year-old one at that. I may not be able to have another one. If he wanted a son and heir—but I don't think he does. He's not in the running for the title. Three years isn't so much difference, after all—not these days—but I'd be all right, without being married to him. Twenty years ago it was a point of honour for a man to marry the woman who'd got divorced on his account. He'd be a cad and she'd be ruined, cut by everyone, but it's different now, and I'd be all right, so would Iris—that's my daughter; my first husband left me quite a bit: of course I'd like to marry Raymond, who wouldn't? but I'd hate to force him into marriage: to have him feel that he'd been trapped . . . no, no that would be . . . oh no, I couldn't, I'd hate myself for ever . . .'

She was thinking of Raymond's interests more than of her own. A man might well think himself lucky to have a wife like that. I was reminded of that talk of mine with Judy all those months ago. I was reminded, too, of my talk only a few weeks back with Myra. Neither of them had been sure, any more than this woman was, how Raymond in his secret heart had felt about her. 'I'll tell him right away,' she said. 'I won't lead up to it. I'll know at once from the expression on his face how much of a shock, what kind of a shock it is. I'll have my answer.'

The boat was now less than a hundred yards from the jetty. 'He'll be able to recognise us in another minute. I'll be on my way,' I said. 'I'll leave you to your drama. Good luck.' I rose but she put out her hand to check me.

'No. Please stay. I don't want to face him alone. I want to take him off his guard, but at the same time I want an exit, an escape route. I've been thinking it out, all the way down in the train. I know exactly what to say if there's that look of a snared jackal. I'll say, "It's a nuisance, Raymond, but you're not to worry. The publicity will soon be over. Good to be rid of him, good for Iris. I'm sorry that you've been dragged into this, but it won't be more than a gossip paragraph. There'll be no damages. No feeling of spite on his part. He's grateful to you, his rescuer. I'm just off now to Monte Carlo, Iris will be joining me there in July for her holidays. You'll be hearing from his lawyers, but no need to worry. Just looked in to warn you and to wish you luck." That's how it'll be if I see that startled look.'

'Even so, I'd better be on my way. You don't want me here.'

'That's precisely what I do want. If you're not here, and if my news is the shock that I rather anticipate it will be he'll have recovered himself within thirty seconds, and be saying, "Now this is something we've got to discuss, mustn't rush into anything. What are you drinking, Dubonnet, I need something stronger. Half a second while I get it." And he'll have started on a scene that'll tear my nerves to shreds, but if you're here, I can make my getaway. It'll be quite easy. I've left my luggage in Nice. I'll say, "Alec, will you walk me up to the Octroi and see me on a trolley." I'll bless you for ever if you will. Well, here they are '

Keith Winter and Raymond were stepping out onto the quay. Their backs were turned to us. They settled with the boatman, gossiped together for a moment, then Winter sat at one of the tables before the bar while Raymond turned to the short flight of steps that led up to the terrace. It was then he noticed us. He started, obviously astonished, but there was no questioning the delight that flashed across his face. 'Eileen, but this is wonderful,' he said.

'You may not think it's so wonderful when you learn why I'm here,' she said. 'Mark has found out about us. He's turned me out of his house. He's starting divorce proceedings.'

She looked at him with a bright carefree smile. She might have been announcing the most casual event. He grinned. No other verb can describe the look of jubilation that crossed his face. 'What thrilling news. All we've got to decide is where to hide our shame until the law courts permit you to make an honest man of me.'

I turned and looked at her. Her face was transfigured, became radiant. I stood up. 'This is clearly a matter for you to decide between yourselves. I'm late for my swim. I must be hurrying.'

They made no attempt to stop me. When I came down from my room, changed into my trunks, they were still on the terrace. They waved at me. When I returned, their table was empty and the glasses cleared away.

In those days the Welcome Restaurant closed in June and residents took their choice for meals among the many small restaurants that were scattered about the lower town—the Spring Bar, then run by Germaine, who was later to open her highly successful restaurant on the waterfront, or the Kit Cat, or the Cabanon on the harbour—now Jimmie's— which I usually patronised. I had expected to find them there, but they were not. I washed down my *friture du pays* and grilled chicken with a half-litre of white Bellet, then returned to my room for a final assault upon my manuscript; most days I left myself an hour's writing after lunch. Then I took my siesta.

*   *   *

72

The waterfront had long since been in shadow,when I strolled along the beach for my final swim. It was half past six before I came down for my evening *pastis*. By now Raymond and Eileen were back before the bar. They waved me over.

'We want your advice,' he said. 'Where shall we hide our shame? It'll take six months at least for our case to reach the courts; then there's a six-months wait for the decree absolute. We'll be lucky if we're married before Christmas 1932. Let's aim then at staying away—who wants to come back to England in January?—until May 1933; so we'll be gone for close upon two years. We want a place where we can enjoy ourselves, but where we can take Iris. We don't want to go where the locals will be censorious. We want some social life, we want a reasonable climate: money's not a problem, or at least not too much of one, but we can't afford to move from one fashionable resort to another according to the season. Also we don't want to move among expatriates. We want to be residents somewhere, temporary residents of course, but we want our acquaintances to be living in the place we settle. That's a lot to ask, I know. But you've travelled a good deal. Where would you suggest?'

'That's quite a question.'

'No need to hurry. Think it over.'

But I did not need to. I guessed that I had the answer. 'How do the West Indies strike you?'

'How's the climate?'

'Healthy, no fever now, never cold, never too hot; quite a bit of rain, for more than half the year the rainless day is as rare as the sunless day.'

'Barbados, Trinidad, Jamaica?'

'Those are the three big British islands. But I'm not suggesting them. Too big and too expensive. My choice is Dominica.'

'Dominica?'

'Between Martinique and Guadeloupe. The French call our Battle of the Saints, the Battle of Dominica. It ought to be French. It was, more often than not, during the eighteenth century. Its natives talk a patois that sounds like French— the same patois that you hear in Haiti and Martinique.

73

It's mainly Roman Catholic with Belgian and French priests. That's one of the things, but only one of the things that make it different. Its beauty, that's the first thing; it has a beauty of its own special kind, but its beauty is self-destructive. Its mountains give it its beauty, but they bring down the rain. Then there's the boiling lake. Two thousand feet above sea level: it would be a tourist attraction, if there were any tourists. As it is, the lake creates clouds and that means more rain. The roads get washed away and the crops have to be "headed" to the coast. It's been unlucky from the start.'

I outlined its history for them. 'The island hasn't been out of the red for years,' I said. 'People have got depressed: all that ill-luck and all that rain, yet at the same time it does attract a remarkable collection of eccentric misfits, men and women who find something there that they find nowhere else. It has a special magic.'

'So that's what you recommend for us?'

I nodded. 'For your particular needs and for the moment, yes.'

'And it isn't as though we were going to spend the whole of our lives there, is it?' Eileen said.

'We can always pull up our roots.' He paused. 'Let's go back to England, see our respective lawyers, supply the required evidence—let's be conventional and go to Brighton, to the Metropole, then find the most convenient sailing. This calls for a celebration. Let's see what champagne they've got.'

The Welcome had a non-vintage Moët. 'We'll need two if we can find the others.' We found them, which made two bottles between six, the right amount for an aperitif-style celebration.

Twenty-four hours earlier Raymond had been boring us with his devotion to Oswald Mosley; now he was asking us to toast his good luck on an extra-curricular adventure. We could join him much more whole-heartedly this evening.

Next evening they drove into Nice to catch the Blue Train home. 'We'll expect you all to come out to see us there,' he said.

Well, and I might at that, I thought.

It was on a Tuesday that they left. I kept my Sundays free for letter-writing. Within five days Raymond would have broken the news at Charminster. I sent a very brief note to Margaret. 'So, there it is. And that kills the plan of Raymond and I opening for the Hall against the village. I'll be back at the end of June, but only for a couple of weeks, I think. Do please lunch with me this time. I shall arrive with a diary innocent of dates.'

My other letter was a longer one, to Myra. I felt that she needed to be warned. I wondered if it would be a shock to her. It was less than two months since he had been in New York; presumably he had spent his last hours with her. Would this elopement spoil the memory of those hours?

Her reply gave me no indication if it would.

It was written on one of those turn-over cards decorated with embossed initials that American socialites affect. 'It was dear of you to write. Am I surprised? Yes, I think I am, but men of that age do things unexpectedly. On Sunday I went to early service to say a prayer for them. I hope that it turns out well. He deserves it should. Do let me know next time you are over here, not only to tell me about Raymond.'

A month later I waited for Margaret at the Jardin des Gourmets, a small French restaurant that had recently opened in Soho and was rapidly establishing itself as a cosy setting for a tête-à-tête. I was feeling nervous. I had no idea how the afternoon would end. I had no idea how I wanted it to end. Everything was different now. The plans that we had made for my coming down for a cricket weekend as Raymond's guest belonged to another world. I arrived ten minutes early, I expected her to be ten minutes late. I ordered a carafe of white wine. I did not want to blunt my alertness with martinis. It was as well I did. I had started on the second glass before she arrived. She glanced at my glass, then at the carafe. 'Not strong enough for me, I fancy. A sidecar, please and it'll save time if it's a double. I'm late, I'm sorry. Now we can order right away.'

She did not, though, hurry over her choice of dishes. 'This

75

is my first meal away from that house for a couple of weeks. I need a good one.'

She treated the first half of her cocktail as though it were her first glass of wine and she was thirsty, not a gulp, or a series of swift sips, but a steady swallow. 'Potted shrimps, chicken vol-au-vent, then raspberries and cream. Now we can talk,' she said. 'Tell me all about it.' I told her all I knew. She listened carefully, interjecting questions. 'But this girl herself. What's she really like?'

'I find her a pretty decent sort.' I explained why I did.

'And Raymond himself, how does he feel about her?'

'Does one ever know how Raymond feels, about anyone or anything?'

She nodded. 'That's true. Takes everything for granted, always convinced that it will turn out right for him. Have you ever known him excited about anything?'

'At Villefranche, before Eileen arrived, he bored us all about the British Fascists.'

'He's well out of that,' she said.

'How's his father taking it?'

'Not at all kindly.'

'He didn't worry about that Oxford trouble.'

'That was very different. Youthful high spirits. A divorce is another thing, with a woman three years older than himself, and with a twelve-year-old daughter.'

'Did he bring her down?'

'No. A great relief for the old man. He came down for lunch to collect his things. He didn't take much away. Two suitcases and a wardrobe trunk; that was all he needed.'

'He can always come back for the rest.'

'I know, I know. It's surprising all the same how little there'll be left him to come back for. He never put down any roots.'

'Did you have any talk with him yourself?'

'A little. He asked me to sit in his room while he was packing.'

'How was he?'

'Couldn't have been more charming. Only worrying about

76

how it would affect all of us. Michael in particular. "It shouldn't embarrass him," he said, "and anyhow kids take a short-term view of things; after all, at Eton quarter of the others have parents who've been divorced, let alone uncles." He didn't seem to worry about his father much.'

'His father never worried about him.'

'Not worried, but cared in an impersonal kind of way. He identified himself with Michael's father, and now of course he's transferred those ambitions onto Michael, but at the same time he and Raymond were very close, closer in a way simply because he had no ambitions for him: more personal, if you get me, because he wasn't involved himself. He wanted Raymond to be happy. He can't be sure now he's going to be happy.'

'How do you feel about it?'

'Me, it doesn't matter how I feel. It's nothing to do with me, though it does make a difference, of course, how the old man feels. We're dependent on his moods. He gets depressed at times. It's hard work keeping him cheerful. And then there's Michael. Raymond is his uncle. There are a lot of things that he could have done for him, advise him about clothes, clubs, things that matter so much in England.'

'Raymond is still his uncle.'

'What's the use of an uncle in Dominica?'

'He won't stay in Dominica all his life.'

'Maybe not, but he'll be there for two years. And such important years. Michael's first half at Eton. Raymond could have taken his father's place. And even when he's back, we don't know how Eileen's going to fit in with us all.'

I felt sorry for her. I remembered how Raymond that first time he had talked of her, had said, 'Someone has to pick up the good hand in every deal.' Was it such a good hand after all? Had Raymond considered for one moment the effect that his elopement would have on her? I doubted it.

'Did he have a real talk with you about it?'

'We've never had a real talk in our lives. I tried to, once, after he'd had his row at Oxford. But it got nowhere. He's self-sufficient. He doesn't need anyone for himself. He can't

77

imagine anybody needing him. He takes each issue as it comes, on its own merits. "Take a short view." That's his motto. He's the least ambitious man I've met.'

'He used to talk about waiting for the right opportunity.'

'He hasn't for several years.'

'He was worked up about Oswald Mosley.'

'Oh, that . . . Forget it. I seem to have been going round and round this subject for the last month. Let's talk about something else. Tell me about yourself. What are you writing? Have you a new book this autumn? How was it in New York?'

I told her about New York, about my apartment on Lexington and 36th, how for four months I had lived as a New Yorker.

'And how did New York and the New Yorkers strike you?'

'To me it's the most exciting city in the world,' I told her. 'Every day something new, a new personality, a new way of seeing things. And the New Yorkers themselves, well, New York is them. They say New York isn't America, but seven million Americans live there. That's enough for me.'

'Are you planning to go back?'

'When I can. I felt a part of it. I want to remain a part of it.'

'That's going to make a difference to your writing.'

She was the first of my friends to realise that. The few who had taken any interest in my visit—the traveller on his return is usually greeted with a few perfunctory questions, then a flood of information about what has been happening in his absence—those who had evinced any interest in my trip had seen it in terms of 'a new market'. 'What luck,' they said, 'you'll sell your stories twice, both here and there.' Not one of them had wondered what impact America itself and the American way of life would have on my whole way of seeing things.

'If you can stay English at heart,' she said, 'yet have New York a part of you, you'll be adding a dimension to yourself.'

I felt singularly at one with her. This was not the kind of

lunch that I had planned but it was a lunch. I knew, that I should remember all my life. It was, after all, nearly a year since we had met. A great deal can happen in a year; particularly to someone as attractive and available as she was. Was someone else filling the place I might have in her life? Why not? Anyhow we were sitting here now, before an emptying bottle of white Burgundy, a sense of exhilaration in my heart and, I hope, some equivalent euphoria in hers. 'We mustn't lose touch,' she said. 'Are you likely to go to Dominica?'

'It's always on the cards.'

5

In the meantime Eileen kept me in the picture.

'Heaven only knows,' she wrote, 'when you will get this letter, but I am writing it on Christmas Eve, to tell you that I shall be thinking of you tonight at the midnight service; and thanking the Almighty for giving us such a good friend, who gave us such good advice. Where would we be, what should we be doing if it weren't for you? How grateful we are. But where am I writing this, you will be wondering; in one of those boarding house hotels in Roseau that you mentioned, Cherry Lodge and the Paz?—no, not at all, on the verandah of our own house, "Overdale". Did you see it? I don't expect you did. It's a heavenly place. We fell for it at sight. I enclose some snaps of it. From the verandah you can glimpse the sea, or at least you can when it isn't raining. There are mountains on either side, they go straight up; yet they're not so close that you feel shut in; right in front, below, there's a deep gorge, a river with banana plants clambering up it's side. It's green, green, green. We're a thousand feet up. That means it's cool at night. Thick socks and a cardigan. And we've got solid club-style furniture, deep sofas and arm-chairs, so that after dinner you can almost feel yourself in England; England in May, that first week when one doesn't need a fire.

'We bought the whole thing as it stood; an American couple had lost their nest egg in the crash: bargain price; I'd have preferred to rent, but they wanted solid cash, on the nail. Never get a second chance like this, said Raymond, but I don't think that's what decided him. He's not the calculating type: if he wants a thing, he goes for it: and he wanted this. "It's a fine investment," he kept saying, but that cut no ice. He wanted it. And why should I object? I can't bear English winters. Christmas with the family, then off for the Spanish main. That's our future programme, and what's wrong with it?'

*   *   *

On a bleak March morning I read on a newsboy's placard 'Peer's son co-respondent'. Raymond already? Yes, it was. But only a ten-line paragraph, at the foot of a column. Raymond was not news; nor was Eileen's husband, nor, for that matter, were the Peronnes. Peer's son, that was all he was in a Pressman's eyes. Was it all he would ever be? I wondered.

Three weeks later another letter arrived from Eileen—'I suppose you saw the announcement of our scandal. Quite a scandal, too, out here. Everybody thought that we were married. We travel as Mr and Mrs. What luck he hasn't got a title. I don't mind calling myself Mrs Peronne when I'm not. But I couldn't call myself Lady something or other if I wasn't. We'd warned the ADC, of course, and signed the book on different days, so that our signatures were a page apart. The Administrator was very nice about it. He sent the ADC round to explain that though he couldn't invite us together to official functions, he'd be glad if we'd come round for a rum punch after church on Sunday. There were one or two others there. It all went smoothly. Seeing us there together made people assume that we were married. Now they know better; but in six months it'll be settled. We don't know where we'll have the ceremony, or when. Even when the decree is absolute, we shall have to wait until the official papers turn up here, but anyhow it must be before next Christmas, and yes, I shall be relieved.'

During the spring I was to receive letters from her, most times that a Lady Boat sailed north.

'My friends ask me to tell them what it's all about,' she wrote, ' "give us a daily picture of your day", they say. But how can I do that? It would sound so dull, all that lying out on a verandah, reading or doing needle work; then those shopping trips into Roseau and the morning rum punch at the Paz, the afternoon siestas; then driving back to the club for tennis, and bridge and swizzles on the verandah; home, dinner, and bed almost at once afterwards, except for an occasional, a very occasional dinner party. It would sound so

81

dull, the same things day after day, with the same people. But it isn't dull. People who would seem dull in England aren't dull here because they're leading unusual lives. Because Dominica is interesting, so are they. Hasn't Maugham said something like that about his Far East characters? At any rate we're loving it, and so is Iris: there's quite a good school here. Her French is getting colloquial. I'm sure that she won't find she has lost anything, when she gets back to England . . .'

She talked about the local characters. They were of two kinds; the local West Indians who had lived here for generations, with names that were well known throughout the islands, Spanish, some of them like the de Freitas, most of whom 'passed as white', and then there were the recent settlers from England and the USA; these two types formed the nucleus of the Dominica Club, which had about forty basic members and to which tourists and visitors were given short-term cards of membership. With several of these forty I was already acquainted. I was delighted to have their news.

'I like the old families,' Eileen wrote, 'but the newcomers are frankly the more fascinating. They *are* eccentric; in the other islands they have a phrase "typical Dominica" which means . . . well, I'll give you an example. There was a widower, whose wife had died in Australia. He started to dig a hole, so that he could pray at her grave. He dug with a cutlass, carrying the earth up in a calabash. He got quite a long way down. I've seen the hole. That's what they call "typical Dominica".'

She told me about Stephen Haweis, then in his late fifties, an excellent painter who before the first war had been one of Gordon Craig's followers in Florence. In the twenties, in a moment of caprice, he had bought an estate in Dominica. When the stock market collapsed, that small West Indian plot of land was his only tangible possession.

'I asked him,' Eileen wrote, 'how he had come to buy it. He smiled at my question. "You know the beachcomber story of a man seeing a pretty native girl on a verandah and letting his ship sail on without him. It was a mango tree that brought me here. Its native owner was about to cut it down. The only way to save it was to buy the ground it stood on. I'd like to save that tree," I said. He pointed it out to me across the valley. It was not yet the mango season. I pictured it as it would be in a few weeks' time, heavy with fruit. "Why on earth did they want to cut it down?" I asked.

'He laughed. "It wasn't any use to them. I didn't know it at the time, but mangoes won't bear above fifteen hundred feet. We're over two thousand here. They'd have sold it as firewood. Charcoal fetches a good price. They were quite right, of course. I see that now." He paused, then smiled. "I felt rather cheated when I found it out. As a man might who gives up his career for a girl who turns out to be worthless. They were right, but so was I, though I didn't know it at the time. I'm glad I spared it. It's enough to be beautiful; there's no need to bear fruit as well." '

There was a lot about Raymond in her letters. 'He's absorbed by the place,' she wrote. 'He wants to do something for it. He insists that something here could be made to pay; "such soil, such special flavours" he keeps repeating. He's as you know, the most patient creature in the world. But he gets exasperated with the "je m'enfout-ism" of the Dominicans. They've given up hope. They let the rain wash away their roads, and then demand a subsidy from Whitehall. He's resolved to make his estate successful, as an example to the others to show them that it can de done. You mentioned in your book that in the bush the small proprietors make bay rum with what you called Heath Robinson contraptions. Raymond believes it's a very good bay rum. He wants to organise an industry. He's bought up several acres and plans to install a plant. Seems ridiculous to me, as we shan't be spending all that much of our time here, but I'm glad to see him occupied. I was afraid that he'd be missing his clubs and all those interests that Englishmen set so much store by. He doesn't seem to, though.'

I greatly enjoyed her letters. That summer two friends of mine, Elma and Lennox Napier to whom I have referred already, settled here. I gave them letters of introduction to the Peronnes. Eileen always wrote of them.

What a lot they would have to tell me on their return. But when would that be? 1933 was passing and still no news of their return.

Eileen continued to be a regular correspondent. 'It's such a relief to have someone to write to who can take some interest in the things I'm doing. It brings them to life for me. I keep saying to myself "This'll make Alec chuckle": and I need something like that, you know, to keep me chuckling. One has to have someone to share one's jokes with.'

Did that mean, I wondered, that she couldn't share them with Raymond? Was he taking his Dominican experiment too seriously for chuckles? He was, clearly, very busy. He had decided to start canning oranges and bananas, and was importing machinery from Canada.

' "Why not from America?" I ask him, but he's caught that "Buy British" tag. Do the Canadians think of themselves as British where business is concerned?'

Was a petulant note stealing into her letters? When I mentioned that mutual friends of ours had produced an infant, she wrote, 'Some people have all the luck.' I presumed that she was trying to have a child, but without success. Would Raymond worry? I doubted it. Perhaps in second sons there is a special antipaternal bloc, an unphiloprogenitive complex. Not having inherited themselves, yet having been brought out in an atmosphere of inheritance, they form a defensive mechanism against jealousy. Trained and resolved not to resent first a brother's then a nephew's better fortune, they do not want their sons to be subjected to ambitions they cannot themselves realise. I had noticed how often second sons in the aristocracy became homosexuals. Was this, subconsciously, a reaction against the occupancy of a second place. Perhaps Raymond was secretly glad that Eileen had not become pregnant. Was he also glad of this excuse for keeping out of England? Was Raymond's absorption in the fortunes of this rainsoaked paradise the expression of a self-defensive mechanism? He was certainly whole-hearted in his resolve to prove that an estate there could be a profitable investment.

'Can you credit this,' wrote Eileen, 'but my lord and master has bought up a large lime plantation in the north, at Portsmouth, where as you know the capital should have been, but there was too much malaria. I won't question that it's a good plantation, but you have to take a launch to get there. It's a four-hour trip. It's not worth going there, unless you spend the night; that means having a house there, so he's converting a ramshackle shed. It's a dreary place, no social life whatsoever: and the malaria's still there. He's also enlarged our own plantation here. Mangoes this time. He's setting up a mango factory.'

As the autumn passed, the note of detached incredulity was underlined in Eileen's letters. 'What next?' she wrote. 'That's more than I can guess. But I can tell you what's come last, arrowroot. It's making a lot of money in St Vincent, so my Lord and Master has decided to launch it here.'

The satiric note was now apparent. References to her 'Lord and Master' became more frequent. She was becoming, too, ironic about the life they led. 'Last week,' she wrote, 'I went to Barbados to have a tooth stopped. There's no real dentist here. I used to feel cheated by my defective teeth. I'd picture myself with snarlers at the age of forty, but now I'm really grateful to these wretched fangs. It gave me a chance to get away, to see real shops and to meet new people. In Barbados they're already beginning to make plans for their Christmas visitors and tourists. No such luck for us. What have we got to attract the tourist? scenery seen through rain, that's all. The same people in the club in January as there were in June; the same talk; gossip about GH, about the AG's capacity, or rather incapacity for rum; about Mrs Jones' car being parked for two hours yesterday afternoon outside the Paz . . . you know the kind of thing. I enjoyed it for the first six months; a place where everyone knows everyone makes every piece of tittle-tattle shine, but oh, for something really new; I'm tempted to do something really outrageous, to give them something to gossip over, make a pass at the Archdeacon's daughter for example . . . When are you coming out? When, when, when . . .'

It was a question that I was beginning to ask myself. I was anxious to see them again. I also, for professional reasons, wanted to have a second look at Dominica. On my next visit to New York I contrived to persuade an editor to send me down there to do a piece about the carnival.

My ship dropped anchor early. To my surprise the sky was cloudless. The mountains glistened and the ochre-yellow houses along the waterfront glowed in the morning sunlight. It was good to be back, to be importuned by voracious boatmen, avid for my custom, who introduced themselves with the cognomina of film stars. 'Mr Robert Taylor, I look after you,' 'Clark Gable, sir, your man, that's me.' And it was good, very good, to be welcomed by Raymond on the jetty. He looked very well, slim and tanned, at peace with himself and with the world around him.

As we drove through the town, I looked eagerly from left to right. 'It doesn't look any different,' I said.

'Did you expect it to, in five years, with a depression on?'

We swung right onto the Imperial Road. Once out of the town the colour dazzled me.

'I hadn't expected it to be so bright,' I said.

'Perhaps it's the first time you've seen it in the sun.'

Perhaps it was. 'I was only here for a week,' I said.

'You should be luckier this time, in two weeks.'

He told me his tentative plans for those two weeks. A cocktail party the following evening to re-meet old friends. 'Iris will be in from her convent for the weekend.' A picnic on the Sunday. On the Monday a dinner at GH. On the Thursday I was to go out to the Napier's, returning to Overdale on the Sunday. Next day we'd come into Roseau for the carnival. 'That's the framework. It gives you plenty of spare time to fit in whatever you may need for that article.'

'It all sounds fine by me.'

'And here we are,' he said.

Photographs in black and white had given me no real impression of the house's charm. They had not told me how the white wood shone and how the red and purple of the

86

bougainvillea stood out against it, nor how the lichen-stained grey stone of the crumbled windmill give it dignity.

'You made a good choice,' I said.

'I knew right away that it was right. As one always does with that kind of thing. The *daemon* that guided Socrates.'

Eileen had heard the car and stood at the head of the steps to welcome me. She was wearing a sleeveless cotton blouse, white with a flowered pattern and a dark blue skirt, cut short below the knees. Her legs were bare and she was wearing sandals. She was not as tanned as I had expected. 'Welcome,' she said, 'welcome.' She looked at the grandfather clock, beside the door. 'Half-past ten. Too early for the first punch, I'm afraid.'

'Much too early.'

'Why don't you let Raymond show you round his factory? By the time he's finished, you'll have earned one.'

By the time we were through it was half-past twelve. 'We lunch at quarter past,' Raymond told me. 'That gives us time for two of Eileen's punches.' She made them on the classic formula, one of sour, two of sweet, three of strong and four of weak, with nutmeg scattered on the surface. They were rich and sweet and cold, creating their own euphoria.

'Did you ever see *Polly*?' I asked Eileen.

'Of course.'

'*Polly*', the sequel to *The Beggar's Opera*, had been put on in London in 1923. Eileen had been between husbands then: no doubt with many beaux, taking her to all the shows that were necessary for a Bright Young Person. *Polly* had run for eight months. 'You remember that opening scene?'

She answered by quoting it. 'Rum, Jamica Rum, 'tis the one commodity that reconciles me to this barbarous climate.'

'How do you find the climate now?' I asked.

'Doesn't looking at Eileen answer that?'

She certainly looked well enough. I had only seen her once before, though that once had covered a twenty-four-hour stretch; at first she had been desperately on edge, gulping at her drink, treating her cigarettes as though they were martinis, then later in the day, radiant and transfigured with all her problems solved. Neither had been the real 'she'. But then what was the real 'she'? How often do we know ourselves to be ourselves? How often are we not filling the series of rôles that chance has cast for us? At any rate she seemed to be cast now in a rôle that suited her.

At lunch she was an easy hostess: noticing what one lacked, not pressing on one more than one really needed. She contributed to the talk without monopolising it. She was full, naturally, of enquiries about England.

'Tell me everything about everyone,' she said. Yet she did not appear envious of her friends; she did not talk as though she missed that life too desperately.

'Of course there are things one misses here. But think of the things you get.'

'What are the things you miss?'

'Music, that more than anything; plays; I loved the theatre, and all that goes with music and the theatre; all the talk about what's coming on, gossip about stars, who's in love with whom; which manager is in the money; hearing things at first hand, being behind the scene. Every party in London's an adventure. London's an adventure. London's the centre of the world. Everything sooner or later comes there, everything and everyone. Yes, one misses that.'

'What takes the place of that?'

'The place itself. Its beauty; the warmth; the family feeling of all of us being in the same show together.'

'What about the rain?'

'There's not really as much rain as one is told. It's terrible, at times, I know. Days and days of it; everything wringing wet. The fruit rotted, the flowers draggled; yet somehow it's the link that binds us all. You were in the war. You know how much better it was in France than it was in England. You shared the danger and the mud.'

'How much of the year do you plan to stay here?'

'How can I tell? As long as we spend a good share of it, I shan't grumble.'

She spoke contentedly; yet I sensed, though I could not define, an air of restlessness, of uncertainty, of questioning self-doubt. There was something not quite right.

88

'How about Iris?' I asked, 'won't she have to spend a good deal of time in England? Aren't you thinking of sending her to a University, or somewhere in Paris or Switzerland to be finished off? How old is she now, fifteen?'

'Not quite. She can afford to spend two more years at least here; and in two years a lot can happen. There'll be air travel soon; then she can come back every holiday—not only in the summer.'

'I'm looking forward to meeting her.'

'She's looking forward to meeting you. She reads a lot. You'll be the first author that she's met. She'll probably bore you blue with questions. "Tell me how you write, Mr Waugh, on a typewriter or by hand? Who is your favourite author?" You know the kind of thing.'

I knew the kind of thing extremely well and was prepared for it. But it was not like that at all. Iris was an enchanting creature; blonde, blue eyed, with a fresh complexion that was barely tanned. Her hair, as was the mode then among young teenagers, was cut in a fringe with coils about her ears. Her legs were slim and straight. She was slightly over five feet tall. She looked sixteen at least. Her breasts jutted against her blouse. Her hips were rounded. She must have become used by now to males in the street following her with their eyes. But she was not in the least self-conscious. She was out-giving without being forward.

As I had been warned, she was full of questions. 'You are the first novelist I've met,' she said.

'What about Elma Napier?'

'She doesn't count; she lives here. Tell me about Rebecca West.'

'That's a lot to ask. She's a complex character.'

'Of course, but what's she like. Beautiful?'

'Very striking. Her friends call her Panther.'

'Do you?'

'I don't know her well enough.'

'I see.' She paused. 'Panther, yes, I can picture somebody with the nickname Panther.'

'Berta Ruck, in one of her novels, described her voice as one of the loveliest she had ever heard.'

'Berta Ruck; I used to dote on her when I was young.'

When I was young. I had the restraint not to smile.

'Berta's one of my best friends. We help each other with our stories. She'll tell me that her hero plays Rugby football; she'll send me her MS and say "in chapter five, half a page about the football match in which he plays." '

'How does she repay you?'

'I send a description of a party. "I want my heroine to feel over-dressed; what would make her feel that way in that kind of party?" '

'I see.'

'Who else do you read?' I asked.

'Rosamund Lehmann, Sylvia Thompson.'

'I've only met Rosamund Lehmann once.'

'Is she as beautiful as she looks in her photographs?'

'Even more.'

'And Sylvia Thompson?'

'Two years ago I crossed in the same liner. She's very lovely too: in every way,' I added.

Iris sighed. 'It must be wonderful to meet all these wonderful people.'

'They don't all seem so wonderful when you know them.'

'I'd like to meet them.'

'You will if you want to.'

'What, out here?'

'You aren't going to stay here all your life.'

'Aren't I? Where am I going then?'

'To a finishing school, to Oxford aren't you?'

'That, oh yes, but that's a century away.'

Fours years a century, and the couple of years ago when she had doted on Berta Ruck belonged to the days when she was young. I was fascinated by her. Not having a sister, I had seen very little of young girls.

Eileen and Raymond had left me alone on the verandah with her. I sipped a Barbadian rum and water while she drew on a coca-cola through a straw. She sat on a cushion, leaning back against the balustrade, her legs crossed beneath her.

'Have you any plans for yourself when you're grown up?' I asked.

She shook her head. 'It's no good making plans. Things happen suddenly, and you make the best of them. My daddy never saw me. I've got the letters he wrote to mummy from the front. "How wonderful that we are going to have a baby. Do I want a girl or a boy? Either way I know it will be wonderful." That was the last letter that he ever wrote. The same thing happened to Uncle Raymond's brother. He never saw his son. Three years ago I had never heard of Dominica. Now it is my home. You can't look ahead.'

'But you have, surely, to make your plans as though they weren't going to be interfered with? You'd never do anything, would you, if you said, "What's the good of arranging a tennis party, it might rain." '

'And that's what always seems to happen here. You make a new party frock: and a rainstorm soaks it.'

'Yet you have to assume that it won't rain.'

'You're right. One has to. Even in Dominica.'

She said it with a laugh. She could take it with a laugh. What was one rain-spoilt afternoon to her? She was so very young, there were so many afternoons ahead.

That night at dinner Iris was full of her plans for Carnival. She was going to 'run mask' with a troup of school friends; a dozen of them were going to put white cotton stockings on their arms to conceal their colour: to powder their faces with flour, mask their eyes; their skirts and blouses were to be striped green and red and orange: black stockings and white shoes: sashes advertising Shillingford's diagonally across their chests: they would take it in turns to strum their quota of three banjos; they had memorised the calypsos. Shillingford's were to renew their vigour every other hour on the hour with cokes and hot dogs. They were to start at ten; at six they were to report back to the convent. Then with their faces cleaned they could rejoin their parents.

'When I was here five years ago, the streets had to be cleared at six,' I told them.

The year before there had been trouble. Old scores had

been paid off; a body with a knife in its back had been found on the waterside. 'That's over now, or at least we hope it is,' said Raymond. 'We're having dinner at the Airds'; then we'll go out on the streets for the last two hours. You musn't miss the last leap. At the last stroke of twelve everyone leaps to his feet, arms on high. One terrific yell; then silence.'

On the Wednesday afternoon Raymond drove me to the Napiers': I was to be back at Overdale on the Sunday in time for dinner. On the Monday evening we were to go into Roseau. We were staying at the Paz. 'I need an hour's rest at least every two hours,' Raymond said.

'My first year,' Eileen said, 'I stayed on the streets all the time. At least that's what I planned to do. But of course I couldn't. I had to have rests. That meant going into bars. Oh, what a head I had next morning!'

Two years earlier I had spent Mardi Gras in New Orleans. I had had an apartment then in Jackson Square, which had been a very useful rallying point. I had settled a number of scores of back hospitality. It had been a big occasion. I expected this to be an even bigger one.

On the Sunday afternoon I was back at Overdale soon after five. Before I had been in the house three minutes, I was aware of a changed atmosphere. Although Roseau was a bare six miles away, and we should be carrying only a handbag each, I had expected to find a restless sense of imminent departure. On the contrary I found a strange serenity. Raymond and Eileen were sitting on the verandah. He was reading poetry to her. There were no drinks beside them. I had heard him read poetry before. I had enjoyed his mellifluous, sing-song way of reading that had stressed and accentuated the rhythm and the rhymes; it had been the fashion when he was at Oxford to break the lines, never giving iambics their full value; reading poetry as though it were prose. Raymond, on the contrary, whenever the actual meaning of the poem permitted, half paused at the end of the line. You found yourself waiting for the rhyme.

Usually at Oxford, he had read very modern poetry. Pound or E.E. Cummings or T.S. Eliot, where the metres and rhyme schemes were unconventional, but now he was reading Victorians—Tennyson, Browning, Matthew Arnold. He offered to stop when I came in. 'No, no, please go on,' I said. 'I so seldom hear poetry read these days.'

He was half-way through *Tithonus*. When he had reached the end, he said, 'Would you like me to change to somebody more modern?' He had the *Oxford Book of Victorian Verse*, which I had seen so often in my father's hands. I was carried back to the bookroom at Underhill, with its two red lamps and my father sitting in his hard, tall-backed chair. Evelyn had written in *A Little Learning* of my father's reading. In terms of my appreciation of poetry, I owe everything to it.

'Is there anything that you'd like especially?' Raymond asked.

'Is "Andrea del Sarto" in the Victorian book? I can't remember.'

'It's not, but I can find it.'

I closed my eyes as he read. 'Here in this melancholy little house we built to be so gay with.' When he reached the last line, I opened my eyes and looked across at Eileen. Her face wore the same brooding expression that my mother's had when my father read to us. 'This marriage is all right,' I thought. I had never pictured their sharing poetry.

'Let's have "The Scholar Gypsy",' Eileen said. It was one of my father's favourite poems. When he had given me at Sherborne a copy of his *Reticence in Literature* he had incribed inside it the verse beginning 'A fugitive and gracious light he seeks'. I waited for that verse to come.

The sun was sinking now. The horizon was lit with red and orange. Fireflies darted above the crotons. Another ten minutes and it would be dark.

'Only time for one more poem,' said Raymond. He turned to the end of the Oxford book. 'The very last poem, "Deus illuminatio mea" appears under the authorship Anon.' My father told me that it was by R. D. Blackmore. It was one of his favourites. I had never heard anyone else refer to it. 'In the hour of death after this life's whim.' I knew the poem so well that my lips framed the words:

> 'When the will has forgotten the lifelong aim
> When the mind can only disgrace its fame
> And a man is uncertain of his own name,
> The power of the Lord shall fill this frame.'

Raymond closed the book. 'Let's move down the verandah and look for the green ray.'

The part of the verandah where we had sat was shaded, but from the end of it we could see the enlarged orange globe already cut by the horizon. 'In how many of your stories have you made your lovers look for that,' said Eileen.

'More often than I've seen it myself,' I said.

We stood and watched, in the angle of the verandah.

'I don't think we'll be seeing it tonight,' said Raymond. He was right. A thin sliver of cloud was drifting towards its rim. It was sinking fast, but that sliver would have reached it before its complete immersion. Raymond sighed. 'I'd have liked to have seen the green ray tonight.'

'That cloud is making a far more dramatic sunset of it.'

'I know, but I wanted to see the green ray tonight. I've a special reason, at least we have a special reason.'

'Don't worry about the green ray,' said Eileen. 'Let's have that champagne.'

I looked first at her and then at him. I was puzzled. They were smiling at one another, in a special way, as though they shared a secret.

'What's all this about?' I asked.

'You'll soon see,' she said. 'We've got a toast to make.'

We stood up to drink it. 'To the future,' Raymond said. We sipped at our glasses. Eileen raised her glass. 'To our future.' We sipped again. They then raised their glasses simultaneously, 'To Overdale that shields that future.'

With this third toast they drained their glasses; and tossed them over their shoulders, among the crotons. I followed their example. 'And now,' I said, 'you can tell me what it's all about.'

'You mean you haven't guessed?'

'Most certainly I haven't.'

'And they say, that novelists know such things by intuition.'

'Put the poor man out of his misery,' said Eileen. 'I'll tell him if you don't.'

'You tell him then.'

'OK. You're the first to hear except the doctor who sent us that mouse test yesterday.'

'Now I've guessed,' I said.

'Isn't he bright?'

'Congratulations.'

'Thank you.'

I understood now the slightly taut atmosphere of expectancy that I had observed over the weekend. Then they had not known. They were awaiting the result of the mouse test. Now they knew that she was pregnant. That explained the atmosphere of serenity that I had found that afternoon. Their future was settled now.

We drank the bottle slowly. 'Will this make a big difference to your plans?' I asked. I knew it would. But I wanted them to tell me how it would.

He explained where and how it would make all the difference. 'When we toasted the New Year,' he said, 'we were wondering whether we ought to go on living here. We had no idea of making a home here when we first came out. As you know, all we wanted was somewhere to be out of the way till the gossip had died down. I bought this place because it seemed a good investment. Then as I developed it, I began to get excited. Dominica is a funny place. It lays a hold on you, like a Voodoo curse. But we couldn't spend our whole lives here. It wouldn't be fair on Iris. We wanted a child, but if we weren't going to have one, we both felt we should go back to England, rent or sell this place and make a life for ourselves in England. It's about time I found some solid occupation.'

'It was such a waste of him, don't you agree?' said Eileen.

I did not answer that. I felt, as we had all felt, that it was

95

high time Raymond started to do something. He had been waiting so long for the right thing to turn up. He was over thirty now. Everyone had said 'There must be the right thing somewhere. He's so wise to wait.' But what was that right thing and where was it?

'I can see what you mean,' I said.

'We agreed to give ourselves a year,' she said. 'If there was no sign of an infant in that time, we'd call it a day.'

'But now that there is?'

'Yes, as you say, now that there is.'

Raymond leant his head back against his chair; he half closed his eyes. 'There's a point now in building up a place like this: particularly if the child's a boy. There is a future in this land for anyone who tries, in the right way. No one can look ahead too far. But it's not impossible that a small country like England will find it more and more difficult to support a growing population; there should be a need for colonies producing food. The West Indies may be as important in the 1960s as they were in the 1760s. You don't need reminding that in 1763 England nearly swapped Canada for Guadeloupe. In 1950 a school boy might well see a future here.'

'If the child's a girl?'

'A girl who has been brought up here might well want to spend her life here. She might well find a husband who would see a future here. Anyhow, it'll be worth my trying to make something of this place.'

Their future, anyhow for the next fifteen years, was settled, and who had so fortunate a fate that he would not be prepared to envy theirs? The sky had begun to darken; but a quarter full moon was shedding its radiance on the garden. There was no need to switch a light on, a smoking coil beside each chair checked the mosquitoes. The heavy sweet smell of frangipani enriched the air. The air had cooled and Raymond and I put on our jackets. Iris joined us. I wondered when she would be told the news that was to make so great a change in her life. I remembered how she had talked the other day about the unpredictability of fate. She sat on a cushion, leaning back against the railing. 'Please read some more poetry, Uncle Raymond.'

'What would you like?'

'Something with a story. Why not "The Highwayman"?'

That, too, had been a favourite of my father's. How much of our family life, Evelyn's and mine, had turned round poetry, and the red lamps in his bookroom. Ours had been a happy home, in large part due to poetry. Raymond was building just such another home for Iris and the children of this new marriage.

6

Carnivals repeat themselves. One is very like another. You
either enjoy them a lot or very little. I, who as a boy was
taken to Easter Monday fairs on Hampstead Heath, have
always found them fun. I have enjoyed their formal in-
formality. The local boys and girls have saved up for months
to buy garish dresses. They are a riot of improvisation. Everything is there. Pierrots, pierettes, sailors, cowboys, men
dressed as women, their paunches padded to suggest advanced
pregnancy. The members of each separate group, known as
a band would be dressed alike. Their small orchestras would
collect alms. Sometimes the bands would parade apart; sometimes they would join with others, forming a solid phalanx
seventy or eighty strong. Each band had its own sequence of
calypsos. Sometimes everyone in the street would be chanting
the same one. Often they resorted to one that I had heard
there five years before; it celebrated a recent suicide:

> Sophia go down to the river to dine
> Wild wild Sophia
> Sophia drink wine and iodine.
> Wild wild Sophia.

Iris' band was under discipline: the teachers took it in
turn to parade with them; but though they indulged in no
unexemplary fantasias, their youth and energy made them
noticeable. We easily picked out Iris, in spite of her mask.

'She's an exquisite creature,' I said to Eileen.

'I think so.'

We ourselves, the elders, kept off the streets. We visited
friends' houses and watched from balconies. We frequented
bars. Sometimes we danced together, in this and the other
drawing room. We had hot dogs at this house, hamburgers at
that. A couple of times I went to the hotel and rested. The day
waned slowly. It had rained the night before and the streets
were puddled. But today miraculously the skies were clear.
Six o'clock drew nearer. We found ourselves on the balcony

of one of the few Georgian houses that had survived the fires and the earthquakes by which time and again Roseau had been destroyed. It had a small garden at the back; its lawn was shaded by a mango tree. A narrow by-path led into the main street; by craning our necks we could see the revellers leaping and cavorting in the streets. The music swelled and loudened, sank, then rose again. I had had it in my blood all day: I found my feet moving to its beat. I suddenly, and to my astonishment, found myself acutely conscious of Eileen's presence at my side. Her shoulder, as she leaned forward, was touching mine. She was wearing a heavy scent of which until then I had been unaware. Her feet, too, had began to move. My arm itched to go round her waist. 'Now this won't do,' I thought. I put my arms behind my back, holding my right hand by the wrist.

'They must have got themselves into a pretty state by now,' I said.

'I'd say they had.'

I had tried to make my voice sound natural. I hoped I had succeeded. My heart was beating. I was the slave of the music. Yes, this was carnival.

A couple turned out of the street and came down the path. They were hand in hand. The man looked young. He was tall and supple. His face was completely covered with a violently grotesque mask. He wore a long-sleeved football shirt. His hands were ungloved. His fingers were long and lean. The girl's eyes were masked; her face was powdered; her arms white-stockinged. Her blouse and skirt were patterned, red and green and orange. A sash advertising Shillingford's was knotted on her shoulder.

'One of Iris' band,' I said.

'Iris herself,' said Eileen. The couple paused. They turned to face each other. They began to dance. Her back was turned to us. He with his mask could not have recognised us on the balcony; even if he could have, would he have cared? They danced, scarcely moving their feet, following the rhythm with their bodies. She raised her arms, she folded them about his neck. His hands slid over her shoulders, down her back in a slow caress, pausing at her waist. He held her close: his hips rotated to the music: she responded in a slow, slow roll. His hands lowered to her haunches. The dark fingers spread against her skirt, tightening their hold on her: they moved together like one body: sometimes quickening their pace; then slackening, till they were almost motionless, quivering against each other: then the roll would become fierce: with one hand he pressed her closer, with the other he caressed her now gently, and now fiercely; each finger separate in its touch. She flung back her head; his back was against the wall, giving him leverage. Quicker, quicker, quicker: more and more fiercely, his fingers on her haunches closed together, lifting the cotton skirt between them; fiercer, fiercer, fiercer, then suddenly a long shudder ran through them both; his hands loosed their hold. They stood motionless, like statues. She sighed, her arms slid from his neck. His hands fell to his side. They stood apart. Then turned towards the road. She took his hand as they walked towards the street.

'She must never know.' That was the first thing Eileen said. 'She must never know we know. She could never be open with me again. No, she must never know.' It was nearly six. We were due at the hotel. In ten minutes Iris would be back to shower and clean up: to make herself ready for the party. 'We must be on our way,' said Eileen.

At dinner Iris sat across the table. With her face washed clean of powder, she looked twelve years old. There was no glow about her: no withdrawn look, as though she were brooding over a secret. She looked in fact as I would have expected her to look ten hours before—worn out and exhausted by the noise, the dancing, the shouting: collapsed, as oarsmen are at the end of a long race.

Raymond and Eileen were both resolved to give her no indication that anything unusual had happened. They asked her the questions that might be expected of a parent; she answered them, not listlessly but without animation. Tomorrow no doubt she would start remembering ... tomorrow.

A dozen places had been laid for dinner; but there were four or five others who had looked in for drinks, had lingered on, had been invited to 'take pot luck', and were now seated on chairs with plates upon their laps.

It was because of them that the party broke up earlier than was planned. They felt that they must not outstay a welcome that they had not in fact deserved, and when they rose, others took advantage of the opportunity to get back to the revels quickly. Raymond and Eileen were among the early leavers. 'All this is new to us,' he said. 'We haven't got blasé yet.' As soon as they were back at the Paz, they sent Iris off to bed. 'You need a full night's rest, young lady,' Raymond said. 'You've got to be fresh for school tomorrow.'

She did not demur. As she stood on her toes to kiss him goodnight, it was impossible to believe that three hours back she had been rocking in that close embrace. She was such a child.

Raymond turned to me. 'Are you desperately anxious to go out again?'

I shook my head. 'I've had enough.'

'You don't feel that in the interests of copy you should go?'

'I've all I need.'

'Then let's have a quiet drink upstairs.'

We had it in their room. They could not run the risk of being overheard.

'Eileen's made up her mind,' he said, 'and I agree with her. She's taking Iris back to England, right away.'

I made no comment. It was no business of mine. But they wanted to have me listen. To see how their ideas sounded when told to a third person.

'Eileen insists on this and I know she's right. Iris must never know, it might set up heaven knows what inhibitions. She could never feel we trusted her. She would suspect that we were suspecting her, watching her, as of course we shall be. A thing like that, happening to a child like that, and with her responding.'

He paused: he looked at me interrogatively; half hoping that I should protest, suggesting that Eileen as a mother had exaggerated what might have been relatively innocent. But I could not contradict her testimony.

'I remember a passage in one of your books, *Hot Countries*, I think it was, when you described the Bal-lou-lou in Martinique. You said you could not describe it literally within the limits of current censorship. That is, isn't it, the way it was.'

'Yes, that's the way it was.'

'I blame myself,' Eileen interposed. 'I should have guessed that such a thing could happen. Juliet was only fourteen. And we're in the tropics, the climate of quick growth. I should have been on my guard. Thank God that we've been warned in time, and can get her back to a cold climate.'

'When are you going back?' I asked.

'Right away.'

'At the end of term?'

'No, sooner than that, on the same ship as you.'

'The day after tomorrow?'

'That's it. As soon as possible. Don't give her a chance to brood on it. Get that music out of her head: keep those dark figures out of her eyes: don't let her see those couples dancing. She's had a taste of it, she'll want to try again. "The fly that sips honey." If we get her away at once, she may forget that it ever happened: feel that it was something that she dreamed. She probably hasn't the least idea who the man was. We're in luck there. She doesn't know who he is. He doesn't know who she is. In a year's time she'll be thinking of it as something that she dreamed; but she must be taken out of this atmosphere. She mustn't be reminded of it. Doesn't that make sense to you?'

It made admirable sense, but there were problems.

'How are you going to explain to her?'

'In the simplest way. I'll tell her that I'm going to have a baby: that I've only just discovered; that I don't want to have it here, in this climate, without proper attention. I'll tell her that I don't want to put it off too late. She doesn't know, or at least I don't think she does, very much about all that; that the first three months are the ones when I'm likeliest to lose it, and that if I were sensible, I'd wait till the fourth month. She won't think of that. She'll be excited at the idea of going home. England is still home to her. She'll regard it all as a piece of luck; missing the last half of a term. You watch her face at breakfast when I break the news to her.'

She had guessed her daughter's reaction accurately. Breakfast was at seven, the three of us were at table promptly: we had agreed on that the night before. Iris was ten minutes late. She was wearing her school uniform: white blouse, blue skirt, blue tunic. 'I'm sorry I'm late,' she said. 'I'm due there at eight. I haven't packed yet. I'll have to hurry.'

Raymond laughed. 'No need to do that. Take all the time you want over your breakfast; make a good one; when you've finished, you can go upstairs and change into ordinary clothes.'

'Why?'

'You aren't going to school today.'

'Why not? The Mother Superior said . . .'

'She may have. But she no longer has any jurisdiction over you, if you know what jurisdiction means.'

'Of course I do.'

'What does it mean?'

'I don't know the exact meaning, but I know what it stands for.'

'That's fine: let's say it means authority. You are no longer under the Mother Superior's authority.'

'How so?'

'You're leaving school.'

'When?'

'You've already left.'

She frowned. She looked puzzled. 'What do you mean?'

'Not what you're afraid I'm meaning. You haven't been expelled. We're taking you away.'

'Why?'

'So that you can go back to England.'

'When?'

'Tomorrow afternoon.'

'What?'

Eileen intervened. 'Darling, something exciting's happened. You are going to have a little brother or a little sister. And you know what that means don't you, when a woman has a baby?'

103

'Of course.'

'A baby gets very heavy, during the last five months. Too heavy a burden for a place like this, so hot, and all these hills and all this rain. So we've decided that I shall go back to England and have it there. And of course I couldn't leave you behind me, could I?'

'Is Uncle Raymond coming too?'

'I'm afraid not, not at the moment—there's too much on the estate to be attended to. He'll join us in the summer.'

'And where shall I go to school?'

'To St James, it's at Malvern, where Jenny goes.'

Jenny, I was to discover later, was the daughter of an English neighbour, and a friend of Iris.

'When does the new term start?'

'The end of April.'

'A six-week holiday, oh goody-goody.'

'It's not going to be a holiday altogether. You'll have to do some work on the ship. Uncle Alec has promised to read you Shakespeare.'

'So Uncle Alec's coming with us?'

'As far as Boston. We go onto Montreal and catch a ship from there.'

That was another of the decisions they had made the night before. There was no American consul in Dominica qualified to give them an American transit visa.

'Where shall we live in England?' Iris asked.

'We'll stay with your Aunt Mildred till we can find a house to rent.'

'In London or the country?'

'Which would you prefer?'

'London. I've had enough of country.'

'You see,' Raymond said, when she had left the room, 'already she's living in the future. She's excited about what she's going to. She's not worrying about what she's left behind.'

Certainly there were no tears in her eyes on the following morning. Nobody had come to see us off. Hardly anybody knew that we were leaving. It had all happened so quickly:

before anyone had recovered from the post-carnival hang-overs. Raymond came out with us in the row-boat to see us settled in. It was raining, and we crouched under our umbrellas, silent, too exhausted for conversation. Eileen and Iris were sharing a state-room on the boat deck. I had a minute cabin to myself. 'I can't stand long drawn out farewells,' said Raymond. 'You're clearly going to be all right. I'll go back to the Paz and have myself a punch. When I hear the siren go, I'll come down to the quay and wave to you.'

But when the siren sounded, the rain was coming down in a succession of torrential waves, one after another, with only a half minute's pause between them. The Morne was covered.

'He won't come out in this,' I said.

'Oh yes, he will. He does the correct thing, always.'

And sure enough, just as the crunch of the anchor started, the red Morris Oxford swung into the quay: its door swung back; an umbrella pointed out, opened, and Raymond followed it. He stood beside the car. We were protected by the roof of the upper deck, and in the shadow. He could not distinguish us, but we could see him clearly. He took off his hat and waved. We waved back, though we knew that he could not see us. He returned to the car, pulling in the umbrella after him. A faint series of hoots came from the car. Slowly he drove off.

'What a casual leavetaking,' she said.

'Scarcely a leavetaking. He'll be following you within four months.'

'Will he? Who knows? Four months is a long time. A lot can happen in four months. And it may be longer than four months.'

'But for sure he'll be back in the late summer for your confinement.'

'He'd better be.'

There was a grim look in her eyes as she said that.

It was a pleasant trip. The Canadian ship stopped at all the British islands. We skirted the north coast of Dominica, pausing at Portsmouth for a couple of hours. We passed Guadeloupe, we were due at Antigua on the following morning: we were to stop at Montserrat and St Kitts; then make north for Bermuda.

St Kitts and Montserrat would be new for me. Eileen, coming out by the French line, had made her first call at Guadeloupe. She had seen none of the other Leeward islands. In fact she had only left Dominica once, that time in Barbados. It was all new for her. We sailed from Portsmouth in the afternoon. The mountains of Guadeloupe were bright with rainbows. 'There's sun there at any rate,' she said.

When we woke next morning, the sky over low-lying Antigua was almost cloudless. We drove out to a nearby beach. The sand was golden and the water blue. 'This is how I thought the tropics would be,' said Eileen.

'In Antigua,' I said, 'they don't have nearly enough rain. There's a lack of water. Do you see those bare patches on the hills? They're catchments to conserve the rain.'

'That's better than having too much rain.'

'You might not think that if you lived here.'

'Mightn't I? I think I would. Why on earth did Raymond have to fall in love with Dominica?'

'That is what he did, didn't he?'

'I'd say he did.'

'That's how it gets some people.'

'It didn't get me.'

'On Sunday night you didn't seem too horrified at the idea of staying here.'

'Sunday seems a century ago.'

'I can't believe that ever happened.'

'It did though, didn't it? I'm glad you were there to see. Without you as a witness Raymond would never have believed it.'

Looking at Iris, it was equally difficult to believe it had. She was exactly as she had been before I went on the trip across the island. I read her *Hamlet, Twelfth Night* and *As You Like It* in *Lamb's Tales from Shakespeare*: when I had finished each play, I would read her certain selected passages from the actual text. She was absorbed by them, asking me questions afterwards, questions that were both naïve and understanding.

I also read to her from the *Golden Treasury*. When we reached St Kitts, I told her of Browning's connection with the island, of how his grandmother was a creole from St Kitts.

'What's a creole?' she asked.

'Someone or something native to, or born on the islands.'

'We were talking about that word at school. One of the girls said it meant having coloured blood. Does it?'

'Not necessarily. You can have a white creole, a brown creole, or a black creole. In Browning's case there isn't any doubt that his grandmother was in large part African. His father was so dark that when he went to St Kitts as a boy he was told to sit on the side of the church that was reserved for coloured people. Browning himself had such an olive complexion that a nephew in Paris mistook him for an Italian. You remember that poem of his wife's we read the other day, "How do I love thee, let me count the ways"? Well, when she got engaged to Robert Browning, her father objected. He had sugar estates in Jamaica, and he didn't want his daughter marrying a man whose grandmother was partly African.'

'Wasn't that very silly of him?'

'It didn't seem so then.'

'But today . . . ?'

'Everything is different in that way today.'

In retrospect I recall the eight days of that trip as a long discussion, endlessly broken off, endlessly renewed between myself and Eileen.

'I've always known that Iris was going to be a problem. Who is there for her to marry in Dominica? There's not a single unattached eligible white man. The young men who are eligible get sent back to England and they don't return. There are tourists, of course, and winter visitors; but tourists and winter visitors aren't out for marriage: they're for a roll in the hay. They'd be no use for Iris.'

'Yet you seemed so happy that other night, when you and Raymond were reading poetry together.'

'Seemed, that's the word, yes, seemed.'

'But weren't you? You looked radiant.'

'Did I? Perhaps I was. It was a relief, a great relief. After all that waiting and all those disappointments. It made me feel differently about myself; to know that I could have a child. No woman likes to feel she's sterile; and then there was Raymond. That was a relief, too.'

'Was it? I've never thought that Raymond was all that anxious to have a child.'

'Didn't you? I don't know that I did either. But then what do I know what Raymond feels about that, or about anything for that matter?'

'That's a strange thing for a wife to say.'

'Is it? I suppose it is. But I don't know him any better than I did three years ago—in the things that really count. I know how he'll react to certain things, about my being punctual, about what I wear, about how our guests behave; he's very punctilious; I know his views on local politics; I know how he'll react when the Administrator puts up a proposition. Yes, I know what he thinks. But how he feels, that's another matter.'

'Three years ago, when you turned up in Villefranche, you didn't know how he was going to take your news.'

'I know I didn't. And I should have done. He did, as I should have known he would, the correct thing for the second son of a British peer. I didn't know then how he ran to type—to an inherited pattern of behaviour. But how he felt, now that's another matter. Even now I don't know how he felt. I never know how he feels.'

'Yet you're saying now that you knew he'd be relieved when he learned that he was to become a father.'

'Of course he was. Isn't that part of the pattern: that a child is the cement that holds a marriage firm?'

I shook my head. 'I may be wrong. I've never discussed it with him. But I don't believe that being a father means very much to him.'

'Then what does mean very much to him?'

'That's something I've often asked myself.'

'And have you found an answer?'

'No.'

'Neither have I. It's puzzling to be married to a man about whom one knows so little.'

'Was it different the other times?'

'I'll say it was. They talked about themselves all the time, in their different ways. How they felt and why they felt that way. Always analysing themselves. With Robert, of course, well, we were kids both of us, you know how it is when you're a kid. We chattered our heads off. It was wonderful. The second time, Mark was well over thirty: nearly ten years older than I was. He was always explaining himself. "What you've got to understand about me is this," he'd say. By the end he'd begun to bore me, but I knew him inside out. With Raymond, on the other hand . . .' She paused, a puzzled, lost expression on her face.

'But he must talk a bit about himself. Everyone does,' I said.

'Yes, of course. He talks about things he's done, people he's met, places that he's been to, but it's all told from the outside. It's all impersonal. He's never inside himself, telling how he's felt. You know how it is in a novel, when you're being told how the hero or the heroine felt, and you get impatient. You say "to hell with how she felt, get on with the story: tell me what happened next". That's how it never is with Raymond. He's always getting on with the story. Never stopping for psychological disquisitions.'

'Does that make him difficult to live with?'

'Everybody's difficult to live with, in some ways: in most ways no one could be easier. He's affable, affectionate, ready to fall in with plans, providing that you remember certain things.'

'Such as?'

'That he hates noisy night-clubs late at night: that meals must be punctual, so that he can get the wine at the right temperature; don't let cigarette smoke drift across his face. Don't interrupt him when he's reading . . . and then, oh well, to get down to brass tacks, in lovemaking one finds out what his particular kinks are—but he's always ready to find out about one's own. He's really the easiest man to live with in the world; at the same time—how shall I put it? I wish he

109

weren't so easy. I'd prefer to have to wonder about him, to be apprehensive about what he's planning ... to be kept guessing.'

The morning after we left Bermuda, the ship's company appeared in blue. The sky was almost cloudless and the sun was shining, but there was a bite in the air. My stewrad, when he brought my morning tea, advised me to put on tweeds.

Eileen was wearing a coat and skirt. 'Oh, the relief of this, to feel cold again, two more nights and I'll be filling a hot water bottle. That clammy Dominican damp: never feeling cool, never feeling dry, never that extra zip: always being under par. Thank heavens I'm not going to have my baby there.'

On my last dinner on board, I ordered a bottle of champagne. I raised my glass across the table. 'Good luck to you both,' I said. 'This has been a happy trip for me.'

'So happy,' said Eileen, 'that I have been wondering ...' But before she could tell me what she had been wondering, a steward had arrived, carrying a sheet of paper folded on a salver. She spread it open. Her eyes widened and she smiled. 'What a surprise,' she said, 'a cable from my father-in-law. Listen to this, Iris. "Very excited your happy news invite you both spend summer here." That's dear of him now, isn't it? What shall I say Iris?'

Her daughter's curiosity was quickened. 'What does that mean, mummy; stay with Uncle Raymond's father instead of going to Aunt Mildred's?'

'That's what it amounts to. How would you like that?'

'Depends on where he lives.'

'You know where Charminster is. I showed it to you on a map.'

'I know. But how does he live; in a palace?'

'You'd better ask Uncle Alec. He's been there and I haven't.'

I told her about Charminster.

'Not a palace, but a big house; quite a big one, with a large garden. You'll like it there, I'm sure: no mosquitoes:

another thing, you'll find your Uncle Raymond's nephew there. Just the right age for you. Two years older. You might fall in love with him.'

'Me, marry him? Then I'd become a Lady.'

'That's right.'

'With Mummy only an honourable. One up to me. Oh, do let's go there.'

But Eileen was still uncertain. 'Tell me more about the set-up. Tell me about his other daughter-in-law. Shall we like each other?'

'No reason why you shouldn't. You're not in any competition with each other.'

'Do you like her, yourself?'

'Yes, from what I've seen of her, a lot.'

'Oh do let's go there, Mummy, do, do, do.'

Later, quite a little later, as much as anything to change the subject, I said, 'Before that steward came along, you were starting to tell me something. I'd just toasted you and said what a happy trip it was; and you said "So happy that I've been wondering" . . . Can you remember what you'd been wondering?'

'Yes of course I can. Have you any god-children?'

'I've one.'

'A boy or girl?'

'A girl.'

'Then it won't be too much of a responsibility, if this child is a boy, if I asked you to be his godfather. You were in at the start, after all, and if that first book of yours is still in print when he goes to school, he might get a kick out of having you as a godfather. At any rate he might think of you as someone whose advice he could ask if he found himself in any trouble. What about it?'

'I'd be honoured, naturally.'

'I'm glad we're keeping you in the family,' Iris said.

7

Most of us, both male and female, would be ready to concede that it is possible to have a satisfactory love affair with somebody one does not like. But most of us would hesitate to admit that we can become friends with someone whom we do not like. Yet it can happen. I did not particularly like Eileen, yet I enjoyed her company, I was always glad to see her at a party. I could be confidential with her, knowing that she would respect my confidences. I enjoyed looking at her, although except for that brief moment at the carnival I was never tempted to make a pass at her. I wished her well. I was curious to know about her. I would have gone out of my way to help her. And when a couple of months later she asked me if I would come down for a cricket match, I did not hesitate to accept. I was curious to know how she was fitting into her new world.

As far as I could judge she was fitting extremely well. Margaret clearly liked her.

'Not unnaturally,' she said, 'I wasn't predisposed to like her. Perhaps it was jealousy. We were in the same boat, after all, in 1919: both of us war widows: one of some two million women, whom the press called "surplus". She had the good luck to find a second husband, of the right age for her what's more. Yet that wasn't enough for her. She had to have a third. Now that's what I call being greedy. Getting more than her fair share. Yes, I suppose it was jealousy; and it was just because I suspected that that is what it was, I persuaded the old boy to ask her here. I made a martyr of myself. My virtue has been rewarded. She adds a lot to our life here: a new young face; and such a pretty one. And Iris is a dear. She isn't spoilt. Eileen's a good mother; that stands out a mile. I'm all for Eileen.'

So was 'the old boy'.

'Must say I felt a bit put out at first,' he said. 'Natural, wasn't it? Divorce, after all. I know things are different now, that it doesn't carry any stigma unless there's a scandal, which in this case there wasn't—all the same, one doesn't want a divorce in one's own family; something that happens to someone else, you know, not to oneself. Made me feel shy in White's: felt I was being whispered about when I left the bar. Fancy on my part, no doubt. Silly of me. Haven't kept up with the times. Still, now that I see Eileen, I feel quite differently about it all. Thoroughly sound girl, you can tell that from her daughter: delightful child: thoroughly well brought up. She'll be a good mother to Raymond's child, I'm sure of that. Glad to be able to make things comfortable for her, at a time like this. Very wise not to have stayed on in Dominica.

'Myself, I've never been to the West Indies. Never heard of Dominica till Raymond went there. Read all I could find about it since. What old Froude had to say: that's all dated now of course. Then I read the chapter about it in your travel book. Very vivid piece of writing, I must say. The place has a character of its own. But how do you think of it in terms of Raymond? He can't surely be planning to settle there for good?'

'Not exactly for good. But to be there, for the winters, say. After all,' I said, 'though it's two weeks from London today, within five years aeroplanes will have brought it within the range of a few hours' flight. He won't feel cut off there any more.'

'I suppose he won't. It's difficult for me to think in terms of air travel. But it'll come: of course it'll come. Far-seeing of him to take aeroplanes into his planning; all the same, to make his base in Dominica—is that what he's really planning?'

'It looks as though it were.'

'It's not what I expected for him.'

'It's not what any of us expected for him.'

'What did you expect for him?'

'That's hard to answer. None of us really knew. But we all felt that he would do something unusual and important.'

'That's what I thought. That's why I didn't press him. I wanted him to find out for himself. There are a great many advantages in being a second son; in being the kind of second son that he is. He has a handle to his name; a minor one, but it sets him just that little bit apart. Then he has money, which a great many second sons don't have. And he has ability; there's no doubt of that: in college, not an oppidan like his brother; he has charm too. Most people like him. There was nothing he couldn't do, I felt. And as I say, that's why I didn't press him. For Michael it's altogether different. His path is cut for him. As an hereditary member of the House of Lords, he has a ready-made political career to take up, if he chooses. Then he has the responsibilities of an estate; he has tenants; he has a position in the county: his time is fully occupied. Myself, I must admit I haven't taken advantage of my opportunities. But they were there for me if I had wanted them. That's what I told Adrian. That's what I'm telling Michael now. If he wants to go into public life, there's every opportunity. At the same time he has to operate within strict limits. There are a great many things that he can do; but equally there are a great many things he can't, because he is inheriting a title.

'Raymond, on the other hand, has no such limits. There's nothing he can't do. He can be Prime Minister if he wants to, which his nephew can't be. That's why a second son can be so lucky. No strings attached. Perhaps I should have explained that to him; perhaps I should have stressed it. Does he feel, I sometimes ask myself, that I neglected him?'

He put it to me as a question that required an answer. I wondered how Raymond would have preferred to have me answer. Would I be serving his interests in any way by making an issue of it? I did not see how I could.

'He's never said anything to me suggesting that he bears any grudge on any score. He realises that there is a difference between his nephew and himself. That row at Oxford provides a good example. If it had happened to the heir to a title, you would have been upset.'

'So he sees that, then?'

'Oh, yes.'

'I'm glad of that, I'm very glad of that. It's sad when a son feels his father has neglected him. I haven't; I've cherished the proudest hopes for him. But I've wanted it to be his career, not mine. Perhaps an estate in Dominica is the answer. All the same there is one thing that puzzles me. How's this wife of his going to take to a life like that? She's not the pioneering type; more urban than rural I'd have said: relies on her English friends. I'm wondering about her.'

So was I, and I was anxious to have a real talk with her. At the end of the day we gossiped together over a final drink. I asked her about St James'. Was Iris liking it? 'Yes and from what Miss Baird writes, they are liking her, which is more important.'

'What about Michael?'

'That's all right, too. He seems glad to have her here.'

'I look forward to seeing them together.'

'You can do that in September. You are coming down, aren't you, for the match against the village?'

'I'm planning to.'

'Raymond should be back by then.'

'How are things with him?'

'Fine as far as I can gather: too fine, I'd be inclined to say.'

'What am I to take that to mean?'

'That without me there, he's getting more and more bound up with Overdale. It's a grapefruit factory now.'

'What's wrong with that?'

'Another chain on him. Does he write to you at all?'

'I don't encourage correspondence. I spend enough time at my desk as it is.'

'You wrote to me quite often.'

'I enjoyed your letters.'

'I see.'

She paused. 'It isn't any good, you know. It isn't any use my trying to pretend it is. I'm not cut out for that kind of life: are you surprised?'

'No.'

'It isn't only Iris. She wasn't an excuse. It's as impossible for me as it is for her. It isn't only the climate; it isn't only the people. The climate is no worse than England's, and the people, they're all right, really. They aren't bores or boors: it's the being cut off from everything that was my life. You can understand that can't you?'

'Yes.'

'Then you'll back me up, won't you, in September, when we thrash it out.'

I laughed. 'I'll sit in as a neutral, or as a neutral chairman.'

'I'll settle for that.'

But when September came, there was to be no need for my unwilling services. At the last moment Raymond delayed his sailing. There was a crisis on the estate. 'If I'm not on the spot, something will go wrong.' he wrote. 'You may think me fussy. But these people are so used to things going wrong that they're more than accident prone; they induce accidents by willing them. I have to be on the spot. But I'll still be back in October for the big occasion. You know that.'

'You see how it is,' wrote Eileen. 'Overdale always first. But you won't, will you, let this stop you coming?'

It was, as far as the weather went, as perfect a September weekend as you could ask for. 1934 was as superb a summer as its predecessor, and the clarets of those two great years linger in our memories and on our palates as symbols of perfection. The sky was blue, with flimsy dove-coloured clouds drifting over it. The faded red brick of Charminster glowed in the amber sunlight. Ivy coloured the space between the bedrooms on the western front with red and purple. Chrysanthemums were in opulent bloom. The scent of hay was in the air. There was scarcely any breeze. Eileen now moved very slowly with the assistance of a stick, 'like a ship in full sail' was her own description of herself; her face wore that look of radiance, when the flesh seems transparent, that women often wear in the last weeks of pregnancy.

'I've never seen you lovelier,' I said.

'Isn't Raymond a fool to miss it?' was her reply.

Michael was the hero of the match. He went in first. He played carefully for the first few overs, then opened his shoulders. He was tall and straight: he had an easy, masterful manner. I remembered Neville Cardus' phrase of Maclaren 'dismissing the ball from his presence'. He looked as though he could have batted all the afternoon, but after reaching his fifty, he took risks that could only end in his dismissal. His grandfather was delighted. 'That's the way that the son of the House should play in a village game. Give the team a good start, show them how to treat the bowling, then leave them to finish the job: not steal the show himself.' He sighed. 'His father would be very proud of him. Damn the Kaiser,' he added.

Iris, too watched him with absorption. 'Isn't he wonderful? Isn't he good-looking? But I mustn't let him know that I think that, must I? I must play hard to get.'

There was dancing that night after dinner. There were a dozen or so to dinner. Those were the days of 'dancing cheek to cheek', but a proper young girl, though she might rest her cheek against her partner's, was careful to hold her body well away from his. As I watched Iris and Michael foxtrotting together with an elaborate variation of trick steps, I remembered how six months back, in a shadowed passage, with the pulse of the carnival drums beating through her limbs and feet, she had swayed close clasped against a masked cavalier, with her head flung back, his widespread fingers straining her hips to his. Did the memory of those dozen minutes inflame her dreams? Did she recall them as something that had happened to someone else? They must be alive somewhere in her subconscious.

Next morning she appeared in the hall, gloved and hatted, in a light grey and blue cotton frock, properly demure, her prayer book in her hand, ready to walk across the paddock to the village church.

The old man was in a black and white pin-stripe suit. He wore a stiff white collar and a grey satin tie held in place by a pearl pin. He had said the evening before, 'There is no need of course for any of you to come to church tomorrow. I have to go myself, naturally, because I read the lessons.'

It was clear that he expected us to go, yet his features expressed appropriate surprise when he saw us gathered in the hall. 'Eight, nine, ten, now this will be most encouraging for the vicar. He'll be as flattered as he'll be surprised. He has a difficult time nowadays, keeping his flock together. It was very different in my father's day. If the grooms and gardeners ceased to attend church, they ceased to be his grooms and gardeners; and on Sunday evening a cold supper was served so that the cook and the maids could go to church—*autres temps, autres mœurs.*'

It was a small Norman church, with a fine rood screen, and hatchments over a couple of sixteenth-century tombs. There was a family pew on the right of the aisle, with a wooden frame that allowed the family to see the vicar in his pulpit, the reader of the lessons on his dais, and the choir in their raised stalls. But they themselves could not be over-looked by the congregation when they were seated, though the tops of their heads were visible when they stood up. In the corner of the pew was a fireplace that had not been used since Raymond's grandfather died. The old man read the lessons in a firm, unctuous voice that was quite unlike the tone he used in conversation. The service lasted for an hour, and was followed by communion. The old man whispered in a voice that could be heard throughout the building, 'Don't you bother to stay for this. I shall, as it's the last Sunday of the month.'

Raymond had told me of this vagary of his. There were too many communicants on the first Sunday of the month: on the last Sunday the service was five minutes shorter.

The sun was high and the morning mists had lifted when we recrossed the paddock. The world could not have seemed more at peace. But on the silver salver on the table in the hall was a sheet of paper, folded over and directed to Eileen Peronne. She picked it up. As she read it, her expression changed. Her lips tightened and her cheeks flushed. She handed it across to me. A cable from Dominica had been telephoned. It was signed Raymond. 'Forgive forgive forgive Plantation crisis Forced postpone return until November Deep deep deepest love.' Her frown was eloquent.

'He treats it like a joke. All those deeps; all those forgives. I'll never forgive him, as long as I live. Never, never, never.'

I remembered how her eyes had hardened on the ship when she said 'He better had'.

8

Early in October Eileen wrote to me that Iris had a brother. 'You remember, don't you, your promise on the ship. I hold you to it. We'll have the christening in mid-November; the third Sunday, if that's convenient for you. I don't know if it will be for the proud father, but I'm not bothering about him. He promises to be back in time. Who can tell? You know that old rhyme about hurricanes in the Caribbean:

> June too soon
> July stand by
> August you must
> Remember September
> October all over

So I'm not unhopeful. Still, you can't rely on rules with Dominica. At the very last moment... who knows, who knows? at any rate you'll be there. His name, by the way, is to be Timothy Alexander, in case you want anything engraved.'

I did not have anything engraved. I did not want to give something that he would discard. I wanted him to have something that he could use all his life, something moreover that would remind him of me. So I went to my habitual silversmith's, Tessier's of Bond Street, and bought a couple of Georgian wine coasters. They were a wise choice; only a couple of years ago I saw them on my godson's table.

The fine weather of the summer survived the first assault of winter. The boughs were leafless by the third Sunday of November, but the sky was blue and though there was little heat in the sun, the worn red brick of the house glowed in its gracious radiance. Raymond shivered, however, though he was wearing a heavy overcoat.

'I suppose my blood has thinned out there,' he said. 'I wonder if I could stand a winter here.'

'You don't call this winter, do you?' his father said.

'It's arctic to me.'

It was a small party for the christening. But it was six before the last guest drove away, leaving those of us who remained in a mood of lassitude. The exhilaration of unseasonable champagne had subsided. Sunday supper was two hours away. It was dark outside: there was a moon. It was not the time of year for an exhilarating walk. It was too early for an aperitif. None of us felt that we would ever want to eat again. We were faced with a ninety-minute vacuum. There was nothing to be done until we went upstairs to change into some kind of evening wear. The sensible thing would have been to take a serious novel to a deep armchair and doze over it. The least sensible thing was to start a serious discussion; yet that is precisely what Eileen did.

'Peace at last. We can relax, and now, Raymond, we can discuss where we are going to make our home.'

'Our home?'

'We've got to live somewhere: not only have we got a son, but I've a daughter at a boarding school in England. She must have somewhere to spend her holidays.'

There were four of us in the room besides herself. Myself, Raymond, Margaret and Iris. We were more or less grouped round the fire.

'You've had a lot of time by yourself, Raymond, since Mardi Gras. You must have thought this out. What have you decided?'

'Nothing.'

'You mean, you've simply pottered round the estate.'

'Pottered isn't the word I'd use.'

'It's as good as any other.'

'I was extremely busy.'

'I know you were; and you've installed a machine for tinning grapefruit; but in the evenings, when you were alone, surely you must have wondered where we'd all be in a year's time?'

'I don't believe I did.'

She laughed. 'And I'm ready to believe you. You were busy and you were happy. You had a succession of day-to-day problems to be decided. You never took a long view about anything. That is true, isn't it?'

'Well . . .'

She laughed. She looked round at us. 'That's true. I thought it was. For eight months he's gone on living in the minute, never looking a year ahead.'

She could not have chosen a less suitable time for a serious discussion. Yet just because it was the worst it might have been the best. We were safe from interruptions, the atmosphere could not be changed by an emptying and filling up of glasses. We were suspended in a vacuum. We had a straight stretch of ninety minutes.

'Shall I tell you what I believe?' she said.

'You tell me what you believe.'

'I believe that you pictured Overdale as your base. That we should spend nine months of the year there. We could either bring Timothy Alexander out with us, or leave him here at Charminster. I left Iris alone with her grandmother, so why shouldn't we leave Timothy Alexander here? Iris has a ten-weeks holiday in the summer. Either she could come out to us or we could go back to England to see her. She could spend her Christmas and Easter holidays here.'

'That would be wonderful,' Iris interjected. Her face lit at the prospect of seeing Michael for at least two holidays of the year.

'That's what I thought you'd say, and that is precisely what I do not propose. I insist on seeing you every holidays. These next four years are your most important, the most decisive in your life. You'll need a mother near you. I'm not at all sure that you don't need me all the time. American and French mothers insist on being around. And they may be right. But the boarding school is the pattern now in England, for girls as well as men. I'm not fighting against the pattern. It's as much an advantage for a girl as for a boy to do what her contemporaries do. But to leave a daughter alone for ten months on end, no, that's too big a risk. You'll agree about that, Raymond, won't you, if you give it a moment's thought.'

Her voice sharpened. I remembered how she had said, 'I'll never forgive him, never, never, never.' Her eyes were fixed on his. I knew and he knew to what she was referring. Margaret was in the dark, and so was Iris.

'I see your point,' said Raymond. 'What are you suggesting?'

This was the showdown. It was strange in a sense that she had chosen to bring it about this way, in public, instead of alone, in a frank husband-to-wife talk. I remembered how that afternoon at Villefranche she had insisted on my staying as a witness when she broke her news to Raymond. Was it a witness, though, she needed: someone who at a later day would testify on her behalf; would say 'Yes, that is the way it was. I was there in the room when the scene took place.'? Was it a witness, or was it support she needed, an audience before whom she would be dared to show her strength; was she afraid that he would wheedle her into dropping her defences? Eileen was not the first to show a reluctance to face a scene with him. All those years ago Judy had begged me to break the news to him of her offer of a job abroad. Was it that women did not trust him? or that they did not trust themselves? The Greek tragedians had always insisted that the big scene should happen off stage; to be reported, not observed. Raymond appeared to have that effect on women.

He was smiling now and his voice was gentle, almost caressing. 'You tell me how you'd like it, and I'll see if we can't arrange it that way.'

His manner could not have been more disarming. I watched Eileen closely. I noticed that the fingers of her right hand were clenched, though her left arm was stretched along the side of her armchair.

'What I want,' she said, 'is something very simple. I want a base in England; I want a home for myself, for us, for Iris and for Timothy Alexander. Overdale can never be that for us. It served a purpose for us, once. But it can never be a home. It can never be a family base. If you'll remember, I did wonder whether we were wise to buy it, but you said it was a good investment: you know better than I do about that; we can let it during the winter. The climate in the West Indies is at its best when the climate in Europe and North America is at its worst. We'd very likely want to go out ourselves every so often. As you said we shan't have to rely on ships in a few years' time. Aeroplanes will bring the

Caribbean within a few hours of London. We're likely to find Overdale more and more useful in the future. We may retire there in the end, but in the meantime what we have to do is to find ourselves a house in England.'

It was said brightly, casually, as though it concerned a trivial project. There was nothing in her tone of voice, in the expression of her face, to indicate that she was delivering an ultimatum. I looked at Margaret. Had she any idea how much was at stake in this discussion? The fire was smouldering warmly in the grate. We were in a small book-lined adjunct to the library, where the newspapers and periodicals were kept on a long table. It was used as an ante-room; where you read the papers at odd moments in the morning, before lunch or after tea: where you retired for a snooze when you felt in the mood. The fire would not be made up after dinner. It was an uncontentious room.

'I see,' said Raymond. 'Yes, I see. Now where do you want to have this house?'

'Within fifty miles of London.'

'That gives us a variety of choice. We'll get a stack of orders to view from Frank, Knight and Rutley. We'll have a great deal of amusement going round them. You'll enjoy that, won't you, Iris?'

'I'll say I will.'

'We must get a house that she approves of for her coming-out dance.'

'You're looking a long way ahead.'

'Not so very. You're fifteen now; this is 1934. 1939: that'll be the year I'd say; or even 1938, or perhaps 1940 when you're through with Oxford.'

'Are you planning for me to go to Oxford?'

'Of course, if you are bright enough to pass your exams, and I'm sure you will be. Anyhow this house will be as important for you as it will be for us. For the first few years, anyhow. So we must get, Eileen, the kind of house that Iris likes. It will be a background for her, so that young men will think "That's the kind of wife I want; someone who comes from a home like that." '

We all laughed.

'You're looking a long way ahead,' said Margaret.

'Not so very far. Not in Iris' case. I'm pretty sure that within a year, young men will be assuring me that their intentions are strictly honourable.'

Again we all laughed together; he did not laugh himself. But there was a broad, benevolent grin upon his face.

'We've got to get the right house for Iris as well as for ourselves. That's why we mustn't hurry this. We mustn't take the first house that comes along. And that's why I suggest that we should rent a furnished house to start with. I couldn't agree with you more, Eileen. We must get ourselves a base as soon as possible. Then when we've once moved into it, when we've got ourselves settled, Timothy Alexander into his nursery, and Iris into her study bedroom, we'll start our quest of houses. We'll take it quietly. There's no hurry.'

This was his ultimatum. He would go a certain way with Eileen, but not all the way. As he had accepted the necessity for marriage, he now accepted her new arrangement of their lives, with Overdale no longer as their primary base. But he was not going to be dragooned into putting down permanent roots in England. He looked very straight at Eileen. She pressed her lips together. Yes, she had got his meaning. She had trumped his knave, but he held the other court cards in his hand. She accepted the inevitable. 'That's fine,' she said. 'We are going to enjoy looking for our real home.'

Raymond moved quickly when he had to move. Five days later I ran into him in Bond Street.

'That was a fine christening,' I said.

'I enjoyed it. I'm glad you did.'

'And now you're busy looking for a house, I take it.'

'Indeed no, I've already found one.'

'That's quick work.'

'Not if you know the ropes. I went into the bar at White's and announced that I wanted to rent a furnished house within fifty miles of London. I'd had three offers before I'd finished lunch, saw all three that afternoon.'

'Which is the one you picked?'

'Bolton's. Perhaps you know it? It was the Ramages'. Near Dorking.'

'What kind of a house?'

'Modern; early Edwardian; imitation Georgian. Good imitation. Red brick: rectangular, three storeys. You know the kind of thing. Easy to run. Eileen will love it.'

'So she's not seen it yet?'

'No need. It would be a nuisance for her. She doesn't want to go traipsing around the country while she's nursing. It isn't as though it was a permanency, after all.'

'When are you moving in?'

'Monday week.'

'That *is* quick work.'

'No reason for delay. It'll be a relief to the old man to have us out. There are bound to be some snags, of course. There always are. We'll find them out soon enough. Then we'll know what we have to be on our guard against next time.'

'For how long have you taken it?'

'A year, with options to renew.'

'And now you'll start looking . . .?'

'For the house that is to be a home. Oh yes, I'll get down to that.' He paused. 'But not until the spring. No good splashing about in mud. The English countryside in February is something to be avoided.' There was a twinkle in his eye as he said that. I suspected that he had put that new house rather low on the list of his priorities.

At the end of March I took him to the Odde Volumes—a small dining club which Evelyn described in *Brideshead Revisited* as 'a surprising association of men quite eminent in their professions who met once a month for an evening of ceremonious buffoonery'. The members chose fanciful cognomina for themselves—Scholemaster, Paginator, Chymicophant. I was Brother Corinthian. Guests were introduced by their hosts in facetious speeches that attempted to ridicule their personalities and achievements.

Raymond was asked to reply for the guests, and he caught

the atmosphere of the club at once. 'I have gathered in the course of the evening that the purpose of your odd fraternity is to provide yourselves with an opportunity of repaying hospitality to persons whom you would hesitate to invite to your homes. I am not surprised that my old friend, Brother Corinthian, should have chosen this way of acknowledging the simple little supper that I gave him many years ago now at the 43.'

'Admirable, admirable,' I said as he sat down. 'I wish you were a member here.'

'So do I.'

'Why not become one, then?'

'I'm not in London enough.'

'You're here as much as I am.'

'Am I? Maybe I am. All the same . . .' He hesitated. 'I'm going back to Dominica very soon.'

It was the first that I had heard of it. 'When?'

'The end of next week.'

It is the OV custom after the Introduction of guests to have a paper read. This time the speaker was my cousin, Philip Gosse. Specialising in the study of piracy, and having compiled a *Pirates' Who's Who*, he had as an Odd Volume chosen for himself the soubriquet of Brother Buccaneer, and the subject for his paper was 'The Brethren of the Coast', the original Buccaneers of Tortuga. He spoke for some twenty minutes, then discussion was invited. My own contribution was appropriately frivolous. I also had specialised in the subject, and had a few years earlier published a chronicle novel showing how a pirate strain had run through three centuries from the French *émigrés* of the seventeenth century to the contemporary gangsters of Chicago. I recounted how on a cricket tour organised by J. C. Squire, I had been correcting the galley proofs of that novel. I had intended to call it *Buccaneer*, but my publishers had complained that readers would be put off, because with that title it would sound too unlike my other books. Squire had interpolated, 'Why not call it *The Jolly Roger*. Any of your novels could be launched under that flag.' It was the kind of speech that was expected of an Odd Volume, and it was greeted with applause.

A couple of other Odde Volumes spoke. Then Raymond rose. 'In my island of Dominica, are to be found the last traces of the Caribs, a cannibal race from South America who were eating their way up the islands—the Arawaks were an idle race, and their unmuscled thighs were succulent—when they were interrupted by Columbus. The Spaniards liquidated the original Indians, the Arawaks, faster than the Caribs, though with less personal enjoyment. I do not know how the buccaneers discovered the *boucan*, the open fire over which they cooked their meat and from which they took their name, but I have sampled meals prepared by the progeny of the ancient cannibals and I have found . . .' His speech did not last two minutes, but it was light, witty and informed. He told us something about cooking by the *boucan* that neither Philip Gosse nor I knew. It was a speech as much in the OV tradition as mine had been. The Odde Volumes had started as and in part still was, and is, a learned society. Speeches could be serious as long as they were scholarly and brief. Raymond in both his speeches had hit the right note, from a different angle.

'That was really excellent,' I told him. 'I can't tell you how completely you are the right person here. Do reconsider your decision.'

'You're very flattering.'

This time he did not refuse right away. I pressed my point.

'Why don't you think it over while you're away. How long do you expect to be away?'

'Three months, four months, I can't tell. It depends on how I find things there.'

'Is anything going wrong?'

'Not as far as I know. Not as far as I'm told, but the Dominicans aren't very literate. And they don't want to worry me: they want to run their show themselves and I don't blame them. But I had a letter from Elma Napier that disturbed me.'

I did not ask him what it was. I probably should not have

understood it. It would have been full of technicalities about crops and soil conservation.

'If things aren't satisfactory, are you considering a cutting of your losses and a selling out?'

'Not unless I have to. I've come to have a very personal feeling about that place.'

'Have you found a house in England yet?'

He shook his head. 'There's always something wrong with every house we see; either the locality or the house itself. We'll find what we want some day. There's no hurry. We're doing quite nicely as we are.'

He did not seem at all disturbed.

'Does Iris like your rented house?'

'Why shouldn't she? There's nothing wrong with it, and it's not a permanency for her. She'll marry and go where her husband is. I've an idea she'll marry pretty young. I hope she does.'

I thought and I was sure that he was thinking of that last carnival.

'How are you going out, via New York?'

'No, by the French Line via Martinique.'

Next morning I made enquiries at the French Line offices. The *Pellerin de Latouche*, the ship on which I had made my first trip to the West Indies, was sailing from Plymouth in ten days' time. The boat train left Paddington at half past twelve. I decided to see him off.

He had not many fellow passengers. The French Line had only reserved two first and five third class carriages on a regular West of England express. Eileen had come alone to see Raymond off. He laughed at the sight of me. 'So you've changed your mind? You're coming after all.'

Eileen looked puzzled, also a little vexed. 'You never told me about this.'

'I'm only pulling your leg. Unless he's suddenly made his mind up on his own.'

'I haven't, don't worry,' I assured him.

I never like station leave-takings. In the old days 'pourings on to boats' in New York were an ideal curtain to a visit:

particularly in prohibition days, when you knew that in a very little while you would be on a bar stool, ordering a legitimate and unbaleful glass of morning beer. But standing on platforms is a strain not only on one's nerves but on one's ankles. The minutes dragged. Yet I was glad that I had come. I might well see it in retrospect as a significant stage in the Raymond saga.

The big clock above the war memorial statue of the soldier with his gas mask at the alert, seemed motionless.

At last the guard's green flag was waved. We both of us gave a sigh as the train pulled out.

'Are you lunching with anyone?' I asked.

'No.'

'Then why don't we go to the Savoy?'

'Why not?'

It was a bright spring morning. The sky about the chimney stacks was blue. The air was cool but the sun had drained out the damp. The pavements were dry and the faces of the men and women who strode them briskly had shed the taut lines of worry that afflict Londoners in winter. Everyone seemed bound on a congenial mission. Eileen sighed as she looked out through the taxi window. 'There's no place like London. Why should any one want to live anywhere else?'

'I'd expected you to bring Iris along,' I said.

She shook her head. 'No point in her missing two days at school. Besides it's better for her not to take a going away like this too seriously.'

'Will she miss Raymond?'

'She'll miss him less, the less we make of his departures.'

'You put it in the plural.'

'It won't be his last.'

'What makes you so sure of that?'

'He's got this thing about Dominica. I can't see it. Can you?'

'In the abstract, yes.'

'What do you mean by that?'

'If a man falls in love with a woman whom you yourself don't find physically attractive, you can say, "I can understand him falling for her, though I can't imagine doing so myself."'

'Is that a fair parallel?'

'I can't think of another.'

'Can't you? No, I see what you mean. It *is* a fair parallel. And I'm in the position of the wife whose husband has fallen in love with someone quite impossible; there's nothing she can do but wait it out.'

'And take no action?' I put it as a question.

'Exactly, take no action. If she says to him "We've got to do something about this" she'll be putting the idea of a divorce into his head.'

We reached the Savoy shortly after one. 'The Grill, don't you think?' I said.

'Either's fine for me. Anywhere in London's fine for me.'

The Grill Room was half full: three or four men were standing round the head waiter's dais. But I was a reasonably frequent client. I was found a table against the wall, near the window.

I handed her the menu.

'What do you not get at home? You'd better choose,' I said. I remembered my lunch with Margaret at the Jardin. She had known exactly what she wanted. So did Eileen. Even though she had not known an hour ago she would be lunching here. 'Whitebait,' she said, 'then omelette Arnold Bennett, a water ice to finish. I'll leave the wine to you.'

'That omelette will ruin a first-class wine.'

'Then let's have a third-rate one.'

'A carafe of rosé?'

'Fine by me. If Bennett was such a gourmet, why did he have named after him a dish that didn't go with wine?'

'I'm not sure how interested he was in wine. He had a very weak digestion. He had to be careful what he drank.'

'Did he come here often?'

'It's a writer's place and it's a stage folk's place. Bennett was both. Did you read *Imperial Palace*? It's all about the Savoy.' She shook her head.

'Are there many of those people here today?'

I looked about me. In those days the Savoy Grill—for that matter it still is—was part of your public relations side if you were in the entertainment game. You went there to see and to be seen. You were careful what you wore. You needed to look prosperous. You were also a little careful as to whom you were seen with. Gossip columnists found it a good source of copy. Hannen Swaffer, London's Walter Winchell, in particular. He was not there that day, but Donegal was, and there were several notables to pad out his column. As I looked round me, I was nodded at from several tables.

'You seem to know a lot of people here,' she said.

'I should do. It's my world.'

'And it could be Raymond's.'

'Could it? I'm not so sure. Raymond's not in this racket.'

'What do you mean by that?'

I tried to explain. 'Raymond hasn't got a job. He hasn't got a career.'

'What a wonderful time we could have here if he had. Don't you think that a woman has a right to expect a husband who does something?'

I smiled at that. 'When she has, she usually complains that he puts that something before her.'

'Does he?' She looked thoughtful. Then she shrugged. 'I shouldn't grumble. I should count my blessings. Do you remember my saying to you in Villefranche that I wouldn't be committing suicide if Raymond started to make difficulties? I wasn't a forlorn love-sick damsel. I had my own reserves. I could make a life for myself if I had to. I had my pension and what I had been left. I was all right: I'm still all right. That was only four years ago. I'm still pretty well the way I was.' Her voice was firm. She was not making a threat. But she was establishing her independence. Was Raymond aware of this hard streak in her? If he was aware, would he let it worry him? One of his most marked characteristics was his refusal to let other people worry him. I felt to my surprise a sudden feeling of compunction for my godson. Eileen and Raymond might take the break-up of a marriage in their stride. But what about Timothy Alexander? If anything went wrong, I must be prepared to pull my weight.

9

Early in June, Raymond cabled me from New York: 'Most important you attend Dominican publicity party evening July 23 international sports club.' I rang up Eileen. 'What on earth is all this about?' I asked.

'I'm as much in the dark as you are; or at least almost. He's got some colour films that he wants to show to what he describes as interested people.'

'And who may they be?'

'I've no idea: he's sending me a list. About sixty of them, so he says. I'm to send out the invitations. They have to be engraved.'

I received mine two weeks later. It informed me that the Honorable Mrs Raymond Peronne would be at home at the International Sportsmen's Club in the Stafford Suite on Tuesday July 2nd at 6 p.m. for 6.30 to see a collection of colour films about Dominica. At 8 p.m. there would be a buffet supper.

Raymond himself arrived back in England ten days before. He rang me up at once. 'You're coming to my binge?'

'Of course.'

'Any chance of our meeting before then?'

'Naturally.'

'What about lunch at White's on Monday?'

'That's fine by me.'

'Just before one?'

'I won't be late.'

He had a half bottle of vintage champagne waiting for me in the bar.

'What a relief to get back to decent wine,' he said. He was looking very well. He was suntanned but he had not put on weight. He was now thirty-two, with his good looks at their peak. He had the same elegance, the same distinctive profile.

'Now tell me,' I asked, 'what is all this in aid of?'

'You'll see.'

He explained what he proposed to do. 'Half an hour of drinking for those who arrive on time. Then we'll go into a small lecture room. You can take your drinks in with you. But there'll be no recharging of glasses—no waiters to interrupt the show. I'll give a brief opening, less than ten minutes, a kind of biography of Dominica, then I'll turn on the film. Not a talking one, that would have been too much trouble; no need either. Let the place speak for itself: though I'll interject some remarks here and there. It should last about half an hour: then back to the bar, and after half an hour of that, there'll be a buffet: substantial but not elaborate. It'll be a meal. But I don't want any hanging around afterwards. Waiters will start clearing away at nine. They'll open a window at quarter past. That'll empty the room all right. Then we'll go back to Derrick Whistler's set in Albany, for a last drink and to talk it over. You know him, don't you?'

'Met him but don't know him.'

'Then that's all settled. Let's go up and eat.'

It might all be settled, but it was still far from clear to me why any of it had needed settling, and what exactly it was that had been settled. 'I still don't see what it's all in aid of,' I repeated as soon as we had ordered lunch. He appeared surprised.

'I thought it would have been obvious.'

'Not to me.'

'No? But it's the simplest thing. Dominica needs publicity.'

'Why?'

'Every place needs publicity; everything needs publicity. Surely you as an author can see that.'

'Yes, when there's anything to sell. Is there in Dominica?'

'Of course there is, there's . . .' He paused. I do not believe that until that moment it had ever occurred to him that Dominica, a place he loved, would not benefit from publicity.

'Are you trying to attract the tourist trade?' I asked. 'Do you think that Dominica has much to offer to the tourist?'

'Only to the exceptional tourist.'

'Do you think publicity will attract capital? Are you hoping that some speculator will buy up property and develop it? Are you planning to turn your own estate into a public company?'

He shook his head. 'Nothing like that.' Indeed, the moment I had set the question I had realised it was a stupid one. Raymond was not that kind of person. He was the last person to wonder what he could get out of Dominica for himself.

'That's not the tack I'm on at all,' he said. 'I'm thinking of the island itself, and of the Dominicans. They've got despondent about themselves. Too many things have gone wrong for them. They have begun to lose interest in themselves. They need to be bucked up, they need to have someone take an interest in them: someone who can help them to take an interest in themselves, so that they can do something for themselves, pull themselves up by their own bootstraps. This party next week may help. It'll be reported in the press. I've seen to that; I've got a couple of fellows from the Colonial Office. They'll talk; when Roseau hears about it, it should make a difference. And that's why I was so anxious to have you there. You'll be able to bring first-hand evidence. Move about as much as you can. Talk to all the people that you can. I'd first thought of asking you to *compère* the show. You'd have done it very well, better than I shall, I'm sure, but I decided that you'd be far more effective as an independent member of the audience. You'll get there early, won't you?'

I did by six o'clock, the first to be there in fact. I watched the guests arrive. Unaware of the nature of entertainment they were to be offered, but suspecting that no drinks would be served after the half-hour, nearly everyone was there by quarter past. There were about fifty of them, with males predominating. Donegal was there, and Tom Driberg, who was then William Hickey on the *Express*. I knew about a quarter of them. Iris to my surprise was there. 'Do you want to remind her of Dominica?' I asked Eileen.

'It's an experiment. I want to see how she reacts.'

At half past six a gong was beaten. A loud official voice

invited us to move into the studio. Raymond stood upon a low dais beside the screen.

'I'm inviting you,' he said, 'to see some colour films that I have taken of Dominica, the West Indian island where I have made—I will not say my home, but *a* home. Though one of the largest it is the least known of the islands—yet in its own way it is the loveliest. I shall be surprised if its beauty does not impress you. During the showing of the film, I shall interpolate occasional comments, and when it is all over I will be happy to try to answer any questions. I hope that you will be interested in what I have to show. I went there by chance, expecting to stay six months—well, that's four years ago.'

He stepped down from the dais, the lights went off, and there on the screen were the towering peaks of Dominica, a merging of green into green, with here and there the dark background stabbed by the pink of the Poi tree and the brilliant yellow of the Cassia. There came from the audience a gasp of astonished admiration, then a burst of clapping, with as it subsided, Raymond's voice laughingly interjecting, 'Thank you. I'm glad. I warned you, didn't I?'

The landscape had been admirably photographed. I had not expected such professional competence. 'He really could have done anything,' I thought, and the editing of the shots was skilful. There was variety of subject and of perspective; there were village as well as rural scenes: many of the sequences were shot in shadow: there were vistas of rain-swept countryside. The local industries were exhibited and explained. Five minutes were devoted to the Carib settlement, and Raymond's occasional commentaries were effective: they were light in tone, informal but informative. It was clear that he knew a great deal about his subject. It was also clear that he was under the spell of a considerable emotional commitment, yet at the same time I found it increasingly difficult to keep my attention on the screen. 'If this was after lunch,' I thought, 'I'd be asleep by now.' I remembered how in *Hot Countries* I had compared the landscape to a reading of *Endymion*, lush and featureless. None of it seemed to be leading anywhere. It was a relief when the light flashed on and Raymond was announcing that that was all, that the bar was open and that a buffet would be ready in half an hour.

It was all admirably stage-managed. There were a number of small tables, seating four to six: there were enough chairs for everyone. Yet there were no seating arrangements: guests could sit where they wanted, or stand if they preferred—which a great many did. A long table was laid with a succession of cold dishes, meat and fish: there were two chafing dishes, containing, the one a rice goulash, the other a chicken stew; there were cakes, fruit salads, cheeses; at each end there were two barmen, the one serving champagne, the other whisky sodas. Low music had been switched on so that guests had slightly to raise their voices. In a very few moments the party had become noisy. I looked for Iris. I wished that she had been near enough for me to watch her face during the film. The dusk had not been so complete that I could not have read her expression. How had she reacted to the shots of the carnival? I made my way to her. 'Did it make you feel homesick at all?' I asked.

She shook her head. 'It was a lovely place, but I'm having so much more fun here than I could there,' which was as satisfactory an answer as any parent could ask to have.

'I'm glad you got your school certificate,' I said. 'When will you be going up?'

'September 1938 if all goes well—though I may have a year in Switzerland or Paris first.'

'And your coming-out dance?'

'I'd rather put that off until I'm through with Oxford.'

'Isn't that leaving it a little late?'

She laughed. 'There are so many amusing things ahead of me, that I can't realise that some have to make way for others. It'll be fun anyhow.'

She was already on the threshold of womanhood. Her face was radiant with expectancy. At this moment, I thought, there is possibly within twenty miles of us some young man bewailing the futility of his existence, who has the supreme enchantment of a lifetime on its way to meet him.

136

I looked for Eileen. I had barely done more than say 'hullo' to her when I arrived. It was a couple of weeks since I had seen her. She had looked tired then, and fussed as though she had too many small things on her mind. Today she was lively, cheerful, glowing. What a difference Raymond's return had made to her. He would be flattered if he could have known how she had looked without him. What a truism it is that we have no idea what our friends and families are like when we are not with them. Oh, for Gyges' ring! Oh, to be invisible!

'It's a lovely party. How well you do this kind of thing,' I said.

'I'd be a fool, wouldn't I, if I couldn't do it? It's only a question of giving an order, of writing out a list.'

'Some people manage to make a mess of that kind of thing.'

'That's because they don't enjoy giving parties. I do. I always wish I could be a guest at one of my own parties.'

'It's because you don't let yourself be a guest that your parties are so good.'

'Is it? Perhaps it is.' She looked slowly round her. 'Yes, they do seem to be enjoying themselves. By the way, have you had a talk with Terence Gilray?'

Gilray was one of the two men from the Colonial Office.
'Not yet.'

'Then let me take you across. Raymond was particularly anxious to have you talk to him.'

She was fulfilling her rôle punctiliously. And I had an interesting talk with Gilray. I asked him if he had ever been to the West Indies. He shook his head. He had not been there. He had not been anywhere in fact. 'That's what makes our job so difficult,' he said. 'We administer these places without realising what they are like. I've got files and files on Dominica. I went over them this morning. I've got all the statistics about limes and coffee, but I couldn't visualise the place. We've got photographs, of course, and reports from Governors. That isn't the same thing.'

'In ten years' time,' I said, 'there'll be a regular airline service. In two weeks you'll be able to make a complete tour of all the islands.'

137

'That'll make a difference.'

He asked me one or two questions about Dominica. He had read Froude; 'It impressed him more than any of the other islands.'

'It has that effect on some people.'

'Are you planning to go back?' he asked me.

'The moment I get a chance.'

'When you do I'd be grateful if you'd look in and see me when you get back. A first-hand independent report is worth a hundred communiqués.'

I told Raymond what he had said to me. 'That's fine, very fine, exactly what I wanted. Gilray will be at the top in a few years' time. When some report comes in, he'll remember this party and what you said. It may just turn the scale one way or another. That's what this party is in aid of. I knew that you'd understand as soon as it was launched. Those last drinks at Whistler's should put the seal on it.'

Derrick Whistler's set was on the west side of Albany, half way down the rope walk. Whistler was in his late thirties. He was what was known in Edwardian days as a man about town. He was of medium height, heavily built; he had dark, short cut hair, he was clean shaven; he was likely to grow fat in his forties. He was a Marlburian. In London he wore dark suits and coloured shirts with stiff white turn-over collars. He was not bad looking; he took obvious pains over his clothes, but he was someone whom you might easily mistake for someone else. Professionally he was 'someone in the city'. Whatever he did there, he must do it profitably to himself. His sitting room was comfortable, deep arm-chairs and a many-cushioned Chesterfield, designed, one suspected, for a girl to curl up on. There were heavy damask curtains, there was a bookcase but no bookshelves. One corner was arranged as a bar, with three stools in front of it; nine of us had come back here, and with the help of three Moroccan hassocks everyone could be at ease. There was a club-style padded fender before the fireplace on which Whistler himself sat, as soon as he had seen that each of us had a drink. It gave him the position of a chairman. 'That was a fine party,' he said. 'I hope, Raymond, that you and Eileen enjoyed it as much as we did.'

'I don't know about Eileen, but I had a good time all right.'

'It was fine for me; I love being a hostess when I have no responsibilities.'

'And did it have the effect you meant it to?'

'I believe it did, yes, in the long run, yes.'

'And what was it that you wanted it to do?'

It was the opening for the same kind of explanation that he had given me in White's.

Knowing exactly what he had to say, I lolled back in my chair, sipping at my port, letting my thoughts wander. To Eileen, too, all this was familiar. She was seated in the Chesterfield, on the other side of the fireplace, lolling back, her eyes half closed. She seemed utterly at peace, relaxed in the relief and relaxation that follows for a hostess the end of a successful party. She was smiling at her own thoughts, or so I guessed.

'And when are you planning to go back there?' Whistler asked.

'In a month or so.'

'And are you taking Iris with you?'

Eileen stirred out of her daze. 'Heavens no, Iris is going to be a good daughter here.'

'So you're not going out either?'

'No, I'm not going out either.'

The smile on her lips deepened. Her eyes were still half closed. It was a rather curious smile. I turned my head and realised that it was turned on Whistler. I could not see the expression of his face, but I had the feeling that in that instant a message passed between them, that it was a moment of recognition and awareness, of stumbling upon a secret. It sent a shock along my nerves.

I remembered how strained and drawn she had looked two weeks ago. She was then fussing over the obligations that would devolve on her through this party. I had gathered, though I could not remember when I had heard it said, that she had scarcely known Whistler, if indeed she had known him at all, before Raymond had suggested that they should end the evening in his set. Presumably Whistler had been in on all the discussions, during the preliminary planning, as to who was coming to the party and who should be encouraged to stay on afterwards, and no doubt Raymond and Whistler had schemed out the scenario of that post-party talk. Whistler had already known—how could he have helped knowing—what was at the back of Raymond's mind. It was for the benefit of those others who had not known, that Whistler had made it possible for Raymond to make his little speech.

For these two weeks they had been constantly in each other's company, scheming this and that, laying out the tactics of the campaign. Had all that time, unknown to either of them, a secret drama had been developing: between Eileen and Whistler, a drama that accounted for the deep look of fulfilment that I had seen in her face at the be-ginning of the evening? Under the surface they might have been unconsciously aware of it; they might only have recognised it now in the realisation that in a month's time they would be alone in London. I supposed that it had to come, sooner or later. Whatever it was that had to come, I prayed that the fabric of Raymond's and Eileen's life might be maintained. And after all, why shouldn't it? Nine times out of ten it was only because two people found it impossible to be alone in any other way that there were elopements and broken homes. These two were spared that, thank heaven, or rather thanks to Dominica.

After the Dominican party, Raymond told me that he did not feel justified in joining the Odde Volumes. 'I'd love to,' he said, 'but you see how it is. I have to be away so much. You need a more regular attendant.'

I was disappointed, I had looked forward to the oppor-tunities for meetings that the Odde Volumes would provide. I was myself expecting to be away a lot and my returns to England might not always coincide with his.

It turned out as I had feared. Indeed in the next year I was to see more of Eileen than of him. We were both members of the Wine and Food Society, and often found ourselves attending the same wine-tastings and dinners.

She kept me up to date with Raymond's movements. Not that she had a great deal to tell. He was still looking for a house to buy, but did not seem in any particular hurry over it. 'Every time he finds a house, there seems something wrong with it. "What's the point of hurrying," he says, "we've all the time there is," and I suppose we have.'

At the start she had spoken with irritation about his refusal to be hurried, but now she seemed to be resigned.

'You are quite comfortable where you are, though, aren't you?' I would ask. She would shrug. 'There's nothing wrong with it. It's well enough.'

'But I suppose you want a place that really is your own with your own things round you.'

'I did.'

'Not any longer?'

'We live in an uncertain world. Perhaps it's better to travel light.'

At that moment the Spanish Civil War was shaking even the most conservative out of their *laissez-faire* philosophy. But was that really the reason why Eileen could shrug away Raymond's procrastinations? Perhaps she did not want to commit herself too far with Raymond; perhaps it was her life with him rather than the European world that was uncertain. Raymond was leaving her alone for four or five months a year. That was a lot for anyone as young as she. Was anything going on below the surface?

I saw her as often as I could. When the Wine and Food Society sponsored a Burgundian lunch, I asked her if she could come with me.

'If only you'd rung me up ten minutes earlier,' she said. 'I've just promised to go with someone else.'

That someone was Derrick Whistler. I was seated two tables away. She had her back to me, but I could watch the changing expression on his face. There was a bright light in it. He was more alive than he had been that evening at Albany. He looked younger too. I wonder, I thought, I wonder.

141

In the following spring my brother Evelyn was married to Laura Herbert. It was the happiest of occasions. Everyone was delighted for Evelyn's sake. His first marriage had broken in the autumn of 1929, and until that marriage could be annulled he had been outlawed in an emotional wilderness. Now, at last, he could begin a new life with someone young and attractive with whom he was obviously in love. The reception was at the house of one of Laura's aunts in Regent's Park. All his Oxford friends were there; it was nearly fifteen years since I had met them at that first party in his rooms at Hertford. Much had happened in that interval; but most of them had started to fulfil their promise, Robert Byron, Christopher Hollis, Douglas Woodroffe, Peter Quennell, Anthony Bushell, Anthony Powell, each in his own way had his feet firmly planted on the narrowing avenue of success. The only one who had achieved absolutely nothing was the one whose promise had seemed the brightest, and yet it was impossible to write off Raymond Peronne as a failure. He looked so handsome, so confident, so potential as he walked up the stairs to be greeted by Evelyn and his bride.

By 1937 a morning coat had come to be worn so seldom that men had ceased to look natural in them. The coats of the older men were usually too tight and the coats of the younger ones had as often as not been hired from Moss Bros. But Raymond, in the cliché of the *Cutter's Journal*, looked as though he had been poured into his fawn-grey waistcoat; the coat lay smoothly over his shoulders, curving away over his hips. The crease of his black and white check trousers broke, but only just, over his polished shoes; his thick brown and white silk tie clung into the angle of his stiff, starched collar, yet at the same time he gave the impression of having been dressed for comfort; you felt that he was ready for immediate and violent action; that he would have been as capable of shouldering a trunk in his formal clothes as he would have been in corduroy trousers and an open sports shirt. He looked, too, in exuberant good health; his skin clear, no sign of a double chin.

I waited for him in the large room where the presents

were on display. He seemed to be alone. 'Isn't Eileen here?'

'No, alas, she couldn't make it.'

We looked at the presents. 'The old boy hasn't done badly, has he?' he remarked. He looked at me thoughtfully. 'You've been away, haven't you?' he said.

'In New York. I went from there to Cuba, then I came back by the southern route and had a few days in Villefranche.'

'Villefranche. I haven't been there since.'

There was no need for me to ask 'since what?'

'How is it?' he asked.

'The way it always was.'

'Then it's about the one thing that is.'

He said it cryptically, as though there were a meaning behind his words. Why wasn't Eileen here?

Three weeks later I went down to Charminster for a cricket match. J. C. Squire had arranged a fixture there for his side of Invalids. I rang up a few days before to ask if Raymond would be there. Eileen answered me. 'No, he won't be there, but I shall. There's a dance in the neighbourhood. Iris is really too young for it, but I'm making an exception in this case.'

'Because of Michael?'

'Yes, in part.'

'Are they serious about each other?'

'As serious as anyone can be at that age.'

'Don't you think one can fall in love at that age, just as seriously as later?'

'One thinks one does.'

'You were married at eighteen yourself.'

'That was in wartime.'

'Maybe we're not so far away from wartime now.'

'Do you believe that?'

'Can you really believe that the world would be so insane? Surely we've learnt our lesson.'

In a few more months it was very clear that the world had not, and it was with a last-time feeling that in the autumn of 1938 I booked myself on a tour to the West Indies. If I don't go now, I thought, I never may.

I chiefly wanted to see the Windward islands, St Lucia, St Vincent and Grenada. The sailings fitted awkwardly and it was clear that if I wanted to visit Dominica, I should have to spend three weeks there, which was more than I could manage. I did find out, however, that the ship I aimed to catch from St Lucia would arrive at Dominica late on Christmas Eve and would stay there overnight. I sent Raymond a warning signal, 'Why don't you dine with me on board,' I wrote. 'There'll probably be better food there than we could get in Roseau. Perhaps you could bring one of those mountain chickens with you. I am sure that we could persuade the chef to warm it up for us.'

But Raymond had other ideas. We anchored in the open roadstead shortly before sundown and there he was, coming out to meet me in a row-boat.

'Get ready as quickly as you can,' he shouted up at me. 'We're going straight out to Overdale.'

'You don't want to dine on board?'

'Good Heavens no, nor do you.'

'What shall I wear?'

'Whatever you like. There'll only be ourselves. It can be chilly out there, though, don't forget.'

I had not forgotten that. I had scarcely used my pullover during the trip, but I should tonight.

'We've a lot to talk about,' he said.

My instinctive need for copy made me wish that we could look in for a moment at the club, though even as I thought it I realised that the club would almost certainly be empty. Boat day was one of the big occasions in the island's life. Residents gave dinner parties on board. And he was right, we had a lot to talk about.

'We haven't met,' I said, 'since Evelyn's wedding.'

'Then you'll have more news for me than I shall have for you. Tell me about that son of mine.'

'My godson, you know.'

'Of course, I'd not forgotten. Is the old man making him another cricketer?'

'I am, more than he.'

In my nursery days I had played endless matches with myself, throwing a tennis ball at the wall above the door, playing it on the rebound. The chairs were arranged as fielders; if the ball landed on one without bouncing, I was caught; a ball that landed on my brother's cot, even if it bounced first, was six and out. I had taught this game to Timothy Alexander. Raymond asked me about Michael.

'What about he and Iris?'

'They're what the Americans call going steady.'

'But I suppose someone will intervene and smash it up.'

For a moment we drove in silence.

'I suppose that you haven't had any mail from England for quite a while,' he said.

'I'm expecting to find a big batch waiting me in Antigua. Most of the ships stop there. If I'd had letters posted to Grenada or St Lucia, I might have missed them.'

'So I don't suppose you've seen any newspapers?'

'You know what one gets in an island newspaper. Local gossip and a few main cables. One can keep up with the cricket scores, that's all.'

'So it's no good asking you if the Peronne scandal hit the headlines.'

'What am I to take that to mean?'

'That a month ago Eileen was granted a decree nisi of divorce in respect of my neglect and flagrant infidelity.'

He said it on a flippant note.

'Is this a cause for condolence or congratulations?'

'Whichever way you choose to rate it.'

'Was there a co-respondent?'

'A nameless lady accompanied me to Brighton.'

I thought of Noël Coward's *Private Lives*. 'Had she a revolting comb?' I asked.

'As a matter of fact, she was rather nice. Does it all come as a surprise to you?'

'Yes and no.'

'Did you know about Whistler?'

'I guessed. I didn't know how serious it was.'

'What made you guess? Was there any gossip?'

'None that reached me. I saw them together once or twice. There was a kind of . . .'

'I know. There's that look in your eyes again.'

'When was all this arranged?'

'The last time I was over.'

'When was that?'

'In January.'

I had been in Morocco then.

'I rang you a couple of times,' he said. 'But I got no answer.'

'It was Eileen, then, who wanted it?'

'Yes.'

'Was it a surprise?'

'In a way, yes. We'd been married for five years—six and a half years we'd been together. I thought we'd worked out a compromise. We never quarrelled. I found her attractive still—in what is called that way. The separations helped. Sailors' wives may grumble, but the spark stays alight and besides, it's very easy for them to indulge a *fredaine* if they want.'

'You were quite happy with things the way they were?'

'Oh, yes.'

'But Eileen wasn't.'

'Whistler wasn't.'

'Why? I'd have thought that he was getting things both ways.'

'I'd have thought so too. Do you know Whistler well?'

'I've not more than met him.'

'How did he strike you?'

'He didn't make any particular impression. He seemed cut to pattern.'

'That's a mistake it's very easy to make where that type of Englishman, the public school type, is concerned. We're all different underneath that pattern. They call women the mysterious sex; I think men are much more mysterious, unaccountable, unpredictable. It was Whistler who issued an ultimatum. Things could not go on the way they were. She either had to marry him or the whole thing was off. That flattered Eileen. He loved her so much that he couldn't do with only a part of her. He couldn't share her with anyone. But I don't believe that that was the real reason. In a curious way, his vanity was hurt.'

'I'd have thought it was your vanity that was more likely to be hurt.'

'You would, wouldn't you? Cuckold isn't a pretty word. But a wise husband, like a wise wife, ought to be able to shut his eyes. Myself, I shouldn't be worried unless a situation was created that made me ridiculous, by which I was humiliated in public. And Eileen would never allow anything like that to happen. But masculine vanity is a peculiar thing. So is English snobbery. You may think this ridiculous, but I believe that Whistler didn't like the idea of Eileen being the Honourable Mrs Raymond Peronne. He was jealous of my courtesy title. It sounds ridiculous. It is ridiculous, but I believe that's how his mind worked. He wanted her to give her title up for him.'

'But she didn't get much kick out of being the Honourable?'

'A very slight one. Nobody minds a handle to their name, even if it's only on an envelope. But she'd never consider marrying for a title's sake; money, well that's another thing.'

'How's Whistler fixed that way?'

'Well enough, but Eileen's plenty of her own. Financially it's a good match for him.'

At that point I did detect a note of asperity in Raymond's voice. Clearly he loathed the man. I was glad of that. It humanised him.

'By the way,' he added, 'don't be alarmed by a dusky female that you'll find about the place. She won't sit with us at the table. She prefers eating off the floor. She won't interfere with us. She never talks. I don't think she bothers to listen. Her English isn't very good. She's a Carib. I talk to her in *patois*.'

She was short and stocky. Her hair was straight and black. She cut it *en brosse*. She was pale skinned, with a straight nose, rather thick lips, very white and even teeth. Her eyes were dark and lustrous. She had a sulky, but not unfriendly look. Most of the evening she lay flat on her stomach on a divan, her arms stretched forwards above her head and crossed at the wrists. Now and again she would turn her head and look at us, but for the most part, with her chin supported on a cushion, she lay motionless, listening to a gramophone.

'She's very restful,' Raymond said. 'In the old days the Caribs had two languages, one for the men, one for the women. Some of the men learnt the women's language, but by no means all of them; as a result the women only chatter when they are together. Another restful thing about them is they haven't the inferiority complex that most West Indians get through having once been slaves. They've always been independent. They were terrific warriors. They probably showed you in Grenada the rock where three hundred of them jumped into the sea rather than surrender.'

When his manservant announced that dinner was served, she did not follow us into the dining room. On our return ninety minutes later, she was still lying on the divan. He said something to her in the *patois* that sounds like French, but is quite unintelligible to anyone who has not learnt it; she smiled when she answered him. 'I told her that you hoped she had a good dinner. She replied that she had been well fed: she hoped that you appreciated what her cook had prepared for you. She supervised the cooking herself. She considers it a great honour to the house that you should eat here.'

'Did she really say that?'

'That's what it amounted to.'

She was seventeen years old, he told me. He had met her when he was conducting a couple of house guests on a tour of the Carib reservation. He had noticed her at the river, busy beside a pile of washing. He had passed the time of day with her; he had liked the look of her and had lingered, gossiping. That evening her mother had called on him with a practical and straightforward proposition. 'Some things are very simple in a place like this.'

I asked him what his plans were for the immediate future.

He shrugged. 'Eileen will get her decree absolute in April. I'll stay out here till then. I'm glad that I never found a house for her. The lease of Bolton's will expire in June. I don't suppose she'll want to take it on. Thank heavens none of the furniture is mine. There's always a bad feeling when you start dividing up goods and chattels. "No, that's not yours. I know Francis gave it to us both. But he was always more my friend than yours," and "Yes, I know that it was your Uncle Frederick who gave us that Chippendale love seat, but he would never have given you as good a present. He took a shine to me. I remember the way he looked at me when he said, 'I thought of you at once when I saw this.' " I'm spared all that, I'm glad to say.'

Had he, I wondered, subconsciously had such a day in mind when he had looked for a house so half-heartedly? If he had really wanted to grapple Eileen to him with bands of steel would he not have built round her a house that she could not bear to lose? He had made it all very easy for himself.

'What about Timothy Alexander?'

'He'll stay with her, of course. She's a good mother. Whistler'll be all right as a step-father. I'll keep in the background, see how the boy develops. He'll probably need me some day. When that time comes, then I'll be there. I've heard it said, you know, that children quite like the idea of a parent whom they don't know too much about. He or she has a mystery and glamour for them. Eventually they react against the parent whom they see all the time. I'm not worrying about him. I am, though, just a little, about Iris. It's happened at the wrong time for her. She would have come out this summer, but for that you need a settled background. Where would she have her dance? She hasn't a chip on her shoulder, but three step-fathers, that's a lot, you know. She must be beginning to wonder who and what she is. But for this she would have had her coming-out dance at Charminster and that . . . well, with this changed situation, there are some things that just aren't possible and that is one of them. And this also means that she won't have opportunities of meeting Michael. Will that mean much to her?'

'A great deal, I'd say.'

'And that's the very thing that might start a chip on that

pretty shoulder. Suppose she marries someone rather ordinary, and the marriage doesn't turn out too glamorously, she might well think "If I'd gone on going to Charminster I'd have married Michael. I'd be the Baroness Peronne instead of the wife of an overworked city drudge who falls asleep every evening while he's listening to the news." If you were writing a novel about her, isn't that the way you'd make it happen?'

'It might well be.'

'Load the dice against your heroine. Isn't that what Hardy did in *Tess*?'

'I reckon so.'

'What are you working on, by the way?'

'I'm hoping after this trip to do a novel with a West Indian background.'

'That'll be a new departure, won't it?'

'I feel it's about time I made one. This isn't the best time for the family chronicle.'

I explained my problem. My last three novels had told how a family had developed over several years. I had started them in the Edwardian period; I had carried my characters through into the thirties. I had brought the various characters to a point where one of them could sum up the direction of their lives, what they had done, where they had failed, what lay ahead of them. 'That kind of novel isn't convincing now,' I said. 'Because you can't tell what the world is going to be like in three years' time. Suppose I were to start a family novel when I got back to England. It would take a year to write. It would take six months to get it published, in June 1940, let us say. No one knows what the world is going to be like in June 1940. We might even be at war. My characters wouldn't have reached any harbour of finality. Suppose the story were to end in September 1938? During the last half of it my readers would be thinking "I can't be interested in whatever point of conclusion any of these characters reach. A war will have broken out which will have altered everything. Families will be broken up, heroes and villains alike may be killed in action." The war is a *deus ex machina* that can't be used. Did you ever read Maupassant's Preface to *Pierre et Jean*?'

'No.'

'In it he wrote that though the number of persons who daily meet with accidental death is large, you cannot have an important character slip under a cab or have a brick fall on his head in the middle of a story. And that's what a war does; it's the equivalent of a brick falling off a roof.'

'How are you going to avoid this problem by setting your story in the West Indies?'

'There'll be no need to date it. It will be the kind of story that can take place any time. It'll be placed in an exotic setting unfamiliar to the reader. It will be apart from the reality of their daily routine. Besides, it isn't going to be a chronicle. It's going to be a story with a plot; a woman murders her husband.'

'How's she going to do that?'

'Leave the exhaust of the car running in a closed garage.'

'I look forward to reading this.'

'I'll try to make it readable.' I returned to the present problem of the novelist. 'We had exactly the same problem in 1919,' I said. 'We couldn't write a contemporary novel that covered several years. If we started it with the hero getting demobilised, the story would have to run on till 1923 or 1924. And the reader would feel "How can he tell what the world is going to be like in 1923? There may be a revolution." If you started the story in 1910, even if you were to finish it in 1913, the reader would say "How can I take an interest in any of these characters when I know that whatever mess they may land up in, August 1914 is going to provide them with a ready-made solution." It's rather strange that we should get the same problem twice in the same lifetime.'

'Isn't that what usually happens?'

'How do you mean?'

'That you get in middle age the same problem that you had when you were young. You see it from a different angle. You may solve it in a different way. But it's the same basic problem. Because we remain the same basic people. You can only ring a certain number of changes on yourself.'

'Has that been your experience?'

'Not yet; but I've seen it in other lives. It'll probably come my way. The second time round I'll see it with different eyes. Then I'll understand what it was about the first time, understand when it is too late.'

I pondered that. We sat in silence on the verandah. In the sitting room the gramophone was purring softly. The Carib girl was on the divan still, her head buried in her arms. The moon was unveiled by clouds. From the garden below us the ripple of the stream mingled its murmur with the multitudinous voices of the forest. It was all very peaceful. A line of Lascelles Abercrombie crossed my memory, 'Oh, the fine world and fine all for nothing.' Was this peaceful beauty doomed? 'What'll you do if there's a war?' he asked me, 'something in propaganda?'

I shook my head. 'I went to Sandhurst and got a regular commission, so in 1919 I transferred to the regular reserve. I've asked the War Office what my position is. If there's a general mobilisation, I go back to my regiment automatically.'

'How old are you now?'

'Forty last July.'

'A bit old for a platoon commander. They'll send you on a staff course, probably.'

'Most likely.'

I was prepared to leave that to chance.

'What are your plans?' I asked.

'I've applied for an emergency reserve commission. It should go through.'

'Did it occur to you to stay on here?'

'Of course, I could argue a case for staying here. There may be important work here for someone like myself. But I want to be in the centre of things. I'm only thirty-four. I've kept pretty fit. I fancy I'm fit enough to drive a tank.'

'I imagine that most of your generation will prove to have been just too young for the first war and just too old for this. I've heard that they're going to have reserved occupations; that they're not going to have technicians and first-class administrators wiped out in front-line trenches. They're not going to interrupt the education of first-class brains and they're going to keep back schoolmasters; they're going

to see that the young generation can have a proper education. Oxford and Cambridge will go on. I should say that
most of your generation who've had no military training
will be of more use to their country in offices and laboratories.'

'Yet even so there are going to be quite a number who
feel that in wartime they should be in uniform. I think your
brother's one of them.'

I thought so too; even though he had only just become a
father and had bought a house in Gloucestershire.

'I'd give a lot,' said Raymond, 'to be able to picture
us all as we'll be two Christmasses from now.' I remembered
an occasion when I had been a prisoner of war in Germany,
in Mainz, in July 1918. A group of some forty of us had been
waiting at the gateway to the dining hall for the bell that
would summon us to what passed for a meal in those
strictly rationed days. One of us had made a precisely
similar remark; another, a more than somewhat class-
conscious member of the upper orders had said, 'I'd like
to switch back four years and see how we all looked in July,
1914.' We all knew what he was thinking. More than a
quarter of the officers gathered there had come from very
humble origins. But as Turgenev had pointed out in *Smoke*,
a wind blows and the top branches of a tree are bent to meet
the lowest.

'Whatever happens in Europe, do you think that anything
will look any different here?' I said.

'Now that's another matter.'

We had not talked a great deal about Dominica. There
was not a great deal to say. That autumn a commission had
come out from England, under Lord Moyne's chairmanship.
'Had he any idea,' I asked, 'what they decided?'

Raymond shook his head. 'The great thing is that there
should have been a commission and it should have come
here. It'll give the people a confidence in themselves. They
feel now that Whitehall is concerned about them. That's
why I gave that party with those films. I wanted the people
who matter in these things to notice that there was such a
place.'

'You think that party helped?'

'It didn't do any harm. The commission spent four days here. They might have spent only two otherwise, or they might not have come at all. They might have asked us to send a delegation to Antigua. It wasn't so easy for them to get here.'

'And did the meetings do any good?'

'The local notables were made to feel important; that was the main thing. That was what I said to you after that party. They've had so much bad luck; they need a shot of something—a *piqure*; that's what that party was. You can't tell whether or not it did good, any more than you can tell whether a tonic you take in the winter helps to keep off colds. You catch a cold, of course you do. But you might have caught a worse one without that tonic. Everything adds in.'

'And if there isn't a war, you'll go on living here?'

'Partially. I'm not going to spend my whole life here. Heavens, no.'

'It might be something for Timothy Alexander one day.'

'That's what I've been thinking. It should be a way of getting back to him, or at getting him back to me. I'd like to have him associate me with a place like this—a father who lives in the West Indian islands is a feather in a small boy's cap. It makes him different. It gives him something to brag about. That's what a small boy needs. He doesn't want his parents to be better than other boys, but he likes them to be different. That makes him special. I look forward to bringing him out here, for a summer holiday.'

He had got the future planned. My godson was not going to feel neglected. He was not going to feel as Raymond himself had done, that no one was bothering over him.

'If there is a war,' I asked, 'what effect do you think it will have on Dominica?'

'There'll be a boom. There always is in war time. There'll be a demand for raw materials. Antigua and St Kitts will have a good market for their sugar, and we, as one of the Leewards, will benefit from that. And there'll be a need for our special products, limes in particular. There'll be torpedoes, of course. But our goods will be insured. We shan't lose by that.'

'If there isn't a war, will you get a flat or a house of your own in England?'

He shook his head. 'More trouble than it's worth. Besides, it would mean an extra tax problem. I can keep my clothes and the few things I have of my own in Charminster. I'll rent furnished flats whenever I'm over.'

'You'll probably marry again.'

'Will I? I suppose I shall. Most people do. But I'm not certain that I'm very satisfactory as a husband. Too selfish, I suppose. As far as I was concerned, my marriage was all right. I thought it was for Eileen too. I was surprised when she broke the news to me. A bombshell, well, that's really what it was. I was perfectly happy the way things were. That proves that matrimony isn't my long suit, I guess.'

It was sad to hear him saying that. The divorce seemed such a pity. Was anyone going to be any the better off? Which is, I suppose, how nine times in ten the outsider feels when a marriage breaks. It could all have been saved so easily. I wished that I had known six months ago. Not that I could have done anything. Anyhow, it was too late now.

10

I wrote to Eileen from New York. 'I have been in the West Indies and have only just heard your news. I wish you the very best of luck. Don't let's lose touch. I expect to be back in England in mid-February. I'll drop you a note. Every best wish.'

A note from her awaited my return. 'Your letter was a great relief to me. I was afraid that it might prove a case of taking sides and you're one of the half-dozen of Raymond's friends that I'd hate to lose. I'm living very quietly, while this case is still *sub judice*; so any day that suits you for lunch is fine with me.'

We lunched at the Jardin. The moment we had ordered lunch, after one sip at a daiquiri, she broke straight into the subject. There was no leading up.

'So you've been to Dominica?'

'Right.'

'How's Raymond?'

'Fine. The same weight, no cold or flu.'

'I didn't mean that. You know what I meant. How is he taking it?'

'It was a bit of a shock to him. He hadn't expected it.'

'I know he hadn't. That's the one part of this wretched business that I enjoyed.'

'What was?'

'Surprising him. He hadn't the right to be surprised. He should have expected it, or something like it.'

'He was contented with the way it was.'

'That's my complaint. He hadn't any right to be, or rather he hadn't any right to think that I'd be. Being left alone for four or five months a year.'

'He didn't want you to be left alone. He wanted you out there with him.'

'And leave Iris behind? How could I do that? You know as well as I do, after that carnival performance, that I had to

156

have her with me, and how could I take her out; how could I run that risk? I couldn't, could I?'

'You couldn't.'

'Then how could he expect me to like being left alone for four or five months a year?'

'Sailors' wives are alone longer than that.'

'He's not a sailor.'

'But he takes Dominica as seriously as a sailor takes the sea.'

'That's what's so maddening. He prefers Dominica to me.'

'To a man who amounts to anything, his career comes first.'

'But I wasn't warned. If I'd married a sailor, I'd have done it with open eyes. "This is what you're letting yourself in for," I'd have told myself. "Do you think that you can take it?" Then I'd only have had myself to blame, if I found I couldn't. But when Raymond and I eloped, he didn't know of the existence of Dominica. He fell in love with it after he'd been with me. For that's what he did, didn't he, he fell in love with the wretched place.'

'That's what he did.'

'Now don't you agree that is rather more than I had bargained for?'

She had so strong a case that I felt I had better change my ground.

'You picked up an unlucky hand, but when you saw how the suits were stacked, well, don't you think even so that the lot of a sailor's wife is not too bad, particularly when she's comfortably off? You had complete freedom, you could do as you liked. No one questioned you. Don't you think that a great many women would be prepared to envy you?'

'I suppose they would.'

'Haven't you heard many married women say—women who've been married for several years, of course—"Yes, I'd enjoy an affair if there weren't so many complications attached to it. It's nearly always more trouble than it's worth." You've heard enough women say that, I'm sure.'

'I've heard them.'

'But that wasn't your position?'

'That wasn't my position.'

'When Raymond was at home he was an amusing companion, wasn't he?'

'I'm not denying it.'

'I got the impression . . .' I hesitated. Should I say it or shouldn't I? Hadn't I told myself that evening on the verandah at Overdale, that it was too late now to interfere. But was it though? The decree absolute had not yet been pronounced. Should I ever forgive myself if I didn't play every card I held? 'I've always felt that Raymond was still in love with you.'

'In his way he was.'

'It's not usual for a husband to be still in love after eight years.'

'So I've been told.'

'Isn't it possible that in another eight years' time you may be thinking "I didn't know when I was well off." '

'Maybe.'

'In that case, then . . .' I looked at her with a question in my eyes. She answered me with a question. 'Haven't you heard it said that a woman in the last analysis will choose the man who needs her most? I may have seemed to be getting it both ways, ninety-nine married women in a hundred would have envied me my life, and wouldn't ninety-nine men in a hundred have envied Derrick? Wasn't he getting it both ways, all the advantages of marriage without the disadvantages? He had me to himself for four or five months a year, all the privileges, none of the responsibilities, none of the dreary routine of domesticity. Isn't that exactly what you at thirty would have wanted for yourself?'

'I would.'

'But it wasn't enough for him. He wanted more. He wanted more of me. He wanted me exclusively. He couldn't share me. He delivered an ultimatum. It had to be everything or nothing. Who could resist that? I couldn't.'

She was echoing Raymond's words. What woman could have resisted that appeal? 'You say that Raymond was still in love,' she said, 'and I won't deny it, in his way he was. But he didn't put me first. He put Dominica first. He didn't come back for his own child's birth. He wasn't with me at that for me so important time, and when I put up my ultimatum . . .'

'No man likes being the target of an ultimatum.'

'It depends on what the ultimatum is. A man expects to have said to him, "You must choose between me or that woman." I said to Raymond, "You've got to choose between me and that island." He chose the island.'

I made no comment. It was not for me to put forward Raymond's contention that Whistler's ultimatum had been inspired not so much by love as by an injured vanity. Raymond might not be right. And anyhow Eileen must be left with her illusions. Perhaps they were not illusions, or perhaps they were illusions that would be turned to truth; that Whistler, once this sacrifice had been made for him, although to Eileen it would not be a sacrifice at all, would become the devoted, concentrated husband that she had not found in Raymond. I lifted my glass, 'The best of luck to you in every way.'

Then we started to discuss other plans. 'Raymond's being very generous,' she said. 'He's not making any difficulties; but then I never thought he would. He isn't that kind of person. Bolton's has another five months of its lease to run, so I'll stay on there till my decree's made absolute. During the time we're waiting, we'll be looking for a house to buy, but not too seriously. We have to be discreet till we've got our decree. The King's Proctor isn't quite obsolete, not yet.'

'Will you keep on the set in Albany?'

'That depends on Derrick, but I don't see the point. If he has to be up alone, he's got his club. When we come up together, it's easier to go to a hotel.'

'Have you told the children?'

'Iris, I have. Not Timothy Alexander.'

'How's Iris taking it?'

'She isn't worrying. After all, Raymond's not her father.'

Whistler would be her third stepfather; perhaps it would be something for her to brag about. Not many of her contemporaries had as many. 'What about her coming out?' I asked.

'We're postponing it for a year. We couldn't give her the attention that she needs. Next year will be time enough.'

It was at the end of March that we had that conversation. A few days earlier Hitler had occupied Czechoslovakia, yet in London we were all still talking as though 1940 would follow the same pattern as 1938.

11

We were very soon to find that we were wrong. September 1939 saw me back again in uniform, with my regiment, and two years later I was posted to the Middle East, to a liaison job with General Spears' mission to Syria and the Lebanon. The day before I sailed, I lunched with Evelyn, whose commando unit had been heavily engaged at Crete. He had now returned to join another unit.

'You'll find a lot of old friends in Cairo,' he informed me.

'I'm expecting to be in Beirut.'

'But you'll be coming into Cairo fairly often. I can tell you one old friend you'll find there—Raymond Peronne.'

I had heard that he was in the Middle East. I had kept up with Eileen. We had lunched a couple of times and she had written to me regularly. Raymond had sailed back for England in that last July. He had seen the West Indians' final test match at the Oval. We had planned to meet in September, he and I, but by then I was with my regiment in Dorchester. I heard him mentioned once or twice. During the phoney war, a number of men of his age and a little younger were at a loose end in London. They were too old to get into the army: the various ministries were full. They were reluctant to commit themselves to air defence squads. They became rather a nuisance. Betty Askwith was very amusing at their expense. She, like most women, had become quickly caught up in war work; and she was a little exasperated by the young men who would waste her time ringing up to tell her how frustrated they felt at not being able to get war work.

'I try to be sympathetic,' she said, 'but it isn't easy. I just haven't the time to listen to their problems. A year ago men were complaining that women interfered with their work. Now it's the other way about. They interfere with ours.'

Raymond was one of those whom she complained about, but after Dunkirk there was room for everyone. I had heard that he was in Evelyn's commando.

'How did he do at Crete?' I asked.

'Very gallantly. He was wounded, in the shoulder, luckily for him. If it had been in the leg, he wouldn't have got away.'

'Was he badly wounded?'

'Not too seriously. He was in hospital five weeks. There won't be any serious effects. It'll probably hurt him later on, when the weather's wet.'

'What's he doing now?'

'Nothing very strenuous. In Censorship at the moment. Cairo's very full of officers who are half employed. It's a very pleasant place if you have a private income. Hell if you haven't, and you're below the rank of Colonel. Far too expensive, and twenty officers to every girl. It's turning the girls' heads, most of them. They've never been so in demand.'

'I shouldn't have thought that that was the kind of life that Raymond would have chosen. Couldn't he have come back with you?'

'He could have but he didn't want to. England hasn't very much to offer him; you've heard about Eileen, haven't you?'

Yes, I had heard about Eileen. She had not found a house by the time the war started. Whistler had been called up right away. He had been in the Territorials and was a major. Within two months his regiment had been sent out to India to relieve one of the regular battalions. 'Not much of a honeymoon for them,' had been Raymond's comment. 'It's the only time,' Evelyn said, 'that I've heard venom in his voice.'

That had left Eileen with the set in Albany, which became impossible when the real blitz began. It was unsatisfactory as a base for Iris. The idea of a finishing year in Switzerland was no longer practicable. Timothy Alexander was going to a boarding school. Six was early for that. 'But how could I have coped with him in London, getting him there in the morning, bringing him back at night; then his trying to do his home-work when the alert was on. He had to be got out of London. And what a place to bring him back to for his holidays.' Thus had she bewailed her situation to me across a lunch table

162

early in November. 'What would you have done in a position like that?' she asked.

How was I to answer that? Everyone had his or her own problems. One did what one could, from day to day. 'I bet you won't guess what I decided.'

'You tell me.'

'I remembered that Timothy Alexander was the old man's grandson. I flung myself on his mercy.'

'You mean to say . . .'

'That's what I mean to say.'

'That you and Iris and Timothy Alexander moved into Charminster?'

'Precisely. Margaret's delighted. She's got someone to play backgammon with.'

'With Michael coming home for weekend leaves.'

'Precisely.'

There was a twinkle in her eye. Six years earlier I had thought that though I enjoyed her company I didn't really like her, but I felt very in tune with her at that moment. We had been raised in the same stable, after all.

That had been when the blitz was at its height. The blitz was over now, but they were still at Charminster. I asked Evelyn what Raymond made of that.

'He mentioned it, of course.'

'Did it worry him?'

'I don't think so, no. He was rather amused by it. What a situation for the old man, after all. His daughter-in-law with his grandson and his heir. His ex-daughter-in-law with his other grandson and her daughter by an earlier marriage. All of them under the same roof. A comic opera.

'If you had been told three years ago that such a situation could arise, you would not have believed it. It would have been very difficult to make it credible in a novel. Yet step by step it has been one logical solution following on the other.

'And what a coincidence if the grandson who is the heir should want to marry the daughter of the ex-daughter-in-law.'

'Is that likely to happen?'

'It's not unlikely. Michael spends his leaves at Charminster. They were attracted to each other. They're the right age for one another. And wartime too.'

'History repeating itself in fact. If it hadn't been for the first war, Adrian would not have married Margaret.'

'And you say that Raymond is amused by the situation?'

'I think he welcomes it. It gives him an alibi for not coming back to England. He'd be a nuisance if he did. Which is the last thing he'd want to be. His father won't be hurt at his not coming home.'

'Does he need an alibi?'

'I think he does. When our commando was disbanded, all the rest came home. We were promised postings to a new unit that was being formed here.'

'Wouldn't that have been in his better interests?'

'I'm not so sure. He had been wounded. He might not have passed for general service. And at his age if you don't get a posting right away, you're likely to find yourself in the unemployment pool. The army's being enlarged so fast. There are all these youngsters passing out of OCTUs. He might have found himself shelved.'

'Isn't the same thing likely to happen to him in Cairo?'

'The pool isn't so large, and he's built up a credit balance of goodwill. Everybody likes him. The right thing is bound to turn up soon.'

Which is what everyone had always said about Raymond. He was so obviously the right person for the right thing. But that right thing never had turned up, and he was now thirty-seven; a mature age in wartime for a captain. 'I look forward to seeing him,' I said.

I reached Port Said at the end of November. I had a week in Cairo before going north to Beirut.

Raymond invited me to dinner at the Mohamet Aly Club, with which he enjoyed exchange privileges through White's. To celebrate our reunion he ordered a bottle of Krug '28, which was then at its majestic peak.

It was three years since we had met. I had wondered how those three years, which included two years of soldiering and

164

eighteen months of campaigning, climaxing in a wound, would have effected him. They had not, so it seemed. He had not put on weight. His hair had not thinned, though it had lost a little of its sheen. His wound had not altered the carriage of his shoulders, though I noticed that he often crossed his left arm over his chest, so that he could support it by holding his tunic underneath his arm. He was wearing a well cut uniform of light cream gabardine. Over his left breast pocket was the mauve and white ribbon of the Military Cross. 'Congratulations,' I said. 'I hadn't heard about that.'

'It's recent. Our unit was allotted two DSOs and four MCs; there were so few survivors that I'd have been unlucky not to draw one.'

He made light of it, but MCs were not lightly earned.

I asked him about his wound.

'Does it worry you?'

'It would if I were a cricketer; but it doesn't interfere with my golf. I'm not sure, as a matter of fact, that it hasn't improved my swing. I've had to shorten it. I'm playing to an eleven handicap at Gezira.'

He was still in Censorship, he told me. 'And likely to remain in it.' he said. He confirmed what Evelyn had said about the difficulty of a man of his age who was not a hundred per cent fit getting taken on by an active unit. 'I'll probably be a chairborne warrior for the duration.'

'That's not a fate worse than death.'

It was my own fate, certainly, but then I was six years older, and six years at that age count as twelve. There had never been any suggestion of my being—with my rank—a combat soldier.

'And Cairo's the best place to be that,' he said.

'Provided you've a private income.'

'Precisely, and as regards that I'm in luck.'

I looked about me. The large room with its tall ceilings, high windows and cut glass candelabra was three-quarters full. Half the tables were occupied by men in uniform, nearly all of them with red flannel on their lapels. There were a number of affluent, obese Egyptians. The waiters wore red tarbooshes, red sashes and white gloves. Long-necked bottles steamed in buckets. Was there any place in the world, except the USA, so redolent of luxury at that moment? It was hard to believe that only a few hundred miles away in the Western desert, lives were being risked and lives were being lost. Egypt was a neutral. The rich Cairenes did not mind whether the Italians won or lost. Life here would go on the same.

Raymond had a second-floor flat near the Gezira Club. 'I play golf most afternoons,' he said. 'I lunch lightly and don't take a siesta. That keeps me fit. Most of the staff eat too much. Have you seen Francis?'

Yes, I had seen Francis Moyston. He was a half colonel in the MS branch. He was my age, and looked over fifty. He must have put on fifteen pounds.

'Are you planning to stay on in Censorship?' I asked.

'I don't see why not. Someone has to do the job.'

He gave me an outline of his day: awake at six; a morning cup of tea. A two-mile walk to GHQ, pausing on the way for a croissant and a cup of coffee; at his desk by eight. Five hours that kept him occupied, without exacting any pressure.

'It's not uninteresting.' he said. 'I learn what people are thinking, not only here but in other countries. And from the instructions we receive I get a glimpse of what's going on behind the scenes. When we're told that certain things must not be mentioned, we ask ourselves why not.'

And it was not as though he had to spend the whole morning at his desk. There was usually a conference in some other office. He could find an excuse for going out for a morning coffee. 'Have you been to Groppi's yet?' he asked. 'There are no cream buns in the world like theirs.'

At one he would knock off work, and make straight for Gezira. A ham sandwich and a glass of beer. He'd be on the first tee by quarter to two. A swim after his golf, then another three hours in his office. 'I begin to feel a little office-weary by seven o'clock; the last hours drags, but there's the evening to look forward to; and that really does amount to something. There's this club and there's the Turf Club; they've got some excellent tawny port. There are a number of good small restaurants. There are films. There's a constant going and

166

coming. Everyone in England is trying to get sent out here on a mission—or for a conference—I've seen more of my old friends out here during the last year than I should have in three years in England. You see them under the best circumstances too. In London everyone is so grand and busy. Here we have time for one another. After those months in Dominica . . .'

He paused, a ruminative expression on his face. Had he felt lonely out there, with the rain beating across the foliage and no companionship but that of the Carib girl who did not speak a word of English?

'What news of Dominica?'

He laughed. 'The kind of news you would have expected, but could not have foreseen. You remember that I prophesied a boom in the Caribbean if there was a war?'

'I do.'

'Well, that's what's happened—in all the islands except Dominica. In the summer of 1940, just after the collapse of France, a committee sat in Whitehall, with that Moyne commission report in front of it, and voted a considerable sum of money, I forget how much it was, but it was quite a sum, to the development of the West Indian colonies. Isn't that typically British, that with invasion imminent, with no one knowing where anyone would be in a week's time, a committee was solemnly sitting down, and deliberating how much could be afforded for the West Indian islands. It has proved very useful; except for poor Dominica, sandwiched between Guadeloupe and Martinique, both of whom accepted the Vichy government. She was completely isolated. I don't know whether or not the German submarines are refuelling in Fort de France and Pointe à Pitre, but in Barbados and Trinidad the authorities believe they are, and that's what matters. Ships are afraid of putting in at Roseau. They'd be sitting ducks. There's another thing, too. I don't know if you've read about the conditions in Martinique and Guadeloupe, but the French admiral who has taken over control in the name of the Vichy government has established a police state. He has maintained the strictest rationing; he has to, of course, with only an occasional ship allowed a safe passage from Bordeaux. He relies on the police and the armed naval and military personnel. He can keep them loyal so long as they are well fed; that means that the population as a whole goes short. Consequently, a number of hungry men escape to Dominica and enlist with the Free French, not out of sympathy with de Gaulle but because they're hungry. By their terms of service they are entitled to a full meat ration, and the island has to supply that out of their own meagre resources. It takes a long time to get these recruits to Barbados or the Windward Islands. In the meantime Dominica is running out of cattle. There will be a serious meat shortage soon. Typical Dominica, in fact.'

He said it with a laugh; but he was clearly distressed for the island's sake. I asked him what his plans were for the future. He shrugged. 'What plans can be made in wartime? anyhow in a war like this. I live from day to day; and I can't say that I don't find it pleasant.'

He was indeed having as good a time as anyone in the world. Amusingly occupied, without any worries, with a surplus of the creature comforts. Moreover, by his service in Crete, his conscience had been assuaged. He had won the MC; he had been wounded; it was because of his wound that he had been transferred to the Staff. In the first war every soldier had prayed for a 'cushy blighty'; a sliver of gold braid on his cuff and the right to enjoy the flesh pots of Piccadilly in the rôle of a rewarded hero. There were few people in the world who would not envy him. But all the same, it did not seem quite good enough for Raymond Peronne. So much more had been expected for him.

It was four months before I was to see him again, and in those four months a great deal happened. First there was Pearl Harbour, and with America in the war, the certainty that in the long run Hitler must be overthrown. But in the meantime, those four months were marked by a series of reverses for British arms, in the Western Desert and in for Eastern waters. Rommel was in the ascendant. *Repulse* and the *Prince of Wales* had been torpedoed. Malaya had been overrun. These calamities had brought two major changes in the narrow and narrowing circle of my personal interests. The first, that Derrick Whistler's battalion had been moved from India and that he had been taken prisoner at Singapore. The second, that Michael's battalion had been posted overseas and that on his embarkation leave he had married Iris. When I learned that Raymond was coming to Beirut for a week's leave I was curious to know what his reaction to this news would be.

He asked me to meet him at one o'clock on the terrace of the St George's Hotel.

It was a warm spring day. The sky was blue. The sun glistened on the snowcapped mountain peaks. I found Raymond seated with a French full colonel, the equivalent of our BGS, at the *grand serail*, the French Headquarters. 'I expect you know each other,' Raymond said.

I knew him by sight, but I did not think he would be aware of me. I had, however, underestimated the extent of Gallic courtesy. 'But of course,' he said, 'Captain Waugh is one of our most valued colleagues.' He rose to his feet. 'I thank you a thousand times for my apéritif and the matter of our mutual friend, that is well understood. I will put the request through this afternoon.'

Raymond rubbed his hands together in self-congratulation.

'Very satisfactory. Very satisfactory indeed.'

'What was that about?' I asked.

'Tony Richardson. I've got him a job as liaison officer with the Free French. You know Tony, don't you?'

Yes, I knew Tony. I had seen him about at parties before the war. He had got a rugger blue at Oxford. He had been one of Mosley's early recruits, as a British Fascist, but later had thought better of it, along with a lot of others. He had been engaged to one of the Ringold girls, but the engagement had been broken off. In 1938 he had been one of those young men who in an indeterminate hour had seemed to be heading nowhere. I had not seen or heard of him since then. I had not known he was in the Middle East.

'How does he fit into this?' I asked.

Raymond explained. Tony had been wounded in one of the

earlier campaigns. He had been in hospital several weeks. When he was passed for duty, his original unit had not applied to have him back. The old colonel had been found a sinecure as a camp commandant at a rehabilitation centre. The new CO had been a company commander when Tony had first joined the unit. At the depot there had been some difficulty about a girl they both had fancied. 'That's Tony's story; at any rate; they did not want him back.' He was posted to BTE, then he got an attack of sandfly fever and was in hospital again. 'I don't know if you've ever had sandfly fever. It's a tricky business. It leaves you very depressed. They take away your revolver in case you get suicidal. Perhaps they sent him back to duty too soon; I gather he put up a black or two; at any rate they sent him on a course. He didn't do well enough on it to get himself an appointment. In the meantime they'd filled his place with his unit. He found himself in the pool, and went back to his war substantive rank—Lieutenant. Then he got mixed up with a girl, a Palestinian ATS, and a subaltern without a private income is not in a position to get mixed up with a girl in Cairo. The competition is too fierce. He might get himself into an awful mess. Tony lacks backbone. But he's not a bad chap. I wouldn't like to see him go down the drain. And as it happens he does speak excellent French, almost bi-lingual. What's more he likes the French; they feel that and like him back. They say about him "One would never think he was an Englishman, though he looks like one"—which is about as high praise as they can give. I remembered that that Colonel was somewhat in my debt. He'd stayed at Charminster. I thought that there might be a string there I could pull. I found there was; so an application is going through for him to come out as a liaison officer with the French, a G2 appointment, and on a major's pay he should do well among the Lebanese houris. I'm told that they are far from unresponsive.'

'I wouldn't contradict you.'

'You shouldn't from what I've heard. At any rate, the posting should be through in a week. I'm seeing Louis Spears tonight. A word in the right quarter there should settle it.'

A smile of satisfaction played across his mouth. 'Every-thing, or at least nearly everything, goes by backstairs in-fluence. It's a funny thing, but I've always had the connec-tions that have made it possible for me to do things for other people. Do you remember that character in *War and Peace* of whom Tolstoy said, "he had realised that the only way to have influence is not to use it". I haven't found that. I've always found that for people on the Tony level, I've been able to pull the right strings. It's been one of my hobbies. You remember Judy?'

'Of course.'

'I got that job for her.'

'She'd no idea you had.'

'I know she hadn't. I took good care of that. If she had, she'd have thought I was trying to get rid of her, which in fact was the last thing I wanted. I was having a fine time; as fine a time as I've had with anyone.'

'Then why did you get that job for her?'

'It was best for her. She wasn't getting anywhere through me. I was spoiling her chances of the jobs that might have been right for her. She wasn't taking her work seriously, and I kept her, through being around, from concentrating on one of the men who would have made her a good husband. She had reached the marrying age. She'd had her share of being wild. Better to start again in a new country. And I was right, wasn't I? It's worked out very well.'

She was married, with three children; her husband a powerful figure in Canadian politics.

'She writes to me every Christmas. I get a real kick out of her letters. I suppose that's what gives me more kick than anything in life; doing things for people and never letting them know I have. I hardly ever let them know. It might spoil a friendship. People don't like having to feel beholden. They like to feel they've done it on their own. Besides I enjoy the dramatic irony of the situaton. Just now and again I do tell them when I'm sure it could do no harm. For instance . . .' He paused. He looked at me thoughtfully, asking himself a question. 'Do you remember,' he said, 'being commissioned by *Metropolis* to do them a piece about the south of France?'

'I certainly do, I look back on that article as a watershed. It started me off on a new tack.'

'I'm glad to hear that. I fixed that commission. I thought it was what you needed.'

'You thought it was what I needed?'

'Um. You had published a novel about post-war London, *Kept*. I thought it pretty good. It showed that you weren't a one-book man. Then you began a serial in the *Daily Mirror*, about the same kind of people against the same background. "He's repeating himself," I thought. "He needs a change." That summer I had been to Monte Carlo. There was no official summer season then, but a few people were beginning to realise how delightful the coast was at that time of year. Another year and a vogue might well have started. I thought of you. You could write about the same people, only against a different background, a background that would make them and their problems different. I thought of suggesting it to you; then at a lunch party I found myself sitting next to the proprietor of *Metropolis*. I talked to him about the Côte d'Azur in August. "It's got everything," I told him. "In three years' time it'll be the most fashionable summer playground in the world. You ought to have a piece on it."

'He was intrigued. He wondered whom he should get to do it. Of course I had you in mind, but I didn't want to mention you right away. He might think he was being got at. I suggested Michael Arlen. He shook his head, "Too expensive. I can't afford him."

' "What about Alec Waugh? He should be within your price range."

'I saw that he was nibbling. But I tried other names—against all of which there would be, I knew, some objection—either too old or tied up with another paper. Finally I came back to you. "I don't think you'd do better than Alec Waugh."

'He pencilled your name on his place card. "I'll get my secretary on to that right away," he said.'

'I'm glad he did. It made a difference to me.'

He laughed. 'I'm glad I told you. Now that it's so long ago you won't feel you've been put under an obligation.'

He paused. He smiled. 'It's a funny thing, but I always seem to have the connections that my friends need, but never the ones that can be of use to me. I'm sure that there's some job at GHQ with red flannel attached to it that I'd be perfect for, but I don't know what it is, and nobody sponsors me.'

'Nobody imagines that you need any help. Everyone thinks that you're capable of looking after yourself, that if you weren't satisfied with what you'd been offered, you'd find yourself the job that suited you.'

'I suppose you're right. At least I'm not worrying, but I do sometimes feel that I might be more usefully employed. Don't you get that feeling sometimes? What's this job of yours at the mission like?' As a matter of fact that was the precise feeling that I was getting. I had arrived in Beirut to find that there was no special niche for me in the mission. There was a publicity department. 'But I can't ask a writer of your standing to take on a post like that,' the chargé d'affairs, whom I had already met in England, said to me. 'It's a very minor sort of work and we've a very junior journalist who's admirably suited for it. We'll make you staff captain Q. so that you can fit into the establishment and draw staff pay, and look around to see if there's not something that really suits you. Something's bound to turn up soon.'

It had not yet and in the meantime my technical limitations had become apparent. I was concerned with transportation. I would attend conferences between French and English as an interpreter. An English colonel would announce: 'And now Captain Waugh will explain to our French colleagues what it is we want from them.' My French vocabulary was adequate to a dissertation on the pleasures of the table and the bed, but not to a discussion of the rival merits in a hilly area of track-lined and wheel-propelled vehicles. I was forced to admit that I did not know what these things were in English, let alone in French. I was beginning to suspect that the military section of General Spears' mission to Syria and Lebanon would soon be needing a new staff captain Q. But I did not want to confide that to Raymond. He would have probably found me an appointment that

173

would have put a crown upon my shoulder. But I did not want to be beholden to him. I preferred to make my own plans for myself.

'It's a funny kind of job,' I said. 'The last kind of thing that I pictured myself as doing when I went back into the army, but it's going to prove very useful for me as a writer. I'm meeting my French opposite numbers for the first time. Up till now the only French men and women I've met have been fishermen or barmaids, the kind that went into the bars at Villefranche, with an occasional colonial official on a French liner, but here I'm mixing with the equivalents of the officers and their wives that I met at Dorchester at the Depot. I'm also meeting the Lebanese and they're a delightful crowd. My posting out here has been a great, great piece of luck for me. I might so easily have found myself a garrison adjutant in a dreary midland town.' I enlarged on the characteristics of the Lebanese; then I changed the subject.

'I suppose you haven't brought any photographs of your nephew's wedding.'

'As a matter of fact I have.'

Here on the terrace of this Mediterranean hotel, surrounded by a polyglot collection of Moslems with long white robes, their head scarves held in place on their foreheads by gold braided cords, by elegant young Lebanese women with their black shining hair falling loose over their shoulders, with smart French cavalry officers with pale blue kepis, with British officers in light gabardine uniforms, with the mountains towering in the background—the beleagured, deprived and rationed Britain that these photographs evoked seemed very far away yet heartbreakingly familiar. It had been a January wedding. The trees that you could glimpse outside were leafless. In the grate was burning a large fire, which must have involved a regime of strict rationing for a week. But there were the family portraits on the walls. There were the Chippendale chairs and table, the Queen Anne bookcase. It all looked as it had four years ago—except that in the centre of the group Michael was in uniform. He looked very handsome, very healthy. Iris was wearing a simple cocktail party dress. She had presumably had an economical trousseau.

'Let's hope it was a real honeymoon,' I said.

'It's strange to think of the life that's going on there now,' he said. 'My father and those three women and my young son. What must he be making of it?'

I asked what were Iris' plans. Was she doing any war work, was she thinking of doing any war work? He shook his head. 'I think that she'll have all she can manage with her share of running Charminster. They used to have six servants, now they've got one cook. Thank heaven I'm not there. Let's go and lunch and compare it with what they're eating there.'

That was in March. During the next three months I was to become increasingly aware that I should need to find myself another posting. I was not the Staff Captain Q. that the Mission needed and I asked for a week's leave in Cairo, in the course of which I could consult the MS branch on the possibility of my finding myself another billet.

At the Canal I changed trains, and took a ferry into Egypt. On the ferry was a young captain with whose face I was familiar but to which I could not put a name. He was wearing an identity bracelet. I edged close enough to be able to read it. Why, but of course, Robin Maugham, whom I had met at the Villa Mauresque five summers before. I re-introduced myself. It was seven o'clock. I had been planning to dine off a sandwich, but this was an occasion that demanded a celebration in the dining car. It was a meal that I remember still with gratitude. We were now on the Egyptian State Railways, and the wagon-lit company was maintaining its pre-war cellar at pre-war rates, content to let its patrons profit. We consumed a superb red Burgundy. I forget its label, but I remember gratefully its depth and richness—and the warm feelings that it nourished. That bottle began a friendship that has been one of the most valued treasures of these my later days; it was a friendship that was also to play a part in Raymond's story.

The next few weeks had for Cairo a curious atmosphere

of suspended animation. As I had been assured, I found no difficulty in getting myself a desk with the military security section of GHQ. A charming and very efficient major was in charge. He did not believe in making work where a need for work did not exist. All he demanded of his officers was a punctilious punctuality. That I dutifully supplied. The war was momentarily at a lull. In July there had been the days of panic when Rommel's tanks had strolled towards the Canal, when wives and secretaries were flown to the safety of South Africa, when the secret files were burnt on the day that was to be called 'Ash Wednesday'; Auchinleck had sent back Rommel 'with a bleeding nose'; Churchill came out to reorganise the Eighth Army; soon it was rumoured that the Eighth Army would be resuming the attack under the new regime. In the meantime life went on, in that bland heavy heat, with party following on party, and the golf club crowded. There were some excellent cricket matches to be watched at the Gezira ground. On Saturdays Wally Hammond was not the only test cricketer to be seen there. I was staying at Shepherd's; and in the evenings I could look out on the screens of two separate outdoor cinemas. At that time the newsreel of the Malta convoy was on show and sleep was rendered impossible by the din of the bombing and the gunfire. That was the only evidence that we were at war. One morning there was a total eclipse of the moon which I watched in broad daylight from my hotel bedroom.

I saw a lot of Robin Maugham during this period. He had been wounded in the head in the Western desert. It had seemed a slight casualty at the time, but its consequences have plagued him all his life. He has been the victim of excruciating headaches. Even then it was apparent that he would be unfit for further combat service. He could have been posted back to England, but he had become interested in Middle East politics. He had the feeling that there was something of use for a person with his powerful connections. This was indeed to prove the case. He was largely responsible for the founding of the Middle East School of Languages behind Beirut. At the moment he was feeling his way towards that. He was a gentleman of leisure, without an occupation;

176

officially awaiting posting in the pool, drawing pay and allowances, staying at the Continental; with his private income he did not have to worry about ways and means.

Not altogether surprisingly, he and Raymond had never met. They belonged to different generations. Raymond had been in Dominica half the time. Their military training had followed different courses, but they, of course, knew a great deal about each other. They could meet now on equal terms, with the same rank, though for someone like Robin, rank and age did not matter. He was, and is, a person of great vitality, great charm, in addition to being a man of outstanding gifts. His father had been Lord Chancellor. He had met and been on terms of friendship with many of the most influential personalities of the day. Yet he met everyone, no matter what their age or position in the social scale, on equal terms. He and Raymond liked each other from the start. And it was through Robin that Raymond became interested in Middle Eastern politics.

It was through Robin that I learned the news that was to re-dramatise Raymond's life. Robin, although he was not occupying an official desk—perhaps for the very reason that he was not—always seemed to get a piece of hot gossip twenty-four hours before anybody else. Moreover he always seemed to have access to an official telephone. It was on the telephone that I learnt that Raymond's nephew Michael had been killed in action.

'I don't know how long it will be before Raymond gets official information. Probably quite a time, and then he'll learn unofficially, through a paragraph in a paper or someone coming up to him in the Gezira, probably the wrong person, in the wrong way. It would be better, wouldn't it, if he learned from one of us?'

'I think it would.'

'From which of us should he learn it, from you or me?'

'From me, I'd say.'

'And so should I. I'll leave you to it.'

I had answered, without hesitation. I had a special reason for not hesitating. I rang Raymond through at once.

'Are you busy now?' I asked.

'Am I ever busy?'

'Are you alone?'

'I am.'

'I've some rather serious news for you. Would you rather I gave it now on the telephone or would you rather we met in private?'

'I'll take it now.'

'Your nephew Michael has been killed in Burma.'

There was a dead silence at the other end. I waited a moment. This was not the only piece of news I had for him. I had a very cogent reason for not hesitating when Robin asked whether he or I should break the news to Raymond. My special piece of news, news which it was unlikely that anyone else in the Middle East possessed, was in its way even more dramatic than Robin's. In a sense my novelist's peeping tom instinct made me wish that I could see how he would react when he heard my news. I wished that I could have seen how his expression changed, but for once my sense of friendship was stronger than my writer's curiosity—it is not so often that it has been, and the fact that it was now is a proof of how very deep my friendship for Raymond was. He was entitled to his privacy.

'I've another piece of news for you,' I said. 'I heard from Eileen three days ago. Iris is pregnant.'

Again there was a silence at the other end. How had he taken this double shock? The silence lasted for fully ninety seconds. When he broke the silence, his voice was firm. Whatever the nature of the shock, he had recovered from it.

'Are you dining anywhere tonight?' he asked.

'No.'

'Then let's meet at the Mohamet Aly at half past eight.'

It was a warm but not an oppressive night. It was good to sit in the open on that wide terrace. 'Let's have half a bottle of non-vintage champagne as an apéritif, then let's order a dish that'll go with a white Burgundy—they've got a good Montrachet here.'

'That's fine by me.'

It would be more than fine, it would be very fine. I was living on my captain's pay and indulgences of which I had taken as a matter of course four years earlier were now no longer within my means. I wondered if Raymond realised this; I questioned it: the rich as a class do not enter imaginatively into the economies that their less affluent friends have to practice. He did not think he was giving me a treat. He thought he was treating the occasion appropriately—as a funeral wake. I had arrived, prepared to leave the strategy of it all to him. Would he talk first about his nephew and his father, or about his own involvement? I was glad that he chose to talk first about himself.

'Do you remember what we were saying about history repeating itself?' he said.

'Of course.'

'That's exactly what's happened, isn't it? Twenty-six years ago I was bidden to the headmaster's study to be told that my brother had been killed in action. He knew, of course, that Margaret was pregnant, but he did not know how much I knew about the facts of life. He said, "This doesn't make any difference to you as far as the title is concerned, your brother was married. That means that he will have an heir. This is an hour of great grief for you because you have lost a brother. You have my sympathy. You have the sympathy of every one of us." Then, as I told you, that young master spilt the beans. "Until we know whether you are going to have a nephew or a niece, we don't know whether you are going to be a Lord or not. It will make a great difference to you if you do become the heir."

'I'm in exactly the same position now. Is Iris going to produce an heir? And do you remember asking me whether I was hoping that Margaret would produce a niece or nephew, and my saying that I didn't care either way, that I was too young to appreciate what was involved, that I had never thought of myself as likely to inherit Charminster, that I was perfectly content to stay as I was? I'm in precisely the same situation now, but today I know what is involved. I've never thought of inheriting a title. I've never said to myself

"If Michael were to be killed . . ." Well, if one were the kind of person who could think that, there wouldn't be much hope for one, in this world or the next, but now that the thing has happened, now that if it's a niece this time and not a nephew, well, I do know what it can mean to me—what it can mean to anyone to be a peer and what it could mean to me in particular . . . it could mean a lot. It's nonsense to say that titles don't mean anything in England where they have a long tradition and a respected one, and where there is a House of Lords—the House of Lords isn't what it was, but it is something, and if I had the right to sit in it and to air my views—well, I'd have a different potential, wouldn't I?'

He looked at me as though he were setting a question which he did not expect me to answer. He was setting the question to himself rather than to me. I waited to hear what he had to say.

There was a pause, a lengthy pause. 'I know what people have said about me. I had promise. A lot was expected of me. I expected a lot of myself. I knew I had special opportunities, special chances. I wanted to make the most of those chances. That's why I didn't hurry. Others might have to hurry but I hadn't. If I waited, the right opportunity was bound to come. But it didn't come. I was getting nowhere. And then there was that curious affinity for Dominica. It seemed to solve my problems. But it couldn't, how could it, an *oubliette* like that, and time went by and I was getting nowhere; it looked as though I never would get anywhere, that I'd missed the bus, as that ass Chamberlain said Hitler had. But perhaps all the time there was at work some hidden providence, that "divinity that shapes our ends", which knew that one day I was going to inherit that title and wouldn't let me get involved in a career that would have been hindered by a title. Suppose, for instance, I'd gone in for politics, as I might well have done. A title would have been the end of that career; it would have precluded me from the House of Commons—maybe that's why I've been disappointing everyone all these years because I have been, I know that . . . it broke my marriage, didn't it, that not settling down to anything; that escape route to Dominica . . . the *daemon*, the inner voice that guided
180

Socrates, without recognising it as such. I've been aware of it, I've listened to it. I've never gone against it; I've heard it at all the points of crisis. I didn't understand it, but something has always said "Don't do that, do this." Perhaps that was because fate knew that one day I should inherit.'

'So this time you're hoping that it'll be a niece.'

'This time I know it'll be a niece. If it weren't to be, then everything that has happened, up to now, would make no sense.'

He spoke with a certainty that astonished me. He spoke as though he had suddenly and at last found himself. My silence took him off his guard. 'Do you think I shouldn't be saying that?'

'I'm surprised at your saying that.'

'Wouldn't it be better for everyone if I did inherit?'

That startled me. For whom would it be better? For himself, yes, no doubt for Timothy Alexander possibly, but what about Iris, Margaret and Eileen? He sensed my reaction. 'Try and picture how it will be if Iris' child is a boy,' he said. 'Iris is twenty-three. She'll feel that she has to stay on at Charminster, because it's going to be her son's. If he's going to inherit the place, he must get accustomed to it. It's exactly the same position that Margaret was in, in 1916. But there's a generation's difference, and that means a lot, in his case. My father was in his late forties then. Now he'll soon be eighty. That can't give him so very many years; picture the place when he goes. A very young boy, surrounded by heaven knows how many women; his mother, two grandmothers; will they both stay on? Margaret will, almost certainly, where else is she to go? She's still in her forties, but even so her whole life's been lived there. And Eileen, in what condition will Whistler be when the Japs have finished with him? Will he be able to re-start his London business? It was a chancy business at the best by all accounts, an income based on commissions. And who can tell what the market for that kind of operation is going to be when the war is over? He might find it easier to live on Eileen's money. Three women under the same roof with an infant schoolboy. Three women and none of them in a position to decide anything. I suppose I'll be one of the trustees of the will, but can you picture me interfering in that hornets' nest? As I say, those three women, and none of them with any authority. For the first few years there'll be my father in control nominally, but will he be in a state to bother? Poor old man, this must have broken him, and then in a few years' time there'll be a schoolboy. It'll be twenty years before he can assert himself. Think of those twenty years. It would be chaos. What a wretched start in life for the poor boy. No, I'm not being selfish. It'll be better for everyone—not only me, if the child's a girl. Did Eileen tell you when the infant is expected?'

'January.'

'Six months. I'm glad I'm spending them here, not there. I don't envy them. The suspense, not knowing how it will turn out, and the general atmosphere of gloom. Poor Iris. This should be the happiest time of her life and it'll be the worst. And my poor father. First his son. Then his grandson. He had transferred all the hopes that he had built round Adrian onto Michael. He's nothing left to live for. He can't start again with a great-grandson. My poor, poor father.'

'He won't let you take Michael's place?'

Raymond shook his head. 'He always saw me in the rôle of the second son. He was a good father, by his own standards. He was fond of me. He did his best for a second son. He couldn't be expected at his age to rearrange his view of me. It'll be easier for him to concentrate on Timothy Alexander. That'll be what I'll do when I go back. I'll make him interested in my boy; arrange cricket classes at Lord's. That kind of thing. I'll try to make his last years as good for him as possible. Try to make him see Timothy Alexander as taking on from Adrian and Michael. That'll be my rôle.'

He had no doubt at all that Iris' child would be a girl. Would he, I wondered, be very disappointed if history were to repeat itself again and for a second time the title were to elude him? This time, however, his prophecy was to prove correct.

12

I was no longer in Cairo when the news came through. As I had foreseen in August, I could not afford to live in Cairo on a captain's pay without exercising economies that would have proved, in the long run, humiliating. I should not have been able to feel myself, and I leapt at the opportunity that was offered by the formation of the new Persia and Iraq force, with its headquarters in Baghdad.

The former city of the caliphs no longer offered the attractions and temptations that it had in the days of Haroun al Rashid. It was a hot and dusty city, with a climate that was considered too exacting for the feminine personnel of the armed forces. There was no indigenous international population. It was a Moslem city. I was assured that a captain on the staff could live comfortably on his pay. And indeed I was never to experience the slightest difficulty in doing so. Moreover I was to find there in a specialised branch of counter-espionage, work for which I felt myself to be fitted by taste and training, and in which for the remainder of the war I was fully and, I felt, usefully employed. My thirty-two months in Baghdad were for me the happiest and most satisfactory period of my military service.

I did, however, feel cut off from what I had considered my real life. In Beirut and Cairo old friends and acquaintances were constantly passing though with news of London and New York. But Baghdad was off the beaten track. It had few personal attractions for the VIP. Robin Maugham was one of the very few friends who did pay us visits. He was still on paper 'a gentleman of leisure' but he was extremely busy organising the school of Middle East languages. Such a school was badly needed; and there had been already many tentative proposals about forming one. Such proposals had proved unfruitful, partially because those who were trying to sponsor them would have personally profited from the scheme; they were colonels who hoped to be brigadiers, and brigadiers who hoped to be major-generals. Robin

Maugham obviously had no personal axe to grind. He would not be on the staff of such a college, and through his family connections he had access to high ranking brass. His low rank was no hindrance to him; in fact it was an advantage. It was easier for a field marshal to meet a captain than for him to meet a brigadier on equal terms. For many years the school of Middle East studies above Beirut has been doing very valuable work; without Robin Maugham it might never have got started—certainly not under such favourable auspices.

Robin's activities in connection with the school brought him to Baghdad more than once. On his first visit, he called at my office on the river, bringing as what he called 'a belated Christmas present', a leather-bound manuscript book. It looked very pretty and its empty pages challenged me. I began to fill them with day-to-day notes about my military peradventures, which were eventually published in a book called *His Second War*. The manuscript book is now included in the Alec Waugh collection in the Boston Universities Library.

It was from Robin that I learnt that Raymond was the uncle of a niece.

'Is he pleased about that?' I asked.

'Apparently. But he didn't seem surprised.'

'Is it making any difference to his immediate plans?'

'Not as far as I can see. He's got interested in Middle East affairs.'

'That's due to you, I guess.'

'It may be. He's certainly excited about the school. He foresees a lot of trouble after the war, in Palestine.'

'I wouldn't contradict him.'

'Nor I. He feels that it's important that the right people should learn all they can about the Arabs, which is what I feel too. The more we understand each other, the less confusion there will be. At any rate we shall know what the issues are.'

'I thought he might feel a need to go back to England.'

'He did, but only for a moment; Charminster is still his father's. He hasn't inherited anything from his nephew.

What there was went into trust for Iris, with Eileen as trustee.'

'Eileen should have control of quite a lot of money.'

'As far as anyone has at the moment.'

I thought of the peculiar atmosphere in that house; the old man nursing his grief, the schoolboy who would one day become the Lord and Master, the infant who might well live to wish that she had been born a male, and the three women, all in their different ways dependent upon an officer in Censorship who at the moment could not be bothered to come back to see them.

A few days later I heard from Eileen. 'It's all very strange here now. The uncertainty is over. And on the surface everything seems the same. My son instead of my grandson is going to be a peer. That's how it affects me. Though my grandson would have been a peer in a few years' time, whereas most likely I shall never see my son sitting in the House of Lords. Margaret is probably the one whom this has touched the most. It makes her whole life seem futile. She had given up everything for Michael. She had done everything to make Michael worthy of the position that he would hold; which would have been her husband's position, after all. And now that Michael is dead, her husband has no real part in the life of Charminster. I feel for Margaret; and I don't feel any the less for her because I fancy that *au fond* she resents me—me with my four husbands, she with her one.

'She feels I've had more than my share; and now she has nothing. We're in a strange position in our relation to each other, both being the grandmother of the child. She said one rather pathetic thing to Iris—not in my presence, Iris repeated it to me. She said it before the child was born. "If you have a son you may feel an obligation to stay on here, because even in these days inheriting a title is some-thing. A peer has a different life from a commoner. That'll be for you to decide for yourself, but if you have a daughter, get out of here as soon as possible; your mother and I can look after her. You're too young to be a slave. You must make a life for yourself; a life of your own." That was very

185

sound advice; and I'll do my best to see that Iris follows it, but don't you think it's pathetic that Margaret should have said just that. She does realise now that she's been sacrificed. What is she going to do with herself . . . I haven't asked her. In one way there's nothing to keep her here and, after all, she's not so old; she's under fifty and she's still attractive, men like her still . . . She might well marry again; it's hard to tell. Myself I'm lucky, I suppose. I've got my path clearly marked; to look after Timothy Alexander until the war is over and Derrick's back again . . . that's enough of a problem —we were only together for less than a year after our marriage, less than that really; and most of our marriage was weekend leaves, hardly a marriage at all. Much less of a marriage than mine to Raymond or to Mark. Mark, by the way, is very grand right now. He's a major-general, in the Ministry of Supply. He's modest about it; or rather I should say, he's rather smug about it. "I had the good luck to be in a lift that was going up," is his phrase for it. He has three children now; just got the third; he was clearly well shot of me; how less real my life with him seems than my life with Raymond. And it's the same with Derrick; none of that seems very real; because I suppose he wasn't as real as Raymond. If the war had come a little earlier, I wouldn't have broken with Raymond. That's funny to think of after all; I should now be about to be a peeress. Titles and all that don't cut much ice with me; but it would have been fun to go to the Abbey for the coronation in those gorgeous robes. I made a fool of myself, I guess, but it's over now. I can't get any more on this air letter card so I'll have to close. Take care of your nice self. I'll keep you posted.'

She kept her word. Every three weeks or so a blue airmail letter card addressed in her neat, back-sloping script lay upon my desk. I was very grateful for them. One lived for air mail in the Middle East. And the new air letter card was the perfect medium for correspondence. It dictated its own length, in the way that a sonnet does. You had to concentrate to get said all you wanted to, yet there was room for some discursiveness. I hoped it would survive the war.

She hardly ever heard from Whistler. When she did, his

letters contained no news; a mere bulletin of trivial facts. It was three years since she had seen him. 'I find it hard to remember that I was even married to him. He seems like someone I had an affair with. Which is really all it ever was. I sometimes wonder why he was so anxious to get married. Does he wonder that himself? Well, anyhow, he's got someone to come back to now, poor chap. I'll do my best to make him feel that I was worth it.'

Some of her information I passed on to Raymond; in particular the references to Timothy Alexander. I presumed that he had links with Charminster, with lawyers, with his father and perhaps through Margaret. They had been good friends. But I welcomed the excuse to keep in touch with him. He was unlikely to come to Baghdad. I was unlikely to go to Cairo. I preferred to take my annual leave in Beirut. As far as I could gather he was enjoying his existence. He was now a major; and was continuing to interest himself in Arab politics. Occasionally a friend of his would present a letter of introduction. Such letters would be preceded by a personal and private letter: 'I have given a chit to an old friend, whom I can best describe as a *boulevadier*. His interests are social and alcoholic. You can accommodate *those* tastes. I gather that females are in short supply on the banks of the Tigris. Don't worry about that. There is no shortage of that here for anyone with funds, which he is,' or again 'I'm not sure if you will like the chap to whom I have given a letter of introduction. But he has a fantastic fervour for your brother and wants to tell you that E is the greatest writer in the world. I know you happen to agree with him but at the same time it's boring, I presume, for a writer to listen to someone's ravings about another writer, particularly if it's one's younger brother, but do be patient; he happens to be my GI and could make life uncomfortable for me if he chose.' Two or three such letters reached me, then in the spring of 1944 a rather different approach was made.

'I have given a chit,' he wrote, 'to an English journalist, a female, a Miss Susan Irving. Perhaps you have heard of her. She works for a Northern Syndicate. She has got a war correspondent's sponsoring. Her bosses in England are responsible for her finances. She is solvent, as far as I can gather—at any rate she has made no trouble here and if she were not solvent, I fancy that I should have heard. She wants to do what she calls "personality articles" about troops in Paiforce. She feels, and I think she is right in feeling, that troops in your command—which has ceased to be an active centre of operations—are getting disgruntled because they suspect that their families in England feel that they are having what you called in 1914–18 "a cushy war". with a good climate, plenty of food and no danger. She wants to write some articles that would present them to the home front as heroic though at the moment unbelligerent warriors. Isn't that what your command needs? At any rate, I'll be grateful if you can help her. She may need permits to get to certain areas. Do help her.'

He was right in thinking that the men of Paiforce were in a disgruntled mood. Two batteries of artillery and at least one infantry battalion that had never been in action, suspected that now they never would be. They were afraid that when eventually they returned to England they would not be welcomed as heroes, but sniffed at as scrimshankers who had had a lucky war. Susan Irving could be doing a very valuable public relations job for Paiforce.

Her name was not familiar to me. Raymond had not told me her age nor described her attractions. Recently the Middle East had been enlivened by the presence of that now widely acclaimed journalist Claire Holingworth. I could scarcely hope that she would be as attractive as Claire Holingworth, but I had a feeling that no female who was not young and reasonably nice to look at would have been posted to an area so deprived of feminine attractions. I greatly looked forward to her visit.

I was not to be disappointed. To say that Susan Irving was as attractive as Claire would be to say a lot, but she was definitely pretty. She was blonde, with one of those appealing pushed-in faces. She had a neat, trim figure. She was *petite*, but she looked resolute and competent. I would have guessed her to be in her later twenties.

Raymond was unaware of the exact nature of my security

activities. Passes for visiting journalists did not come within my parish. But Baghdad—as a military fortress—was a small place. I could be of use to her. Or rather, I could introduce her to the top brass who could be useful to her. I planned a small dinner party in her honour. But I thought that I would first ask her to a meal *a deux*, so that I could find out what was on her mind.

I invited her to lunch at the Alwiyah, the Baghdad country club of which resident officers were honorary members. We could bring over and pay corkage on wine that we had purchased at the Naafi. We were issued with chits, on which the club profited by issuing us with ninety dinars' worth at the cost of a hundred dinars. It was very useful. To entertain in one of the town hotels was beyond my means.

The Alwiyah was at its most charming in April. Winter was over, but summer had not begun: the swimming pool was not yet open. But it was neither too hot nor too cool to lunch out of doors. I looked forward to my lunch. By now I had been there twenty months and this was only the third time that I had had a meal there alone in feminine company. She looked very lush and appetising in a light cotton frock.

'Usually,' I said, 'one shouldn't talk business till the coffee's reached. Let's break the rules and get our business settled right away. Then we can gossip.'

She laughed. 'I really haven't any business to discuss. What little I have is managing itself. I wanted to meet you. Let's gossip right away.'

We did. We soon found that we had a number of mutual Fleet Street friends, but I very soon realised that it was not to talk about them that she had asked Raymond to give her a note to me. She wanted to gossip about him.

'He tells me that you're his oldest friend,' she said. 'I'd have given anything to have known him when he was an undergraduate.'

'He wasn't so very different.'

'He wasn't? No? I can understand that. How old is he? Forty-one? He doesn't look that old.'

'He hasn't lost his hair. He hasn't put on weight.' I might have added, but I did not, that time and trouble and adversity had not drawn on his face the lines that both age and give character to a man of forty.

'When did you meet him first?'

'Autumn 1922.'

'When I was four years old. When I could scarcely speak. Now I've caught him up. To think of all the things that were happening to him when I was in a nursery, when I was a kid at school. To think of all the women he's been in love with. Twenty years . . . at the rate of one a year . . . at least one a year.'

'He was married part of that time, remember.'

'That wouldn't have hindered him, would it?'

'I've an idea it might have done.'

'But his marriage didn't last that long. And half of that time he was away.'

'That's true.'

'What was his wife like?'

I did my best to describe Eileen. She listened attentively. 'She sounds good fun. I'd like to meet her one day.'

'That shouldn't be difficult. You could say you wanted to interview the mother of the future Baron.'

'Could I? Yes, I suppose I could. It's useful to be a journalist. You can manage to meet anyone you want. Was he very much in love with her?'

'I wouldn't say so, no.'

'How come then? How did she trap him?'

I explained to her what had happened.

'I see. It doesn't sound too romantic. Tell me about the others. Was one of them like me? I think I should tell you, by the way, I'm having an affair with him.'

'I was beginning to suspect you were.'

'Were you? Am I that obvious? Well, I suppose I am. There's a glow about one, isn't there, when one's in love. That's one of the nice things about being in love. One's like a honey pot; all the men stare at one. Tell me about the others.'

'I've only met one or two.'

Three to be exact, I reminded myself, apart from that Carib girl. 'But he must have talked about the others.'

I shook my head. 'He doesn't talk about that kind of thing.'

'Doesn't he? I'm rather glad he doesn't. Some men do, don't they? Another scalp upon a belt. I wouldn't like that; no, not at all. I don't want to be bragged about. Yet at the same time, I'd like him to be proud of me. Do you know what I'd really like?'

'You tell me what you'd really like.'

'To be able to think that twenty years from now, you and he should sit over dinner in one of your clubs and reminisce about the past and wonder which was the most satisfactory of all your love affairs, and for him to say "You know, by and large the best times I ever had were with Susan Irving."'

'I don't see why he shouldn't be saying that.'

'You don't? That's dear of you. Now I don't need to ask you about those girls. If you think that in twenty years he might put me at the head of the list that does mean, doesn't it, that there hasn't been anyone up to now so glamorous as to consign me to a second place, and if that is so, then I've got a right to hope that there won't be anyone in the future to outshine me. After all, he's forty now. When would you say a man was at his prime?'

'Do you mean physically?'

'Yes.'

'Then he's just past his prime.'

'In one sense, yes.'

'What do you mean, "in one sense"?'

'That a man can have the grand passion of his life when he's past his prime, a desperate recovering of youth—a last time feeling. Doesn't history tell us that? What's your experience?'

'I'm forty-five—nearly forty-six. I'll give you my answer to that in ten years' time.'

'I see.'

It was a side of the subject that she was not anxious to explore. She tried another tack: 'Would you agree that in an affair there's nothing more important than the setting?'

191

'What do you mean by setting?'

'The opportunities to meet: the background; the chances of privacy. How much you can be together; the places, the times you can be together. Is there anything worse than the sandwiching of someone into odd half-hours; having to make the most of stolen moments. Did you ever read Maupassant's *Notre Cœur*?'

'It's one of my favourite novels.'

'Do you remember how exasperated the heroine felt at having to be available on fixed days of the week, at fixed times, of how unromantic it all became. Wouldn't you say that nothing can kill love faster than all that?'

'I would.'

'You'd say, wouldn't you, that there are times when the first excitement has worn off, that the whole thing becomes more bother than it's worth.'

'I'd go further than that. I'd say that women who have had that happen to them are reluctant to go into an affair that'll be a repetition of that same situation.'

'Then that's where we are so very lucky, Raymond and I. We've got the perfect set-up. Cairo in the first place. If you know of a more glamorous place, well, is there one? And Raymond has that delightful flat in Gezira. He doesn't share it; he has it to himself. I'm in a hotel, but it's a discreet, no question-asked hotel with a well-tipped night staff. Then I've my car; you can guess what a difference that makes.

'We don't have to worry about money. Our schedules can be made to dovetail easily. He has a fixed routine: 8 a.m. to 1 p.m. and 5 p.m. to 8 p.m. six days of the week. About once in a blue moon he's duty officer. I always know where to find him. I, on the other hand, am at an editor's beck and call. I have to go where the hot story is. But Cairo is my base, I can never be away for long. And those separations give the affair the kick that an affair needs. I may be sent to Alexandria or to Tripoli. "I'll be away five days," I tell him. But I'll work like blazes so that I can telescope those five days into four. Then he'll be sitting at his desk at half past six and suddenly his telephone will ring and it's my voice. "Are you doing anything this evening?" "Nothing that I can't cancel if you're around," he'll say. "Then expect me at your flat at half past nine. And have a lively bottle on ice." I have a key to his flat. Sometimes I play pranks on him. He has a dinner that he can't avoid—he has that sometimes—not too often, once every three weeks or so, then maybe I'll let myself into his flat during the evening and when he comes back, he'll find me in a kimono, curled up on his sofa, reading and there'll be a bottle cooling in a bucket. Sometimes I'll get back from an assignment early in the morning. I'll go back to my hotel, I'll shower, change my things, then hurry over to Gezira. I'll let myself in very quietly; undress like a mouse, slide into bed beside him. He's got a heavenly great double bed, and quite likely he won't wake until his usual waking time, you can guess what kind of a laugh we have when he wakes up and finds me there. I'll bet he's not had that kind of fun with any other girl.'

'I certainly haven't.'

'Then there's another thing, about having an affair in wartime. You can't look ahead. You can't make plans. You have to live in the moment. You know how it is in peacetime. When the first excitement of a new thing has passed, you begin to wonder where it's headed; what's it all leading to. You feel that everything ought to be leading somewhere. You may not want to be married, but you want marriage to be discussed. You want him to want to marry you.'

I set myself a mental sum. Peacetime was four and a half years ago. She had been barely twenty then. Out of how much experience was she speaking? I remember how Judy had discussed the problems of an affair when she was relatively inexperienced. I guessed that Susan now, as Judy then, was talking to impress herself.

'One knows an affair can't last,' she was continuing. 'Just as one knows that love itself dies down, that you can't live at that high peak forever, but in marriage, because you expect the marriage itself to last, you can pretend that the love that started it will last. That's how it is in marriage, isn't it?'

'It's supposed to be.'

193

'But in an affair you know that it can't go on forever and that can't help spoiling it, just a little. There's a niggling feeling that you should be doing something to preserve it, but in wartime there's nothing to be done. You can say to one another "When it's all over, we can start wondering if there's anything we can do." '

'Have you actually said that to Raymond?'

'Not actually, but it's been inferred.'

I smiled. 'You've the perfect setting for an affair,' I said, 'I'm pretty sure that twenty years from now Raymond will be saying "the peak of everything was those months with Susan".'

'You believe that; you really do? Oh, I'm so glad, that's what I wanted to hear you say. You've made my day for me. You've made my whole visit to Baghdad. You know him better than anyone else knows him and if you can say that ... Oh, I'm so happy, happy, happy.' Her voice glowed. Her eyes shone. I envied Raymond.

'When are you coming to Cairo?' she was asking me.

'That depends upon my Lords and Masters.'

'Couldn't you pull strings? Everyone has some strings to pull. Come to Cairo and we'll have a party, such a party. When you see us together, you'll recognise how right we are for one another.'

I would have enjoyed that party, but it was not till the following February that the chance to pull that right string came my way, and by then it was too late for the party she had envisaged. Early in June, the second front had opened, the Middle East was a back number. Susan had been recalled to England, on her way to France for stories about the D-day landings, and both Raymond and I were visualising an early return to civilian life.

The Germans were on the run, and the formula for demobilisation had been announced. As soon as Germany had surrendered, the process would begin. We were arranged in groups according to our age and length of service; I was nearly forty-seven, I had been in the army since the start. I was listed in the second group to be sent home. Raymond, who was five years younger, and had not managed to get into the army until Christmas 1939, would not arrive in England until three months after me at least. We talked a little about Susan, but most of the time we discussed our own immediate plans.

'What are *you* planning?' I asked.

'I've made no plans. I'm waiting to see how things are. I want to see how my father is. He's eighty but his health is sound. He may well last another ten years; you've heard Iris' news, I suppose.'

Iris had got engaged to a young American, an Air Force pilot. 'Have you any details about him?' I asked.

'Nothing that doesn't make him eminently eligible. Twenty-eight years old; Groton and Amhurst: a corporation lawyer. Seaboard society.'

'It almost makes him too eligible.'

We laughed at that. We were both remembering the carnival at Roseau.

'I wish you'd go down to Charminster . . . see how they all are, and write and tell me. I'd like to be put on my guard.'

'I'll do my best.'

I left Baghdad in the first week of June. Within a few hours of getting back, I started to pull strings for a passage to New York. With any luck, I was told, I should be able to get one early in September. I got in touch with Eileen and arranged to go down to Charminster at the end of August, and then a week before I was due to go there, a bomb was dropped on Hiroshima and the world became a different place for everyone. For Eileen as much as anyone.

She met me at the station in a pony trap. 'We have to be very careful of our petrol,' she explained. She had come alone. 'I wanted to have a gossip with you first. Nothing's the way it was. You'll realise that right away, but I thought I had better put you in the picture. It's made more difference to Iris than to anyone. It meant that her boyfriend won't have to fly against the Japs. For him the war is over. Think what that means to her. After losing Michael?'

'Has she got over that?'

'She's very young. You can't stay wedded to your grief.'

'Will she get married right away?'

'I don't see why not. He's twenty-eight. He'll want to start a new life as soon as possible.'

'What about the baby?'

'I guess they'll leave her here—for the present. Iris is not maternal. She's never had a chance to be. She was in khaki the moment the child was weaned. Two years at her age is a long, long time.'

'And you'll soon have Derrick home.'

'I know.'

There was a pause. It was a complicated situation. One day, one day soon, probably, but no one could tell how soon, Charminster would belong to Raymond, but in the meantime it was the old man who made the decisions.

'How is the old man?' I asked.

'You'll see; he's in good health. He had the good sense to lay down a cellar before the war. He's never had to miss his glass of claret.'

A lot of change can take place in four years in a man of his age. There is a point when a man who has scarcely changed in thirty years will become an old man in seven weeks. But Raymond's father looked very much as he had that afternoon, nearly four years ago, when I had come down to say goodbye before sailing for the Middle East. He still stood erect. Everyone in England looked shabby in those days of clothes rationing, but his rough tweed suit fitted smoothly over his shoulders; he wore a Rambler bow tie, so that you could not tell if his collar was frayed; his worn brown brogues were well polished. His colour was good. He walked slowly, but steadily; he walked with a stick but did not seem to need it.

I told him that I had seen Raymond in February. 'Oh yes, dear Raymond. He's had a good war; an MC and a majority. Does his wound worry him?'

'It doesn't seem to.'

'That's good. That's very good. You know what everybody wanted in the first war; a cushy blighty; that's what they wanted and then leave in London. London was different then. No real bombing, no real rationing, just those shaded lights: "The Bingboys are here." "If you were the only girl in the world" . . . a different war that first one. How I wished that I'd been young enough. But I wasn't . . . that's how it was. I wasn't.'

'Raymond should be back in a couple of months,' I told him. 'He'll find a change in Timothy Alexander. Five years is a long time.'

'Five years is it, as much as that? A real schoolboy. Another year at Summerfields, then Eton. I'll bet he'll play at Lord's, as his uncle did—you never saw his uncle, did you?'

'No, I didn't know Adrian. I didn't meet Raymond till after the war. But of course I knew Michael.'

'Ah, yes, Michael. He was a good batsman too, not quite as good as his father would have been. Adrian's style, so smooth, so easy, a Spooner in embryo; such a sportsman too. I remember a match for the village against a side from London. Adrian went in first, made his fifty, was seeing the ball like a balloon, but he got himself out; didn't want to steal the show, even though the match wasn't won yet, by a long chalk, but he wanted the boys to win it or lose it on their own. That was the spirit.'

It was Michael, not Adrian, who had played that innings, I remembered watching it. The old man was confusing his grandson with his son; history had repeated itself. The same tragedy a second time; and now he concentrated on Timothy Alexander in the same way that he had transferred his allegiance to his grandson after Adrian's death. He did not seem particularly interested in Raymond. He had never pictured him as the heir to Charminster. Charminster should go to a young man who cared for cricket; Adrian, Michael and now Timothy Alexander.

My godson had certainly grown into a good-looking boy; he had not the dramatic good looks that his father must have had at his age, but he was tall for his age, he was well proportioned, he had the Peronne profile. I had kept in touch with him, sending him a packet of dates every now and then.

'I've seen your father in Egypt several times,' I said. 'He'll be home soon. He's very excited about that. He'll hardly recognise you.'

'I'll recognise him. A man doesn't change much at that age. You look the same.'

That was a rather adult remark for him to make, I thought. 'Daddy tells me that you were catching spies in Baghdad. Did you catch a lot?'

'Seven.'

'That doesn't seem very many.'

'One spy, if he's a good one, can do a lot of damage.'

'What kind of damage?'

'In our case, he could tell the Germans if we had a lot of troops in Baghdad. If the Germans knew we had a lot, they would believe that we were going to attack through Turkey, so they would have to have troops on the Turkish border.'

'But we didn't attack through Turkey.'

'I know, but we wanted the Germans to think we would.'

'Why?'

'Because then they'd have to keep their troops on the Turkish frontier instead of sending them to the Western desert. We made one of the spies we captured send false information to the Germans. We called it our deception campaign.'

'That's clever. How did he send his message?'

When I had been engaged in counter-espionage work—work that was as exciting as anything that I had ever done—I had warned myself that I should have to be very careful not to reveal secrets when I got back to England. Everyone, I fancied, would be fiercely inquisitive about how counter-espionage agents work. But I found that no one took the slightest interest in what I had been doing; they wanted to tell me how they had dodged buzz-bombs and how they had wangled clothing and food coupons. Timothy Alexander was the first person to take any interest in my exploits. I explained to him how spies used secret inks. 'They had pencils that looked like matches, and they would put them in their collars instead of stiffeners. They would smuggle them into Baghdad on the Orient Express.' I told him about water writing. 'Have you got a paintbrush?' I asked. He brought one and a glass of water. I worked the paintbrush into a fine hard point, dipped it in some water, then wrote on a white sheet of paper. 'Now let it dry,' I said. We waited. The sheet was blank. 'Now warm it in front of an electric fire. Do you see?'

The water handwriting showed dark against the white. 'They were beautiful script writers,' I said. 'They would write their messages in between the lines of an ordinary letter.'

'How did you find them out?'

'There might be something suspicious in the letter. It might be very dull. We'd wonder why anyone should take all that trouble to write so dull a letter. Or again we might feel that someone was writing too often to someone he did not seem very fond of. It's funny the kinds of thing that make one suspicious; when you're on the scent.'

His eyes widened with excitement. He examined the paper carefully. He hesitated. He seemed to be about to say something. Then changed his mind. 'Did you actually arrest any men?' he asked.

'Yes.'

'How many?'

'Five.'

'Were they very frightened?'

'Not in the least. They pretended to be surprised. They pretended to be innocent.'

'And they were guilty all right?'

'Oh yes.'

'I read a story about a murderer. When he was arrested he said "Thank god; the strain of being on the run had become too great." '

'There was one fellow our group arrested who fainted dead off when our man came behind him with a revolver. But that was in Teheran, I wasn't there.'

'I wonder how I'd feel if I was on the run,' he said.

'I hope you never are.'

'It would be exciting all the same.'

At lunch I sat next to Iris. I was curious to see what style was maintained in war conditions. The table looked much the same. The silver *épergne* in the centre—a pattern of ostriches and palms—was brightly polished. A row of dishes had been arranged along the sideboard. There was a salad: there were potatoes in their jackets; there was a bowl of cabbage. There was a loaf of bread; and various jars containing jam and pickles. There was a bowl of fruit. An entrée dish was simmering above a flame. It looked like a buffet meal. There were no servants, but there was no free-for-all atmosphere. The three women had apparently allocated their respective duties. Neither I nor the old man had to rise from our seats. We were each given an ample helping from the entrée dish, which proved to contain sausages and kidneys. We were then presented with our vegetables. In front of my plate and the old man's was a small silver dish containing butter. Otherwise there was no butter on the table. The sausages and kidneys proved to be excellent. Two decanters containing red wine stood in front of my host. One of them was unstoppered. A wine glass had been set in front of my place and of his. Before the others were glass tankards; there was a large jug containing cider, from which they helped themselves. 'These young people say that they can't take wine at lunch. Makes them sleepy, they say; what's wrong with that, I ask: mustn't make a fetish of this war effort, particularly now that the war is over; a short siesta is good for everyone. Still, if that's how they feel, who am I to interfere and in this case it means all the more for us. We'll finish off this bottle; it's too old to be kept hanging about, after waiting all this time.'

He raised the glass to the light, examined, then held it above his mouth. He sniffed, 'Good on the nose,' he said. He sipped appreciatively.

'I remember that you were a Burgundian not a Bordelais,' he said. 'This is an Alare-Corton; a '34; not an estate bottled wine, but I think you'll like it.'

'It's heaven to me,' I said. The stoppered and half-full decanter contained a Cockburn '34.

'Too young for it,' he said, 'but I'm keeping the '27s until Raymond's back. We'll have to work out a policy together. With all this bombing, I didn't see any point in holding back. I've had my glass of port every night I've dined at this table since I came of age. I saw no reason to stop just because there was a war. How do you like this port?' he said.

'It's nectar to me, but then I'm prejudiced. I've had no vintage port since 1941—only a glass or two of tawny in Cairo at the Turf Club.'

'Port's what you set most store by, isn't it?'

'I'm probably laying up a heritage of gout; but when the time comes, I hope I'll have the decency not to grumble.'

The old man chuckled. 'I don't believe in that old canard about vintage port and burgundy being bad for one. I think that it's a piece of propaganda put out by the Bordeaux shippers. I'm eighty. I've never had a twinge of gout.'

I may add here in parenthesis as I write these lines, that at the end of my seventy-fourth year, in spite of my addiction to red burgundy and vintage port, I have not yet suffered any discomfort in my big toe.

The old man took a second sip—'I wonder if there's anything in my life that has given me so much pleasure as vintage port. I enjoyed it at twenty; I enjoy it now at eighty. What else can one say that of? But I shall have to work out a new policy when Raymond's back. The port we've got may be irreplaceable. All these import restrictions. They may force the shippers to start bottling in Oporto. It won't be the same thing.'

Talk at lunch was general for the most part; but while the entrée was being cleared away and the fruit and cake set upon the table, Iris and I did have a brief three minutes of talk together. 'This is strange for me,' she said, 'seeing you again, just when I'm going to say goodbye to this particular world forever.'

'Oh, come now, surely . . .'

'Yes, oh come now, surely . . . I'm going to America in October and will I ever come back? I question it.'

'Come now, I hate to repeat myself, but you've an English daughter.'

'Have I? yes, of course, but will she think of herself as mine? will I, and this is more important, think of her as mine? Three years ago I was a widow, pregnant, saying to myself, you may be carrying under your heart the heir to a title two centuries old; then suddenly I discovered I was not going to be that at all; that my daughter was going to be Miss Mary Peronne, that and no more, and that I was simply a war widow. One of a million others, that my child's lot was to be no different from any other child's, and then before I knew where I was, I found that I was a GI's bride-to-be; and I was issued with a brochure, explaining to me how I should behave as a citizeness of the great Republic; that I wasn't English any longer, and as I sat with this brochure in my hand I said, "So this is who you are after all." Then I added, "Well, and perhaps that isn't so bad. At least someone has taken the trouble to write this brochure to explain to me who I am," and I said to myself, "Maybe that isn't at all a bad thing to be, so don't start feeling sorry for yourself." And do you know what I thought then, maybe this'll surprise you, I shan't be Uncle Raymond's step-daughter any more, and that just a little saddened me, because that's something I had rather enjoyed being.'

'May I tell him that?'

'Of course you may. It's true. When Mummy told me that she was going to marry Uncle Derrick, one of the first things I thought was "That means I shan't see Uncle Raymond any more." And one of the afterthoughts to Michael, I mean to the happiness of falling in love with Michael, was being able to think "he's Uncle Raymond's nephew. I'm not going to lose him after all." And now once again I am going to lose him.'

'You needn't say that, need you?'

'Oh yes, I need. I'm not going to fool myself. This is the end of England for me. I'm in love with Franklin. I'll make him a good wife and that means I've got to be a good American.'

'You may not find that so difficult.'

'Why do you say that?'

'It's a wonderful country; they're a wonderful people. I can't help envying you—just a little.'

'Have you ever thought of becoming an American?'

'It's different for a man.'

'Is it? Perhaps it is. A man has to go on being what he starts as. He can't change his name in the way a woman does. She's the wife of the man she marries, ninety-nine times in a hundred.'

She paused. I half changed the subject.

'What made you feel that Raymond was so special?'

'That's something that I've asked myself. It wasn't only his looks, and they are something, aren't they?'

'He's the best looking man I've ever seen.'

'You don't use the word "beautiful" for a man; it sounds effeminate, but beautiful is the only adjective that's right for him. It was a delight to look at him. But it was so much more than that. Does restful sound an odd word to use? He was so restful to be with.'

I knew what she meant. Most human beings are trying to be something, or to appear something. That puts a strain on them, which in its turn puts a strain on you. Raymond never did that. 'Have you ever heard anyone read poetry the way he did?' she asked.

'My father read poetry beautifully.'

'Did he? Then you were lucky. That explains you and Evelyn. Uncle Raymond reading poetry was . . . well, it was so effortless. He let the poetry speak for itself. I shall never forget those evenings at Dominica, sitting out on that verandah, with the colours changing on the mountains, all those shades of green, and the rain sweeping across the valleys, all those valleys, and all that rain and all those greens.'

'Do you often think about Dominica?'

'I often dream about it.'

'Are they happy dreams?'

'Yes and no. I wake up thinking that I'm in Dominica. Then I realise that I'm not. For a moment it's a relief. Then I feel rather sorry. I'll never see it again, I tell myself.'

'Is Raymond in your dreams of it?'

'That's again, yes and no. He's never there but he's always about to be there, if you know what I mean. He's always expected to be arriving any moment.'

Was that symbolic of Raymond, I asked myself? Never quite on the stage in other people's lives; expected, in the wings.

'I wonder if I'll ever see him again,' she said.

'Your daughter is his great-niece, don't forget.'

'There's the Atlantic in between; that's quite a stretch of water.'

'I'll often be coming over. I'll liaise between you.'

'Oh, do do that.'

Our talk made me a little wistful on my journey back—wistful on Raymond's account. I had had only a few words with Margaret. She had sat at the foot of the table, away from me and directly after lunch she had gone up to the nursery, to relieve the village girl who came in for baby-sitting for a few hours every day. She had asked me about my plans, in a way that no one else had done. Most of my friends had assumed that a writer went back to his desk and picked up his pen where he had left it. 'Won't you find it difficult to begin again, to know what to write about and whom?'

'That's why I'm going to New York.'

'To write about New York?'

'No. To get an idea of what the people are like who'll be reading what I write about post-war London; one needs to be conscious of one's audience.'

We talked for a moment about the perpetual, persistent problem of the writer, the need to visualise the people with whom he is trying to communicate. I felt very much in tune with her. Fifteen years earlier I had hoped that a romance might grow between us. On both sides there had been a flicker. It had not developed. No reference had ever been made to it, but we were both conscious of its existence. It enriched now our relationship. There are few pleasanter things in middle life than this sense of oneness with those with whom one nearly fell in love.

But though we talked about my problems, no mention had been made of Raymond's; he was in precisely the same position that I was, a man of over forty returning to civilian life after six years in the army, four of them abroad. No one was worrying about him. No one ever had worried about him. Everyone had taken for granted his eventual success 'in whatever walk of life it might please God to call him'. Why had they taken that for granted in his case, and in no one else's? Because of his looks, because of his air, I will not say of promise, but of certainty. His father had not been concerned when he was sent down from Oxford. Was it because he took himself for granted too, that he made no demands on anyone? He had remarked, himself, that while he had helped others to get jobs during the war, he had himself lingered on in the *cul de sac* of Censorship, finishing up with a routine majority. Was that unconcern with the furtherance of his aims and interests, the reason for his being at the age of forty in an equivalent position emotionally? No woman's life was closely involved with his. Was that because he had made no demands on any woman; he had never made any woman feel he needed her—for the simple reason that he never had? Perhaps he had never really given himself in love, and was not that in the last analysis what a woman really needed—to feel that a man belonged to her? I felt wistful on his account as the train hurried me back to London.

In the spring of 1941, when I was a staff captain in the Ministry of Mines, I had taken a very small one-room apartment in a block of flats called The White House near Regent's Park. It was on the top floor and when the bombing was on, top floor flats were not in active demand, so I got it for a ridiculously small rent. I had kept it on while I was in the Middle East, and I had found it unlet on my return. I proposed to keep it on. It was very convenient and so cheap that I could afford to leave it unlet when I was abroad. One of its great advantages was that it had a central telephone service that took messages. On my return from Charminster, I found a message that Susan Irving had called and was desperately anxious to get in touch with me.

I rang her back right away.

'Oh, it's you. At last. I've been hunting for you everywhere. You're as slippery and elusive as a piece of soap. I heard you were back. I wanted to see you but I thought "what the hell". I was due for the Far East at any moment, with Colombo as my base. But now that's off. I'm back at the London desk. Just where I was three years ago. I must see you as soon as possible.'

'Where are you speaking from?' I asked. She had given me a Flaxman number. 'I've a flat in Swan Court.' That was just off the King's Road, Chelsea. 'If you caught a 30 bus, at the top of your street, you could be here in half an hour.'

'I'll do just that.'

Within quarter of an hour, there was a ring at my front door.

'I was in luck,' she said, 'I found a taxi.'

It was two years since I had seen her. She was now reaching the peak of her good looks. She had thinned a little; it was hard to look smart in London at that time, but she managed to. It was a cool evening and she was wearing a long, tight-fitting coat. It had an un-English look. An American offering maybe, from a PX store. At that time a London girl's looks depended on whether she had a Pole or an American as her beau.

Alcohol was in very short supply right then, but I had allowed my ration and credit to accumulate at my wine merchants.

'I've got whisky,' I told her. 'But I've also, if you'd prefer it, I would myself, a half bottle of champagne on ice.'

She laughed. 'I could have guessed you would,' she said.

'How so?'

'There was a girl you rather liked who told me that you always had exactly the right drink at the right temperature.'

'Who was that?'

'I'll let you guess. There can't have been so many that you can't guess. It became a kind of game with her. She would especially go back to your flat, when you had not expected her, even when she really wasn't in the mood, just to see if she could catch you off your guard. She kept the thing going longer than she really wanted, simply to catch you unprepared. And she never did.'

206

'I know who you mean.'

'I should hope you would.'

She sipped at her glass, appreciatively. 'She was right, dead right.' She looked at me quizzically, as though she were asking herself a question. Then she laughed.

'But it's Raymond that I'm here to talk about. When is he due back?'

'Almost any day. He was booked two sailings after me. I got back six weeks ago.'

'Did you see him on your way through Egypt?'

'We sailed from Alexandria.'

'Then when did you see him last?'

'Over two years ago.'

'Not since his nephew turned out to be a niece?'

'No.'

'Have you corresponded?'

'Only notes; when anything came my way or came his that was likely to amuse the other.'

'You've no idea how he's feeling about things?'

'About what things?'

'Oh, you know. The title, what he's going to do about it, and me, that's the main thing, what is he planning about me?'

'He's never discussed that kind of thing with me.'

'I don't like being classified as that kind of thing.'

'What else am I to call it?'

'Oh, you know,' she smiled. 'You know perfectly well what I want to ask you.'

I helped her out. 'Whatever there's been, he's been discreet about it. There's been no gossip. And if there had been, I think I would have heard.'

'That's something to be thankful for. If there was anything in Cairo, he's left it there behind him. But all the same, coming back to England . . . mayn't there have been something here, something that would be waiting for him? Would you say that was likely?'

'I wouldn't know. He hadn't been in England for a while; when he was, he was a married man, have you forgotten?'

'You sure there was no one here?'

'Not that I heard of. There may have been, during the phoney war. He was at a loose end for several weeks, but the moment he got called up he was posted out of London.'

'What about Dominica?'

'Nothing that can be any competition.'

'What was she like?'

'She was very silent.'

'I wonder if I talk too much.'

We laughed at that. She was someone with whom it was difficult to be serious for long.

'It's about time,' I said, 'that I started asking questions.'

'Fire ahead.'

'What do you really want? Would you like him to come back, with a heart at your disposal, or would it be a relief if he said "We had a fine time, didn't we? Weren't we lucky that fate intervened without our getting tired of one another? Now we can have wonderful memories of each other." '

'That's just what I'm asking myself,' she said.

'But you yourself,' I asked, 'is your heart at his disposal?'

'What do you mean by that?'

'You know very well what I mean by that.'

'I suppose I do. After all, two years . . .' She paused. 'You'd be surprised, wouldn't you, if there'd not been anyone?'

'I'd have been astonished. I'd have been more than astonished, I would have been shocked. Is there anyone now in London, about whom you're wondering "shall I break it off or not"?'

She shook her head. 'The real one's gone already; he was an American. It would have meant breaking up my life here, my career, my friends; it was too much, I wanted to . . . but no, I couldn't. At my age, and at an exciting point in my career. I'd never forgive myself if I didn't give myself the chance. And what's more, I couldn't forgive him if because of him I stood up that chance . . . It wouldn't be fair to him. It broke my heart but he had to go.'

'How long ago was this?'

'Six weeks; it seems six years. Something that happened in another life.'

'And you're ready now to pick up your old life, as it was before.'

'I had no real life before the war. I have to start in fresh.'

'With Raymond, if . . .' I hesitated. I did not want to say 'with Raymond if he's disengaged'; I said instead, 'if you feel you can put back the clock with Raymond.'

'It's a long way to put it back. I was such a kid in those days.'

I smiled at that. 'You didn't sound a kid from the way you talked at the Alwiyah.'

'I guess I didn't. I was being knowing, wasn't I? putting on an act. I wasn't letting Raymond or any friend of Raymond know how inexperienced I really was.'

'And you're afraid now that two years later Raymond will look less glamorous.'

'He'll always look glamorous; no, it isn't that. It would be wonderful if it could be as wonderful in London as it was in Cairo, but . . . oh, I don't know, I don't want those memories to be spoilt. You can understand that, can't you?'

'I can understand that.'

'It's . . . oh, well, when are you leaving for New York?'

'In about ten days.'

'Then he probably won't have arrived here before you leave . . . give me your address. I'll tell you how it works out.'

In mid-Atlantic I prayed that it would turn out well. Two weeks later there was a cable at the Algonquin signed Susan. 'Wonderful wonderful wonderful.'

And now what next, I wondered.

I got back to London on the last Tuesday in January. I crossed in the *Queen Elizabeth*. She was still operating as a troop-ship and no alcohol was served. Only the big sitting room was open. The cabins had been converted into dormitories; at all hours of the day announcements were being made to the military personnel on the telecommunication system. It was a dismal journey. We docked at Southampton at three in the afternoon. It was a grey, cold day. On the quay a small army band was playing us a welcome.

Somehow this seemed pathetic; a pretence that we were returning to a joyful homeland.

I was spending my first night in my mother's flat in Highgate; several letters were awaiting me. Among them was one from Eileen. It was duplicated, with my name written at the head in ink.

'Dear Alec,' it ran, 'Derrick is due back the twenty-eighth. His train is expected at Waterloo in the afternoon. You could get the exact time from the P & O office. I thought it would cheer him up if as many of his old friends as possible could be there to welcome him; we might all come back afterwards to my suite at Athenaeum Court for drinks. I'll bring up something pre-war from Charminster.'

From the smudged nature of the type, I assumed that a good many copies had been sent out. At the foot of mine was written 'Do, do come.' I looked at the date on the envelope. The seventeenth. It had showed great reliance on the efficiency of the Peninsular and Oriental Steamship Company to assume that a ship's arrival could be guaranteed ten days ahead. Next morning I rang up the P & O. Yes, I was informed the *Ralcunda* would dock at noon; the boat train was due at Waterloo at 3.15. I arrived at the station shortly before three. The train was due at platform 3. There was a barrier across the entrance. Less than twenty people were waiting. I looked for a familiar face; did not see one, then recognised Eileen. She was surprised to see me.

'So you've come after all,' she said.

'What do you mean, after all?'

'You didn't get my message?'

'What message?'

'That I had changed my mind; got cold feet at the last moment. I rang up everyone. You included.'

'That must be the confused message that my mother's woman didn't understand.'

'The message wasn't confused at all. Your mother's woman, as you call her, seemed rather dense.'

'She is. I'll be on my way.'

'No, now that you're here. Do stay. I may need support. It's good to see you, anyhow. Was New York fun?'

It was, I told her, but I did not enlarge on that. Anti-Americanism was on the increase. The English had had six dreary years. The war was over; but the restrictions, if anything, were stricter. The English did not want to be reminded that their former allies were enjoying a bonanza. Better to change the subject quickly. Besides, I wanted to hear about Charminster. 'How's my godson?'

'He's fine. They say that he ought to get a scholarship.'

'How did he find his father?'

'Fine. Raymond came down for Christmas.'

'How did *you* find him?'

'Just the same. He doesn't alter.'

'Do you know what his plans are?'

'You are as likely to know that as I am.'

'I only got in last night.'

'So you did; it was dear of you to come here. But you will be seeing him, of course. He'll probably tell you more about his plans than he would me. It's a little awkward, between us. I can't go on living at Charminster now that Derrick's back, yet Charminster is going to be Timothy Alexander's home. He thinks of it as his home.'

'Where's Raymond at the moment?'

'In a furnished flat in Queen Anne's mansions. Rented it furnished from a friend.'

'That doesn't sound a very permanent arrangement.'

'It doesn't.'

'I wonder if he'll go back to Dominica? That's what I'm wondering.'

'His heart's there, isn't it?'

'It ruined our marriage.'

I wondered how Susan would cope with Dominica. If she had the chance of having to cope with it. She was a career woman. She had put her career before her American.

'I didn't manage to see Iris,' I told Eileen. 'But I talked to her on the telephone. She sounded happy.'

'She'll be all right.'

'And what about her daughter?'

'She'll probably let that slip her memory. Something that happened to someone else. Margaret's happy with her.'

'And the old man's happy to have her there?'

'He's devoted to Margaret. She's been a daughter to him, and after all she isn't all that too old for the child. She isn't fifty yet. They'll be quite good companions for each other.'

'Someone has to pick up the bad hand in every deal.'

'Has it been all that bad a deal for Margaret? From what Raymond told me and from what I've guessed, she had a lively time in the hectic twenties.'

'What different lives the two of you have led. And in January 1919, you were in identical positions.'

'I know. I know. Look . . . here's the train.'

The barrier was moved back. There were two ticket collectors on it. But the waiting group was not let through. Eileen and I stood back. The train was crowded. It was a miscellaneous collection, some of them in uniform, most of them shabby, and all suntanned. They had come back through Suez. There was first a sprinkling of those who had jumped out of their carriages before the train had stopped. Then there came a thick jostling crowd: 'Line up there, please; one at a time,' the ticket collectors were exhorting them. 'No hurry; no pushing please, one at a time, one at a time.'

The press was over now. It was once again a thinning stream of stragglers. Eileen raised herself upon her toes, looking to the right and to the left. 'He must be here. He can't have missed it. I had a telegram from Suez. He couldn't have got off the ship. I'd have been telegraphed if anything was wrong . . . There's hardly anybody left; it can't oh, no, it surely can't, it can't . . .'

I could see where she was looking: a tallish man was walking very slowly, supported by a much shorter man. He was very thin, and very pale; his clothes, which were shabby, hung loosely from his shoulders. His feet dragged as he walked; as he drew closer to the barrier, he raised his head. His face was drained of animation. He looked straight at us. 'It can't be, it can't,' she said. A flicker of recognition crossed his face. He raised his arm, to a level with his shoulder; his fingers flickered, in a half salute; a phrase out of *Jurgen* crossed my memory, 'like a face drowned in

212

muddy water'—that was how he looked. 'What have they done to him?' she said. Then with a little cry, with her arms spread wide, she stepped towards the barrier, to meet with a smile of welcome, whatever the years might hold for her.

That night I wrote to Timothy Alexander.

'I am afraid I have bad news for you. This afternoon I went with your mother to meet your stepfather. It was a great shock to us both. He is very thin and very feeble. He is almost unrecognisable. I don't know whether he is seriously ill; all the ex-prisoners return in sorry shape; they have been starved for months. It may be that there is nothing basically wrong with him. I pray that there isn't. But he will need very careful treatment for quite a while. I thought you needed to be warned. It is bound to be a very difficult time for your mother, and she will be very largely dependent on your help and sympathy. It is worse for her than anyone. Now to more cheerful matters. I am going up to Lord's tomorrow and I will ensure that your name is down for the Easter classes. You'll find that it'll make all the difference when you're back at school. You'll start the term with your eye in . . . good luck in every way . . .'

Three days later I was rung up by Raymond. 'When can you lunch with me?' he asked.

'Almost any day.'

'What about Thursday?'

'Thursday's fine.'

'At the Jardin, then, at one.'

It was three years since I had seen him. He was out of uniform, in a blue pin stripe suit. It was faded, but its cut made him look well-dressed. His eye ran me up and down. 'You're looking elegant,' he said.

'I replenished my wardrobe in New York.'

'Smart of you. But it's not the done thing to be smart in London. People will think you've picked up coupons in the black market. Put women against you too. You ought to give your coupons to a female. It's a mark against you to look like that.' He looked very well, and he was in high spirits. 'As a matter of fact,' he said, 'I've quite a number of new suits, ordered them during the phoney war, but I'm not wearing them yet awhile; one has to watch one's step in this brave new world.'

The waiter handed him the menu. He looked at the wine list first. 'Let's decide what we'd like to drink. Then we can decide on the right food to go with it.'

'I feel like a rich red wine, a burgundy.'

'Then let's choose a good one. They've a Beaune '37. It costs three pounds. That should warrant a steak. This isn't black marketeering. They do have legitimately a certain amount of steak. The commodity's not non-existent. It's fair that their steaks should go to the clients who provide them with a profit on their wines. What use to them is a man who orders water? I've no complaints about the workings of this brave new world.'

'And it is a good steak, isn't it?' he was saying half an hour later.

'A notably good steak.'

'As good as you'd get at the Algonquin?'

'It would have to be very good for that.'

He laughed. Through the beginning of the meal we talked of mutual friends. Who was doing what and where? Then he brought up the matter that was, I knew, the reason of his invitation.

'You were at Waterloo when Whistler arrived. How did he strike you?'

'As someone who wasn't really here.'

'And how did Eileen take it?'

'A moment of utter shock. Then she put on an act.'

'She would. That's like her. And she'll play her part through to the end. If he does recover, he won't ever be able to think she's made a martyr of herself.'

'Have you had a medical report?'

'Not a thorough one. You know what doctors are: "give it time", they say. There doesn't seem to be anything definitely wrong. He's been starved, but then so have several thousand others. He may have picked up a bug. But there's no sign of anything. The doctors are right, I reckon. Give it time. And he has all the time there is. One thing

214

about it, for me at least, it makes the next step easy. I was wondering what I ought to do. Now I know. To be honest, I was puzzled as to my next step. It's simple now. I haven't an alternative. Maintain the status quo; Whistler and Eileen can't be turned out of Charminster. I can't live under the same roof as Whistler. I must make myself scarce.'

I had wondered how he would accept Whistler's disablement. I should have known. He always had an eye for the immediate solution, the simplification of any issue. He trusted his own instinct; he had not hesitated on the terrace of the Welcome Hotel. He did not now.

'Does that mean Dominica?'

'What else? I've been to the French Line offices. There's a sailing in early March. I should be able to get on it. I've every priority, as a landowner. To find out how everything is I need to go there. I'll bet it's in a mess.'

I asked him what news he had. 'The usual news. Everyone in debt, an appeal to the government for a grant in aid. A temporary boom in vanilla. A scheme to construct an airport.' He mentioned one or two mutual friends. 'Most of them are still going strong. You remember Archer? He's checked out.'

His voice took on a deeper tone. He was clearly excited at the idea of getting back there. I wondered how Susan fitted into this new planning. He switched to Timothy Alexander.

'In a way it's a pity about him. But I don't know. It'll maintain the continuity. It's not a good idea to have a boy dividing his holidays between separated parents. It makes him take sides. It's better to have him thinking of me as someone in a different world. I'll bring him out to Dominica one summer holiday. There'll soon be a regular air service to Antigua. There's an American base there and of course he'll know that later on I'll be coming home: though heaven knows when that'll be. The old man looks in fine form. He may last ten more years. When the time comes, I'll make the decisions that are needed. Live in the day. When you're writing a novel, you're not thinking about the next one, are you?'

'I've a pretty clear idea what the next one will be about.'

'And I've a pretty clear idea about what I shall have to do when the time comes. In the meantime, I have to deal with each separate situation as it comes up. I won't pretend that I wasn't worrying about this last year when I knew that I should be coming back soon, and didn't know what I was coming back to. One's stupid to worry; fate nearly always takes the decision out of one's own hands.'

He spoke with assurance. It is not so very often that one meets someone who is at peace completely, self-confident and assured—particularly at a time like that. A period that was not yet post-war.

His temper was contagious. I began to feel reassured about myself, which was something that I was very far from feeling. The burgundy helped. Raymond poured the last half-inch into a separate glass. He raised it to the light. It was unclouded. 'What luck,' he said. 'But quite often burgundy doesn't throw any sediment.' He divided the small measure between us. 'I'm afraid I can't offer you vintage port,' he said, 'but tawny when it's good can be endured. Let's have a large glass each with a slice of fruit cake.' Ten minutes later he was saying, 'If in twenty years' time our doctors tell us to eschew vintage port, I don't think that a good tawny constitutes a fate worse than death.'

'You won't get this in Dominica.'

'Very likely by the time . . .'

The headwaiter interrupted him. 'A lady on the telephone, sir. Miss Susan Irving.'

He raised his eyebrows. He rose and slipped past the table. 'I won't be a minute. At least I hope I won't.'

He was back in less. 'As I was about to say,' he said. 'By the time I'm ordered off vintage port, I'll be glad to have an excuse for not regretting it. Another reason for feeling grateful to Dominica.'

He paused. He frowned. 'She said that she had to see me right away, urgent and important. I'd told her that I was lunching with you here. She said "OK by that." I wonder what's on her mind? Well, we'll know soon enough.'

She was with us within ten minutes. She was looking harassed. She was carrying a briefcase.

'I'm sorry to interrupt you but you'll soon see why. Yes, I'd like a coffee, and a cognac. My nerves need steadying.' She opened her briefcase and took out two copies of a new shilling weekly. *The Clarion*: she opened the copies, handing one to each of us. 'Read that,' she said, 'and you'll see why I'm fussed.'

She had opened the paper at the column headed 'Charivaria'. This particular column was at the moment inspiring constant comment. It was a gossip column: and frankly a malicious one; it was also well informed. There was a good deal of conjecture as to who supplied the news. 'It's the third paragraph,' she said. It was headed 'Peers putative and proper'.

'Putative prose, I suspect,' said Raymond.

We read the paragraph. 'Now that the social scene is being restored to focus, it is not uninstructive to speculate on the rôles that will be played by personalities who on March 14, 1939, the day before Hitler marched in on Prague, no one had expected to achieve high prominence. No one, for example suspected that Lord Gerald Wellesley would soon be the Duke of Wellington. No one could have presumed that within four years his nephew would have fallen in action and without an heir. Nor could anyone have foreseen that the end of the war would find the enchanting and enchanted Raymond Peronne similarly placed, through a nephew's untimely fate, though still, in his case, waiting in the wings. What difference will the imminent prospect of nobility make to him? He has a son, so in his case there is no problem about an heir, but the mother of that heir changed her matrimonial obligations shortly before the outbreak of war. So that when the heir apparent enters the ranks of the nobility, Charminster will be without a chatelaine. Who will she be? Surely it is certain that there will be one. Raymond Peronne's susceptibility to feminine attractions is well known. During the last half of the war when he was on the staff in Cairo, he was frequently seen in the company of an exceptionally attractive member of our profession. After eighteen months' separation while she was covering the Second Front, they have met again in London. They appear to be inseparable. But so she tells us, there is no likelihood there of wedding bells. Who then will it be? We are all eyes and ears.'

'I'm sorry. I'm terribly sorry,' Susan said.

'Why should you be?'

'Because I'm responsible. I gave him the information.'

'Who is he, by the way?'

'I'm sorry. I can't tell you . . . a professional secret. It's not important. *That* isn't important. I mean to say, the professional secret isn't. It's about you—this personal publicity and I know how you hate personal publicity. It isn't my fault. Yet it is my fault. He came round to see me. I thought I could trust him. We're both journalists, after all, dog doesn't eat dog, but then you're not a journalist. That's what I hadn't realised—I could trust him as regards myself, and after all he didn't mention me by name. He had a gossip with me and I told him about us. I never dreamed he would use it in that way; when I saw the new issue an hour ago—it won't be out till tomorrow: you do realise that? If you feel too strongly, I could stop it; even at this late hour. It isn't impossible. It could be done. You do see . . . you must see . . .'

Raymond checked her. 'It doesn't matter, nothing could matter less. Calm down, calm down . . . Here's your cognac sip it and compose yourself. Alec and I were talking about old times. Relax, enjoy yourself.'

His eyes were twinkling. He was completely self-composed. He was not putting on an act.

'Do you realise,' he said, 'that this is the first time the three of us have ever been together? Let's make the most of it. Relax, have fun.'

We did. He had a contagious composure. He was obviously undisturbed. He and I were in the afterglow of a dry martini, a bottle of Beaune and a double port. Cognac was creating for her a common multiple with us. We were soon chattering and gossiping about the Middle East; having the best of times. There was no strain. 'They are a team,' I thought. Time passed. The restaurant emptied. The waiters were starting to look restive. Raymond signalled for his bill.

'This has been fun,' he said. 'We must have another party soon.'

He looked at the bill carefully. 'Always as well to check these things,' he said. 'If you don't, you're putting temptation in their way, encouraging them to put on that extra brandy that you haven't had. It isn't fair to them, and in the long run it harms oneself. They harbour a grievance against one because they've swindled one. It seems all right this time.'

I had watched Susan as he talked. I was puzzled by the expression on her face. I could not diagnose it.

'You're really not angry about that paragraph?' she said.

'Heavens no, why should I be?'

'I wondered . . . oh, I don't know. You seem to set so much store by privacy.'

'I do, but I don't call a paragraph like that an invasion of it. It's so badly written and so silly. So silly that one's tempted to ring those wedding bells, just to prove the man's an ass, but I was never one for cutting off my nose to spite my face.'

'So you see,' she was saying to me two days later in my White House flat, 'it's quite impossible.'

She had rung me up that same evening. 'I've got to talk to you. I've got to explain.'

Here was the explanation. 'You see how impossible he is,' she said.

'No,' I said. 'I don't see it at all. In what way impossible?'

'It's obvious, I'd have thought.'

'It's not to me.'

'Oh surely . . . his . . . well, what's the word—imperturbability . . . that's as good as any. He can't be shaken out of it. You must see that.'

'I might; if I wasn't in the dark.'

'Oh you, you're as impossible as he is. Even that paragraph didn't work the trick. You realise that I wrote it, don't you?'

'Of course I don't.'

'You don't? Then you're as obtuse as he is. It was my last attempt to bring things to a head.'

'What things to what head?'

'Him and me, of course; we're headed nowhere. We're back to where we were three years ago in Cairo.'

'What's wrong with that?'

'Everything. That's what I tried to explain to you in Baghdad. What's all right in Cairo in wartime, isn't all right in London in peacetime. Then you couldn't look ahead. Now you have to look ahead. You must be able to answer the question "where shall I be in two years' time?"'

'But you cabled me that everything was wonderful.'

'So it was, to start with. We picked up the threads exactly where we'd dropped them. I was so afraid we wouldn't; that so much had happened to us both that we'd be different people. But we weren't. We arranged to dine. He asked me to have a drink first. Before we were half-way through our drinks we were in bed. We never did get out to dinner. It was exactly the way it was. First thing next morning I fired you that cable. I was so happy, so fulfilled, so thrilled. The whole world was changed: the war was over; a new life was starting, a rich, rare future was beginning and then . . .'

'And then?'

'There was no then. It was just the same; exactly as it was in Cairo. And the days went by and nothing happened.'

'What did you expect to happen?'

'I don't know; but I expected us to talk about it; to plan a future, discuss a pattern for ourselves, assume that we meant something special to each other; I don't mean marriage necessarily, but we'd say something some time about why we didn't marry.'

'You've been seeing each other pretty often?'

'Two or three times a week and on days when we don't see each other, we telephone. We always know what we are doing. That's how I know that you were lunching together, and at the Jardin. That's when the idea of that paragraph occurred to me.'

'I had no idea you wrote that column.'

'Not more than half a dozen people do. And I don't do

all of it. Not by any means. There are five of us, and we've worked out that distinctive style. It's ghastly, isn't it? Raymond was quite right. Every Monday we have a lunch together; and plan our column. How we laugh over it. They were delighted with that paragraph.'

'What effect did you expect from it?'

'I didn't know. But it would have some effect, I was sure of that, and I wanted to have you as a witness.'

'What was the idea of that?'

'I can't be sure; but I wanted someone who'd been in at the start to be in at the finish.'

I remembered how Judy had wanted me to break the news about her assignment and how Eileen had insisted on my remaining on the terrace at Villefranche when she broke the news of her divorce. There was something about Raymond that made women reluctant to have a direct showdown with him. They wanted someone else to break the news, or they wanted a witness. Judy, Eileen and now Susan. What was it in Raymond that produced this effect in women? Susan had used the word 'imperturbability'. Not a definitive word, in this case; and one with which she was not satisfied herself. I repeated my question. 'Did your bombshell have the effect you wanted?'

'It showed me where I stood.'

'And where do you stand?'

'Not here; not any longer. I'm getting out.'

'Where to?'

'South Africa. I've got an assignment from the paper.'

'Have you warned Raymond?'

'Not yet, and I don't suppose I shall. If that paragraph didn't galvanise him into action, nothing will. One day he'll telephone and there'll be no answer. Then a week later he'll get an air letter card with a South African stamp on it.'

'It'll probably catch up with him in Dominica, three months later.'

She laughed at that, a little ruefully. 'I wish it hadn't to be this way,' she said. 'It's all been fun, and glamorous. He's such good company. He makes everything more enjoyable. I really love him, but when I think how much I could have loved him if he'd let me. It wasn't that he held me off, but that so much of him wasn't there. I wish I knew what makes him tick, in what's called "that way".'

'I'm afraid I can't help you there. I am as much in the dark as you are. As I've told you, he doesn't talk about himself.' It was indeed five years before I got a clue as to what it was that 'in that way' made him tick.

13

Though Raymond was to come little to England during those five years, I was to see him regularly. The development of the Pan American and the BOAC air networks created a tourist boom in the Caribbean which I exploited professionally with articles and short stories. I was one of the first in the field and my pre-war experience of the area gave me a start over my competitors. I concentrated upon the smaller islands, and because of Raymond's presence there I specialised in Dominica. He was there half the year.

'What,' he said, 'would I find to do in England?'

On his father's death he would have a seat in the House of Lords. He would have duties and responsibilities as a landlord, but waiting for a father to die was no life for a man in his middle forties. Moveover he could not make Charminster his base as long as Eileen was still there, and he was reluctant to turn her out until he had to. The problem of Whistler was insoluble.

The doctors had found no organic defect. They were convinced that his trouble was emotional. Psychiatrists had done their best without success. He seemed well enough. He enjoyed his meals. He took wine in moderation. He played golf. He read novels and the newspaper. He was reasonably good company. But he was afflicted with a basic apathy. He discussed politics but without commitment. He did not appear to care.

'I wonder,' Raymond once remarked, 'if he makes love to Eileen.'

'That's something that I'd like to know.'

'You couldn't ask her?'

'I suppose I could; I don't know that she'd resent it. But somehow I prefer not to know.'

'Poor Eileen.'

It was easy to see why Raymond preferred to stay on in Dominica.

Myself, I was still seeing quite a little of his family.

Timothy Alexander was my godson, and I appreciated the opportunity this gave me of watching a boy become a man. I enjoyed going down to Eton, taking him out to lunch and giving him a pound note at the end. I watched him at Lord's at the April cricket classes. The pros there were convinced that he showed real promise. I was not surprised when he got into the eleven at the age of seventeen; he did not have a chance in the big match as it rained the whole of the first day, but next year he would be captain. He would be the first Peronne to lead an Eton eleven past the white seats in the Pavilion. Raymond would be over for that. He had promised to arrange for a coach. How proud the old man would be. The future could not have been more roseate, and it was at that very moment when so many dawns were breaking for so many people, that the calamity occurred which as a corollary brought me an answer to the problem that had perplexed Judy, Eileen, Susan and no doubt many others.

Shortly after Christmas 1950 I set out for what had become for me a routine trip to the West Indies. As I was travelling by a French ship that made a call at Roseau, I decided to start there. I invited myself for a ten-day visit.

Raymond was there to meet me.

'Would it be convenient for you to stay a little longer?' That was the first thing he asked me.

'If it isn't,' he went on, 'if you've only a limited time and need professionally to spend a week in St Lucia, could you go across there in a couple of days, and then come back?'

'I'm not limited by time. I can go to St Lucia later.'

'That's fine. I'd be particularly grateful if you could stay on. I want you to be here the week after next.'

'Why?'

'Timothy Alexander's coming over. I'd like you to be here when he is.'

Timothy Alexander in mid-January; with the new half starting? 'How on earth has that come about?' I asked.

'I'll explain when we get back,' he said.

The ship had anchored at half-past ten. It was after midnight when we got back to Overdale.

'You ate on board, didn't you?'

'Of course.'

'Then you won't be hungry. I've got some sandwiches in the icebox. While I'm fixing you a drink, you can read this letter. It'll put you in the picture.'

It was headed Wharrcliffe House, Eton College, Windsor, Berks. It was written in the small letter-by-letter caligraphy of a man who has learnt Greek.

'Dear Mr Peronne: This is a difficult letter for me to write. It will be a sad one for you to read. I am asking you to remove your son from my house. I have discovered that he has been engaged in sexual activities with a fifteen-year-old boy in another house. We take now a less stringent attitude in such matters than the authorities did when you and I were school-boys. It is rare to expel a boy for a first offence, and your son's conduct up to now has been excellent. He has worked hard and he has played hard. He has been an influence for good in the house and in the school. It is for these very reasons that I have in his case to take disciplinary action. He is a member of "Pop"; next summer, he would have been captain of the eleven. He is, in fact, a school hero, and we cannot have as a school hero a boy who has been involved in a serious scandal. He has, in fact, to pay the price of his own achievements.

'I learned about this matter a few days before the end of the half; on that account there is no question of "expulsion". He will just not come back next term. Apart from the fact that he will by this be robbed of the prizes which he had earned by his previous achievements, it will not make a great deal of difference to his future. He has his certificates, and he can go up to New College in October. Oxford will not be informed of this scandal. There may be rumours. But the fact that you yourself live out of England will be an excuse for his staying abroad for the next few weeks. Or perhaps you will prefer him to take his military service right away. There is a lot to be said for that. It is unsettling to have the prospect of it overhang a university career. You yourself will make whatever decisions may seem appropriate. I wish your boy the very best of luck. I am most sorry that this has happened. I am confident that a successful career awaits him.'

I handed the letter back to Raymond. 'Well, what do you make of it?' he asked.

'It's bad luck, isn't it?'

'It's cruel luck for the old man. He had so looked forward to having someone of his own name an Eton captain. That's one reason for letting the boy take his military service. He'll understand military necessity.'

'It's one of the few things that he is capable of understanding. Anything that's in the present, that's to say. Most of the past is as clear as ever.'

'You've seen him since I have. Is he very confused now?'

'He mixes things up,' I told him. 'He confuses Michael and Adrian already. Now he'll mix up Timothy Alexander with the other two.'

'I suppose he'll mix up Korea with the Somme and the Battle of the Bulge.'

'That's more or less how it is.'

We laughed at that. It seemed easier to speculate on a very old man's senility than on the very present problems of a very young one.

'The boy's coming out here soon,' said Raymond. 'That's why I'm so glad that you'll be here. You'll know what to say better than I shall.'

'I question that.'

'I don't. To me the whole thing's incomprehensible.'

'What thing?'

'This business of boys and boys. It's never come into my life, any time, not even at school.'

'You're an exception.'

'Am I? I suppose I am.'

'Not many of us had such an obliging aunt.'

It was the first time that I had ever mentioned her to him. As I had told Susan and Eileen, and Myra earlier, Raymond was not one of those men who discuss their experiences with women. 'That aunt,' he said. He paused. 'Do

226

you know that she's still alive? Why shouldn't she be, after all? She's only in her sixties. I saw her a few years ago at a cousin's wedding. The first time I had seen her for over twenty years. I must say she looked pretty good. She's kept her figure. She is trim and neat. There was still a glint in her eye. I bet she still gets into her share of mischief. In fact, she as good as told me that she did. She was a grass widow when I met her. It was in the war. Her husband was in Egypt; with a territorial battalion. A very cushy war for him. She had no qualms about deceiving him. She's been a widow now for several years. We had a real gossip at the wedding. I felt so in tune with her. We sat together with our champagne and let the party follow its own momentum. I asked why she hadn't remarried. "Because I don't want to marry a widower older than myself. A man who is older than myself is too old for me. I've always liked quite young men." There was a twinkle in her eye as she said that.

' "Then why not marry one?" I asked.

' "I'd feel ridiculous. So would he. Besides, I wouldn't want to marry the kind of young man who'd want to marry me. There'd be something phoney about him. I have much more fun playing it the way I do. I'd made up my mind about you when you were twelve. I enjoyed those two years of waiting. Perhaps you did, too?" What a twinkle there was in her eyes when she said that. We'd never referred to it before. But I had a suspicion that one day we would.'

I had, as I sat there on the verandah, with the rich tropic night about us, a suspicion that Raymond was at least in the mood to tell me about that past. He only needed, I felt, the least encouragement. 'How did it begin?' I asked. 'Tell me about those two years of waiting.'

He laughed. 'You'll never guess how it began. It started with her whipping me.'

'Whipping you?'

'Don't look so surprised. You know about flagellation, don't you?'

'In theory.'

'You know how it's linked with sex, particularly with youthful sex: Haven't you noticed that the school stories

227

we used to read as boys, that's to say when we were between ten and thirteen, had luscious descriptions of boys being caned? Nearly every school story had a scene or two of that. A schoolboy's pornography.'

I had indeed noticed it. My own preparatory school, that had been started in the year I went there and that had only ten boys in my first year and only forty when I left, was completely innocent. We knew how babies were born but we did not appreciate the nature of paternity. We evolved between ourselves a ritual routine of flagellation. We belaboured our bared sterns with hairbrushes and knotted bootlaces. We got a thrill out of our courage in accepting pain, as Indian braves did, but we also got, without recognising it for what it was, a sexual kick. I remember in the changing room when we were discussing beatings, one of us pointing to his own manifest emblem of excitement with the remark, 'It's funny that I always get like this when I talk about beatings.'

I recounted this incident. Raymond nodded. 'That's how it was, in our different way, with us.'

'I used to stay with my uncle in the holidays. In wartime it was the only change of scenery that I could get. My aunt was living in the house. She had no home of her own, with her husband at the war. We were thrown into each other's company a lot. She was fun and sympathetic. We played tennis and golf, and in the evenings chess together. She was very interested in everything that interested me. She looked at my stamp collection. She asked me about the books I liked. She read me poetry. She introduced me to a number of poets that I had missed ... the silver poets ... Landor, Coventry Patsmore, Swinburne. We became very confidential. She asked me if I got caned at school. "Yes," I said, "every now and then." '

In retrospect I recall his confession as the dialogue of a film script.

' "What with?" she asked.

' "A cane."

' "Where?"

' "On the place appointed." '

' "Where's that?"

' "As a matter of fact when the headmaster beats me, it's just below the place appointed."

' "On the leg?"

' "Yes."

' "Here?"

' "No, a little lower."

' "Here?"

' "Yes."

' "That's funny."

' "Why?"

' "It's better higher up."

' "Better?"

' "It's where it should be, isn't it?"

' "I suppose so."

' "And do you take off your clothes for it?"

' "We let down our trousers."

' "Doesn't that leave weals?"

' "It makes scars."

' "Does it make you bleed?"

' "Not quite."

' "How long do the scars stay?"

' "Three weeks."

' "When were you caned last?"

' "About a month ago."

' "So it's no good asking you to show your scars?"

' "I'm afraid not."

' "Afraid?"

' "Well . . ."

' "Would you like to have scars to show me?"

'I did not answer.

' "I believe you wish you had," she said. The talk excited me in a funny way.

' "You do wish you had, don't you? Next time you come down, the very first day you're here, I shall ask if you have any scars to show me."

'As it happened, next term I was caned tens days before the end of term. The following day there was a letter from my father. "The question arises whether it would be better if you

229

went to your uncle's at the start of the holidays or at the end. It's a question of the train fare. One has to remember war economies. You don't want to cover the same ground twice: which would you prefer?"

'I wrote back. "I'd like to go to my uncle's first. I always want to spend the very last day of the holidays at home."

'That was the explanation that I gave my father. And he, I knew, was touched, but that was not my real reason. I wanted to arrive at my uncle's house with unfaded weals.

'My aunt met me at the station. Was there or did I fancy that there was a look of interrogation in her eyes? I found myself blushing. She smiled. It was a conspiratorial smile. My heart began to pound. That evening when she came up to say goodnight, the same smile flickered in her eyes. She stood beside my bed. She said, "Haven't you anything to show me?"

'I could not speak. I was as hypnotised as a rabbit is supposed to be by a snake. "I think you have," she said. "You have, haven't you?"

'I could barely bring out the "Yes".

' "I thought you had. Turn over on your face." She pulled back the blankets; she put her hand under me and undid the knot of my pyjamas; she drew down my pyjamas. "Oh yes, I see you have."

'She drew a hand over my legs. "This must have hurt," she said. "I've brought you up some ointment."

'She had a small tube in her handbag. She squeezed it over the scars, then very gently massaged them. The ointment was very cool. Her fingers were very soft. She moved up slowly over my legs, upwards towards my waist; lingering over my haunches. Her fingers sent a thrill along my senses. "I wonder why he beats you there," she said. "This is where he should beat you."

'Later, a long while later, she was to tell me why. "He was afraid that he might excite you if he whipped the place appointed. He wanted to give you pain, not pleasure."

'On that first evening, she sat beside me on the bed, slowly stroking me with her soft finger tips. "This is where he should whip you. This is where I shall whip you if I have

230

to; and I may have to one day if you're not good. I'm rather sure that I shall have to one day . . . like this." She raised her hand and brought it down hard; very hard. She let her hand rest where it had struck. Then slowly once again her fingers began to stroke me. "How often do you get whipped at school?"

' "Every other week or so."

' "That is what you need then. And in the holidays you're not getting it at all. That's bad for you. Your headmaster wouldn't do it unless it were good for you. Yes, I shall have to whip you; I shall, shan't I, Raymond?"

' "Yes."

' "Say that I'll have to; say, "Auntie, if I'm not good you'll have to whip me." I said it. It excited me to say it.

'She talked about whipping quite a lot. "What'll I whip you with?" she said. "I haven't got a cane. I'll have to use a birch. Yes, that's what I'll do. I'll use a birch. We'll have to make one."

'Next day when we were walking in the coppice, she said, "Let's get the twigs now for that birch. You choose them. It's for you, remember." And we chose the twigs together. "No, that's no good," she'd say. "They have to be flexible and springy. They mustn't be too heavy. They've got to sting, remember, not to hurt, to cut, not bruise." We collected about a dozen twigs. "That'll make a very good birch," she said. When we got back to the house, she took the twigs up into my room and hid them in a drawer under my shirts. That evening she brought up some ribbons. "We'll make a pretty birch of it," she said. And she tied up the twigs. She swished it through the air. "This'll do," she said. "Now I'll have to use this on you, just one stroke, so that you'll see what you're going to get if you're not good. Down with those pyjamas now. Yes, that's right. Now how do they whip you at school?"

' "We bend across a desk."

' "We haven't a desk here. You'll have to lie on the bed or across my knees. I think on the bed. Yes, that's the way, and I'll put a pillow under you. Yes, that's it now." It was quite a hard blow. It hurt. Yet the pain was followed by an agreeable glow; she laid her hand on me; then stroked me

231

gently. "It'll be harder another time and it won't be just one stroke."

'As her fingers stroked me, I found myself getting excited. I didn't know what it meant. I was afraid she'd notice. Yet I hoped she would.

' "Now you know what you'll get, when you deserve it . . . only a lot more strokes."

' "How many?"

' "It depends on what you've done. Not less then six."

'Three days later I did deserve it; or at least appeared to. I overslept and was late for breakfast. My aunt called me every morning. She said she had called me that morning. I have often wondered since whether she really did. At any rate, when I came downstairs she was sitting at the foot of the table with a mocking, meaning smile upon her face. My uncle had already taken *The Times* to his study.

' "You know what this means," she said.

' "How many?" I asked.

' "I'll tell you at lunch."

'She made no reference to the matter during the morning. It was just like any other morning. We played a couple of sets of tennis. She read some poetry. Just like any other morning, except that there was this undercurrent of excitement. I was nervous, yet I was expectant.

'At lunch she looked up from her plate and said, "Seven." My uncle looked surprised. "Seven what?" he asked.

' "He knows, it's our secret."

'The fact that we had this secret gave me a delicious sense of intimacy. It made me feel grown up.

'That evening when I went upstairs, she said, "Better have a bath."

'When she came up to say goodnight, she asked if I'd had one. "Yes."

' "That's good. It won't hurt so much. That means I can whip you harder. Lie down on your face now." She slipped a pillow under me. As she did, her fingers lingered between my legs. The effect was instantaneous. She made the beating last as long as possible. She paused between each stroke. "Yes, that was hard, but the next one will be harder."

232

'It was. "That'll leave a mark tomorrow." She counted the strokes. "Six, now for the seventh and last." It was as hard as she could hit. It hurt, but as the pain subsided, the glow returned. "Now for a little ointment." The ointment was cool, her fingers soft. "You've been very brave," she said. "I'll give you a goodnight kiss."

'I had flirted with girls at children's parties, but this was my first real kiss. Its effect was immmediate and electric. Her hand slipped down over my stomach. "Oh," she said. Her fingers lingered. "Do you often get like this?" she asked.

' "Now and again."

' "Does it worry you?"

' "No."

' "It will one day. I'll have to explain to you what to do about it. In the meantime . . ." She got up. She went over to the basin. She soaked my flannel in cold water. "This will cure that for now," she said. Sure enough my rampancy subsided. "How old are you?" she asked.

' "Thirteen."

' "In another year's time that won't be enough. Don't worry. When the right time comes I'll show you what to do."

'I spent a week or two with my uncle every holiday. Each time she found an excuse for whipping me. Always after whipping me, she kissed me, and always she subdued me with a cold damp flannel. During the Easter holiday before I went back for the last term at my prep, she said, "I shan't be using this flannel again. Next holiday you'll be too old for it. I'll show you what to do instead. Next term, in your last week your headmaster will give all those who are leaving an address about the dangers that are awaiting you at Eton. I've an idea that you won't understand what he is talking to you about. Don't worry. I'll explain it to you when you come here."

'She was quite right. The headmaster did give us an address and I had no idea what it was about. I remember him saying, "How can you ask some pure woman to be your wife if you've been a filthy beast at school?"

' "Well, was it the way I said?" That was the first thing she asked me when I arrived back for the summer holidays. I nodded. "And you didn't understand a word of it?"

' "Not very many."

' "Then I'll have to show you tonight, practically."

'I could hardly wait for the day to end. I was now considered old enough to stay up for dinner. I was so excited that I completely lost my appetite. I could barely swallow a mouthful. "Not hungry?" she said. There was a conspiratorial flicker in her eyes. She did not keep me waiting long. She had brought up the birch, which when I left she always took back into her own room. "This is the last time we'll be needing this," she said. "You're too big for this. You're not a boy any longer. You're about to be a man. It's time to say goodbye to this. And this last time, it shall be as if you were a little boy, not on the bed, but across my knees, between them." She was seated; I was standing in front of her. She undid my pyjama cord. As she lowered my pyjamas, her hand brushed against me. She opened her knees. She held me tight between them. She had hitched up her skirt. She was not wearing drawers. Her skin was very soft. "Bend over now," she said. She struck once, twice, three times. Then she flung the birch across the room. "Goodbye to that," she said. "Lie down." She knelt across me, guiding me. It was . . . well, you don't need telling what it was . . . the first time and with such a one . . . We lay beside each other, silent, recovering our breaths, then she began to talk.

' "Now you know what your headmaster meant," she said. "And now you can forget nearly everything he told you, except one thing; not at school, and not with other boys. Lovemaking is the loveliest thing in life; it will bring you all the happiness you can take; only you mustn't spoil it. That's what I'm going to teach you, how not to spoil it. I'm going to teach you everything, show you all the things that please you most and then, what is more important still, I'll show you all the things that a woman enjoys most, because a man can't really enjoy himself unless the woman is enjoying herself too. By the time you go to Eton, you'll realise how ridiculous it is to make love with boys; it'll seem so tame, so futile after what you've done with me. And now," she said, "for the second lesson."

'There were many lessons during that long summer holi-

234

day; then there was the Christmas holidays, and at Easter she came to Charminster again. But that wasn't all she taught me.

'In the following summer, when I went to her home again, she welcomed me with the news that she had a pleasant surprise for me—a highly attractive young female was coming for the weekend.

' "Why should that be a pleasant surprise?"

' "I've an idea that you'll attract each other."

' "But why should I want that, when you're here?"

' "Sooner or later you'll have to do without me; you'll have to find replacements; the sooner you start finding them the better. Mary should be a good start."

' "But . . ."

' "There's no 'but' about it. She's coming for three nights. She'll arrive on the Friday afternoon. Pay a great deal of attention to her. On the Saturday night go into her room. However that works out, it'll be a start; then on the Sunday night, you should reap your harvest."

' "But . . ."

' "No, no, listen now. Confidence is the great thing. Assume that she'll do what you want. I've explained to you what women like; if she resists, persist. And here's a useful tip for you . . ."

'We were in bed together when she told me that. "Spread me out, spreadeagled, just like that. Yes. You're on my right. Now lie on my right arm, with your full weight on it, like that, you're on your side; now with your right hand move my left arm above my head, it shouldn't be difficult; now grasp my left wrist with your left hand; see what I mean? I'm pinioned, my two arms helpless and your right hand is free. If you can't do something with that right hand, you don't deserve me. Got the idea, yes, I see you have. Yes, oh yes, oh yes . . ."

'Whether it was a put-up job between the two of them, I've no idea; but it worked out. On the Monday morning when Mary left, my aunt patted me on the shoulder. "I'm proud of you. Mary was impressed. You're a good pupil."

'That evening my aunt talked to me long into the night.

235

' "So much of your happiness in life is going to depend on women, and so many men don't get the full amount of the happiness that they've a right to; women are ready to give happiness; never forget that. It's their pride and privilege; they bring life into the world, they want life to be enjoyed. It's a safe assumption that if a woman attracts you, you attract her; there's an instinctive reciprocity. It's like safety matches striking on certain boxes. If you want to make love to a woman, it's probable that she will want you to. But she needs to have her mind made up for her. Make it as easy for her as possible; make it easier for her to say 'yes' than 'no'. Take it for granted that she'll say 'yes'. Take *her* for granted when it comes to that. It's what she wants herself, provided that you attract each other; and that's something that you ought to know instinctively, and now," she said, "you've had a busy weekend. You need a rest. I'll come back —tomorrow . . . Oh, well, perhaps you don't need a rest all that much . . . no, well, well yes, I see . . . oh well . . ."

'Later, quite a little later, she was to say, "But tomorrow I really must insist that you have a rest. On Wednesday well, I've one last lesson for you. I won't say it's very necessary; it's not something that I'd recommend, that I myself set much store by, but . . . well, your education has to be complete. I don't want one day to have some sultry catamite offering you a pleasure that you've not had from me . . . my pride forbids it . . . For you, I have to be the works."

'So you see,' Raymond concluded, 'why I don't find it easy to enter imaginatively into this particular problem of Timothy Alexander's.'

It was the first time in over thirty years that Raymond had talked about himself to me. It explained a lot in him that had puzzled both me and the various women with whom he had been involved. I compared his amatory education with that of the majority of his contemporaries as Evelyn has described it in *A Little Learning*. I thought of all the strain and worry that had been caused to my generation by misinformation and prejudice on those issues.

'You were very lucky,' I said to Raymond. 'You should be very grateful to that aunt.'

'I suppose I am. I suppose I should be. I usually think I am, but sometimes I wonder whether everything was not made too easy for me. I took it all for granted; and by doing that I went for the things that could be taken for granted. I've asked myself whether the most valuable things cannot be taken that way. That they have to be earned. I wonder. I often ask myself.'

14

Timothy Alexander was travelling out by the French line's *Colombie*. She was due to drop anchor at night, at half-past ten. 'In one way the worst time to land. In another way the best,' said Raymond. 'No question of getting anything said that first night. One drink and then to bed. It'll probably be raining, too.'

It was. A steady downpour, not a wave of showers. But that did not deter Raymond from going out in a lighter. 'Mustn't miss a chance of getting a better glass of champagne than we can at Overdale. I signalled the purser, at Guadeloupe, to ensure that there'd a magnum upon ice.'

Raymond was resolved to make it an occasion. We sat in the small bar where I have spent many cosy hours.

'This is a big day for me,' Raymond told the venerable white-haired barman with the air of a Russian emigré. 'You may not believe it, but this is my son's first visit to my island. Up to now something's always intervened. Lack of an airport, that's been the trouble here. Still is.'

Timothy Alexander caught his mood. 'You can think what it means to me. I've seen so many films, so many photographs. I've dreamed of my first sight of Dominica, and now that the great day's come, I can't see a thing.'

His father laughed. 'In the dark and in the rain. Typical Dominica. You wait till you see it in the morning.'

The rain and the wind were beating so hard against the car that conversation was difficult on the drive to Overdale. 'Is the old man worried about your leaving?' Raymond asked. That was the sole reference to the situation.

'He hasn't really grasped it. "Wars interfere with all my plans." That's all he said.'

It was midnight before we arrived. 'What'll it be?' asked Raymond. 'The wine of the country as a nightcap?'

Timothy Alexander shook his head. 'Bed right away for me.'

'Very wise. But may I recommend a glass of coconut

water: clean and refreshing, good for the kidneys. Marie, a jelly nut,' he called to the girl who was waiting up for us, 'and take a glass to my son in his room. Breakfast at half-past eight. But don't set an alarm clock. Sleep right on.'

'I will.'

But when I came on to the verandah at six next morning, I found him already there, stretched out on a long chair, in his dressing gown. 'I can't get used to this change of time,' he said. 'The clock going back an hour every other night. I've been waking up earlier every morning and dropping off to sleep directly after dinner.'

'How well I know that, it's the same with me.'

I sat beside him. I was impatient to get to my desk. An habitually early riser, I like to get an hour's writing finished before breakfast, but I could not leave him alone on such a morning. There was something I ought to say. I wondered what, and I felt ill at ease. He smiled. 'This'll make you laugh,' he said.

'What will?'

'What I'm going to tell you. Do you know how I got found out?'

'You tell me.'

'Through that water-writing trick of yours. I used it for my notes to him. He was so amused by it, that he showed them all round his house.' Timothy Alexander was right. I did laugh at that. And our laughter removed embarrassment. The day before there had seemed so much to say. Now there seemed nothing at all.

'This is a lovely place,' he said. 'I'm not surprised that the old boy's sold on it.'

It was a bright sunlit morning. 'When after the rain and with never a stain, the pavilion of heaven lies bare,' I quoted.

We sat in silence. A couple of humming birds darted from bush to bush. The air was full of sounds and scents. 'Do you think you'll care for this place as much as your father does?' I asked.

'Not as much, but I shall care.'

There was another pause. But not an awkward one. He

was someone with whom it was possible to be silent; once one had got on friendly terms with him.

'Charminster's my home,' he said. 'It always has been and it always will be. It never has been for the old man. He's never belonged there. As a boy he thought of it as somewhere that he'd have to leave some day. He wouldn't let himself become attached. Now it's too late. His heart's here.'

'What are your immediate plans?'

'To do my military service right away.'

'I think that's wise.'

'I've done a lot of thinking on the journey out.'

'Half of my plots have come to me on liners.'

'I hope that my plans will work out as well as yours. In the first place I've decided not to put in for a commission.'

'What?'

'I thought that might surprise you.'

'It astounds me. Why?'

'I'll learn how the other half lives. I'll never have such another chance.'

'Do you think you'll like it?'

'I'm not worrying about that. Within a very little while I shall be cut off from the other half by that handle to my name. If I don't take this chance, I won't get another.'

'Do you think there's all that difference nowadays between the one half and the other?'

'That's what I want to see. I suspect there is. But I don't know. If there is a difference, I want to learn what it is. There's another thing too. I want to see how I come out when I'm in competition with the other half, on equal terms. Shall I get promoted? Shall I finish up as a sergeant or only an unpaid lance-corporal? You see that, don't you?'

'I see that.'

'Another thing too, I'm not going up to Oxford. Harvard instead. A degree in business administration. Iris is there, remember. She'll be the greatest help. As a private soldier, I'd learn about the other half, socially; by going to Harvard I'd learn what the new world's like.'

'Not thinking of becoming an American?'

'Heavens no, I'm planning to fit myself to make the most effective use of the opportunities that I'll get through Charminster.'

'Do you think you'll make a better use of those opportunities this way than by becoming an ensign in the grenadiers, getting a blue at Oxford and a first in law?'

'Under these changed conditions, yes. If everything had gone conventionally, I'd have done my best to fit into the accepted pattern, but owing to this—what shall I call it?'

'Piece of bad luck.'

'That's charitable, yes; it was bad luck, but it's effect has been catastrophic. It's broken the pattern. Being Captain at Lord's was part of that pattern; an essential part of it. Without that captaincy the pattern would be incomplete. I'd rather start a whole new pattern.'

I shook my head. 'Think again,' I said. 'Look ahead six years. You'll be twenty-four. You'll have had your military service. A commission in the Guards. You'll have had your four years at Oxford. You'll have got your blue. You should get a good degree, and be in exactly the same position as if you hadn't had this bad luck.'

'The bad boy who made good, in fact.'

'If you care to put it that way, but I don't think I should.'

'It's what it amounts to, isn't it?'

'I suppose so, yes.'

'It's a rôle I prefer not to fill. I'd rather find myself going into competition with my contemporaries with a different equipment altogether. Eventually, in some way or another, I'll be in charge of personnel. I believe I'll be better at that by having seen the problems of the less fortunately placed through having shared them. And when I go into business, in London, I believe I'll handle situations better through having seen London's problems through transatlantic eyes.'

'What kind of business do you have in mind?'

'I'll know when the time comes. It won't be in one of the professions, that's all I know.'

He checked, then smiled. It was a very winning smile, rather like his father's. It contained both modesty and confidence. 'I'm being very vague, but all this is very new to me.

It's been quite a shock, you know: when I came home at the end of the half at Christmas, everything seemed cut and dried. I was starting on the final lap of the race that had been planned for me since the day I was born. Everything was going according to plan. Then everything fell apart. It wasn't till I got on that ship that I began to think. But of course you see that.'

I nodded. 'And the great thing is,' I said, 'that you don't have to make an irrevocable decision now. You can see how you like the Army, before you decide to stay in the ranks for your whole service.'

Though even as I said that I was pretty sure that his mind was made up.

'How do you think your father will take this?' I asked.

'How did he take the news from Eton?'

'Philosophically; he thought it was cruel luck.'

'He doesn't feel he's been let down?'

'Heavens no, why should he?'

'Some fathers would; they'd talk about all the sacrifices they had made, and this being all the return they'd got for them.'

'He'd scarcely be justified in saying that.'

'Indeed he wouldn't.' He smiled. Was there a wry twist to that smile: a wish that he had had the kind of father who would have been justified in saying that—the father that in fact the majority of young men do have, that I had had myself?

'How's your mother taking it?' I asked.

'She's not realised all its implications yet. She's a lot on her mind, you know.'

'Such as?'

'Derrick, in the first place. A constant invalid. A husband who isn't a husband.'

'How is he?'

He shrugged. 'He has his good days and his bad days. He's brave about it. He doesn't grumble. He pretends to be absorbed in his various hobbies. His stamp collection: crossword puzzles, football pools, television.'

Not much of a life, I thought . . . but still. 'Sometimes,' I said, 'How shall I put it—when you become incapable of something you don't miss it. The need goes with the capacity. Twenty years ago cricket was half my life. I don't grudge its going. Perhaps it's like that with him.'

'It's dull for my mother, though.'

'At least he keeps her busy.'

'Is there a housewife now in England who isn't busy? No, it's not too bad for her. And there's the grandchild. A delightful poppet. Then Iris. She writes every week. My mother plans to go over in the spring.'

'There's you as well.'

'Oh yes, there's me.' Once again that smile that might be wry, flickered across his lips. Had this unusual household, with so many involved cousinships, made him feel lonely and unwanted? He wasn't the self-pitying type. 'When you talk about going into business, have you any particular side of it in mind? Big business is a large, vague area.'

'I know: that's what I expect to learn at Harvard. When I come back, I ought to be able to see where I can be most useful.'

He was talking very much as his father had talked thirty years ago. 'I'll bide my time,' Raymond had said. 'When the right moment comes, I'll recognise it.'

And we had been confident that Raymond would, because of his good looks, his charm and manifest ability. But the years had gone by and in the end it had all come to nothing.

At breakfast Timothy Alexander told his father that he wanted to do his military service right away. He did not, however, mention his idea of not applying for a commission, nor of taking Harvard instead of Oxford. Later in the morning we went down to the pool. Raymond and I were suntanned, but Timothy Alexander's skin was white from an English winter. 'I'm going to take this slowly. I've been warned about sunburn. Not more than quarter of an hour the first morning.'

He left his father and myself to linger by the rocks. 'You had a long talk with the boy this morning,' Raymond said.

243

'I could hear your voices but not what you were saying. Did you say anything?'

I shook my head.

'During the last few days I've been thinking out a whole lot of things I might say, but when it came to the point it all seemed pointless. What could I tell him that he doesn't know already? He's practically adult. He's thought the whole thing out himself. If there's anything that's on his mind, he'll tell us of his own account.'

'That's what I feel. We'll behave as though it hadn't happened. There's a change of plans. Ours not to reason why.'

'Exactly.'

But though I had agreed with Raymond, I had a plan of my own worked out.

Freemasonry flourishes in Dominica and three days later, I was a guest at the monthly meeting. At the banquet afterwards I managed to sit next to a Dominican in his late twenties who was one of the most effective batsmen in the island cricket side. He was tall, very dark, handsome. We had talked together once or twice on the cricket ground. I had felt an instinctive liking for him. He seemed exactly the right man for the project that I had in mind. If it turned out the way I wanted, I should be able to recruit his cooperation.

It went the way I had hoped. Long before we had raised our glasses to the Tyler's toast, I knew that he was my man. 'Let's have a final drink at the Paz,' I said.

We were both in a mellow mood.

'I've a problem,' I said. 'I've an idea that you could solve it.'

'Man, you tell me what it is.'

'It's a woman problem. I know that there's no such thing in Roseau as a regular prostitute, but there must surely be one or two attractive females who would be ready in return for a financial consideration . . .'

'Man, man, if that's your problem then your problem's solved. What type do you prefer?'

'No, no, it's not for me.'

I explained the situation. 'Raymond Peronne's son has

come out here. You may have seen him: he's seventeen and a half years old. He's very good looking. I'm his godfather and I feel responsible for him. You've read about the way it is in England at those boarding schools; they herd together for eight months of the year boys who are almost men and boys who are almost children. They never see a woman from the beginning of term until the end. Of course things happen. If a man says that he's never had one of those experiences at his public school, he's either a liar or he's undersexed. Usually it doesn't matter. The first time he goes to bed with a woman, he knows that that's the works. He'll never look at a boy again. But now and again there are complications. He acquires habits that he finds hard to break. Now I don't say that that has happened to my godson, or that there's a danger of it happening. But I want to make very certain that it won't. So this is what I have in mind. There's a dance next Saturday at Chancellor's Hall. We're all going to it. I want some girl to make a pass at him. He's inexperienced; he'll be shy. She'll have to make the running, but if before the dance, she has a present of—what would you say, fifty Beewee dollars.'

'Man, man, for fifty Beewee dollars . . .'

'Too much?'

'Much, much too much.'

'Twenty, then, and another twenty afterwards, but he mustn't suspect, he mustn't have any idea that she's been put up to it. That would spoil everything. He's got to believe she's fallen for him.'

'She'll make him believe anything for twenty beewees.'

We arranged to spend the night in town, taking rooms at the Paz. I arranged for a dinner first at Kingsland House— of which Froude had written with such warmth in 1888, and where his host's daughter, Miss Maggie, now ran a boarding house. I ordered mountain chicken and champagne to go with it. It was too early for mangoes but there was a delicious sour-sop fool. As regards guests I had not, apparently, been too successful. The men outnumbered the women two to one. But that was intentional. I did not want Timothy Alexander to be enslaved to duty partners.

We arrived in high spirits, just as the dance was getting lively.

As a dance it was much like all the others at that time in the smaller West Indian islands—nothing elaborate, no luxuries for tourists: there was noise, and a steel band, paper streamers festooned from the central electric light globes; reproductions of Royalty from the *Illustrated London News* upon the walls; rows of wooden chairs; a buffet; a bar. It was like any village hall in Britain upon dance nights, except for the fact that it was in the Caribbean, that faces were darker, blouses brighter, voices louder, except that it was all gayer, livelier, that everyone quite obviously was having a fine time. My spirits lifted. I love the Caribbean, I love its people, I love their way of life. I felt at home here.

I subjected myself to my share of duty dances. Then I moved over to the bar. I leant against the wall. I looked for Timothy Alexander. The floor was jammed. I took a long time finding him, then at last I saw him. A dusky cheek rested against his. She was shorter than he; six or seven inches shorter, but not so much shorter that her height looked incongruous. Her arms were bare. One lay along his shoulder. Her fingers touched his neck. Her fingers were long and thin. Her hair was straight; Carib stock presumably. I could not see her features. I shifted my position so that I could see his face. His eyes were closed. His hands were on her hips. Slowly but with mounting fierceness, her body undulated against his. She swayed with a slow deep rhythm, pressed close, pressed closer, one of her arms hung loose beside him. She swayed, swayed, swayed. She lifted the loose lying arm, crossed it behind his neck; she sank back on her heels, then lifted herself upon her toes, never breaking the rhythm, but tautening then lessening its pace. Couples on every side of them were held by the same fierce congo beat; their feet scarcely moved, but every vein, every nerve cell was responsive, captive, dominated; yet with each couple proud of, exulting in the dominance. I thought of Iris all those years ago.

Two afternoons later I ran into my brother mason. 'Man, did I do my job,' he said.

'What did she have to say?'

'Was so good that she'd have paid for it, she said.'

'Then perhaps she'll give him a second session free.'

'That's what she's doing at this very moment.'

Seventeen years earlier at the altar, I had renounced on his account 'the devil and all his works, the pomps and vanities of this wicked world and all the sinful lusts of the flesh'. I felt that I had fulfilled my duty as a godfather.

15

That was in 1953. In the autumn of 1956, the old man died.

During those three and a half years I had kept in touch with the Peronne saga. I had seen Timothy Alexander during the early days of his basic training. He had looked very well and he had consumed a prodigious lunch. 'How's it making out?' I asked.

'I'd hate it for a lifetime, but I don't mind it for two years.'

'What about that commission?'

'I'm not applying for one.'

'You still feel you'll get more out of it that way?'

'In the last analysis every enterprise depends on whether the man in the field, the man at the wheel is happy. By the time I'm through, I'll have an idea what makes him tick.'

'What about Oxford?'

'I'm in touch with Iris. She's sending me the Harvard papers.'

'You certainly thought it out during that ten days' trip.'

I was to see him again shortly before he left for the USA. His eyes were bright with anticipation.

'Oxford would have been so obvious,' he said.

I met Eileen a few times in London. I asked her if she was happy about Timothy Alexander's plans. 'It's his own life,' she said. 'He knows best what's best for him.'

'You'll miss him, won't you?'

'Of course.'

It would be the first time she had been alone. Derrick had long since ceased to be a partner in her life. I asked her how he was. She shrugged. 'He's well enough. He doesn't grumble. He doesn't make a nuisance of himself. No one seems to know what's really wrong with him. I guess it's mental: delayed shock. Three years in prison, in that kind of prison.'

'Does he ever come up to London?'

'What would be the point? He'd only embarrass his old friends. He'd rather they remembered him the way he was. He's resigned from Boodle's.'

'You come up yourself though, don't you?'

'As often as I can manage.'

'You haven't changed.'

'Not too much, I hope.'

She was in her middle fifties. She had not put on weight. She was still attractive. Did she have a beau or beaux in London? I presumed she did. Her life wasn't too unlike what Margaret's had been thirty years before. I asked about Margaret. 'Absorbed in the granddaughter,' Eileen said.

'I'm told she's a delightful creature.'

'She is, but tiny tots have never been my long suit. I left Iris with her grandmother, remember.'

'And life keeps ticking over?'

She shrugged again. 'And I can tell you what it is that makes it tick. There's never been a money shortage. We're the one family I know of which you can say that. I don't know how it's come about, but no one has been extravagant. No one's gambled.'

'If Timothy Alexander goes into business, the pattern may change there.'

She laughed at that. 'If he does, I won't be here to worry.'

Raymond certainly was neither gambling nor indulging fantasies. He was losing money on his estate, but his losses were deductible against income tax. He could not have lived anywhere else on such a scale. At that time I was paying yearly visits to the Caribbean, and I made a point of including Dominica in each trip. One quarter of each visit I spent at Overdale. We had many good evenings, Raymond and I, sitting out on the verandah reading poetry, gossiping about old friends. He came over to England every year, but he did not enjoy his visits very much. He did not like going down to Charminster with Derrick around and rarely spent the night there. Not too many of his old friends still lived in London. White's was full of ghosts. 'It's all rather ghoulish,' he said, 'waiting for the old man to die.'

He had nothing to do in London. London had ceased to be a place for playboys. 'I read an article by Partick Kinross the other day that was very much to the point,' he said. ' "You can't do nothing in London now," he wrote. "There's no one to do nothing with." Out here there's plenty.'

'Is Dominica any nearer to getting in the black?'

'It never will be. Always at the last moment some unexpected thing goes wrong. But the island still attracts eccentrics; mercifully, too, it attracts a few monied people who can afford to take a tax loss, instead of cutting into capital.'

'John Archbold and yourself, for instance.'

'Precisely. John Archbold and myself.'

'How much is he down here?'

'Three, four months a year.'

'And is that what you intend to spend here, when you inherit?'

'Probably. I suppose so. It'll be easier in a few years' time; there's bound to be a proper airport soon.' At the moment there was only a precarious hydroplane that carried a dozen passengers and on which it was very difficult to arrange a passage.

'No place for Timothy Alexander?'

'Oh no, Charminster will always be his base. He's doing his wandering now.'

Timothy Alexander's decision not to go to Oxford had surprised him. 'I suppose the boy knows what he's doing.'

I made no comment. I did not tell him that the news had not come as a surprise to me. It might have hurt his feelings to learn that his son had confided in me first.

'I'll be hoping to see him over there,' I said.

'I'd be grateful if you would. I'm writing to one or two people who might be useful to him.'

'Myra, for example?'

'Myra?. . . I suppose I should . . . But after all those years. I don't know her address. For that matter I don't know her name.'

'I can give you both. She lives in Georgetown. She's rather grand in Washington. Wife of a senator.'

'Fancy your keeping up with her.'

'She wanted to keep posted about you. Did you know that she was planning to come to London that first October?

She wanted to see what you were like on your own home ground.'

'I'd no idea of that.'

'I fancy that you wouldn't have stood much chance if she'd been satisfied with what she found.'

'I don't think I should.'

'You might have done much worse.'

'She's done much better.'

So we gossiped, night after night, visit after visit, in the cool of the verandah, with the fireflies flickering over the plants, and the bullfrogs croaking in the jungle.

I was abroad when the old man died. I read the news in a London paper, four days old, on the day of the funeral. I wished I could have been there for it. Eileen and Raymond have both talked to me about it; so has Timothy Alexander, who could not get back in time to see his grandfather, but was there for the funeral. I feel as though I had been there.

The occasion had its own tragic beauty; its chief poignancy lying in this, that though Eileen and Raymond both knew what was in the other's mind, they left the essential words unsaid.

It had been a very short illness, a chill on a cold evening that became pneumonia. Luckily Raymond was in England at the time. His father was in his middle eighties. He did not know that he was dying. He talked a lot about his grandson, 'Mustn't give up his cricket. Not too late for him to get a county cap . . . too late for his blue . . . too bad . . . one son, two grandsons, each good enough for a blue and not one getting one . . . the Army's fault . . . these wars . . . young men have to go of course . . . came at the wrong time for each of them, these wars . . . two grandsons and one son . . . not a blue between them . . . a little luck and it would have been three blues . . . these wars, these wars . . .'

It was a rich gold September; misty mornings, boughs dripping with dew, then amber sunlight upon yellowing leaves and reddening ivy. When Margaret was watching at the bedside—the two daughters-in-law took turns—Raymond and Eileen patrolled the tennis court. Each knew what was in the other's mind. How different it might have been, how different it should have been. This would have been anyhow a sad, sad time for them, with the old man whom they had both loved, dying in that room that looked upon the copper beech that he had planted, a sad, sad time: yet even so it would have been the day that marked the start of their new life—as owners of this house that had come down to them from eight generations. It would be the opening of a chapter that they had been waiting to read for over twenty years. On the day after the funeral they would have been discussing the joint plans that in the old man's lifetime it would have been unseemly to discuss. A dimension would have been added to their lives. That was how it could have been, that was how it should have been. Why wasn't it that way?

They could not say that in so many words, but the implication of it was inherent in every sentence they exchanged. They had never felt so close—not even in their days of courtship.

'What do you plan to do?' she asked. 'Of course you'll want Derrick and myself to leave.'

'I can't turn you out.'

'But we can't go on living here now that the house is yours. We were a nuisance to you before.'

'Oh no you weren't.'

'Of course we were. It was one of those situations you drift into. It was so easy to drift into it in 1940 when London was being bombed, with you and Derrick away; Timothy Alexander had to have a home. No one could foresee it would all turn out the way it has, with Derrick getting ill, then Iris becoming a widow with a baby, then her going to America; and the old man liked to have us here. I kept saying to myself "this can't go on". But weeks became months, months became years. While the old man was still alive, there was no alternative. You had the same feeling, hadn't you?'

'I had.'

'Living from day to day, feeling that nothing could be decided while he was alive. We had to give him a sense of continuity. We couldn't start pulling up roots when he was liable to check out at any moment. And that's how it did happen, didn't it, suddenly, without warning. On the Monday he catches a chill, on the Wednesday night he's dying. Our hands have been forced all these years. But now we've got to make decisions. It's your house now.'

'It's also Timothy Alexander's home.'

'I know, I know. But it *is* your house. Derrick and I can't go on living here.'

Derrick—that was the problem. He took no part in the discussions. He would sit at a table, or over drinks, for half hours on end, not exactly like a zombie, because he was completely aware of what was going on, but silent and abstracted, only joining in the conversation when some subject in which he was interested was discussed—and those subjects were few and at such a time in no one else's mind—a television serial that he followed, a sale at Sotheby's, his weekly football pool, the results on Saturday evenings. Most of the time they were not aware that he was there. Why had he to be there? How had it come about that he was there? The active rôle that he had played in their lives had been so brief. A year-long affair, a few months of marriage; a marriage that had never been cemented into a home, a nursery, the bonds of shared possessions. And then the years as a prisoner in Japan when there had been no exchange of letters; after six and a half years' separation the return of an invalid, who had long since ceased to be the brisk, purposeful City man who had bullied her into marriage. Now there was this amiable animated cabbage. Why had it had to happen? It could so easily not have happened. If there had been a war over the *anschluss*, it would not have. If there had been no Munich, it might not have. October 1938. The case was not heard until December. It would have been awkward then, with Derrick posted to his regiment and Raymond in Dominica. Eileen on her own, at a loose end might well have cabled, 'Why not postpone it for a little.'

They never actually said that, but each was thinking that. Each, later, was to tell me that. It was obliquely that they talked about their past.

'I never wanted to break it up,' he said.

'I know you didn't.'

253

'I was quite happy with the way things were.'

'I know. Perhaps that's what worried me: the fact that you were.'

'I was still in love with you.'

'In your way, you were.'

'It's the only way I know. Everyone's supposed to have at least one grand passion, but I never have. 'I've never felt the world well lost for love. I've never felt "if I don't get this woman I shall die".'

'That was our trouble, maybe.'

Never had they been so close. They felt an imperative need to explain themselves to one another.

'The moment I saw you, I wanted to make love to you,' he said. 'I never stopped wanting to make love to you. You were the tops, that way.'

'It's nice to be told that.'

They looked at one another. They were, after all, only in their middle fifties. They could so easily have picked up the threads where they had dropped them.

'But you can understand, can't you,' she said, 'how differently a woman feels when a man tells her that he can't exist without her, that he refuses to share her, that it must be everything or nothing.'

'Yes, I can understand.'

'That's how a woman wants to be loved, crazily, exclusively; in the last analysis she goes, or is tempted to go to the one who loves her most. And when she's left alone . . .'

'I know, I know.'

For hours, for days it was a long, renewed, interrupted, re-renewed going over of their times together: their first dates in his London flat; the excitement, the lure of the forbidden. Then that day in Villefranche. 'I didn't hesitate that morning, did I?' he insisted. 'I was delighted, wasn't I?'

'If you hadn't, I'd have been lunching in Monte Carlo.' They talked of their elopement; of the thrill of discovering Overdale. Of Iris at the carnival.

'She's survived that all right,' he said.

'She wouldn't have, if I hadn't rushed her right back to England.' They talked of Bolton's, of their weekend guests, of their London parties: 'Did that Dominican party with the films have the effect you'd hoped for it?' she asked.

'I've an idea it did.'

'You still love the place as much.'

'It's laid its hold on me.'

'You said that you don't know what a grand passion is. What else was Dominica?'

'Maybe, maybe.'

'Will you be able to give it up?'

'Why should I?'

'If you're going to make Charminster your base ... can you run the two?'

'There'll be a real air service soon.'

'Even so ...' She paused. 'It all depends on you, you know: the decisions that we'll have to make, we others. When do you plan to move in here?'

'Not right away.'

'I didn't mean tomorrow afternoon.' They laughed at that. They were on very easy terms with one another.

'You may re-marry if you make Charminster your base.'

'I don't think that's very likely.'

'Why not? You're only fifty-three. You haven't given all that up, I hope.'

'Hardly.'

'How are you managing in that way nowadays?'

'You know me.'

'Tourists and local *houris*?'

'More or less.'

'You may not find your quarry over here quite so accommodating: they'll see you as matrimonial timber, particularly now that you've a title.'

'That's one of the very reasons I don't want to marry.'

'Why do you say that? Most women would like to be Her Ladyship. Why shouldn't they?'

'I daresay. At the beginning; but she'd sooner or later resent the fact that her son would have to play second fiddle to my son by a first marriage.'

*   *   *

Later Eileen was to discuss with me at some length this aspect of the situation. 'Don't you think that's ridiculous?' she said. 'Nobody bothers about titles nowadays.'

'Oh yes, they do: particularly those that have them.'

I reminded her of how Hemingway had made fun of Scott Fitzgerald for saying that rich people were different from themselves. 'Of course they are,' he had said, 'they've got more money.'

'But I'm not sure,' I said, 'that Scott Fitzgerald wasn't right in thinking that there is a basic, inherited difference about a family that has been protected by wealth for several generations, that has been spared the strains and compromises that are forced on those for whom the demands for livelihood are an actual and persistent contest. In the same way there may be a basic difference even today in those who are born into the aristocracy.'

I remembered how Raymond had believed that it was the fact of Eileen being an 'Hon.', though only through marriage, that had made Derrick insist on her divorce. She must give up her handle for him. I did not mention this to Eileen: though Derrick was nothing to her but an encumbrance now, she needed to remember him as the man who had loved her so much that he could not share her. Had Raymond been mistaken in imagining that that 'handle' had been an influence on Derrick? Impossible to tell now; but the fact that Raymond had considered it a probability did show how acutely aware Raymond was of that basic difference. It was not fancied if it was real to him. And it was influencing his action now. There was also Timothy Alexander. He had another year to run at Harvard.

He returned two days after the funeral.

'How do you feel about it all?' he had been asked by both his parents.

He had shrugged. 'It's something that's up to you, to both of you. My job is to get back to my courses, do as well as I can, then when I've got my degree see what there is for me to do with it.'

'You do mean to come back here?'

256

'Of course: that's why I'm there. So that I can make a more effective prospect of myself.'

'You couldn't imagine settling there?'

'Heavens, no. I'm English. My life is here. More now than ever. By the time I'm back, you'll have settled on *your* plans, and I can decide how I fit into them.'

Myself, I was back in London for two months. Within a week I had had long talks with both Eileen and Raymond. Raymond was in a puzzled mood. 'For twelve years,' he said, 'I've been waiting for this moment, and now that it's come I don't know what to do. It seems ridiculous, it is ridiculous, at the same time . . .' He paused. 'All my life I seem to have been waiting for *the* moment. At Oxford I said there wasn't any hurry. I was relieved when I was rusticated. 'Now,' I said, 'I haven't to go into one of the conventional professions. I luckily haven't to worry about money. I'll look around. I'll see what I'm likely to be best at.' You'll say I took it all too casually. Perhaps I did. But I thought I was taking a long view. The depression—and what I saw of the results of the depression in places like Chicago—convinced me that the system was wrong at root. Two alternatives were offered or seemed to be offered, Marxism as interpreted by the Russians, a police state as interpreted by Mussolini; I preferred Rome to Moscow. It seemed for England in 1931, that Mosley had the answer. Then Eileen intervened. There was no choice for me at that point, and, as you know, after eighteen months in Dominica I had become enchanted with the place. I saw it as an interlude, but then . . . well you know what happened. Divorce, then when the war came, I had no doubt that my first duty was to get myself into uniform. By the time the war was over, I found myself the heir to a title and a country seat. As a divorced man in the Army I had resolved to get down to something solid the moment the war ended, but as it was, there was no point in getting launched on a career I'd have to abandon in mid-stream. I had to sit and wait till the time came: and where could I wait better than in Dominica? I fulfilled a function there. So I sat and waited. I sometimes wonder whether I haven't been providing myself with alibis all my life.'

'It wasn't easy for you.'

'Most people would say it was too easy.'

'Oh no it wasn't. It's much easier for people like myself, who have to develop and exploit whatever talents we are born with.'

'In other words the camel and the needle's eye.' He said that with a smile; the particularly winning smile that I had noticed the first time that I had met him, all those years ago at Oxford; the smile that accepted and dismissed the changes and chances of this world. Then he said the one thing he had not said to Eileen, though she had known that he was thinking it, just as she herself was, 'Damn that man Whistler.'

It would all have been so easy but for him.

'I can't bear to turn them out,' he said. 'Yet they can't stay on. And think of me living there all by myself. I don't want to marry again. I can't start all that over again. And it's Timothy Alexander's home. What kind of a home would it be for him, just me there, me whom he scarcely knows?' He paused, he shrugged. 'I'm going back to Dominica before Christmas. Have Christmas at sea. Christmas in Charminster; that would be impossible. I'd spoil it for everyone, myself included. I'll have to issue some kind of an ultimatum before I go. I'll stay away for six months. They should be able to arrange their lives in that time. Money isn't any problem, thank the Lord. And you can get houses now, but there's one thing I have to do before I go, make my debut in the House of Lords; I've taken my oath of allegiance, been sworn in. I've got to make my maiden speech, introduce myself; most of my fellow peers have never seen me; for those that have it's a question of twenty, thirty years. They don't know what I'm like today. I've got to show them. If I'm going into public life, they've got to realise who it is that's going there.'

'Which party are you joining?'

'Neither. I'm going to be an independent. I can do more that way.'

'Such as?'

'I don't know yet, but if I make a mark, I'll be invited to join committees. I'll sit on commissions. One thing will lead to another. The great thing is to make a start. The moment I see the right opportunity I'll take it.'

The opportunity was to come sooner than he expected. A few days later Britain embarked on what history would come to know as 'The Suez Fiasco'. Raymond was on the telephone within a few hours of the news making the headlines. 'This is my chance. A subject that I feel strongly about, that I've got the facts about. I'll wait till the fog lifts, then I'll put a question.'

'I'd like to be there when you do.'

'You shall. I'll give you warning.'

He called me a week later. 'It's to be next week on Wednesday.'

'What's your question?'

'To ask if Her Majesty's government appreciates the damage that its military operations in Egypt are doing to our national image in the Arab world.'

'That should put you in the public eye.'

'The purpose of the exercise. My question's number five. Kick off two-thirty. I should be on soon after three. I wish I could ask you to lunch, but I don't want to have a real meal first: coffee and a slice of cake'll suit me best. But let's dine later. Then you can tell me how it went. Shall we say Pratt's at eight?'

'Fine.'

'You've been to a Debate before?'

'Once or twice.'

'Then you know the ropes. The peers' entrance: the man at the door will have your card of entry.'

I arrived just after prayers, with proceedings already started; the Lord Chancellor was on the woolsack with the gold mace behind him, and a noble peer was on his feet. I had been placed in the gallery, half way down the hall: a good place from which to watch and hear a speech from the cross-benches. Raymond was wearing a black pin-stripe suit, a white shirt with a stiff collar and a polka-dot black tie, with a white handkerchief at his breast pocket. Though he was dressed so formally he had a casual air. He had not lost his tan from the West Indies. He looked fit and well.

A noble Lord was discussing some problem about civil aviation. He had his back to me, and he was not very audible. My attention wandered. I tried to absorb the atmosphere of the chamber, which with its red and gold decorations, its classical murals and its high lamps, might so easily have been garish, yet managed to achieve dignity and splendour. The chamber was fairly full. There was a certain air of casualness about it all. It did not seem that anything of very high importance was under consideration, but that perhaps is the British way of conducting matters of big moment; to appear casual about what is of high significance and to become worked up about a cricket match or a referee's decision.

At last it was Raymond's turn. As he rose to speak, I felt the same nervousness that a father has on the cricket field when his son goes out to bat. I was desperately anxious for his sake that it should go off well. For over thirty years I and so many of his friends had been assuring ourselves that one day he would fulfill his promise. The moment had come at last.

As he stood up, there was, or did I fancy it? a stir of interest. Without having become a legendary figure, Raymond was someone about whom a great many had felt curiosity. An exile who had unexpectedly become an heir, who had a property in an obscure West Indian Island, who had been one of the best-looking young men of his generation, who had figured twice in the divorce courts, who had been talked about in the days of the bright young people and then had vanished. Here he was at last, there was a stir of curiosity, but also of well-wishing, of welcoming. He was one of them; a member of the same club, no matter what his politics.

'My lords,' he began, 'this is a very proud moment for me; to stand here for the first time among you, and to be privileged to address you on a subject that lies close, very close to my heart, and I would ask the indulgence of the

House towards my inexperience as an orator. I am most anxious that my speech should make the impression that the occasion needs, that the occasion demands, but I am only too well aware that my achievement may fall far short of my intentions. I repeat, my Lords, that I crave your indulgence.

'The question that I wish to ask is "Does Her Majesty's government appreciate the damage that its military operations in Egypt are doing to our national image in the Arab world?" I want to explain first why I ask that question.

'It was my privilege to serve for four years in the war in the Middle East, and I returned with a very deep, a very real affection and respect for the Arab peoples. I am not the first Englishman to have had that feeling, many of us have, and that feeling of trust and affection has been reciprocated. The history of the last fifty years tells us that.' His voice was clear and resonant. It was almost affable. He was uncontentious. He talked as he would have done to a group of friends round his own table. He was so affable that it was almost as though he were inviting them to interrupt him, to make a dialogue of it. 'This is going to be all right,' I thought. 'He's found himself at last. This is where he belongs.'

'I am to speak,' he said, 'of our national image in the Arab world. May I ask you to consider the nature of that image.'

He started on a historical survey of Britain's involvement in the Middle East starting with Kitchener of Khartoum. 'Oh,' I thought, 'Oh, he's on the wrong tack here. They won't want to be read a lecture.

I looked away from Raymond, turning to the faces that were turned to him. Was there a puzzled expression in them? There was still a welcoming, a well-wishing feeling, but was not there also an air of awkwardness? He was hitting the wrong note. I wondered why. Was he as a new boy showing a lack of deference? Was he missing the atmosphere of his audience? It might well be, since it was the first time that he had spoken here. Or was he missing the political atmosphere of the moment? England was in a difficult mood. The country had embarked on a military operation and then been criticised, had been more than criticised, had been called to order by the United Nations. The country had been humiliated

by John Foster Dulles. No one knew where we stood. Had
we as a nation made a colossal blunder? Was the House
feeling that there were certain things that it did not want to
have said now and here, and in this way. The sense of embarrassment increased. Was Raymond aware of it? He did
not seem to be. He went on and on. His speech was much too
long. He was not asking a question, he was delivering an
address. In a way it was a good speech. It was well phrased.
He spoke, if not with fervour, at least with feeling. He was
obviously sincere. This added to the embarrassment. He was
thoroughly enjoying himself, and he was, there was never at
any moment any doubt of that, a thoroughly nice person.
Everyone was liking him. It was for his sake that they were
ill at ease. 'Will he never stop,' I thought. 'What am I going
to say tonight at dinner?'

He did not stop: he went on and on. He repeated himself.
He became autobiographical. He told how his travels, particularly his travels in the USA during the depression, had
convinced him that the world was afflicted by a faulty distribution of the world's resources. It was a digression that had
no bearing on the question that he had posed, but he
appeared to be at the mercy of a resolve to get everything off
his chest. He had told me that he had wanted to present, to
introduce himself to his fellow peers, and he was indulging in
a complete apologia. He had been so long in the background,
so long in the wings, that now he was on the stage he had to
deliver himself completely.

He went on and on. He appeared to be utterly at his ease,
to be having the time of his life. He was quite unconscious of
the mounting temper of the house; the atmosphere of irritation, almost of indignation at having such a performance
inflicted on it. Looking down from the gallery, I was acutely
conscious of the glances that members were exchanging, of
the whispers, the turned heads as though counsel was being
taken as to the correct procedure. Somehow this had to stop,
had to be stopped. But how?

On and on he went. He must have been speaking for half
an hour. On and on and on. And then, suddenly, without
warning, without premeditated planning, the end came. He

was warming to what would in any other speech have been a peroration, but in this looked likely to be only the winding up of one more digression. He was back now on to the operations in the canal.

'In this current campaign,' he said, and his voice took on a fuller, rounder tone, 'we have abandoned a friendship, a trust that has been built up over fifty years by honourable men, by men of honour, at the cost of blood, at the cost of lives; abandoned it for what, for a flimsy pretext, a device that deceived no one, abandoned it for whom? The French and the Israelis. What a choice, what a preference; this picture, then on that.' He paused. He looked round him, his face wore a triumphant look. 'The French and the Israelis. I have nothing to say against our new-found allies, but . . .' Again he paused. With his voice fuller, rounder, he delivered himself of the eight words that were to become a cliché, 'The Arabs, my Lords, after all, are gentlemen.'

As I heard those eight words, I gasped. Heavens, I thought, what has he said, what has he done? There was a moment's silence, then from the Opposition benches came a single laugh: or rather a guffaw. The outcome of nervousness, of embarrassment, an equivalent of the little laugh that the Chinese give when they are made to feel ill-at-ease.

On Raymond it had the effect of the sudden slap or dash of cold water that a doctor will administer to a patient on the edge of hysteria. It brought him out of his trance, recalled him to his senses. He looked round him helplessly. He tried to continue his speech, but he had lost the thread of his ideas. 'I must apologise,' he began, then stopped. He could not think what to say. It was more than anything a need to put him out of his misery that made one of the senior members of the assembly avail himself of the House's traditional weapon of defence. Rising to his feet, he said, 'I move that the Noble Lord be no more heard.'

Raymond looked round him again, helplessly. Then sat down. A minute later he stood up, walked towards the wool-sack, bowed to the empty throne, then left the hall. The House continued with its business.

I waited for a moment or two, then went out. I wondered

if I should find him waiting for me in the cloakroom. I did not. I asked the attendant if he had gone out. The attendant shook his head. I decided not to wait. We had our date that evening, in four hours' time. If he wanted to call it off, he would assume that I was in the Athenaeum.

He rang me there at five. 'I gave you a fine piece of copy, didn't I?' he said.

His voice was light and cheerful. I did not know how to answer that. He did not expect an answer. He went straight on. 'Perhaps Pratt's isn't such a good idea after all, this evening. Some of the people who were in the House this afternoon might be there. I don't want to embarrass them. They'll probably want to talk about it. Let's go to the Jardin.'

'That'll be fine.'

In the autumn of 1927 Noël Coward put on a play, *Sirocco*, with Ivor Novello and Frances Doble in the leads, that on the first night was booed and yelled at. There was pandemonium in the house, with Hugh Walpole standing up in the stalls, shouting 'un-English, un-English,' and the gallery and pit shrieking 'Author, author, come out you Coward, come out and face us.' That first night is part of the history of the stage. In his autobiography Noël Coward said that during the next few days he made a particular point of going to restaurants like the Ivy which were frequented by the stage, to prove that he could carry off a failure with *panache*. Raymond was avoiding Pratt's, not because he was afraid of showing himself in public after a humiliation, but because he thought his presence would embarrass his fellow members. The two situations demanded different techniques. Each took the course that was right for him.

In the Athenaeum drawing room I wondered what I should say to him. I need not have. He was already in the Jardin when I arrived, a half bottle of champagne was cooling in a steaming bucket. 'We'll treat this as an apéritif,' he said. 'I'm having oysters, which I can't get in Dominica. I remember that you can't take them, so I've ordered you smoked salmon. Is that all right?'

'Smoked salmon's fine.'

264

'And then a grouse?'

'That's better still.'

'And a sound red burgundy. They've got a Corton '49, a Château Grancey.'

'This is going to be a memorable meal.'

'That's what I need after an afternoon like that, yes,' he said. 'I certainly gave you a fine piece of copy. I've made enquiries. It's years since a peer has been called to order.'

'When was the last time?'

'In the middle of the war.'

'What happened then?'

'An eccentric peer was speaking about Hitler, said he was really a pretty good chap, only we had used him wrong. It wasn't the time for that kind of speech. I suppose that that was what was wrong with mine today. The wrong time for it. Did you feel I was hitting the wrong notes?'

'Didn't you?'

'No, that's the curious thing. I thought it was going very well.'

'It was a very good speech, very well phrased, I mean. It was very well delivered. But . . .' I paused: how was I to put it? 'The country's in a funny mood. It's been humiliated. It doesn't want to have salt rubbed into the wounds—not by its friends at least.'

'Where did I start going wrong?'

'With the bit about T. E. Lawrence.'

'Ah, I see.' He frowned. 'Do you think I've been out of the country so much, so long that I've lost touch with it?'

'I wouldn't say that; at the same time,' I gave him an example, 'there was an American who'd been writing a soap opera for radio for fifteen years. He took a house in the South of France. He didn't see why he couldn't write his opera as easily there as he had in Connecticut. The thing, so he thought, was automatic. He loved life in the South of France. His soap opera came out as easily as ever, but within six months his sponsors found that he wasn't gripping his audience as he had. He had lost contact with his audience. He needed to see every day in the streets, the supermarkets, at the post office, the men and women and the children who were switching on to him every weekday afternoon at half past five. He gave up his house in Grasse, he went back to Connecticut. The soap opera got back onto its old tracks; the sponsors were delighted. Yet he himself can't see what was wrong with the stuff he wrote in the South of France. It seemed all right to him. Is that pertinent?'

'I suppose it is. His eye was out. That's what it amounts to, isn't it?'

'Yes.'

'And mine is too?'

'It looked like it, this afternoon.'

'And that's what's rather frightening. One's eye's out when one thinks it's in. It's a lesson that I've got to learn.'

He changed the subject. He asked me about myself. For the year or so before he came back for his father's funeral, our respective visits to London had not coincided. But he was soon back onto his own problems. 'Did you hear the six o'clock news?' he asked.

'No.'

'I wonder if I was on it. I've been besieged by telephone calls. There was only one reporter there. The *Daily Mail* scooped it. Is the *Express* mad! They want me to go on television.'

'Are you going to?'

'I might as well. What have I got to lose?'

'I'm glad you're taking it as a joke.'

'How else can I take it?'

'Some men wouldn't.'

'When you are faced with an ultimatum you have to do your thinking quickly.'

'How do you make it out to be an ultimatum?'

'What else is it? My eye is out when I think it's in. There are only two courses; stay here till my eye is in, or get right out and stay out.'

'You've decided to stay here?'

'On the contrary, I've decided to get out: get out and stay out.'

There was a challenge in his eyes. I did not take it up. I waited for him to explain. 'When we lunched two weeks

266

ago,' he said, 'I was in confusion. I didn't want to turn Eileen out of Charminster. I wanted Charminster to go on being a home for Timothy Alexander: I didn't want to live in Charminster by myself. Yet if I was going to make a life for myself in England, I had to make Charminster my base. I was on a spot. Today's fiasco has let me off that spot. I know exactly what I've got to do—make Charminster over to my son. It'll save him a lot in death duties when the reckoning comes. It'll ensure his coming back to England. He says he's English, that his life is in England, but the whole situation might seem very different if he met an attractive girl out there. I'm quite likely to last another twenty years. Twenty years is a long time when you're only twenty. The sooner he comes back the better; let him strengthen his roots here: avoid my mistakes. There are two types of Englishman, the type who is fretted and confined by an island life, who goes abroad: and the type who stays behind, whose character grows stronger with his insularity. One type built the empire; the other type administered it. You yourself are the type that goes away. I've become that type, though I don't believe that nature meant me to be: perhaps a great many of the old Empire builders weren't meant to either, circumstances forced them . . . Botany Bay, you know . . . Anyhow, I don't want circumstances to force Timothy Alexander out of the groove that's natural to him. Let him come back here as soon as possible, and start right in on an English life based on Charminster.'

'While you go back to Dominica?'

'Why not? I've roots there and I love the place. It makes sense, doesn't it?'

'It seems to, but . . .'

'But what?'

'That evening in Villefranche, when I suggested Dominica, how little I guessed, how little any of us could have guessed that it would turn out this way.'

'It's not a bad way.'

I supposed it wasn't. We had all been so certain that a great future lay ahead for Raymond, and after all what he had achieved in his sidetracked way was far from negligible.

An MC in the war; an estate in an island that needed the belief in it of men like himself, and a son who would carry on the family tradition. He was the ninth holder of the title. His eight ancestors would accept him with pride as one of them, and yet, and yet . . .

Next morning the *Daily Mail* ran the story across two columns. The evening papers starred it. Both the *Spectator* and the *New Statesman* had it in their notes-of-the-week columns. *Time* took it up. Within a week the phrase 'The Arabs, my Lords, after all, are gentlemen' had passed into the language along with such accepted clichés as 'many of my best friends are queer'.

Then the story broke that Raymond was making over Charminster to his son. That, in view of his current publicity, rated a TV interview. 'Has this decision of yours been at all influenced by the scene in the House of Lords the other day?' He smiled. 'Yes and no,' he said, 'or rather I should say it confirmed me in my suspicion that I had been out of the country too much to fit into public life. I've lost touch. During the war, I was in the Middle East five years. Everyone who served in the Middle East found it difficult to adjust himself to the changed conditions here. The England to which the demobilised soldier returned in 1945 was very different from the country he had left in 1940. Because I had my estate in Dominica, to which I returned the moment I was out of uniform, I never made that adjustment. I had suspected that I was out of touch, I was convinced of it the other day. The responsibility, the obligations and I will say at the same time the rewards that accompany Charminster are far better in my son's hands than in mine.'

He spoke lightly, graciously, without rancour or self-pity. He appeared thoroughly satisfied with the way everything had turned out. He must have made a very agreeable impression on the viewers.

'Does this mean,' he was asked, 'that you are saying goodbye to England?'

'Heavens, no. I've far too many good friends here. Besides, I need to go to Kew Gardens fairly often for advice about my garden.'

Before he left, he gave a small masculine dinner party at the Café Royal. There were a dozen of us, five of whom had been at that Oxford party to which Evelyn had brought Judy. It was a sentimental but not a wistful occasion. He seemed so thoroughly contented with it all. 'This isn't a leave-taking,' he said. 'I'll be over every year, and I'm expecting you to visit me.'

The last thing he said to me was, 'I'll be expecting you. If not this January then the next.'

'I'll take you up on that,' I said. And I thought I would. For the six previous years I had been going out most winters. But a change had come in the pattern of my routine. During those six winters I had been acquiring the material for a West Indian novel; with the novel written, I needed fresh material. I looked for it in the Far East, in Thailand and Malaysia.

I did my best to keep in touch with Raymond, but I always seemed to be missing him when he came to London. We exchanged letters once or twice a year. I paid visits to Charminster. I saw Eileen at London wine-tastings. Timothy Alexander was now a member of MCC and we watched the test matches from the top gallery at Lord's.

He was now a man. Without having his father's striking good looks he had developed into a very handsome creature. He had a gracious manner. He was popular with women; his photograph appeared regularly in the illustrated society weeklies, and his name in the gossip columns. Born in Berkshire, he was scoring enough runs in second class county cricket to make his friends wonder why he did not take out a qualification for a first class county. He shook his head. 'First class cricket is a game for professionals.' And in that he was probably right. He had a seat in Lloyd's and was associated with a large firm of insurance brokers. I have the vaguest idea of what people 'in the City' do, but whatever it was he did he seemed to be doing it successfully. Eileen had no worries on that account. 'He's sensible,' she said. 'He's not extravagant. He's adventurous, but he doesn't gamble.'

'What about his girl friends?'

'Plenty of them.'

'Anyone in particular?'

'Not as far as I can judge, but I suppose when the time comes, it'll be the very last one we expected.'

In the early autumn of that year, he invited me to lunch. 'There's someone I want you to meet,' he said.

'Is this the one?' I wondered.

'No,' I was to decide as I came into the Savoy Grill, a few minutes late, to find him sitting beside the blackest female I have ever seen in a London restaurant. 'No, this is not the one.' In the thirties some men used to wear very dark blue dinner jackets which at night looked blacker than black, they argued. That was how black she was—blue-black. She was small and trim. Her teeth were very white. Her hair, dragged back from her forehead, was held in place at the crown by an ivory and enamel comb: large thin gold circlets hung from her ears. It was hard to tell her age. She seemed very young. She was wearing a light yellow blouse, loose-sleeved, buttoning at the wrists: its collar was a scarf that tied in a wide knot. The light yellow and the black were an effective combination. She wore no jewellery. I am a little deaf and I did not catch her surname when he introduced her. Her Christian name was Ada.

'Ada's a Nigerian,' he said. 'She won a scholarship and is reading history and law at London—Queen's College. Her class was taken to Lloyd's. That's how I met her. She said she had never met a novelist so I thought of you.'

She asked me the usual questions: Did I keep regular hours, did I take my characters from real life, how did I get my plots? She had a pleasant voice, with something of a singsong accent. She was very natural. The Nigerians at that time were a happy people. They did not think they had been exploited by the English. They were grateful to the English for the modern methods, the machinery, the medicine, the education they had acquired.

'Is Ada the first Nigerian you have met?' he asked.

'No, there was a very attractive one in Tangier.'

'Was she at all like your West Indians?'

'Not in the least. Neither to look at nor in herself.'

'That's what I would say. The West Indians will take a long time to forget that their ancestors were slaves, though a lot of those ancestors did come from Nigeria; the Nigerians themselves have always been free.' He paused. We were half-way through our lunch. 'I think, Ada, that it's time you put on your rings.'

She laughed. Her laugh was the one thing about her that reminded me of the Caribbean. It was loud, it was high-pitched, it was a cackle. She opened her handbag. She took from it a small round enamel box. She laid it on the table. She opened it. It contained two rings. The one was a large emerald in a silver setting: the other a single gold band of alternating diamonds and rubies. She slid the gold band onto the fourth finger of her left hand. Then she slid on the emerald.

'Allow me to present the Honourable Mrs Timothy Peronne. Could I knock you down with a feather?'

'You wouldn't need anything as powerful as that.' We laughed together.

'When did this take place?' I asked.

'Officially last week. Unofficially two months ago.'

'I'm slowly recovering my breath.' I raised my glass to Ada, 'Good luck'; to Timothy Alexander, 'Congratulations.' Then I started asking questions. When were they moving down to Charminster? Was she going on with her course at Queen's? Did Eileen know? What had his father said? Those questions took a while to answer. Yes, she was going to finish her course. Yes, Eileen knew: she had met Ada and was delighted. No, his father did not know, not yet. They could not move down to Charminster until he knew. As soon as the wedding was announced they would take a flat in London. Until then they were continuing the unofficial pattern of the last two months, his staying in his club and visiting her in her flat.

'When are you going to tell your father?'

'As soon as possible. That's one of the things you're here for. I want him to get letters from all four of us simul-taneously: my mother's the fourth of course. I want each of us to mail a letter in London at ten o'clock on Monday morning. On my envelope I'll mark "please read this first". Ada's will be the second, my mother's the third, yours the fourth. How do you think he'll take it?'

'He should be delighted.'

'Yes, but will he? He may not fancy the idea of a coloured grandson in the House of Lords.'

I laughed at that. 'By the time that grandson comes to take his place there, the world, and the House of Lords along with it, will be a very different place.'

Ada looked puzzled at that. The House of Lords was an unreal issue to her.

I endeavoured to be reassuring. But I could not help wondering a little bit how Raymond would take it. He thought of colour, after all, in terms of the West Indies. In my letter I would point out that Nigerians were as different from West Indians, in spirit though not in blood, as Syrians were from either. I wondered how Eileen felt about it. I rang her up that evening and next day we lunched. She was happy all right. 'A thoroughly nice girl; responsible, and clever. I'm sure that they're in love. And she's not self-conscious about being black. That's part of her appeal for him. She thinks that marrying a white man's a great joke. The fact that he's the heir to a title cuts no ice. It's simply a little extra sugar on the joke. With an English girl or an American, he'd have kept wondering how much the prospect of being Her Ladyship affected her.'

'You always come back to that question of the title.'

'You can't ignore it. Raymond himself was always aware of being a second son, though he never mentioned it.'

Except, I thought, where Whistler was concerned, but that point I wasn't mentioning. I wondered how soon we'd have the answer. 'I wonder if he'll cable us,' she said.

He did. Four enthusiastic cables. Mine said, 'You told me exactly what I needed to know. See you very soon.' To Ada he cabled, 'Welcome into the family. Your father-in-law longs to meet you.' His cable to Timothy Alexander announced his immediate return. By now Dominica had an airstrip, and daily BEA connections with Antigua.

* * *

He arrived in the highest spirits. 'I'm delighted,' he told Ada. 'It was time he married, and I was terrified lest he'd marry some simpering, designing debutante who'd set her cap at him. I'm sorry you married secretly: but I see your point. It would have been difficult with your parents in Nigeria. But it would have been an adventure to have us all flying out there for a tribal feast. However we'll do the best we can. We'll have a celebration party that'll make London talk.'

It was to be at the House of Lords. He discussed it with Eileen and myself. 'There's not to be anything hole and corner about this,' he said. 'It must be done on a grand scale. We'll have it in costume. Ada will look superb in her national dress. Have you ever seen it? Terrific. Long skirts down to the ankles. Very bright tunic in primary colours, broad diagonal stripes, and an elaborate headdress. I'll get the High Commissioner. He'll be delighted to come in his full war paint.'

'Do you know him?' Eileen asked.

'Not yet. But that's the kind of thing it isn't difficult to manage.'

'For me to manage' he should have added. I remembered how he said all those years ago in Beirut, on the verandah of the St George, that he always seemed to know the key man who could further a friend's interest, though he was never able to pull the right string in his own. He was very tactful with the High Commissioner. He asked him to choose a day that would be convenient. 'It is most important that you should attend. I want this marriage to start under the right auspices.' He made the High Commissioner feel that the wedding would be a valuable piece of publicity for the new Dominion. And indeed it was. Raymond insisted that all Ada's friends should come in their national costume. And the High Commissioner arranged for the presence of one or two prominent nationals. The House of Lords has rarely in recent years been afforded such a chromatic spectacle.

It was a warm October day; though the reception was held indoors, it was warm enough for the guests to stroll along the terrace. The invitations had gone out in Eileen's

name as well as Raymond's. She and Raymond stood together with the High Commissioner beside them. Seeing
them together sent a nostalgic wave along my nerves. How
different their own wedding must have been, in a dingy
impersonal office in Dominica. They looked so right standing
there together, she so elegant and he so handsome; never had
his good looks been so striking. There was a glow about him.
He looked more like a bridegroom than his son did. 'One
would think you were in love too,' I said. He laughed.
'I haven't yet reached the Sophoclean calm,' he said.

Ada was enchanted with him. 'He looks so young,' she
said. Her face was transfigured with a bright, broad grin.
She was like an exotic jungle creature, something out of a
Rousseau canvas. 'I never thought I should have a wedding
anything like this,' she said. And indeed I would question if
there has been a wedding party quite like that: with the river
flowing below it to the sea, Big Ben counting the minutes;
and the brilliantly robed Nigerians mingling with the
fashionably dressed English men and women; the setting sun
spread its benediction on them.

Next day it provided the press and on Saturday the social
weeklies with a series of decorative photographs. The photograph in the *Express* was captioned 'Nigerian females, my
Lords, after all are ladies'.

Later at the Beefsteak that caption was to be the cause of
comment. I was sitting next to a youngish man in the foreign
office who was largely responsible for Dominion and Colonial
postings. 'I've an idea,' he said, 'that Peronne's stock must
stand high now with Africans and West Indians. Dominica
will be needing a new Administrator shortly. In a very little
while Dominica will be getting its independence. Peronne
might be the man to bridge the gap. It might be easier for
him than for a career diplomat. When were you there last?'

'Five years ago.'

'I don't suppose it's altered very much in that time.'

'It hasn't altered much since I went there first in 1929.'

'Is Peronne popular?'

'Yes, and respected too.'

'Just what's needed in an Administrator. I wonder how he'd like the job.'

'I'd say he'd jump at it.'

'I'll think it over.'

A week later I met him again. 'I've had a talk with Peronne. The idea appealed to him.'

'Will you be able to fix it up?'

'As far as one can be sure of anything, it's settled.'

'I couldn't be more pleased.'

The Administrator of Dominica, during the period of changeover, was the equivalent, on an infinitely lower level, of the rôle that Mountbatten had played in India. It was good to think of Raymond, sitting in Government House, presiding over the legislative assembly, exercising authority over an island and a people that he had loved so long. It was far from being a fulfilment of the promise that he had showed as a young man, but it was not negligible. And he would do it very well.

I rang him up next morning to congratulate him, but to my surprise I learnt that he had left the country. I had believed that he was planning to stay on for another month. Presumably the offer of the Administratorship had hurried his return, so that he could organise his new routine. How soon would it be before the appointment was confirmed?

I myself left London a little later. On my return I got in touch with his son. 'What news of Dominica?' Presuming that I had missed the *Times* that announced Raymond's appointment, I expected to be told 'Oh, haven't you heard? The old man's very grand. His Excellency now.'

But the reply was as it had always been. 'As happy there as ever. Very proud of having developed a White Anthurium.' No reference to GH. I assumed that the projected appointment had been sidetracked in the corridors of Whitehall. I felt sorry for Raymond. It must have been a considerable disappointment.

It was a couple of years before I again ran into my friend at the Foreign Office. 'What happened about Peronne's appointment to Dominica?'

'That's what I've asked myself. He was most enthusiastic

when I put up the idea. In fact he returned to Dominica two weeks before he had intended, to reorganise his commitments. I thought the whole thing was settled. Then I got a letter six weeks later saying that now he was back, he felt that the job was more than he could manage. A great pity. He'd have done it very well. Now and again it pays to have a non-career diplomat in a special post and Dominica always has been a special post.'

I wondered what had happened. Had Raymond felt that his strength would not stand it? He had looked so surprisingly well at the wedding party. I did not mention it in my letters to him, nor did I mention it to either Eileen or Timothy Alexander. Raymond had a regard for privacy.

16

Two years after his marriage, Timothy Alexander became the father of a son, eighteen months later of a daughter. He took a flat in Dolphin Square. His business commitments were now too many to let him spend more than his weekends at Charminster. He had fingers in a great many pies. 'Those two years at Harvard are invaluable to me now,' he told me. 'They gave me a global view of business.'

'What about those two years in the ranks, do you think they helped?'

'Ultimately, yes. If I'd gone into the Brigade I'd have met a number of useful people, and I'm not sure that being an officer in the Brigade isn't a better training for handling men than having a more intimate knowledge of what I used to call "the other half". But I believe that those two years in the ranks made it easier for me to fit into American life. If I'd been a Guardee I might have adopted a patrician attitude that would have put people off. That row at Eton was a blessing in disguise.'

His marriage seemed to be going very well.

London was rapidly becoming a four-and-a-half-day city. Men went down to the country on Friday afternoon. Many clubs were closed on Friday evenings and Ada came up to Dolphin Square in the middle of each week. On Monday and Thursday nights Timothy Alexander saw his men friends; dining at Pratt's or White's. On Tuesday and Wednesday nights he and Ada entertained or were entertained. Twice a month they would go to a play.

'It's turning out very well,' said Eileen. 'They're very good friends and there's still electricity between them. Everybody likes her. She looks so unusual, yet actually she's natural and straightforward. She takes herself for granted, which is more than a lot of people do.'

One Saturday I went down to Charminster, on a warm July afternoon. There was a cricket match and Timothy

Alexander was captaining the village side. It was all very much as it had been, thirty, fifteen years ago: the only thing I missed was the old man in his straight-backed chair by the pavilion. Ada with her two dusky infants was the only addition to the scene.

I stayed the night. Timothy Alexander looked very patriarchal, sitting at the head of the table in a bottle-green velvet dinner jacket with elaborately frogged button-holes, like a French Hussar's. Iris's daughter was now fifteen. She looked five years older. She was fresh and pretty, with an air of *race*. She joined unassertively but independently in the conversation. She did not wait to be spoken to, but she did not interrupt. She asked me about women novelists, just as her mother had done on the *Lady Nelson*. What was Elizabeth Jane Howard like; had I met Iris Murdoch? It was consoling to an ageing writer that she should be curious about two of the same writers that her mother had— Rosamund Lehmann and Rebecca West.

Eileen and I had a long talk about her. 'It seems to be turning out all right,' she said. 'She's had a strange up-bringing, never seeing her mother and not feeling curious about her. She doesn't feel underprivileged with two devoted grandmothers, and Timothy Alexander's wonderful. Better than most fathers.'

'Doesn't Iris want to see her?'

'Not much. She had a curious childhood. All those step-fathers. All those changes of home. And then that marriage that hardly had time to become a marriage. The first solid thing in her life was this American. She's got her feet on solid rock. To her all this life over here must be very unreal in comparison with what she has.

'I've had a funny life too, you know,' she added, 'one thing and then another; my roots being pulled up so often. But I've a good feeling about things now. After all these broken marriages, it's a relief to see a marriage that you feel must last. If you marry someone as unlikely as Ada you do stick there.'

'What would the old man have made of her?'

'Oh, he'd have liked her. Everybody likes her. She's so real.'

278

Eileen herself was looking wonderful. She had kept her figure and the lines in her face had given her character. She was now in her middle sixties, yet she was still a woman at whom a man, seeing her across a crowded room, would bother to look twice. Margaret, however, had greatly changed. There are some men and women who from thirty on will not seem to change at all. Year after year they will look the same, then suddenly in the course of three months, they will put on thirty years. That had happened to her. She had neither grown thin nor put on weight. But suddenly, inexplicably, she had grown old. I asked Eileen if she had been ill.

'No.'

'What's happened then?'

Eileen shrugged. 'The kind of thing that happens. One week one looks twenty years younger than one's age. A month later one is old.'

It sent a quiver along my nerves. I remembered how all those years ago, nearly thirty now, there had passed between us that flicker of recognition. She might have been my fate. We might have been each other's fate. Had things gone that way, how should I be feeling now?

I didn't feel that she would be around much longer. But it was Whistler, not she, who was the first to go. He made so few demands upon himself, that one had imagined his vegetable existence going on for ever; then one morning he did not come down for breakfast. There was no more any reason for his dying than there had been for his inability to recover from his three years in prison.

'I miss him,' Eileen said. 'It's absurd that I should. There was no, what's the modern word?—communication between him and me—but in his curious way he was companionable. I don't suppose I'll ever watch "Coronation Street" again.'

Another landmark: and the years went by.

I was not aware of the pattern of my own life altering but when at the end of each year I took stock of the last twelve months, I would find that I was spending less and less time in England. Not so very many of my friends were left. 'Do you know that I haven't seen your father since your wedding?' I was to remark to Timothy Alexander.

'Nor've I. I'm getting worried.'

He looked at me, thoughtfully.

'How often do you hear from him?'

'At Christmas always, and when I send him one of my books.'

'Does he talk about coming back?'

'Vaguely, but not as though he meant it. He keeps asking me when I'm coming out.'

'When are you?'

'Heaven knows. The West Indies aren't in my parish any more.'

'You still go to New York, don't you?'

'Every year.'

'When are you going next?'

'In March, to file my income tax return.'

'In that case will you let the estate offer you a return ticket, New York—Dominica? I'm worried about the old man. He keeps saying he's coming back next year but he never does. I need to know what's cooking. It would be most inconvenient for me to go out there and I doubt if it would be a good idea if I did. There may be something that he wants to conceal from me, that it would embarrass him for me to know. I want an independent report. You're the one person who can go there without arousing his suspicions. You've got a perfect alibi. You can be going there in search of copy.'

'That's true.'

'You can write and tell him that you're planning another West Indian novel; that you want to see how changed the islands are; and you're particularly anxious to see Dominica because it's the one island that hasn't been affected by the tourist boom. It has so little to offer the tourist; no beaches; no luxury hotels. And all that rain. As a matter of fact you probably will be able to make some use out of your visit.'

'It's not unlikely.'

'You've so perfect an alibi that you'll be able to believe

in it yourself. He'll never think he's being spied upon. But something must be the matter. I don't know what it is. Are his letters cheerful?'

'Perfectly. He gives me the island gossip. He asks me about mutual friends. One or two comments about politics.'

'What's his position there?'

'Tory, a little right of centre. Only a little right.'

'He doesn't sound bitter? He isn't harbouring a grudge?'

'Heavens, no.'

'It isn't that then, but it must be something. Why on earth shouldn't he come home? He can't surely be harbouring a grievance about my marriage. He was wonderful to Ada. Look at that party at the House. I keep thinking of excuses. Has he got disfigured by some accident or illness and not want to show up in England? Has he got himself tied up with some ghastly floosie whom he's ashamed of, but doesn't like to leave behind? Has he lost his money? That is possible, you know. An estate that wasn't properly insured could get washed away by rain. There must be something, and you're the one person who can find out. I'm devoted to the old boy, though I can't say that he's ever taken a great deal of trouble over me. Perhaps I should be grateful to him for that. Parents who live in and for their children can be a responsibility. But if he's in any kind of a mess and is shy to tell me, I want to get him out of it. I wish that he'd come home. Why shouldn't he make his home here? It is his home, after all. Ada and I aren't here so much. After all this wandering, we have been such a scattered group, it would be nice if we could finish up as a united family. And there's an idea I've had. You may think it ridiculous, but . . .' He paused. He looked at me interrogatively.

'You tell me about this idea of yours.'

'That he and my mother should remarry. They never quarrelled. From what each has told me they slipped into that divorce, with war coming, and everything uncertain. That marriage with Whistler was never a real marriage. When my father and mother are together they seem so much at one. Their marriage *was* a real one.'

'That's what I've always felt.'

'It's worth considering.'

'It's the kind of idea that Ada could very well put up to them.'

'You're right. I can hear her saying it, opening those big eyes, all those teeth flashing in a grin. "Why don't you two get married?" I can hear her saying it.'

We sat in silence, pondering it. Yes, it did seem a very good idea.

That night I wrote to Raymond, explaining that a professional need for copy would be bringing me back to Dominica. Two weeks later I got his cable. So that here I was on an April afternoon sitting out on that familiar verandah looking towards the sea. I had already found the answer to four of the questions that Raymond's son had set me. Raymond was in perfect health: he had not suffered a disfiguring complaint. No female was installed in Overdale, and there was no obvious sign of a financial crisis. My plan of campaign was simple. I would stay two weeks. I would act as though I were seeking material for an article. I would see as much as I could; I would interview as many people as I could; and who knew that as a result of my researches I might not find material for an article? At the end of my visit, I would try to persuade Raymond to come back to England: anyhow for a little. If he did come back for that little, he might very well stay on. In the meantime I should spend a pleasant fortnight.

I did. The weather was much as I had expected. A first-visit tourist would have been disappointed and depressed at the long hours that he would have had to spend on a verandah, watching the rain sweep like the waves of the sea across the mountains. Everything got damp. But I expected that. I waited for and gloried in the hours of incredible splendour, when rainbows curved over the valleys, when one green mingled with another, when the wide plumes of the bamboo glistened in the sunlight, and the green and violet crested hummingbirds darted from bush to bush.

I made a couple of trips across the island that would only have been possible on horseback when I went there first.

In 1948 it had taken me a full day to get to La Plaine on foot and pony. Then it had been a thrill to reach a midway point from which I could see, through a gap in the hills, the Atlantic skyline. That particular thrill, compounded of exhaustion and achievement, has been removed by progress. I went to Elma Napier's house at Point Baptiste on the north point of the island facing the Atlantic. I got there by car within two hours. In 1948 I had had to make half the journey by boat and it had taken half a day. At that time the fishing village of St Joseph, a few miles north of Roseau, had had no road. Its inhabitants had grown very independent. Now it is linked by road with Roseau and the air of independence is less acute. Beyond St Joseph there was a beach club, The Castaways, where you bathed off sand, and where you could get an admirable club sandwich. Sixteen hundred feet up, along the Imperial Road, was the Riviera la Croix Estate Hotel, with five honeymoon bungalows and a swimming pool. It had a candlelit dining room and served an admirable red table wine, brought to Guadeloupe in tankers and bottled there. It cost only $2.50 a carafe.

There were a few changes such as those, but for the most part the island had changed very little since I had seen it first in January 1929.

In Roseau, of course, the changes were more marked. Old buildings such as Kingsland House had been replaced by supermarkets. The library had been modernised and re-catalogued; and no doubt improved to the extent that it was easier to find what you wanted: but the rearrangement of the shelves had necessitated the closing of the verandah looking out over the sea, where I had spent so many happy and profitable hours. A hotel restaurant had been built inside the walls of the old fort, and had become, since the Paz was burnt down, the town's social centre. Daphne Agar ran a snack bar—the Green Parrot—where I lunched several times.

There were a number of new government buildings, but the general feel of the town was the same, with its cluster, seven blocks long and eight blocks wide, of small two-storey houses, built on ochre brown stone foundations which have contrived to resist successive hurricanes because when they were built it was the practice to mix syrup with the mortar. Unpainted wooden balconies, now as then, projected over the pavements. There were no gardens, no trees, no flowers.

Among the new government buildings a massive concrete police station was under construction. Five other such buildings were being built over the island. 'This will soon be a Police state,' I was assured.

'What does it all amount to?' I asked Raymond.

He shrugged. 'Did the customs at the airport ask you if you were bringing in any arms?'

'Yes.'

'That's the one thing they're worried about—armed revolution. I expect that all these small islands will become minor dictatorships. That may sound terrible in England and the USA, but I'm not sure that a dictatorship isn't the best form of government for an underdeveloped community such as this.'

I remembered that he had been an embryo follower of Mosley.

'Under a dictatorship, law-abiding people like myself can lead our lives undisturbed. And the trains run on time,' he added with a smile.

Among the majority of the white Dominicans I found the same kind of anxiety that I had found recently in Morocco. When I went there first, Tangier was an international zone; now it is part of the kingdom of Morocco, and its residents are alarmed about the government's plans. Is income tax going to be imposed? What are the currency restrictions? What may be imported and what not? House agents, dressmakers, lawyers, hoteliers are in a constant twitter of anxiety. I found the Dominicans in exactly the same state of dither; owners of businesses did not know if they would be allowed to take their profits out of the country. If you owned property, you could only sell it to a Dominican, therefore you would not be able to get the full value for it.

'Does this mean,' I said to Raymond, 'that the contemporary equivalents of people like yourself won't come here any more?'

'That's about what it amounts to.'

284

'Does that mean that there'll be no more eccentrics here?' He laughed at that.

'Can you imagine Dominica without eccentrics? The island will create its own eccentrics, instead of importing them.'

Luckily John Archbold was on the island. We went with him on an excursion to Point Mulatre, and dined with him a couple of times. He had enlarged Springfield, building on a whole new wing, so that it could now accommodate a dozen tourists in considerable luxury. 'Does it pay?' I asked him.

'Nothing pays in Dominica. I don't lose very much.'

He is a rich man, with many concerns and a large estate in Upperville, Virginia. Springfield's loss was deductible against other gains. He ran it as a hobby, because he loved the island.

'You still love it as much?'

'Even more,' he said. 'It lays its hold on one.'

Because he was not a British subject, because his main financial interests lay elsewhere, he stood outside the political arena. He was on good terms with the Prime Minister, a good friend of the Governor. But he was not involved. The island knew that it was lucky to have him there.

I asked him if there was any racial feeling. 'There shouldn't be,' he said. 'There wasn't in the past. Some people think there is; the old residents, that's to say. The whites are called Huskies; sometimes they are shouted after in the streets. A woman who runs a dress shop was rung up and accused of discriminating against the blacks. "Black power'll get you if you don't look out." But I don't think it meant a lot. This has always been a happy island. Of course there's a certain amount of xenophobia. Foreigners can't get a job here. But that's how it is in all new countries.'

I told him how it was in Morocco. 'New countries are touchy. There's press censorship. Criticism is resented. And of course, the new officials aren't as competent as the old colonialists.'

During my talks with various people for my projected article, I made such enquiries as I could about Raymond himself. As far as I could gather, I should have no sensational news to carry back. Raymond was in excellent health. Everyone was agreed on that. 'He leads a regular life,' they said. 'He's a moderate drinker. He takes exercise. I've never heard of him being ill.'

I made tentative enquiries about his amatory existence. 'He must get lonely,' I said. 'Does he have a special girl-friend?' Shoulders were shrugged. 'No one that we've heard of. He's nearer seventy than sixty. He's probably packed up.'

'What about ex girl-friends?' I had thought that someone out of the past would give me a clue as to his reluctance to return to England. Heads were again shaken. There had been someone some while back, whom he had appeared to be taking seriously, but she had gone to Trinidad. There had been, as far as they knew, no one since.

'And before that?'

No one that appeared to matter. There had been an American tourist who had come down three years in succession, then she had married. There must have been others in earlier days, but nothing that had stood out. Some of them had probably been merely friends. He enjoyed feminine society.

Once I met his bank manager. I did not try to needle him, but I was on the watch for any clues as to Raymond's financial status. I had asked him about the difficulties of taking money out. I told him that that was one of the chief problems of living in Morocco. 'It's so difficult to find out what the laws really are,' I said. 'I doubt if the Moroccans know themselves.'

'The laws here are quite straightforward,' I was told. 'The trouble is that nearly everyone is trying to avoid them, with some fiddle or another: a concealed account in Zurich or New York: if only all my clients were like our host, with a comfortable wad of blue chips, whose funds come in regularly, with tax deducted at the source, so much easier for me and what a relief for all of them. What a lot of worry they cause themselves with their fiddles, and in the long run how very little they really save.'

'As most of them are retired, I guess that that's their equivalent for going to an office.'

'Maybe you're right, but it's a headache for me: our host's account takes up no time at all and it pays a large proportion of my salary.'

That settled the issue of Raymond's finances. I had found the answer to all the questions that Timothy Alexander had put to me. It remained for me to try to persuade Raymond to give England at least one more chance. I could see a great many reasons why he should. Most Britons who expatriate themselves do it for tax reasons, but I do not think that Raymond saved very much by staying abroad. Taxes in Dominica were high, and as regards climate, I should have thought that the rains of Dominica were as rheumatic and arthritic as the damp and chill of England. It was probably more than anything a reluctance to feel a stranger in the country of his birth that kept him at Overdale. And perhaps he would not feel a stranger at Charminster, now that Whistler had checked out. Charminster looked the same.

At the end of my visit I would bring the matter up. On the last night, or perhaps the night before, so that he would have a whole day to think it over; on the final night I was giving a party at Springfield to those who had entertained me. Perhaps during my last afternoon Raymond would give me a message to take home. I prepared myself for the last night but one. As it happened, however, our decisive talk came earlier than that.

Half way through my second week it began to rain, in the true Dominican fashion. As I went out for my morning swim, I was aware of water on my face. The sun was shining, there were no clouds in the sky, but a thin veil of rain was passing across the mountain. By the time I was dressed for breakfast the sun was dimmed, the veil had become a mist, the sky had darkened.

'It's going to be a wet day,' said Raymond. 'We'll probably have to call that picnic off.'

By the time we had finished breakfast it was quite certain that we should. The rain was beating on the iron roofs; the crested coconut palms were swaying; the bamboos were rustling in the wind. 'This is a day to spend with a good book,' he said.

There were a number of books on the shelves that I would have been glad to read, there were several of which I would have liked to refresh my memory. After sixty, one is wise to re-read old books that one has liked, if only to appreciate how often such books lose their magic. It makes one more tolerant of new books that puzzle one. I made a small pile of old books, set them on a table and swung up my feet on the leg rests of one of those long expanding chairs which I had first encountered in the twenties in Penang. I dipped into one and then another. *The Green Hat* was one of those that I picked up. I had not read it for nearly twenty years. Michael Arlen had said of himself, 'I was a flash in the pan, but luckily there was a good deal of gold dust in the pan.' I had half expected it to date, but to my surprise and pleasure, I found myself unable to put it down.

The morning wore slowly on. The rain beat down, the wind began to get upon my nerves. A window on the second floor was rattling. I went up and wedged it with an envelope. Raymond joined me on the verandah. He, too, swung open the leg rests of his chair and began to read. The grandfather clock chimed twice. 'Is that half-past eleven or half-past twelve?' he asked.

'Half-past eleven.'

'Early for a punch but I think we need one.'

We swung back our leg rests and sat upright. The cool, sweet drink was a strong restorative. 'I cancelled the picnic half an hour ago,' he said. 'If this weather doesn't change soon, I'll call off dinner. I can't drive out to The Castaways in this.'

'There are worse things than drinking punches in the rain,' I said.

'Many worse things, many worse things.'

We sipped slowly, with reverent appreciation. 'If a genie from a bottle were to give us the choice of having one friend from our past beside us here, whom would you choose?' he asked.

We went over one list of those whom we had both known. Most of them were from the twenties. Raymond had not been in London much since then. We had more to choose from than we might have expected, since they were all well over sixty. 'A lot of your contemporaries were too young for the first war and too old for the second,' I said.

'That's true, very true. How's Patrick Kinross?'

'He's put on weight. But he's ageing well.'

'It would be good to have him here.'

'It would be very good.'

The clock struck twelve, our glasses were almost empty.

'We'd better put lunch forward,' Raymond said.

'But not too far forward.'

'No? . . . Yes, I see what you mean. How many more punches do you think we need? Two or three?'

'It depends on whether we're having wine.'

'Of course we're having wine.'

'Then I'd say two.'

'Yes, I think two's right. How long does it take you to consume a punch?'

'Twenty-seven minutes.'

'That's fair. The third punch at half past twelve and lunch at one o'clock. *D'accord?*'

'*D'accord.*'

'And how about wishing for John Sutro to share one of them?'

'Or perhaps John Betjeman?'

'Why not James Laver?'

'We've quite a few to make our choice among,' he said.

'Don't you feel lonely for them, now and again?'

'Of course.'

'It wouldn't be so difficult to come back and see them.'

'I've been away too long. I might . . .' There was a pause. The maid arrived with the second punch. He changed the subject.

'I miss the club life here. I miss Pratt's and White's,' he said.

'You'd find them just the same.'

'How are they in New York?'

I told him about the Coffee House and the Century.

'We never went to Clubs, did we, when we were over there.' he said. 'They used to give me cards of temporary membership, but I never used them.'

'Wasn't that because of prohibition? Speakeasies were our clubs.'

'But you must have been able to get drinks in places like The Century. Members must have had lockers.'

'Or else they carried flasks.'

I remembered drinking highballs in the Harvard club: before a dinner in a private room.

'When I was last in New York,' I said, 'I was trying to find out how they managed in the Coffee House. The premises there are very small, no private rooms, no space for lockers. I was taken there in 1927 by Charlie Towne. He didn't offer me a cocktail. And he would have if he could. I asked several of the older members. Nobody could tell me.'

'It's a long time ago.'

'Forty years. And after all, it's not a club for the very young, except sons of members. That means that anyone who could remember prohibition would be over seventy.'

'And at that age one's very near retirement.'

'Writers don't retire.'

'But do they go on living in New York? Don't they build houses in Connecticut?'

'There are cemeteries round New York, and there are crêches. But no one seems to be born or die there. They come to New York to make their killing and then go home.'

'Do you ever see Myra nowadays?'

'She died last year.'

'Myra. I can't imagine Myra old.'

'She never did look old.'

'I'm glad of that.'

For lunch he served a heavy red wine that put us in a sentimental mood. We talked about the past. The twenties and the thirties; our years in the Middle East during the war became very real to us. He asked me about Susan. 'I always get a Christmas card from her. It arrives either too early or several weeks too late. Invariably with a foreign stamp on it.' I told him that she was a very senior reporter now, that she was always on the move, that she was sent wherever the top story was.

'She hasn't married?'

'She's involved with someone rather high up who's not free to marry.'

'Isn't that bad luck?'

'Not in her case. It leaves her free to work. I don't think she wanted children.'

'Two years ago there was a photo of her on her Christmas card—on horseback against a date palm. Tunisia, I think. It looked as though she'd put on weight.'

'She has, it suits her.'

'I wondered looking at that card if I'd recognise her.'

'You would.'

'I'm not so sure. My eyes are my weak spot. If you're seeing someone every month you don't notice the change, but a five years' gap, that's another thing. A year or so ago someone came up to me in the Dominica Club with outstretched arms, "Wonderful to see you. No idea that you were here." He was a man of fifty or so, rather bald, rather gross, with very prominent false teeth. I could have sworn I'd never seen him. I had an awkward ten minutes, finding out who he was, without actually asking him. He'd ask me things like "Do you see any of the old gang now?" How could I tell? I didn't know to which gang he was referring. It was all Christian names, old Frank, old George, old Shirley: a most awkward ten minutes. When he'd gone, I asked the barman. "That's Major John Sinclair." Of course I knew then. But the Sinclair I knew in Cairo had been slim, hadn't been bald and had his own teeth. How false teeth can alter the whole look of a face. No resemblance whatsoever. If I went back to London, I'd be terrified of not recognising someone I'd known all my life.'

I could see his point. I was finding it increasingly difficult to recognise old acquaintances; worse still I was forgetting the names of those whom I did recognise.

'There's one odd thing,' I said, 'if it's someone that you

knew at school, you recognise him right away, however much he's changed and you don't forget his name.'

'Ah yes, those early days; first faces and first places, they cut in deep.' He looked at the decanter. It was half-full; we had reached our cheese. Usually after two, let alone three punches, he would stopper up the decanter at that point. But it was raining with unchecked violence. 'We'd better finish that decanter off,' he said.

I slept till four o'clock. I did not feel livery or hung over; but I felt the need of exercise. I would have enjoyed a swim. But the rain was falling with undiminished force. A walk was not practicable; a drive down to the aquatic club was unattractive.

'We could go down to the pool, of course.'

He said it without conviction, a slithery slide over wet stones; no, no. Four o'clock. We could not start drinking again till six.

'I've got some notes that need writing up. I'll get down to that,' I said.

I did not really want to write up my notes. I set my travelling clock on the desk in front of me. The minute hand moved very slowly. The room grew darker. I switched on the reading lamp. No light appeared. Bulb's gone, I thought. I did not want to bother the staff; I put a candle on the desk. The matches and the match box were damp. It was not till the fourth attempt that I struck a light. I returned to my manuscript, not because I had anything to say, but to keep myself occupied. At ten minutes to six, I showered and changed and went onto the verandah. I arrived there punctually at six. 'I need a new bulb for my reading lamp,' I said.

'That's not what you need: all the lights are off. It may be a fuse: or it may be a connection at the works. The man who knows how it all works has taken the day off. In the meantime, what'll it be? Whisky, or gin or rum or what?'

'I see you've got Campari. I'd like that with ice and soda and a slice of lime.'

I needed something with a sour flavour. The maid came in to light an oil lamp. 'That'll give a soft light to read by.'

There was nothing I wanted to read particularly. I had been reading through the morning.

'Is tonight's dinner off?' I asked. He nodded.

'I don't fancy the drive there in this weather. I tried to get them on the telephone. No luck. I expect their line's down.'

The rain was falling now, not in a steady downpour but in a series of gust-driven waves.

'What does the radio say?' I asked.

'Nothing but static on the radio.'

'Have you any of those long-playing poetry records?'

'I've Eliot and Frost.'

'Why not some Eliot?'

'Why not.'

It was like distant days to sit there on the verandah hearing poetry read.

When the record came to its end, I said, 'You had good times, didn't you, with Eileen?'

'Very good times.'

'She doesn't look so very different now.'

'That's good to hear.'

In the half light I could not see the expression of his face. I felt I was laying the seed for what I meant to suggest on that last night but one.

'Looking back,' I said, 'after all it was the merest chance that you and Eileen ever made a life together. You didn't mean it to be anything serious when you began, and nor did she. And if that morning at Villefranche, she hadn't thought you welcomed her, she'd have made another life for herself without any illwill on either side. There was no need for you to have welcomed her.'

'Me being myself, there wasn't anything else that I could do.'

'Do you sometimes wish it could have happened differently?'

'It's no good thinking things like that. Things happen to one in character. If it isn't this, it's that.'

By a natural association of ideas, I asked if he had read Mosley's autobiography. 'Of course. Did you?'

'Yes.'

'What did you think of it?'

'He makes out a good case for himself.'

'He was right in so many ways, more right than so many of the others were. I've sometimes thought . . . Everyone knows now what the trouble with him was, not his actual opinions but the fact that he could never get one solid man to work with him, for more than a few weeks. John Strachey and Harold Nicolson . . . I've sometimes wondered . . . if he'd had someone with him whom people could both like and trust . . .' He checked. I knew what he was thinking. He himself was someone whom people could both like and trust. If Mosley had had Raymond and the others that he would have brought with him . . . But no, Raymond shook his head. 'It couldn't have worked. The whole thing. Something that "ailed from its prime foundation". In public life, in England, you've got to be able to work with the right people. I don't mean the aristocracy or the plutocrats, I mean the solid people who run the country whatever party's in. You have to have them with you. What about some Robert Frost?'

It was another very cosy evening, the long-playing poetry records alternating with talk about the past. We stayed up till midnight, without drinking very much. 'Myra,' he said, 'I can't realise that she's not here any more. Perhaps it'll be a better day tomorrow.'

It wasn't. The sky was grey and sodden, the wind had dropped and the rain was falling in a steady, unbroken sheet. Too wet for a morning swim. I was glad that Raymond had installed a hot water system. When I had first come to the West Indies there had been no such thing. You took a cold shower or splashed yourself from a large tub with a dipper; a small jug of hot water for shaving was brought with your morning tea. That was all you needed. I had always maintained that the provision of hot running water to please American tourists was quite unnecessary and had largely contributed to the heightened cost of living. Before the war you could live in the best hotel that the smaller islands had to offer for eight shillings a day all found. But I was glad, however, on this particular morning that I could luxuriate in a deep hot bath. I was out of luck, however; the water from the tap marked H ran cool.

'No hot water in my bath this morning,' I told Raymond.

'I know; the wick's got damp. I'll have to put in a new one.'

'Do you have to keep a stock of them?'

'We should do. But I expect we're out of them. Francis hasn't shown up yet.'

'What about the electric light?'

'That's out through the whole valley. I've been trying to call Roseau, but I can't get through. As likely as not my line's out of order.'

'Does that often happen?'

'When it rains a lot.'

'So that's fairly often.'

'Exactly.'

We ate our way through a substantial British breakfast; orange juice, papaya, cornflakes, eggs and bacon. I did not feel hungry but there was nothing else to do. It was eight o'clock. The morning stretched ahead of us: a day that would reproduce in every detail the one that had gone before, and as likely as not the ones that were to follow. In weather like this, there was nothing one could do out of doors.

'Another morning at my desk,' I said.

'You're lucky to have a desk to go to.'

There was no alternative: but my mind moved sluggishly, and the tip of my soft-point pen kept sticking in paper that was becoming porous. Nine o'clock became ten o'clock. Only half a sheet covered. Punch time two hours away. Ten past ten, twenty past, then, without warning, my ears were outraged by the roar of what sounded like a large scale explosion that was succeeded by a rattle of small clashes, as though a basketful of stones was being scattered over a corrugated iron surface. I jumped to my feet. I hurried onto the verandah. Raymond was standing by the railing. 'What on earth's that?' I asked.

'A landslide.' He pointed down the road. A cloud of dust hovered over it.

'Is that serious?' I asked.

'Hard to tell yet. Last time the road was blocked three weeks. That was higher up. This one will be more of a nuisance. No direct route into town. We'll have to go north to the roundabout. Half an hour longer at least.'

Raymond fetched a pair of field glasses. Slowly the cloud dispersed. The whole road was covered. A boulder crashed down the hillside, and bounded into the valley below. 'Not safe to go down there yet,' he said. 'Give it an hour to settle.'

'Is this going to be serious for you?'

'Not serious, but a nuisance. Add an hour onto every journey in and out of town. You can guess how that impedes the working of an estate. Nothing to be done about it now. Only half-past ten. Still, we can't sit here doing nothing. Marie,' he raised his voice, 'bring two punches.'

The cool, sweet, strong liquid was very welcome. We sat back in our long chairs, sipping at our glasses, looking through the screen of rain at the scar upon the hillside. 'You can see how it is here,' he said. 'No wonder people go crazy. No wonder people take to drink. For days on end this kind of thing goes on, rain, rain, rain. There's not a thing that one can do. All work's held up on the estate. And every day something new goes wrong: no electric light, no telephone, no hot bath; you sit here looking at the rain: and all the time that rain is ruining the crops and roads, the projects you've been working on for months. You can't get your bananas to the coast, and those that are stored in sheds go rotten. Is it any wonder that people take to drink?'

'Yet you still want to go on living here?'

'Where else?'

His smile had the winning quality that had over the years endeared him so to many; the smile that disarmed criticism. Yet even so . . . Why had he got to go on living here, when so full, so satisfactory a life was waiting him in England; why, why, why . . ? I had planned to set out my case on the last evening but one, in the warm glow that follows a good dinner, when mind and body are at peace. You write your script, but then fate forces you to deliver it at what you would have thought in advance was the least auspicious moment, yet when it comes you recognise it as the one, the only time; what novelists used to call 'the psychological moment'. Now, on a bleak, rainswept morning, was the hour to get said the things that I had come out to say. Even so the opening had to be prepared.

'Since Dominica means so much to you, I wonder why you didn't take on that administrator's job.'

'So you heard about that?'

'Williams asked me if it would appeal to you. I said I was very sure it would. He told me that you were enthusiastic, most enthusiastic, you left London earlier than we'd expected. I thought you were going back to make sure that you could manage both it and the estate. Williams thought the same. Then there came a letter saying you couldn't manage it.'

'I know.'

'What made you change your mind?'

'That's a long story.'

'I'd be glad to hear it.'

'It may surprise you, but—here goes. You were quite right in thinking I left in a hurry, and that I left because I had to see how I could reorganise my life here at Overdale in terms of being Her Majesty's representative in Roseau, but you couldn't be expected to guess at the exact nature of the life that needed to be reorganised.' He spoke slowly, carefully, as though he were delivering a speech that he had rehearsed. Perhaps he was. It might well be that he had had something he wanted to say to me in the same way that there had been something I needed to say to him; that he had been waiting, as I had, for the psychological moment. Only he had got in first.

'I don't know if you remember,' he said, 'but you told me how well I was looking, how young. "You must have fallen in love," you said. Well, that's exactly how it was. I had. She was a Dominican: part Carib, I'd have thought, part African, part French. She wasn't very dark. She had delicate features. She had straight hair. She was about sixteen. I met her at one of the carnival dances; you know how it is at Carnival: how you dance with everyone: how you let yourself go. I went to the dance expecting something. There hadn't been anything of that kind in my life for several weeks. After all, I was nearing sixty. But I wasn't quite ready for the Sophoclean calm. "Let's see what I can find at Carnival," I thought. As soon as I came into the hall, I noticed her, our eyes met in a look of recognition. As I walked towards her, she moved to meet me. Before I'd danced a dozen steps with her, I knew that this was it. From the way she danced, the way she held herself, you know the way it is. One can't mistake it. As always at Carnival, I'd taken a room in town. I took her back. To my astonishment she was a virgin. I couldn't believe it. A Dominican, and at her age; someone who danced like that. "But surely," I said, "it can't be."

' "Oh yes it is."

' "The first time?"

' "The very first."

' "I can't believe it."

'She roared with laughter.

' "Do you know," I told her, "that this is the very first time I've had a virgin."

' "Isn't that wonderful. So it's the same for both of us. How wise I was to wait."

' "To wait?"

' "Till I found someone I could really go for. I knew I must sooner or later, but I did want the first time to be very special. I'd marked you down. If only it could be somebody like him," I thought. "If only it could be him."

' "Someone as old as me?"

' "Age doesn't matter. You're so good-looking. And with such style. If only it could be you, I'd think. When you came into the room tonight, I willed you to look at me. That's why I danced the way I did. Now that I've got you, I won't lose you. I'll put gri-gri on you."

' "I shouldn't mind if you did," I said.

'She laughed. "It won't be for you to decide," she said. She was chuckling to herself. I had never seen anyone so happy. I'm not going to let this go, I thought.

'Next day I made enquiries about her. She came of a good family. Her father, who had died a few years back, was some kind of a contractor in the import–export business. She had three brothers and four sisters. I heard nothing but good accounts of them. I went to see her mother. That's the way to do things here. You don't need telling that West Indian society is matriarchal. If the mother's content so's everyone. Her mother was easily appeased. There was a piece of property she needed. I saw she got it. I took a small house for the girl—let's call her Jannek. I didn't want to have her installed in Overdale. Occasional evenings and weekends, but not a permanency. She'd be happier in Roseau, too, where she could see her friends: be on her own. I arranged for a cousin of hers to live with her, a considerably older woman, to keep an eye on her, to look after her. Jannek was going to the convent school. I wanted her to keep that up. I wanted the thing with her to last as long as possible, but there was a limit set; the disparity of age, my age. I wanted to make her feel secure.

'It all worked out wonderfully well. I suppose everyone on the island knew what was going on, but no one minded. Appearances were maintained, and that's all that matters in a British community. I've never been happier. I was in love, which I'd never expected to be again, at my age. I'm not surprised that you should have thought I looked well and young. That's how I felt; at the same time the situation was complicated by that offer from the Colonial Office. Her Majesty's representative has to be above suspicion. He could not maintain an obscure subject in "guilty splendour". If I accepted the Foreign Office offer, I should have to give up Jannek. But that was the last thing I wanted: for her sake or for mine. If I was to go on with Jannek, then I would have to marry her.

'It was the first time that I had thought of marrying her. It was for that matter the first time that I had ever thought of marrying anyone. I had accepted marriage with Eileen, when it was inevitable, but I had never wanted it. With Jannek it was different. I wanted her. I did not want to lose her. If that was what I wanted, then I must marry her. There was no alternative. I was as delighted as I was surprised to realise this. I had never felt so excited about anything. I recognised at once all its advantages, for me, for Jannek and for Dominica. How thrilled Jannek would be. It would have been false modesty on my part not to have realised that. How proud she would be. How proud Dominica would be, at my marrying one of them. How much more effectively, because of that marriage, I should handle my post as Administrator. The Foreign Office had first thought of me as an Administrator because my son had married a Nigerian, and because I had honoured that marriage with a party at the House of Lords. By doing so, in the public eye I had identified myself with the new idea, with the principle of race equality. They had felt that on that account I was the right man to shepherd the island during the difficult transition from Colonial subservience to Commonwealth independence. How much further I should have identified myself with the new idea, by marrying a Dominican. I should have proved myself to be one of them. I was so excited by the prospect that I could not wait to tell Jannek. I did not want to write to her. I wanted to see the expression on her face when I told her. How those big eyes would open. I must get back right away.

'I didn't let her know that I was coming. I did not let anybody know. I wanted the surprise to be complete. I had been expected to stay in London for at least another fortnight. This truant, this secret return added its special spice to the adventure. Old though I was, and, as you know, there've been quite a few women in my life, I have never had such an intense excitement at the prospect of coming home to someone. I was too excited to sleep on the plane.

'I arrived at Dominica in the late afternoon. The perfect time. I would stop off at Overdale: shower and shave and change and then drive into Roseau. I should be there by nine. She would have had her evening meal. She would be listening to the radio, probably on the verandah. Perhaps with that cousin of hers. Should I ask the cousin to go away, to leave us together? No, that would be too contrived. Better play it casually: be off hand, say something like "I've just got an idea, why shouldn't we get married." The drama of the undramatic. That was the note to strike. How often we could relive that scene during our years together.

'Never have I felt such tense anticipation as I turned my car into the road that runs towards the club. I could see the roof of her house. I parked several yards away. I did not want her to hear the sound of a car drawing up. There were lights on in the house, but no one was on the verandah. I could hear the sound of music, soft muted music, the radio was turned low. Three steps led up to the verandah. I was wearing rubber shoes: the music came from the sitting room. What a surprise I'd cause. I pushed the door open carefully, and then . . .

'Jannek had her back to me. She was kneeling on the floor. Her cousin was lolling back among the cushions of a low wicker chair. She was a large, stoutly-built, not unhandsome woman. She was wearing unbuttoned a thin silk housecoat. Her bare legs, widespread, were rested on the arms of the chair; it was between her legs that Jannek knelt. The cousin's hands were in her hair. They were pushing her head down. They were pulling her head forward. Jannek was completely naked. She was like a priestess worshipping before a shrine. The cousin's eyes met mine above her head. There was in them an expression of gloating greed, of sensual obscene delight. I have never experienced such horror—it was, well, you know as I do that to a great many normal men the idea of two women together is far from unattractive. You've written a novel about that, after all . . . You made it pretty, graceful, a minuet in porcelain, but this, this was completely different. It wasn't jealousy, no, no, not that. It was the look on the cousin's face, with all that it implied; its air of challenge, and its air of triumph; its assumption of complicity: as though she were saying "Were in this together". The spirit of evil was incarnate there. Then she closed her eyes in voluptuous surrender. I turned away. I left the room. Jannek had no idea that I had been there.

'Next morning the cousin drove out to Overdale. She came alone. She was wearing tight-fitting dark blue pants, and a white silk, short-sleeved jacket. She was much darker than Jannek: her hair was crinkled and she wore it short. She looked "butch" all right, but she was not without her fascination. She was not fat but she was firmly built. Her manner was slightly regal. It was the first time I had really looked at her. I asked her what she would like to drink. She asked if I had a jelly nut. I had.

' "A glass of that."

'She sat down facing me. She was completely composed. "I'm glad this has happened," she said. "I wanted to talk to you about it. But I did not know how to start. It was easier to let things drift. But you had to know sooner or later. Better sooner, and in this way. You will want to know how all this began, when it all began. That's an easy question. From the very start. When the war started, I was in England. I was just fourteen. My parents had come over for the summer, so that my father could see the West Indian cricketers. He liked it there. He decided to stay on. He sent me to a boarding school. You can guess what that did to me. It taught me about myself. It taught me what I wanted and how to get what I wanted. In the last year of the war I joined the ATS. That taught me even more. I liked England. I decided to stay on. I'd have stayed on for ever if there hadn't been a scandal. But there was. I was warned to leave, to come back to Dominica. That's when I first saw Jannek. She was barely ten. I knew at once that she was what I wanted. I only had to wait. I made friends with her mother: I helped her mother in the house. I helped her with her work and in her office. I made Jannek my special care. I endeared myself to her. That wasn't difficult. I led her slowly, oh but so very slowly, in the way I wanted. She did not know what was happening. We used to bathe together in the streams. I dried her afterwards. 'You like being dried, don't you?' I would say. She would nod her head. 'And I like drying you,' I'd say. 'Wouldn't you like to dry me too?' That's how it began. First with drying, then with massages. 'Today,' I'd say, 'I'm going to give you a very special massage.' Afterwards I'd say, 'Didn't you like my special massage?' 'Oh yes, oh yes,' she'd say. 'Then don't you think it would be nice if you gave me a massage?'

' "The massages became more elaborate. One day I said

302

'Wouldn't you like to give me pleasure in the same way that I give you? You may not like it at first,' I said, 'but you'll soon learn. I love giving you pleasure. You'll soon love giving it to me.'

' "I made everything seem natural. We couldn't have been happier. It never occurred to her that what she was doing with me could not be right. I protected her from the young boys who were in wait for her. 'You don't want them when you've got me,' I said. 'There's nothing they can do I can't, except give you children, and you don't want that. Not yet. You can ruin your whole life by having children before you're ready. Look at Mabel, look at Isabel, you don't want to be like them.'

' "I knew that sooner or later she would be needing a young man. Her curiosity had to be set at rest. She didn't want to be out of it when the other girls were comparing notes. I had made her promise not to tell them about us. 'They wouldn't understand,' I said. 'They'd laugh at you. When the time comes for a young man, I'll tell you: not before you're sixteen.'

' "What I should do then, I didn't know. I should have to play it by ear. I was apprehensive, but I was not going to be a coward. When she was fifteen and a half I said, 'It is time you went with a man. But you are too young to marry yet. And you don't want to have a child. You don't want to choose the kind of young man who can be troublesome, some men can be. When you see a young man you fancy, ask me, I'll advise you. You mustn't make a mistake.' I spoke as though it were a simple matter. I made her think it was, but I knew it wasn't. I was terrified of losing her. After four years, after all, and every year it had been getting better. I can't tell you how relieved I was when she picked on you. Nothing could have been better from my point of view. When it worked between you, when she told me that she was in love with you, that she believed you were in love with her, it was precisely what I had prayed for, though I hadn't dared to hope that it could be so good. There's only one thing that was missing. Something we must work out ourselves, the three of us together."

303

'She spoke very quietly, with complete assurance. She had a masterful manner, yet at the same time her smile had a disarming power. It fascinated, dominated, cast a spell. "Have you ever thought how it could be, the three of us together? No, of course you haven't. But you have looked ahead and wondered how it will work out for the two of you. You are not an old man yet: far from it, but you are over forty years older than she is. You are able to suffice her now. But for how much longer? For three, six years, perhaps for even longer, but all the time you will be becoming more and more conscious of your waning powers. Another year and a year after that, but sooner or later you will have to lose her. You will foresee a date upon the calendar, the year 1970 shall we say, by then certainly it will be over. Between now and then the break will have to come; and because that calendar date stares at you, out of nervousness your powers will decline faster than they need. In a very few months you will have begun to dread the future; that is, if you are just the two of you, but not if I am with you.

' "She will never leave you, if you are, in her eyes, one with me. Have you ever tried to visualise a trio? I presume that in your youth, you took a girl friend into a brothel, made a *partouze* of it. And it was fun, you enjoyed yourselves, the occasion was a link between you, but for that other girl, for your paid partner it was nothing. Think of what it would be if all three of us had our hearts in it. You cannot think how Jannek could be, if I were with you. I have trained her from her girlhood. Dared by me, she would do delightedly things that you would not have the face to ask her. She would keep you young. She would give you the price that Faust sold his soul, for recovered youth. She must never know that she has been discovered. That would shame her. I would not have her shamed. You must install me here as your manager. You need a woman to run this house. Jannek will come out with me as an understudy. She can continue going to school. She must not be robbed of that. Once we are installed, you can leave everything to me. We will not so much share her, you and I, as all three of us will share each other. One night she will sleep with you. One night she will sleep with me. One night it will be the three of us together. And those are the nights that will mean the most to you. Think it over well, my friend. You are being offered what nine men in ten, if they were offered it, would sell their souls for."

'She stood straight up, and without another word, without a backward glance, walked across the patio. Within thirty seconds I had made up my mind. That *daemon*, that inner voice that guided Socrates, that voice that must never be denied, said "No, no, no". First instincts never lie. I had had the sense the night before of being in the presence of incarnate evil. I must act at once, decisively. I should be lost if I hesitated, if I brooded over the monstrous proposition. For I was not immune to the temptation. I could feel its power. I might have become its slave. I must act at once. For Jannek's sake as much as for my own.

'Jannek was in school. Her class would end at noon. I drove into Roseau and parked outside the building. I was standing on the pavement when the steps were suddenly crowded with a stream of blue-skirted, white-bloused urchins, chattering across their satchels. I had a sense of my heart turning round and over. She was so very pretty. And she looked so young. She had to be protected.

'Her face lit at the sight of me. Not a lover's delight, a child's delight. She had to be protected.

' "You back so soon," she cried.

' "I've news for you," I told her. I took her out to lunch; it was something I had never done before. I had preserved appearances as far as possible. It was a great treat for her. She had not very often held a menu in her hand. She deliberated her choices lengthily. "Now for my news," I said. "I made some enquiries while I was in London. I've not been very happy about that school of yours. It's good enough, of course, but its standards are not as high as the universities in Trinidad and Barbados. I want you to have the best there is. I want you to go to Trinidad. You'll stay there with friends of mine. You'll go there just before the new term opens. If you get a degree there, you'll be able to get yourself a good job anywhere. A girl with your abilities and looks." She was enchanted. I had of course not made any such arrangements, but that's the kind of thing that I've always been able to work out, for other people. Jannek was thrilled. To be going to Trinidad. What an adventure! How her friends would envy her. "And we shan't be losing touch. I'll be coming down to see you. You'll be coming back here for your holidays," I assured her. Not that she was worrying about us, about her and me. She was far too excited. And all the clothes that she would be buying.

'To her mother, however, I was quite explicit. "This relationship with me is bad for Jannek," I explained. "I had thought it would be something that would be over in six months. But it hasn't turned out that way. She means much more to me than I had expected. If she were to stay on here, I couldn't keep away from her. She must go away. And she must stay away. She mustn't come back. Probably she will marry there, quite soon. When she marries I will make her a quite large present. Within a very short little time, she will have become part of a new life. She mustn't be reminded of Dominica. That cousin of hers mustn't visit her. Is that understood?" It was understood completely. None of the Dominicans have any money. The man who has a little money is all powerful. I had more than a little money.

'The arrangements went even more quickly than I had expected. Within ten days I had the bookings fixed. The next day the cousin came out to see me. Her face was set in a grim, fierce frown. "You are a very foolish man," she said. "No man can cross me and not suffer. If Jannek goes away, you will never leave this island." '

Raymond checked. He had told me his story without interruption. Now he asked me a question. 'Do you believe in the power of the evil eye?'

I nodded.

'If you believe in the efficacy of prayer, you must also believe in the power of a person to will you harm,' I said. 'In the New Hebrides, planters told me how a native whose pride has been hurt will turn his face to the wall and die within three days. They commit hara-kiri with their minds.'

'You wrote a story about a Frenchman in Martinique

whose girl put a spell on him, so that he could never leave the island. Every time he tried to leave, he had a dizzy spell.'

'That was the first West Indian story that I wrote, forty years ago.'

'Was it true?'

'It was told to me as true.'

'You believe it happened?'

'Yes.'

'That's what happened to me. "Every time you try to leave the island," she said, "you will have a dizzy spell. As a warning, on the day that Jannek is due to go, you will wake with a headache so fierce that you will not be able to get out of bed. I will come and visit you. I will deliver my ultimatum."

'And that is what did happen. I had been careful to spend a very quiet evening the day before. I left Jannek among her friends. I would call for her in the morning. I ate only soup and drank a small bottle of beer. But I woke with a cracking headache. When I tried to get out of bed, I collapsed. I could not even crawl to the bathroom to get an aspirin. I waited for the maid to bring me coffee. The smell of the coffee made me vomit. I lay there waiting, sweating. At ten o'clock she came. On her face there was a look of gloating triumph. "What did I say?" she said. "I don't make empty threats." She had a piece of paper in her hand. "Sign this and when it has been delivered you will feel well again."

'She read me what was written on the paper. It was an order countermanding Jannek's passage. "Sign this," she said. "I will take it to the airport. The moment I have delivered this paper to Jannek, you will recover. If you do not sign it, I will stay here beside you. The plane is due to take off at eleven ten. It may be late. The moment the plane is in the air you will feel well again. Come now, sign." I shook my head. I had not the strength to speak. "Very well," she said, "I will sit here and wait."

'She sat silent, motionless, watching me. I was not in pain as long as I did not move. I watched the hand of my bedside clock move round. Quarter to eleven, eleven, five past eleven. "Nearly time," she said. The minute hand moved on,

307

reached the two and covered it. "The plane's late," she said. "I'm sorry." The minute hand moved on. Quarter past, twenty past; suddenly she stood up. "All right. The plane's taken off. You can get up now." My headache had disappeared and I felt ravenous. I swung my feet onto the floor. The floor did not move beneath them. "Now you know I was not fooling you," she said. "You will never be able to leave this island. You will be foolish if you make the attempt, but if you ever become weary of Dominica, you have only to bring Jannek back and all will be the way it was."

'That afternoon I made enquiries at the airport. The southbound plane had taken off twelve minutes late. Yes, she had put her gri-gri on me.

'But would her spell be effective if she did not know the exact time of my departure? That I must find out. I must make an attempt to get away when she couldn't possibly know that I was leaving. She could invoke her powers if I was leaving on a scheduled flight or sailing, but what if I went unannounced. I would avail myself of the first chance I got.

'I hadn't long to wait. A yacht from the north put in at Portsmouth. Its captain had a letter of introduction to Elma Napier. She invited me to lunch to meet him. He was to leave for St Lucia that afternoon. I took a small suitcase with me. "I wonder," I asked, "if you could take me with you. There's a matter I'm very anxious to discuss with the Administrator." "Nothing easier," he said. I asked him that at the very end of lunch, when we were alone; when no servant could have overheard. I had brought my gardener with me. He could drive back the car. I would tell him at the last moment. My excitement mounted as we took our farewells. I could see his yacht at anchor. In half and hour I should be on her. I took my seat at the wheel. I would not tell my gardener what I was planning till I was out of earshot. He might have an arrangement with the cousin. She could not possibly know that I was leaving. The news would reach her when I was beyond her powers. I had fooled her. I was free. I released the clutch. I put my foot on the accelerator. The car moved slowly forward. And then without warning agony convulsed me. I fell across the wheel: I shut my eyes.

The car swung into the ditch. I did not lose consciousness. I knew precisely what was happening. The pain I had felt when I was wounded in the war was trifling in comparison. I was incapable of movement. My gardener called for help. I was lifted out of the seat. "It's no good," I said, "you'll have to drive me back." Though the pain did not diminish I was in complete control of my faculties. I apologised to my prospective host. "I'm very sorry. It's nothing. I have these attacks. It's not unusual. It'll pass in half an hour. Don't worry. I'm all right."

'As his car swung out of sight, my pain vanished as suddenly as it had come. There were no after-effects. "So this is that," I thought.

'Two days later I met the cousin in the market. There was a look of triumph on her face. "You see," she said. "I warned you. There is no escape." She looked me up and down. "The remedy lies in yours hands," she said. "You have only to bring Jannek back. Then you can go."

' "I shall never do that," I said.

' "Then you will never leave this island. You will be my prisoner."

'That was seven years ago,' he said.

I stared at him, believing and yet not believing him. I believed in the power of gri-gri. Everyone does who has spent any time among those peoples. Yet it seemed incredible that he could have spent seven years upon this island. 'A prisoner for seven years,' I said.

He laughed. 'They've been my seven happiest years. For the first time I've known complete peace of mind. There was nothing to be done about it. That was what made everything so easy. I remember you telling me of the relief you felt in September 1939 when you rejoined your regiment. For twenty years you had been plotting the graph of your personal career, wondering what books you should write, what editors you should work for. You were making decisions all the time. From now on, until the war was over, you had only to find out what the man immediately above you wanted and carry out his orders to the best of your ability. Life is very simple

309

when there are no alternatives. That's what you said to me in Cairo, that was how I felt here in Dominica a quarter century later. I knew what I could do. I knew what I couldn't do. I knew for instance that I couldn't be an Administrator. I should be unable to go to other islands for conferences. I should be unable to visit London for discussions. I wrote to the Foreign Office, expressing my deep regret, and assuring them how more than happy I should be to assist the government in any way I could, and in point of fact I have been able to do quite a lot. If there is only a very little you can do, if your work is limited by a short radius, it's surprising how much that little can amount to. I fancy that our own Royal Family, though it has no constitutional powers, is able to achieve more than many absolute monarchs can. That's in our small way what John Archbold and I do here. We're both above the battle, above and outside it. John's a very rich man, of course. I'm not; but I'm not poor. We've neither of us got an axe to grind, our advice is often asked. And we're able to get people together who might otherwise not know how to meet each other. John being an American is a help in one way; it gives him an independence. And my being English helps in another. John and I complement each other. I'm not nearly as much involved in the island as John is, but I've got enough to keep me busy. What's more I'm doing all I can. Which is something I've never been able to feel before.

'I've always from the start felt that I should be doing something, that I'd been put here for a purpose. But I couldn't find out what the purpose was. I was irked by that. I always felt that I ought to be doing something different, something more; there was a basic central dissatisfaction. That's over now. I'm doing all I can. It's enough to keep me busy. And I like doing it. That's as much as any man has a right to ask of life. And besides, this is a lovely island. It rains too much, but even so, it doesn't rain all the time, even today I shouldn't be surprised if it doesn't clear up in the end.'

Already it had grown lighter. There was no break in the clouds, and it was raining still. But the rain had become a mist rather than a downpour.

'Let's have another punch, and let's move lunch forward half an hour. I bet we'll be able to manage a walk after our siesta.'

The punches were brought: and he changed the subject. 'Tell me more about all our friends. There's so much I want to hear. Francis Beaumont-Palmer. Tell me about him.'

'He and Sylvia live in Brighton now, they're fine. I'm planning to go down this summer.' We went from friend to friend. But soon inevitably we returned to his own position. 'What's happing to Jannek?' I asked.

'She's fine. She's married—to a lawyer, quite a rich one; they've got two children.'

'Surely, in view of that, that cousin would cast off her spell?'

'She might, I don't know. I haven't asked her. I don't like to ask her. I don't want to ask favours of her.'

'But surely you want to get away from here?'

'No, I don't think so. I've got used to it. Tell me about Peter Quennell. I was very fond of him.'

'Me, too. He's fine. I see him now and then.'

'And Tony Powell?'

Name followed name. I felt very close to him, talking over the past. The past that was as real to him as it was to me: the past that for him, an exile. could never merge into the present. In all human probability this was the last time that we should meet. It was unlikely that I should ever come again to Dominica. And since he was resolved never to return to London ... It was strange to think of him a prisoner on this island. 'Don't you miss your old friends?' I said.

'I do and don't. It's wonderful to have you here, to pick up the old threads. It's wonderful when any old friend comes out; quite a few do, you know. They look in on cruises: and those that do look in are, in terms of health, staying the course. But I don't want to hang around in London, while my friends check out, seeing them go one by one: thinking, "his colour's bad; he won't last much longer." There was a fellow I knew in the thirties. He wasn't old, not much over fifty; but he was dying, of cancer. He'd been given a few months to live. He kept coming into White's: each time he looked thinner and more drawn. I could see his point; he wanted to get the most out of his last weeks alive, but he did depress us. I made a vow then that when my time came I would keep to myself.

'No, I don't want to see my friends grow older. When I read their obituaries I want to be able to picture them in their prime. That's the way, too, I want my friends to remember me; as I was in my big days. After all, I had something, hadn't I?'

'I'll say.'

'That's how I'd like to stay, for them, the way I was. Out here it doesn't matter. I quite relish the idea of growing decrepit here. I'll enjoy making jokes about it, here where I know everyone, where I can say to some young stalwart, "Your father can remember the time I climbed up to the boiling lake. Couldn't do that any longer." "No, man, you couldn't." There'll be something rather cosy about growing old out here, with familiar sights and sounds around me and familiar faces. I love the Dominicans and they love me. I'm an institution here. Besides, here, in this country of easy growth one lives and feels and thinks in terms of the Old Testament; the coconut palm rises, the nut falls, man goes to his long home.'

We went into lunch. At last it was easy for me to ask him the essential question. 'After Jannek, what?'

He shook his head. 'Nothing. I called that off; one has to some time. Better on one's own terms than later upon nature's. I've heard two men talk of the humiliation of going to bed with someone and have nothing happen. I've spared myself that shame. The Sophoclean calm. Best to anticipate it if you can. End on a high note. "Just once in a while we can finish in style." Jannek was the tops. What news of Iris?'

Name followed name; place followed place. He asked about London's clubs. Did I belong to the Savage still? 'As a country member; we've amalgamated with the National Liberal. It's still got the feel of Adelphi Terrace.'

'Adelphi Terrace. How I hated seeing that go. And the old curve of Regent Street: as it was in that line-drawing of Pennell's in the first number of *The Savoy*. There's so much about modern London I'd detest; to walk out of White's, turn left and at the end of the street to see St James' Palace, not against the sky but against a skyscraper.'

'London's the same at heart.'

'Is it? I suppose it is. If you've seen the changes coming year by year. What about that network behind Brompton Road? Rutland Street, Montpelier Square?'

'As Soames Forsyte knew it.'

'For how long, I wonder.'

Name followed name. 'Myra. I can't get accustomed to the world without her.'

The room had lightened as we lunched. 'We'll get a swim all right this afternoon,' he said. By the time we left the table the rain had stopped, the sky had cleared. We walked to the edge of the verandah. We stood in silence, looking out over a world refreshed and radiant. I am old, I have travelled far, I have seen some majesty; but I have seen nothing more regal than the pageant of Dominica's greens that afternoon.

'Italia, oh Italia, thou who hast,' he said.

To myself I finished the quotation: 'The fatal gift of beauty.'

The mountains that were its glory brought the rain; the rain gave the foliage its special splendour, the rain washed away its crops and roads and bridges: the one was the complement of the other. The fatal gift of beauty. Raymond and Dominica. Were not their fates identical? He had been too good-looking, had had such grace and graciousness. He had showed such promise, seemed destined for the world's rewards. He had only to stretch out his hands to take them. The race was won before the pistol went. He had been born to what others had to earn. Love had been given to him so freely that he had taken it for granted. Now he was alone. No one had ever thought that he needed to do anything but wait for the right opportunity: the opportunity that had never come. Yet even so he was at the end of it all as happy as any man I knew. I could relieve Timothy Alexander of his anxiety.

The crested plumes of the bamboo waved in the breeze: the ragged leaves of the banana plant glistened in the sunlight, reflecting it like burnished shields. The humming birds darted above the crotons. 'A siesta and then a swim,' he said.